What others are saying about D. Barkley Briggs and *Corus the Champion* . . .

"*Corus the Champion* is everything we waited for . . . full of surprises, with layers of legend, faith and magic. Highly recommended."

—KACI HILL, co-author with Ted Dekker of *Lunatic* and *Elyon*

"D. Barkley Briggs more than delivers with this rousing second installment, deftly weaving Arthurian lore with mind bending fantasy. Surprises and twists lurk around every corner while characters and stunning locations leap off the page. *Corus the Champion* will capture your imagination and leave you begging for more."

—FictionAddict.com

"The Legends of Karac Tor is an epic, thrilling series and D. Barkley Briggs is a major new voice in fantasy fiction. Don't miss your chance to discover destiny in these pages."

—WAYNE THOMAS BATSON, author of THE DARK SEA ANNALS (Living Ink Books) and THE DOOR WITHIN TRILOGY

"Once again, D. Barkley Briggs has managed to capture the mystery of Arthurian legend, the enchantment of fairy tale folklore, and the valor of Celtic and Norse mythology. This rousing second installment of the Legends of Karac Tor delves deeply into the heart of heroism, its joys and sorrows. Read and let yourself burn with adventure."

—M. C. PEARSON, director, Fiction in Rather Short Takes (FIRST) Blog Alliances

"Using engaging and totally credible characters, prose that is nearly poetic at times, and a complex but comprehensible plot, Briggs has matched the quality of the book's predecessor, *The Book of Names*. This is some of the best Young Adult Fantasy work available."

—CHRIS MCCALLISTER, Rambles.net Book Reviews

What others are saying about D. Barkley Briggs and *The Book of Names . . .*

"Briggs braids ancient strands of Arthurian myth together with his own homespun thread into a complex tapestry of magic and meaning, bravery and brotherhood."

—JEFFREY OVERSTREET, author of
Auralia's Colors and *Cyndere's Midnight*

"D. Barkley Briggs has a fresh, unique voice. His writing style brightens every page. The lyrical prose suits his intriguing tale and heightens the feel of another world. *The Book of Names* is sure to gather a following among young and old fantasy lovers."

—DONITA K. PAUL, author of
THE DRAGON KEEPER CHRONICLES

"In the same vein as such master fantasy writers as J. R. R. Tolkien and C. S. Lewis, author D. Barkley Briggs has penned a superb fictional tale. *The Book of Names* is fast-paced and compelling, and readers will be clamoring for Briggs's next installment in this exciting and worthy new series.

—Teenreads.com

"A rousing fantasy packed full of Norse and Celtic mythology with a hearty dose of Arthurian legend. Strap on your armor, pull out your sword, and get ready for an adventure!"

—M. C. PEARSON, director, Fiction in Rather
Short Takes (FIRST) Blog Alliances

"Everything . . . about the story is fascinating and intriguing."

—*CHRISTIAN FICTION REVIEW*

"*The Book of Names* weaves a tale that is both thrilling and wrought with hope. D. Barkley Briggs is a new and welcome voice in fantasy fiction."

—WAYNE THOMAS BATSON, author of THE DARK SEA ANNALS
(Living Ink Books) and THE DOOR WITHIN TRILOGY

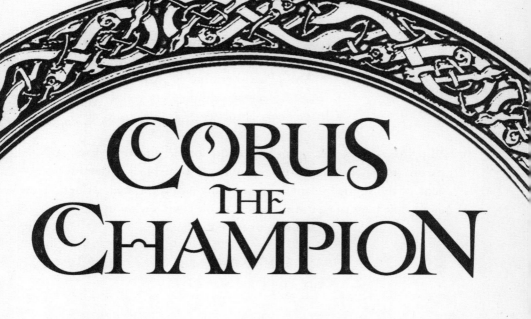

CORUS THE CHAMPION

LEGENDS OF KARAC TOR

LIVING
INK
BOOKS
Writing Worth Reading

D. BARKLEY BRIGGS

Corus the Champion
Volume 2 in the **Legends of Karac Tor** series

Copyright © 2011 by Dean Briggs
Published by Living Ink Books, an imprint of
AMG Publishers, Inc.
6815 Shallowford Rd.
Chattanooga, Tennessee 37421

ISBN 13: 978-0-89957-864-4
First Printing—May 2011

LEGENDS OF KARAC TOR™ is a trademark of
AMG Publishers.

Cover illustration by Kirk DouPonce, DogEaredDesign.com

Cover photo by IstockPhoto, Shutterstock, and Dreamstime

Cover layout by Daryle Beam at BrightBoy Design, Inc.,
Chattanooga, TN

Interior design and typesetting by Kristin Goble at
PerfecType, Nashville, TN

Creative Team: Rebecca Guzman, Michael Van Schooneveld, Reagen Reed, Darla Hightower, Arvid Wallen, Sharon Neal, and Rick Steele

Look for *The Song of Unmaking*—the next book in the
Legends of Karac Tor series, releasing fall 2011

Printed in Canada
16 15 14 13 12 11 –T– 7 6 5 4 3 2 1

For Joe, Thom and Steve,
Fratres quondam, semper mihi carus

What if sorrow was a doorway,
And memory, a gate?
What if we never passed through?
What worlds would go unfound?

In final days / Come final woes
Doors shall open / Doors shall close
Forgotten curse / Blight the land
Four names, one blood / Fall or stand

Great one falls / Fallen low
Rising new / Ancient foe
Darkest path / One turns back
Blade which breaks / Anoint, attack

Once and future / Lord and land
Hidden tomb / Burning brand
Bone and earth / Warriors rise
Haste the day / Of bloody skies

Aion's breath / Aion's curse
Making song / Made perverse
Cold beginnings / Wild cry
Truth revealed / Fates divide

Secrets lost / Secrets found
Eight plus one / Hel unbound
Beast shall come / Some must go
Doors shall open / Doors shall close

Hanging prince / Vision seen
Ancient gate / 'Neath crimson green
Nine shall bow / Nine shall rise
Nine shall blow / Nine shall shine

Falling fire / Burning pure
A thousand cries / For mercy heard
Plagues on water / Horns of dread
End of days / Land be red

When final days / Bring final woes
Doors shall open / Doors shall close
Fate for one / For all unleashed
War of swords / Slay the beast

                    —The Ravna's Last Riddle

CHAPTER 1

Taliesin

Darkness like a blindfold. Warm air close to his skin. Garret felt panic rising. For some reason, it stayed in his belly. He heard his own voice, as if from a great distance: *"Who are you? And where am I?"*

So much had happened in such a short period of time. Only moments ago, he and Gabe had scampered to the back of the tunnel with scrolls in hand. Winter cold, this morning. Cool light, falling from the sun, rising from the gray earth. Strange marks, glowing. An arch of rock. He hadn't known what to do. Neither had Gabe.

Curiously, Garret went first. Not the usual way of things. But there he was, under the arch. Through the arch. Behind him, Gabe followed. That's when the darkness came, when light was swallowed up. He had heard Gabe, laughing like it was a ride at Six Flags or something. Even felt him nearby in the brush of arms and legs. There was a swirl of air, a sensation of movement, of falling. Something like wetness splashed over him, like plunging into water headfirst. Yet he remained dry. In the confusion that followed, they were separated.

"Gabe!"

Faint and far away, he heard his brother calling his name too. Then another voice, chuckling. A near, touchable voice. Not mocking, not vindictive. Amused. An old man's voice.

"Who are you?" Garret asked nervously. "I don't like this."

The voice that answered from the warm darkness was clear:

"Before my release, I was many shapes:
I was a slender, enchanted sword,
Raindrops in the air, a star's white beam,
A word in letters, a book in origin;
I was a lamp of light for a year and half again,
A bridge that stretched an estuary for sixty and six;
I was a path, a kestrel, I was a coracle in blue water."

The voice was pleasant, crackling with humor. "Many words have been written about me. For me. Words like these, wondering how I survive through time, how I move between worlds." A pause. "It makes for nice poetry, at least."

"Where am I?" Garret demanded. He was blind in the darkness.

"In between is the best I can tell you. We're on a journey, you and I. You'll see your brothers again, soon enough. All of them. Don't worry, lad. I've been waiting for this for a long time."

Garret's tone became quite serious. "How do you know about Hadyn and Ewan?"

The old man's voice became even lighter. "Ah, how many times have I been asked that question? Eh? *How do you know? How did you do that?* How, how, how! I know the same way I know about your letter—signed by the High Prince himself, no less. I just *know.*"

"So you know about the scroll, too?"

The old man chuckled. "Many things, lad. I know many things. I have lived a very long time."

He spoke another poem:

O'er the nighttime winds that howl,
O'er the darkened roar,
Comes the whisper calling me,
Enticing me to more.

Garret tried to sound calm. "Tell me your name, then. I can't see you."

In the darkness, he felt a firm, gentle hand on his arm.

"Tal Yssen," answered the old man. "My name is Tal Yssen."

The rushing sensation came again. Gabe's voice became distant, then became nothing. The next awareness Garret had was of sudden, pale blue skies and the smell of goats. His feet stood on firm ground, no more floating or plunging. He took a step, moving through something. Turned. Energy vibrated around him. At his back was another arch, similar to the one in the briar patch but much larger, made of fitted, mortared stone. They stood alone, he and the man named Tal Yssen, on a solitary hill of green, surrounded by flatlands.

Other than hedgerows of wild hazel and scattered oak and elm, the hill was the only major feature, like someone had dropped it there by mistake. It rose, tall and sudden, shorn of trees, utterly alone, with vast sweeps of green on every side. A worn footpath wound down the hill, past a stand of trees, toward a clutch of wattle-and-daub buildings. One of them, larger than the rest, was circle shaped, with a cross made of beams rising from the center of the thatched roof. It looked to Garret like an old church. Near to these simple structures, small brown figures worked in rows, tilling the earth. The way they were hunched over made Garret think of giant mushrooms. He stood very still, trembling, not quite willing to believe his eyes.

"What is this place?" he said softly. He looked at Tal Yssen, saw a man perhaps sixty years old, with a short-cropped, silver-white beard and a nose like a hawk's beak. He wore long leather breeches, a blue tunic, and a dark blue cloak, fastened at his neck with a silver brooch. His eyes were the color of new-tilled earth and just as warm.

"You have not merely come to a place, but also a time," said Tal Yssen. "You stand in Ynys-Witrin, in the year of our Lord 539. This is your world, my boy. A long time ago."

He spoke calmly, almost calmly enough to soothe Garret's nerves.

"Ynys whatdja say?"

Instinctively, Garret put his watch to his face. The timepiece, shaped with the red arrowhead logo of the Kansas City Chiefs, seemed strangely out of place here. It had been a gift from Dad last year for Christmas—their first Christmas without Mom. The Chiefs were Mom's favorite team, and Garret never took it off. It kept great time. Now, however, the digital display was frozen at 7:13:28.

"Ynys-Witrin," Tal Yssen repeated. "But don't trouble yourself with words. By the time of your day and age, it will be known by other names."

"Okay, but the *five thirty-nine* part? As in AD 539? Is this some sort of joke?"

Garret tapped his watch. *Maybe when I entered the arch?* he wondered. Minutes and seconds were frozen. This made no sense.

"That device will do you no good here," Tal Yssen informed him equably.

Garret whirled, hoping to find a hidden camera and some reality game show host smiling behind a microphone. Up until now he had felt strangely calm. That feeling was beginning to fade.

"Please tell me what's happening," he said, not discourteously. "Did we come through that arch? Is it like that Stargate thing on TV?"

"We stand on the great tor, the hill at the heart of all of Breton." Tal Yssen swept his hands below and to the west. "Not long ago, this region was a seaport for Caesar's troops. Later it became an impassable marsh, and the ships withdrew. Now, after heavy rains, it often becomes a vast, freshwater lake. The waters rise, making an island of the tor. The abbey, below, usually remains just above the water's reach. And this"—the old man, who did not act old at all, swung round to the stone arch—"this is called Myrddin Esgyll."

"Myrddin what?"

"A doorway, like the one on your father's land. Centuries hence, another structure will be built atop the tor. But the builders, fearing the magic of this rock—both to lose it and to keep it—will be very clever in their design. They will hide this arch in the shape of the main entrance of a church. And so it shall endure."

Garret put out his hands as if to steady himself, though there was nothing to lean on. His voice began to rise. "I don't understand anything you're saying."

Tal Yssen began walking down the footpath, motioning him to follow.

"It is a holy place with a holy purpose, Garret ap Reginald Barlow. Here the king shall return. From here . . . *emitte lucem et veritatem*. And the truth shall spread to all of Breton."

"You aren't making any sense!" Garret said with exasperation. He began walking faster to catch up. "What king? Where's my brother, my dad? Why have you brought me here?"

Yes, the calm had definitely worn off.

As they strode down the hill, a flock of black-and-white-spotted goats came trotting up, amiably chewing their cuds, neck bells tinkling. A young monk in brown with a bald pate and a pleasant face nursed them along the footpath with his staff. His head was down at first, then lifted. He stopped.

"Taliesin the Merlin?" the man whispered hoarsely. For several seconds, he seemed transfixed, even confused. Then, over and over, he began to shout excitedly. "Taliesin the Merlin! Taliesin the Merlin!"

His words rolled down the long waving grass to the monks busily tilling the earth below. They all looked up. Paused.

Garret, too, paused mid-stride. He was a bright, meticulous child, with patterns of thought much like his older brother, Hadyn. He tended to absorb information quickly—structuring, categorizing, digesting, interpreting.

"Wait a minute. Hold it! *The* Merlin?" he blurted out.

"That is what they call me, yes," Tal Yssen said, almost embarrassed. "In truth, it is what I *do*, not who I am. I am a mirling. But they think it is my title, and it does no good to tell them otherwise, I assure you." His expression sobered. "Stay close. It is about to get even more strange."

They drew near the base of the hill. In the circle of huts, a dozen monks halted their garden tending. They held their crude tools close to their chests, watchful, but avoiding eye contact.

Presently, an old, wrinkled monk emerged from one of the huts. The younger ones dissipated to make room for him, bowing slightly as he passed by. His skin was weathered and cracked with age, and one eye was blind, but his sight was not so poor that he could not recognize his visitor.

"Ah, Taliesin! Welcome again, my friend. It has been too long."

He hobbled toward Tal Yssen, and the two embraced. Garret strained to hear what they said. Tal Yssen whispered something. Garret heard only the reply.

"Yes, yes, she is here. Don't worry," the old monk gestured back toward the hut. "The autumn rains will bring the water to us. We have a vessel ready. She waits inside for you."

"And?"

"And what? She waits. She sits and speaks nothing. She trembles. She writes. She cries. She hardly eats. Since spring, nothing but tears, since *he* passed beyond . . . to wherever he has gone." He said the last part nervously, low under his breath, glancing toward the sky as if he feared some sort of divine retribution.

Then she came. The monk fell silent. From the same hut, as if beckoned, stepped a woman of bruised, exquisite beauty. She was a contradiction in her plain woolen slip, her doe eyes, wide and innocent, and weary with secrets. Seeing Tal Yssen, she lowered her gaze. Strands of hair feathered in the breeze, covering her face. She did not bother to push them away.

"My queen," Tal Yssen said. Garret could not tell if his tone was one of kindness or sorrow. Or whispered, silken judgment.

The woman kept her eyes to the ground for a long while. When she finally looked up, they glistened in the sun.

"So you have come all this way to mock me then, Merlin. Is that it? I am no queen, and you know it. I am a beggar. I am the shame of the kingdom."

"I do not mock," Tal Yssen said gently. "You are, and ever shall be, the wife of my lord."

The breeze that had blown earlier now became still.

"Artorius is no more," the woman said. Touching her fingers tentatively to her lips, her voice faltered. "A queen must have a king."

"And love must pass beyond the grave, or it hardly counts as love. Will the queen stay true? Can she become true once more?"

The woman raised her chin, clenching. Specks of pride and fire glinted in her dark eyes.

"Ever the puppet master, eh, Merlin? The wise sage, the prophet. The kingmaker. Well, what do you do when the puppet dies? What then?"

"Gwenhwyfar, Artorius has passed into another world. He is not dead." Tal Yssen's voice dropped even lower. "At least, I hope not."

"I saw him fall!" she shouted. "I felt the coldness of his skin. Do not contrive upon my heart!"

Tal Yssen's voice stretched to something thin and sharp, like a razor. "I am not the one who has dallied with hearts, my queen. Not I. Not Artorius. I loved the king with all my soul."

"And you imply I did not?" Gwenhwyfar cried. "You think I *meant* to betray him? To hurt him so? You think I shall ever forget the look in his eyes? To the day I die, I tell you, old wizard, I shall not."

Tal Yssen nodded slowly. "Indeed, my queen. I think the grace to forget will be all too rare. You and the king's champion shall grow old with memories. And guilt. Paid for dearly. "

Gwenhwyfar hushed her voice, dropped her chin. "Thus, I go to Almsbury. To live out my days in seclusion, in service to the Lord. As penance." She clutched a handful of the loose fabric of her dress, balling it in her hands. Her tone allowed neither pity nor hope. "Some wounds never heal, Merlin. They are beyond even your art."

"'Tis true, especially for wounds of the soul. True enough of my lord's mortal wounds, had I left him in the care of mortals. But I did not."

Gwenhwyfar turned livid. She lashed out, "Stop it! He's dead! I know you, old man. You would have me believe he sailed to Avalon, these very shores, when the rains came last. And from here to . . . where? With your lover—the faerie and her sisters? Is that it, Merlin?" She laughed bitterly. Such a beautiful face, dark molasses hair. So much lost in the gray mist.

In four strides, he was upon her, looming. Gwenhwyfar looked caught, like a rare bird trapped in a cage. Shame covered her face.

"I do not have time for your doubt, much less your accusations," Merlin intoned. "I have come to ask a simple question. Will you be *true*, my queen? Once you had a lord who loved you. For all the truth of that love, the tender memory of it, what will you give, in hope of redemption?"

Gwenhwyfar slowly regained her composure. Rising to her full height, she met Tal Yssen's fierce gaze. There was a flickering moment of cold connection before something broke loose behind her eyes, and the challenge passed. She turned without a word, and ducked under the low-framed entrance of the hut. Returning moments later with a small note, folded and sealed with red wax, she pressed the paper into Tal Yssen's hands. She also removed the only ring which adorned her fingers and gave it to him as well.

"These," she said flatly. "These are what I will give."

Without another word, she spun, reentered the hut, closing the door with a loud, wooden smack. Tal Yssen stared at the place where she had stood, at the door through which she had gone. His shoulders sagged. He took a tentative step toward her, to follow. Stopped. Looked at the letter, the ring in his open palm. Turned.

"Come, Garret ap Barlow," he said. "We are done here."

CHAPTER 2

Mount Agasag

Saliva and blood spattered the wall, flung from the face of a broken man. A Champion once. Now in chains. His head flopped as though his spine were no longer attached. The fist that had struck him, gloved in leather and mail, tilted up his bloody chin, held it there.

"I told you to look!" thundered Baron von Gulag. His prisoner had limp hair and a long, ragged beard, laced with gray and knotted with frozen water like pearls on a necklace. His face was bruised almost beyond recognition. His eyes, haggard. The baron rumbled with laughter at the sight of him. Pitiful creature. Fool. Mighty Corus. He struck him again. "Look, I say!"

The two were alone in a chamber of blue cold, a hole in a mountain of snow and ice—Mount Agasag. Though he practiced the baron's shape now, there was no real need to use the dead man's

11

voice. Not here in his own domain, save for how it advanced his cause among the S'Qoth.

Of all his human shapes, von Gulag's was the one Kr'Nunos most enjoyed. It served him well and would continue to, according to plan. He no longer even tried to hide from Corus the antlered mark on the skin of his wrist—a mark he could not forsake even with countless shapechangings. He was lord of this realm. While Karac Tor slumbered, her last Champion watched, caring nothing for pain or life. Corus knew each day only as grinding torment. If he could have been granted any gift, the choice would have been simple: death.

And so Kr'Nunos took pleasure in keeping him alive.

It was a long, meticulous torture. Deep in the bowels of Mount Agasag, he would let Corus rot for weeks in the iron cages of Hel, known for darkness so thick that it cut off all life and hope— darkness no human light could penetrate. It was a place of sulfur and nightmares and spirits of the dead: creatures best left asleep in the cold earth. Kr'Nunos would abandon him there with only enough food and water to keep him alive, then bring him up into the blinding light to taunt and beat him.

The baron took perverse pleasure in this routine. He would lift the former Champion thousands of feet through the rough, sulfurous shaft of Agasag's volcanic past, from the labyrinthine corridors of Hel to the very heights, and force him to look across the empty miles of vast, frozen tundra, toward the Frostmarch. South, to Elkwood first, and then all of Karac Tor, lost in dream and darkness beyond the silver peaks. He would describe his plans of coming devastation in delicious detail: the army of Goths, unformed below, lurking in the mud and rock of Hel; the Watch- ers; the secret armada of ships he was building in the frozen ocean of the Cruel North. Day by day, week by week, Corus was made to endure it all. Worse still, to live. It had been years now since he had been taken from the Fey, yet whenever it pleased the Horned Lord, he would bring Corus to this place and taunt him. Then he would cast him once more to the lower regions, engulfed in darkness that penetrated the mind, surrounded by caged beasts that never slept.

Baron von Gulag sneered at his captive. "Do you see the lands you once protected, now ravaged, now raped?"

Corus neither answered nor moved. He was stripped nearly naked, left to shiver where he hung from thick iron manacles. His breath was frost, his once-proud physique nothing but skin and bones and pain, thinned with hunger and striped with the whippings of a bone lash. He didn't even try to focus his fevered eyes. His mouth drooled freely.

"I will destroy it all," said the baron. "Down to the very last tree. Down to the very last maiden and child. Down to the last seed in the cold ground. The Hall of Ages will be no more. And when all is finished, I will make Mount Bourne my footstool."

He spoke these and other blasphemies over and over. He reminded Corus of his great love, Nemesia, now a witch in the baron's service. Told him of the Staff of Shades, the darkening of the land, the stealing of names. Told him of a governor, ruling in Stratamore, who was weak and easily controlled. Told him of a shamed and shameful champion, rotting in Hel, too weak to escape, as would a real man, and do his duty.

What he did not mention was the interruption of his plans. Nor did he speak of the coming of the Outlanders. Such trivialities were minor annoyances.

When he was done, the baron descended into Hel, leaving Corus to freeze in the bitter wind. The deep world was impossibly vast, a network of subterranean chambers and countless pits scraped out of hard, blood-stained rock. The main level of Hel was called Angwyn, which was accessible by a single pair of great black gates. Other places had other purposes, and below all, deep in the bowels of the earth, lay Undrwol, a place outside and beyond even the baron's power. But here in Angwyn, the great forges burned. Massive beams connected complex wooden frameworks to arched bridges, to pulleys with ropes, to buckets and carts and long extension arms. Kr'Nunos was building. The clang of hammers on anvils, the burst of sparks was unceasing. Here, fire brought light. Deeper still, darkness ruled.

Angwyn had great pits beyond number, stone craters full of gears, of machinery; pits of iron ore and copper, even algathon, so rare. The raw materials progressed through smelting pits and smithies, eventually forming huge mounds of long iron spikes and coppery nails. Smaller pits sparkled with jewels and gold, and there were great piles of dirt and rock. But most terrifying of all were the bones. Great piles of bones, like mountains, stretched as far as the eye could see.

Thousands of men labored in firelight and steam, with hammers, axes, and rope. Their oiled bodies moved and struggled in the dark like maggots on a carcass. They were S'Qoth man-slaves brought from Quil, dressed in animal skins, with faces painted green and black, and strange markings on their arms. Loops of silver pierced their ears, their cheeks, their lips. Big, beefy overlords commanded them, perched on platforms of wood, shouting curses in the brutal language of the S'Qoth. Others mingled amongst the slaves, snapping whips.

"We are nearly ready, Great One," said a tall overlord, his feral grin revealing several missing teeth, and the rest filed to points. He bowed to Baron von Gulag.

"You have earth?" the baron said.

"From High Röckval, as you commanded, my lord."

"Then give me a test, Oruuwn. Let us make a creature in my image."

The man took a short gorse horn and blew. Immediately, overlords began barking orders, whistling, gesturing. Slaves scrambled, crying out as whips nicked their skin. Wood was brought. Another fire was lit. A barrel of dark, oily fluid was poured into a large cauldron, where it soon began to boil. Next, bones were hauled in—bones of bull and jackal and human—along with shovelfuls of rock. Sharpened iron spikes went in, and a handful of copper nails, then mud, water, sawdust. All were thrown together into the bubbling cauldron. Pleased, Baron von Gulag folded his great arms on his iron-plated chest, his robe billowing in the drafts of hot air rising from the fire. When the time was right, he stretched out his hand, spoke a command. The bubbling intensified. The liquid began to thicken, coagulate. Slaves and overlords gathered round, whispering gleefully, clenching their fists in toothy delight.

"Arise!" the baron rumbled.

Something took form. From inside the cauldron arose a crumbling beast of earth and bone. It was man-shaped, but faceless, bulging with nondescript features. It had a rough outline of head, torso, arms, legs. A cavity of ribs was clearly visible along its midsection. Long iron spikes protruded from the stumps of its fingerless hands. Lurching to its feet, dripping mud, it showed a gaping maw and a jagged mess of copper nails for teeth. A noise came from its mouth, a sound like the movement of wind through winter-crusted leaves—a gasping, nothing sound. The beast stood eight feet tall, looked as thick as a tree. It had no eyes.

Kr'Nunos took a clump of new soil from a separate pile. He pressed it like clay into the beast's belly, then stepped back, spoke a final word.

Shivering, the creature became aware. Then it started killing.

No roar of rage, no warning. No emotion or cause. Only the cold grind of rock and bone and heavy arms swiveling left and right. It was not fast, yet it punctured half a dozen S'Qoth through chest and skull as easily as a man might snap a twig or put a knife in a tomato. The strength of the beast was the strength of the earth, the hardness of stone, the bite of metal. One S'Qoth, leaping upon it from behind, shouted and pounded the beast's head with an iron rod. He struck wildly. The beast neither flinched nor cried out. It clamped upon the slave and, as a child might bite into an apple, ripped the man's arm from his shoulder, letting it drop to the ground. The Quil man hit the cavern floor screaming, fumbling about in shock for his severed limb. The other S'Qoth fell back, unsure. They formed a loose circle beyond the beast's reach, out of its path. It no longer lashed out, but began moving relentlessly in one direction, toward the baron. The beast raised its arm, ready to strike. When it drew near, Baron von Gulag stepped out of the creature's path. A test. The S'Qoth hissed in fear. The beast did not veer to attack. It lowered its arms, lumbered on. Straight path.

"Strike it from behind!" the baron commanded.

Overlords and other S'Qoth grabbed shovels, spikes, axes. They rained down blows upon the creature's backside, then jumped back warily. The beast was unconcerned, unfeeling. It made no attempt to retaliate. One direction drew it like a magnet. Its mouth opened in a silent cry.

Eventually it reached an impasse, a wall of rock. It did not bother to change course, searched for no door, just methodically began assaulting the stone with crushing force.

The baron smiled, pleased. It would go through, not around. He spoke a word that rattled on his lips, made the S'Qoth cover their ears. Instantly, the beast crumbled, collapsing into a loose heap of bone and rock and mud.

"Behold what I have created!" he cried aloud to the men cowering around him. "The first of my great army of Goths." His voice dropped to a low rumble. "Let the people of Röckval tremble."

CHAPTER 3

Faielyn

Befitting its preeminence among the Five Dominions, Vineland carried a lofty place in the minds of many. "The Crown of Aion," it was fondly called, with good reason. The province boasted beauty, culture, and history unsurpassed by any other dominion. Was there an abbey more noble and glorious than the White? Or a city more resplendent than high-towered Stratamore, capital of all the realm? Were there wines so delicate to the palate, or poetry so lovely, as that which grew from Vineland soil? Even holy Mount Bourne and the sacred waters of Avl-on-Bourne found refuge . . . where? The awesome spectacle of the Rim, where? All in Vineland. Perpetual counterclaims, raids, and feuding by Midlands earls over the centuries only reinforced the obvious: everyone wanted a stake in Vineland.

Citizens of the other dominions grumbled and wagged their fingers in spite. "Nothing but rich, sniveling drunkards, the whole lot of them," a decent family man, a fisherman, or a farmer from Greenland might say, based on the most popular, well-circulated rumors. Highlanders hurled insults too, but nobody in Vineland cared what Bird Men thought.

Jealousy, all of it.

Besides, the very pretense of moral disdain tacitly acknowledged the truth. Here, strewn amongst verdurous fields with gushing rivers and groves of olive trees, in the shadow of the towering, majestic cliffs—here was the splendor of the Hidden Lands under Aion's wide blue sky. It was the cradle of philosophy, art, religion, wealth, not to mention vines. If nothing else, Vineland earned *that* name. Fat clusters of sweet grapes were everywhere. Nearly every family had a root stock of some sort, fermenting spicy Eligoté from the hillocks north of the White Abbey, deep hued Berberi from the southern flatlands, costly Brnallo for the rich, and sweet Muskot or Tarusi for the poor. Midlands had its mead; Greenland had its thick, hearty ale. But Vineland was wine country.

Thus, the importance of Faielyn, the port city to which all wine eventually flowed, home to a renowned sweet wine of the same name. A city for lovers and thinkers—"Drinkers, more like!" some would jest—Faielyn was home to Vineland's noble family, as well.

It was a charming, sprawling, terribly ill-planned city, being raised on a cluster of mud banks that formed dozens of small islands amidst the slow-moving Deeps drifting into Champion Bay. Sinking structures had been stabilized over time with pilings of wood and concrete driven into the mud. Eventually, it all started to work. The various lagoon townships, called *vestrinias,* were connected by a latticework of canals, slender boats, and innumerable bridges. It made for robust tourism, as now the most common site for which Faielyn was known was that of men pushing visitors along the liquid streets with long sweeps, singing loudly to one another from dusk to dawn. The city was a mess of homes, theaters, libraries, kirks, small clutches of mud-brick buildings, and giant edifices of marble columns and granite block. A stirring, lovely mess.

It was here in Faielyn, at a blacksmith's shop along a narrow alley far outside the sight of the royal residence of Giovanni di Etrascus, that Gabe Barlow found himself the sudden apprentice of a burly man with beefy arms, shoeing hooves. His role was nail boy, it seemed.

Remedial nail boy.

"Lad, you daft? Stick 'em in the fire, I told you three times . . . ah, there, finally, that's it. Turn 'em real slow now. Hold it . . . hold it. See the glow? Wait until it's white, not orange. Now, pinch them with the tongs, one at a time. Pull 'em out and lay 'em there, careful. Now . . . no! Mama's good tooth, lad, do I have to tell you every time? Shield your eyes!"

He swung. Sparks flew. His name was Ulavo.

Kichang—clink—kichang!

"Next!" he barked, as if Gabe couldn't hear.

Gabe wore a junior-size leather apron that was still much too big and leather gloves that reached to his elbows. After removing the nail, he let it steam in a bucket of rainwater—no lack of those, for sure—then plopped the cooled wedge in a barrel full of more nails. He reached into the fire for another glowing shard.

It was a busy day for Ulavo the blacksmith. He had guests. Gabe was one, still trying to figure out how he got stuck holding the tongs, though truth be told, even with the yelling, it was pretty fun stuff. It didn't look like Hadyn was having much fun, though.

He stood in the alley, damp-skinned, holding his sword, glumly staring intently into the flames. Gabe knew it frustrated him to no end. He could name so many things and, with the name, summon control. That was his gift, the truth of a name, as bird language was for Gabe. Hadyn was getting more creative, more skilled with rope, wood, stone.

Yet two things eluded him: iron and fire.

So it must have been tough, watching Gabe play with iron and fire. As any little brother would in such a moment of minor triumph, Gabe grinned, stuck out his tongue. Hadyn grimaced, then jerked, barely having time to raise his sword. A Creed was leaping.

"Thus do all men perish against the mighty Creed!" cried the swordsman, lunging, then arcing his blade. Hadyn rolled just as the sword whistled past his ear. He scrambled to his feet, flashing with anger. As they formed up against one another, the student slowly began circling his teacher, parrying and thrusting into the air with exaggerated form, just as Cruedwyn had taught.

"Nice, old man. Is the mighty Creed getting slower?" he taunted.

Cruedwyn feigned an invisible stab wound to his heart. But his eyes twinkled. He raised his hand in front of his face and snapped his fingers twice. "I say stay away, snap away to your jesting curse. Creeds are spry as young lambs—improving with time like a fine wine. However, *you* are another matter." He shook his head in a gesture of deep pity. "Truly, my friend, it pains me to inform you that your brother Ewan is twice the student you have been. In half the time."

"Careful now," Hadyn said. "Don't let your sword hear. You might burn yourself."

Creed attacked again. Soon the two were clanging about, laughing with relish. Hadyn was no match, of course, but showed real improvement. Neither seemed to mind the thin gray drizzle curling over the various rooftops of clay tile, or thatch, or rusty metal. Their hair was wet and glistening. Two months, and the sun had only shone three days. Faielyn was not meant for such a deluge. Water was everywhere. Always, the rain.

Va'nya, the Highlander, stood off to the side, watching in silence. Three weeks ago, it was Va'nya who had escorted Gabe to the White Abbey to reunite him with his brothers. He was a young Bird Man, short and acrobatic, brown-skinned. Like most Bird Men, he didn't walk so much as glide. He carried a pack on his back for his wings, was hairless except for a stubby, dark band down the middle of his head. A thin needle of steel pierced the skin of his lower lip. He rarely spoke. The Highland Jute, K'Vrkeln, had assigned him to deliver the boy safely. Having completed his task, Va'nya refused to leave. He would not say why.

Three Bittermen traders had also come to Ulavo's shop today. They stood casually, arms crossed, joking amongst themselves in their own tongue. They had come to meet with the exiled Vineland prince, Diamedici. They had come selling gorse.

As he worked, Ulavo motioned with his chin to a table full of horseshoes.

"What will you be wanting, m'lord?" he asked, swinging, sparks bursting like fireworks beneath his hammer. He was unaccustomed to so many visitors, but only Diamedici made him nervous. "I've got heel calks, toe calks, wedges. Plain. You name it."

"Heel calks," the prince replied, stroking his neatly trimmed goatee. "Just don't be stingy with your coal this time. I don't want

poor welds from a soft fire of peat and cinders. Besides, I can get
heel calks anywhere. I come to Ulavo for his mighty nails."

Ulavo puffed up red with heat and strain, grinning like a
crocodile.

"Nothing better in the Five for ice and mud, m'lord. Except
maybe some of them Bittermen nails."

"These *are* Bittermen nails," said one of the traders in his thick
northern accent, examining a cooled piece. Two were fair, dressed in
rough leather and fur-lined boots, even though summer was full on.
They wore necklaces of bead, bones, and bear teeth. One, cloaked,
showed a hint of rare, pale skin underneath his hood—unusually
pale, like freshly skimmed cream. Another had a bow and quiver at
his back. Actually, Gabe thought, as he plucked another nail from
the fire, they looked more like warriors than traders. He was truer
than he knew, not yet understanding that *all* Bittermen were warriors, or once had been, in the olden days of the *viks*.

Ulavo made a nervous sound, hasty to agree. "No smiths anywhere like the Bittermen, m'lords. Old Ulavo has learned a bit over
the years. From your kind, I mean."

"Not entirely," said the hooded Bitterman, tossing the nail back
in the heap. "You should have paid more attention. Your alloy needs
more iron. And your coal less sulfur."

Ulavo tightened his grip on his hammer, swung again, harder.

Diamedici turned to the one who had spoken. A sly smile crept
into his narrow eyes, if not his lips. "Clever Thorlson, too clever by
half. Ulavo's nails are not my chief concern, and you know it. What
I want is assurance that you've brought me decent gorse this time.
Or do I need to speak to the Lady Odessa myself? Are their hooves
quarter-cracked and full of corns? Knucklers, as before? You told

Archibald the herds were puny. You said many were born lame. I heard your complaint at High Council."

"Amongst thousands, yes, too many," Thorlson said, slipping his hood off his head. Gabe almost gasped to see the washed pink of his eyes. "But these . . . I culled the best myself. A thousand fine gorse."

"I'm shoeing gorse?" Ulavo paused mid-swing. "A thousand?"

"A little different than horse, eh?" Thorlson grinned. "The hoof is narrower and longer. You can trim the wall some, but not too much. Gorse need to stay nimble."

"Four thousand new shoes?" Ulavo swallowed. "When?"

Diamedici tossed the blacksmith a jingling bag. "That and three weeks. Another bag when you're finished. Does that help? South of Faielyn, past Toleda Hill. Bring your tools to the house of Milangino. He is a friend. Thorlson will also be there, with his fine herd, which I will inspect *before* any shils are paid."

Thorlson shrugged. "Inspect all you want. Ber Skellinson will manage the trade. I ride hard tomorrow."

Diamedici shifted his gaze to Gabe. "In the meantime, I shall make sure my young guests are brought safely before my uncle."

Thorlson appraised both brothers with dawning recognition. "So these are the Outlanders? I saw the one who came before Archibald. These two have his look."

"That was Ewan you met. He's with Har Hallas," Gabe said cheerfully. "I'm Gabe. That's Hadyn. We don't know where Garret is."

"They bring news for my uncle from the high priest. For all the land barons."

"Also for the House of Cloven Hoof, then?" Thorlson said, narrowing his gaze. "What news for my lady?"

Hadyn, on cue, sheathed his sword, inserting himself into the conversation. His mock battle had left him flushed and panting, but he procured a gilded note bearing the wax seal of Alethes with a flourish. This he gave to Thorlson. "Tell the Vanír of Bitterland that war is coming. It cannot be avoided. We do not yet know when, but on this the abbeys are of one mind. The witch Nemesia has unleashed Watchers, and the Ravna's riddle is being fulfilled. I and my brothers are proof of it. The land barons need to prepare now, or it will be too late. Arm yourselves. *Be ready.* That is the message."

The alley grew quiet, with the only sound being the low whoosh of Ulavo pumping at the bellows, pretending not to hear. Strangely, it was Va'nya who broke the silence, his eyes fixed on the Vineland prince.

"A thousand will not be enough." He paused. "The Jute will expect more."

Diamedici tilted his head as if smelling the air for a change in the wind. He arched a brow, though whether in warning or surprise it was hard to tell. Regardless, the Bittermen watched him carefully.

"Time and patience," the prince replied in slow, even tones. "Layer upon layer, day upon day. K'Vrkeln must steady himself. We do not want to draw too much attention."

The Highlander withdrew in silence, but not before sharing one more brief, wordless moment with the prince. Gabe knew the look contained more, but didn't exactly know what. Caught in the moment, he fumbled the tongs, accidentally dropping a hot nail on the bed of straw underfoot. The stalks sputtered, but were too wet from the rain to catch fire.

"Easy, lad," Ulavo said softly, snuffing the smoldering straw with the heel of his boot.

"Your uncle will kill you if he catches you," Thorlson said, not soft, not loud, not threatening. A fact observed. The only thing more stark than his coloring was the ruggedness of his features.

"For taking the lads to him, you mean?"

The Bitterman refused the bait. "All of it. Any of it."

It was no great revelation, but once again, Gabe sensed more beneath the diplomatic vagaries. Tensions between Diamedici and his uncle Giovanni were well known. The prince had been cast out, disinherited, though no one knew precisely why. Giovanni had no other heirs, leaving Vineland without a clear line of succession.

"My uncle wants to kill me no matter what," Diamedici replied. "With these boys or without. In the city or in the country. Any reason will do."

Hadyn tried to assert himself helpfully, "We can find our way to the castle without your gracious aid, my lord. Cruedwyn knows the way."

"Nonsense," the prince scoffed. "Getting there doesn't get you in. Not for an audience with a ruler on his deathbed." He paused. "But I cannot be seen with the Bird Man. That is a fact."

"Va'nya is my name."

"Yes, of course. But not yet."

Va'nya set his jaw. "I will not leave L'ka. He hears wing speech. You place him in danger. I must be there."

Gabe grinned at the compliment. Hadyn seemed troubled, but kept silent.

"Friends, friends," Diamedici said, making a placating, calming motion with his hands. His fingers sparkled with rings. "I know the streets of this city like the lines across my palm."

"It is not you I fear. It is your uncle."

The prince flashed a broad, easy smile, but his eyes hardened to blue crystals. "I have been outsmarting my uncle since I was eleven years old. Another day is no great feat."

CHAPTER 4

Diamedici

When Gabe first entered Karac Tor through the runestone, strange as it was, he didn't think twice. When he heard birds talking to him, he didn't try to second-guess. He didn't doubt. He didn't think he had been conked on the head or wonder if all of it was a dream. He saw the birds, heard them speaking simple words, and spoke back, boy to bird. The reaction was mutual surprise. The birds croaked louder and ruffled their feathers. When the Highlanders found him sitting on the ground, talking to a cactus wren, they instantly revered him. Birds were sacred to the Highlanders. They gave him a knife inlaid with *quoi*, the color of the sky, where birds fly. They called him L'ka—Wingtalker.

His entire arrival had been a fairly breezy affair. No angst nor fear to speak of. A fluttery stomach, sure, but not rocks-in-the-belly dread. On the calendar back home it might be Thanksgiving break, but Karac Tor seemed more like a field trip. If he had taken even half a minute to stop and think about it, he might have grown afraid. But he didn't. Not in more than two weeks. He had been swept away, happy for the ride.

Gabe Barlow was one of those in-the-moment kind of kids. Some might casually label his tendencies as selfish. And on his worst days, the label fit. But Gabe was more thoughtful, more tenderhearted, than a truly selfish person could ever be. Though plenty bright, he wasn't cerebral like Hadyn or Garret. And if Ewan was intuitive, Gabe tilted more toward impulsive. Part of that could easily get him stuck in a mood. But the other part was more like a launching pad. Whatever he felt like doing, he did.

Walking double-time to keep up with the adults around him, he decided to check out of their conversation and tune into the birds around him. A part of him was surprised at how naturally it came, even after so short a time. His thoughts drifted to the cooing of the pigeons, the crisp trilling of the sparrows perched on their rooftops. Over the days of their journey to Faielyn, he had learned the cry of hawks and eagles wheeling overhead, speaking of freedom and wind. Owls, telling of night and moonlight. Crows, of magic and memory. Here in the city, the pigeons spoke mainly of bread crumbs, mice, and wetness. Gabe didn't speak back. He was the one brown-eyed Barlow boy—brown like his daddy's—with short blond hair and an open face that showed everything he was feeling. At the moment, what he felt was conflicted. A part of him still felt jealous and secretive about his gift, while the other part wanted to show off a bit. Caught in the middle, he simply perked his ears and smiled.

Before long, they reached an impasse in the streets, where the lane abruptly terminated at water's edge. A boat and oarsmen were there, waiting for passengers. Gondolas were everywhere, part of the rhythm of life in Faielyn.

"Along the Outers. Stick to the lanes all the way to the Fountain of Virgins at Costellana," Diamedici told the gondolier, handing him a fare three times the journey's worth. "And no shortcuts through Caregio."

The man held his long oar close to his chest. His eyes were on Va'nya.

"I don't carry his kind," he said.

"There's another shil for you on the other side. That's four times your fee, and more than enough to buy your prejudice."

The oarsman, a tall, lanky man, remained in place. He was visibly agitated. "It's not right, my lord. A highborn Vinelander like yerself keeping company like that."

"Really, now? And yet here I am, keeping company with you, thinking how much better the world would be if gondoliers would shut their mouths and do their jobs."

His lips formed a smile of wine and steel as he spoke. Va'nya's expression remained implacable. Still, the oarsman hesitated. The prince took a small, almost imperceptible step toward him, a movement felt more than seen. Point made. The gondolier jutted his chin to show his courage. Spat once, took the money.

"Think 'cause you got gold around your neck you're a real dandy," the gondolier said. "Think you can just buy off a man and forget your own obligations."

"Think of me whatever you like," he said. "So long as you're stroking that oar."

They pushed back from the dock, drifting swiftly along back alleys of still water. Diamedici stayed close to the gondolier, his hand resting on his sword with casual intent.

They glided past women hanging out their back windows with wet laundry in hand, stringing it on twine or wire stretched between the buildings on either side of the canal in search of a few moments of sunshine. There were pots of flowers sitting in windows and pigeons lofting in the breeze. As the mists gradually rolled back, both petals and birds seemed to warm to the meager sunlight. It was nearly noon.

After some time, the gondola came to rest. The five exited the vessel.

"I'll be taking that extra shil," the driver said warily.

"You'll be thankful you still have a tongue," Diamedici replied.

They melted into the convoluted mess of dusty streets, moving aimlessly enough that Gabe began to wonder if they were lost, not realizing that was precisely the point. Within a few short moments, they passed a busy courtyard paved with brick. In the center, the Fountain of Virgins featured three pretty young copper maidens, giggling, pouring water from a pot onto the statuesque form of a sleeping man, startled awake. Gabe thought it humorous.

"So, Giovanni is dying?" Cruedwyn asked. "I hadn't heard."

A pained look crossed Diamedici's face, which Gabe thought odd. After all, Giovanni was the one who had placed the bounty on his head.

"The castle staff has done well with the secret, but my uncle is not getting any better. When he dies, I will be given the crown."

Gabe didn't understand the politics, and didn't really know what to think of the prince. All he knew was that the flurry of activity had never stopped since entering Faielyn. They had literally bumped into the prince at a tavern in the Poor Quarter, only to find out later that his spies had been trailing them for days. Apparently, the rumor of their coming to Faielyn had preceded them. Once Diamedici knew the date of their arrival, he arranged to be ahead of them. A typically cunning move for the prince, as Gabe would come to learn. And so they had come to Ulavo, the Bittermen, and whatever Diamedici was plotting. Strangely, it seemed to include the Highlanders. But Diamedici was a hard read. He carried himself the same way he carried the smile on his face—too confident by half, with just enough twinkling humor that a person was left wondering if the joke was on him or if the prince was merely laughing at himself.

Diamedici kept his head down as they walked. He was brash, but no fool. Obviously, he preferred to remain recognized by the general populace.

"So you're really a prince?" Gabe said, impressed. "Son of a king?"

Diamedici's answer was both polite and a trifle bored, as if he had explained this a thousand times. "There are no kings. Not anymore. I am of the line that once ruled Vineland, when the royal line began to falter. A long time ago." He held out his hands, spun once, putting himself on display. "I know, I know. You were about to tell me how much I look the part, yes? Flattery, my boy. Remember, flattery will get you everywhere."

Gabe didn't know what to do until Diamedici winked. He grinned, mostly with relief.

Moving through back alleys, past low canopies and knots of people, their party gave no greeting. The streets were a blinding maze of sunlight, cobblestone, and soft blue shadow.

Cruedwyn whispered in Hadyn's ear, loud enough to be heard.

"Many guilds here. Guild of Glassblowers. Guild of Mosaicists. Guild of Sculptors, Painters." He gave Hadyn a knowing look. "The League."

"Ah, the Cutters and Gutters!" Diamedici said. "Assassins are quite entrenched here, yes. Can't seem to uproot them. Too much money and fear. Frankly, I think my uncle has given up trying." Taking note of Cruedwyn's pained, furtive glance, he smiled. "In a bit of trouble?"

Cruedwyn shook himself, as if casting off a wet cloak. "None worth speaking of."

"Better not to speak of such things, eh? Everyone fears the League, friend. Nothing to be ashamed of."

Creed waved dismissively. "A Creed fears no man."

It was the sort of statement Gabe had come to expect from Cruedwyn. He cringed, waiting for the soft protest of the magic sword to begin. He watched the ornate shape of the dragon-jawed haft, the glowing amber orbs. In their short time together, Gabe had witnessed the spectacle half a dozen times. Each began with a playful boast, followed by exaggerations without repentance; next, the bard would wiggle and twitch, talking faster as the metal blade grew hot in its scabbard; finally, red-faced and humiliated, he would tear off the sword and swear.

This time, no swearing, no heat. The sword was quiet.

"See a ghost, little friend?" Diamedici laughed, noticing the surprised expression on Gabe's face. He turned to Cruedwyn, crooking his mouth. "Seems you have a reputation for one reason or another. Never fear. I plan on steering clear of League streets and taverns, so your pride can rest easy. Besides, it's for my sake, not yours. There's a bounty on my head."

"Oh, the bounty," Creed said, a little too hopefully. "Right."

"A small fortune, really," said the prince.

Hadyn flicked at a mosquito on his arm. "What kind of fortune?"

"I dare say it's up to a hundred shils. Are you plotting to turn me in?"

The oldest Barlow seemed impressed. "Coppers? Or silver?"

Diamedici huffed. "Obviously you don't understand the color of royal jealousy. Gold, my friend. Gold. The people like gold. The League likes gold. Uncle promises gold."

Cruedwyn tried to act nonchalant. "Well then, of course, we should avoid those places you mentioned. Definitely, so long as it helps *you*. That's all I care about."

A high, familiar twang began, coming from the bard's person. Gabe grinned at Va'nya. He had almost made it. Cruedwyn quickly added, "Probably help us all, I reckon. I mean, we all need help, right? I know I do."

The twang faded.

Just ahead, six soldiers in leather armor and green sashes turned down their street. The guards had a casual stride but were aimed straight for them. Diamedici kept his pace.

"Palace guard, probably a shift change," he said coolly, slipping into the shadows of a nearby alehouse. "Better to be safe than sorry."

They entered a small, low-ceilinged room with a handful of rickety blackened tables and a single crooked window facing the street. The greasy air was layered with smoke and body odor. Gabe choked. Behind the bar, a large, rough-looking woman lazily chewed some unidentifiable piece of meat, staring out the window with a dull gaze. All the tables were empty save one, where a fat man and a small, wiry fellow were deep in conversation. The fat man paused briefly to consider the new entrants. Unaffected, he resumed his conversation. But a moment later, his eyes darted up again, narrowing.

"What'll it be, gents?" the barkeep asked, wiping her mouth on her sleeve, letting her eyes finally come to rest on Diamedici. For a brief moment, she seemed surprised. It passed.

Cruedwyn gagged at the smell. "Would a good vinegar scrub be too much to ask? Good grief, woman, have some pride." To Hadyn, he whispered, "That *is* a woman, isn't it?"

The barkeep didn't move. Mouth open, she laughed. "You're a funny one."

Hadyn whispered back: "Lucky man, I think she likes you."

The two men at the next table rose suddenly, ready to exit. Before they could take a single step, Diamedici had placed the tip of his sword at the fat man's throat. Both men raised their arms. Everyone froze. The prince pulled three silver coins from his pocket with his free hand. He flipped a shil through the air to each man, a third to the barkeep.

"Don't think I've ever met the man who'd hurry off with his glass still full."

The barkeep snorted, bit the coin. "Dinbalo, you is a fool."

Gabe saw then. A plate of cut meats. Two glasses of ale, more than half full. Obviously, the men had barely begun.

"Just makin' room, m'lord. You looked thirsty."

"Very polite, I'm sure, but take a seat. All we ask is a few minutes' time. No questions. No leaving."

"'Course, m'lord," the fat man said, returning nervously to his chair. "Mighty generous of you now, not killing us or nothin'. I'm a friend of the League, truth b'told."

Gabe fidgeted in the center of the room, searching the window for a glimpse of the guards outside. Hadyn had his hand locked on his sword as if he might actually use it. What did he think he would do? Yell and swing, hope he hit something?

As the man named Dinbalo returned to his seat, the tension in the room slowly eased. Diamedici edged away from both men, still gripping his weapon. He approached the window, taking care to stay outside any angle of light or visibility. He peered down the street, saw the six guards standing in the middle swapping stories. Nothing suspicious.

"Dinbalo, eh?" the prince said, glancing back. "By your accent and look, I'd say you're from Desora. Certainly not Faielyn, or you'd know I'm not with the League."

Both men exhaled, visibly relieved. They licked their lips nervously, while the barkeep carefully polished the face of her new silver shil. Not many of those came through a place like this. Satisfied, she revealed a mouth full of brown teeth.

"I've got a nice ale for you, lord," she said, cheered and grateful, as if a bit of service might bring more silver. "Ale and a wedge of Eldoran cheese, maybe? Doesn't that sound nice?"

"We thought you was the Black Hand," the smaller man said, his eyes darting from his food to Diamedici and back again. "We heard tell he's been roaming 'round these parts looking for one of them magic Fey swords. Heard it on the road here. Idle merchants waggin' their tongues."

"Quillian, the Black Hand?" Diamedici mused, flicking his gaze toward Cruedwyn, who by now had turned a shade or two lighter in color. "Nonsense. Are you blind? Am I wearing black gloves? Black anything?"

"Reckon not, now that you mention it. Sorry, lord. We're but simple folk."

Diamedici edged his face away from the light as the soldiers finally passed in plain view of the window. "An honest mistake, I'm sure," he said, putting fingers to his lips.

"Honest might as well be my name," said the fat man, grinning. He had begun to sweat profusely, and the smile on his face looked plastered there. He kept talking, even louder. Gabe wanted him to be quiet. "Honest and truthful, that's me. A fine, upstanding citizen. Which means you'll be forgivin' me for wantin' that reward I seen hung on a post." Then, with startling volume, Dinbalo began shouting. "Diamedici! Diamedici! Prince Diamedici. In here! Guards! Guards!"

He was very nearly dead before he finished his last word. Or would have been, with the prince's blade buried in his heart, had Cruedwyn not caught Diamedici's wrist and shoved him forward.

"No time for blood! Out the back. Go!"

The barkeep did nothing but grin and watch, slurping grease from her lips. Cruedwyn grabbed Gabe, pushing him toward the door at the rear wall. In the tumult, the little man with Dinbalo turned brave. He stuck his foot in the walkway, thinking to trip one of them. Hadyn kicked his leg ferociously, leapt over, sprinting for the door. The man jerked and howled. Va'nya, on cat's feet, tipping tables behind him to block their path, hauled a small bench out the door with him.

The voice of the fat man rang out, laughing, mocking. "Apologies, lord! And to think I almost settled fer yer silver! Bah!"

Cruedwyn glanced back once more, then slammed the door shut. From the inside came sounds of table legs scraping the wooden floor. Agitated voices. Movement. The barkeep, laughing.

The five of them were cramped in a narrow alley barely wide enough for three. Va'nya wedged the bench under the door bolt. It held, but probably not for long.

"This way," Diamedici said. He darted down a long, cramped lane. Behind, Gabe heard pounding, heard the alehouse door burst open. He heard angry voices shouting. A jolt of fear hit him. After weeks of play and fun, suddenly, came revelation. Karac Tor was a place of danger, not some fanciful game. As they rounded the corner, he caught a flash of green uniforms behind, the color of the House of Etrascus. At least two of the guards were in pursuit, maybe more. He saw Dinbalo bulging into the alley, shaking his fist, screaming.

"Let's fight," Cruedwyn breathed as they ran. "They aren't many, and I count for three."

"More will come. Keep moving."

So they ran. Left, right, left, left. Straight. Double back. Onward. Keeping to narrow alleys, shadows, darting across traffic, amongst bodies and carts and great wicker baskets lining the streets, baskets full of fruits and vegetables and bolts of cloth. Then back into shadows again. Gabe caught glimpses in between buildings of the waters of the canal not far off, the sun glinting on its rippled surface. He was tiring out. It hurt to run.

"Faster, Gabe!" Hadyn urged." You can't quit now."

His legs and lungs were burning when a familiar sound on the rooftop drew his attention. Not a chirp or squawk, not a coo as the others heard, if they heard at all. Instead, skimming the tops of the roofs like a leaf carried by a river, the noise of birds became words in his ears. Two silverdoves, descending in a torrent of wings, lit on a gutter, murmuring nervously to one another. It took Gabe a minute to realize they were saying something important.

"No, no, no!" he blurted out suddenly. "We can't keep going that way! Soldiers . . . headed toward the arch. They're coming toward us. We'll be trapped."

Diamedici stopped short, heaving for air. He was clearly annoyed. "Nonsense, boy! We've nearly lost them. Do you think I don't know my own city?"

With surprising calmness, Hadyn said, "Gabe, are you *sure*?"

Gabe raised his eyes to the roof, hoping he would not have to say more. Following his gaze, Hadyn saw the two silverdoves. Back to Gabe, then to Cruedwyn and the prince. Cruedwyn also looked up.

"I know it doesn't make sense, but you've got to trust him. I trust him."

"I agree," Cruedwyn said. "We should change direction. Quickly."

Diamedici growled. "Obviously, the three of you know something I don't."

There were three shop back doors. He hurriedly yanked on each, but all were locked. To the right, another narrow lane curved around a building.

"What's that way?"

"It drops down to the canal and dead ends. There's a ledge. It's a retaining wall for the canal." His face suddenly brightened. "We can crawl it, I'll wager! It's fitted rock and has plenty of grips. From there to Sandovar Bridge, then hide under the bridge and cross later. They'll never see us."

"Too late," Cruedwyn said, flicking quick eyes to the Barlows. Calm, sure eyes. "This is not yet the end," he whispered.

Gabe saw four soldiers enter the shadowed alley, swords drawn. But Cruedwyn was already sprinting to meet them, his own sword singing silver in the sultry air.

Hadyn put his hand on his scabbard, but Va'nya pushed against him. The Highlander wheeled about, pulling two short double blades from leather holsters on his legs. They were like long metal claws extending outward from both ends of his fist. *Jirq* knives, a Highland specialty.

"Take the L'ka and his brother," he told Diamedici. "Go." He put his hand on Gabe's shoulder. "I *will* find you, L'ka. My fate is with you."

"The shop of Milangino, across the bridge," Diamedici said. "Find us there."

The Highlander nodded once, then dashed away, like a leopard leaping toward its prey. Joining Cruedwyn, whose blade flashed in the sun.

CHAPTER 5

Meetings

*N*ope . . . *can't do it*, Gabe thought, panting. *Not this time.*

Sweat poured down his face. He felt like a wet cloth flung against a wall, pressed flat, stuck by a mix of suction and willpower. He groped blindly for another careful handhold, got it. His fingers were tired and his ankles throbbed from bearing his weight. The climb wasn't difficult so much as tedious. Very tiring. All he could think about was Cruedwyn and Va'nya, risking their lives so that he could escape. He kept glancing down the wall, anxious and hopeful to see their faces peering over the rim of stone. Cruedwyn was a cunning swordsman, right? Darn good, really. One of the best. And Va'nya . . . well, Bird Men were raised to fight.

None of it brought comfort. They could still die.

He stopped for a minute to catch his breath. They were scut-
tling along the backside of a stone levee barely taller than Diamedici. Water skimmed their toes. His fingers were rubbed raw.
This part of the canal passed directly under Sandovar Bridge. They
just had to get to it.

"Hadyn, they'll be okay, won't they?" he whispered.

Red-faced, Hadyn managed a rough grunt, nothing more. His
sword banged about, getting in the way of his movement. He was
frustrated.

"Am I missing something?" he whispered harshly, as if blaming
Diamedici. "We're official emissaries of the White Abbey for crying
out loud! Vineland is the abbey's protectorate. Shouldn't it be a little
easier to get to Giovanni?"

Diamedici had rotated his scabbard to hang off his backside.
Moving with relative ease, he paused. "Politics, my friend. You are
missing politics. Court intrigue, like fleas on a dog. Uncle's advisors
pull their little strings, but I know them all. Selfishness makes men
utterly predictable. I trust one man in the whole wretched court.
You will never get your message into the right hands unless we go
through back channels."

"Back channels," Hadyn repeated, staring up and down the
watery path. "Right."

They made it to the bridge, a wide, gentle arch of mortared stone,
one of two bridges connecting the Poor Quarter to the Palazzo,
where merchants and artists formed a beehive around the royal
palace. In the Palazzo, wealth, culture, and snobbery made revelry
in the streets. Marble buildings with tall, fluted columns dazzled

the eye with their stately grandeur, colorful mosaics and tiled
courtyards, while entrance to the private bathhouses clearly distin-
guished elite from humble peasantry. Elegant silver-haired ladies in
flowing gowns glided past galleries of fine porcelain, glassworks,
and sculpted stone, looking for pieces of sufficient quality to elevate
their status, while old men and young men gathered in streets,
pubs, and parks, arguing over the teachings of the latest popular
philosopher, whose works they barely understood.

Having finally reached the bridge and crawled up the wall,
Gabe, Hadyn, and Diamedici found enough space to rest and pass
the time. They crouched on a slope of earth underneath the bridge,
listening to sounds of foot traffic and grinding cart wheels. Gondolas passed in steady succession, slender fingers of wood trawling
the water. Most bore passengers; a few were empty. Regardless, no
one paid them any heed. What was noteworthy about a few beggars
finding shade under the bridge? After roughly two hours with no
sign of Cruedwyn and Va'nya, nor any guards, Diamedici scampered out and around the side of the bridge, peering past sculpted
shrubs to survey the milling crowds.

"I think it's safe," he said. "Don't dawdle and don't look guilty."

He said this to Gabe more than Hadyn, which sort of bothered
Gabe. Too hot to fret much. They crossed, dissolving rather easily
into the crowds on the other side. Though Gabe still worried about
Cruedwyn and Va'nya, he found himself starting to breathe easier.
Hadyn didn't seem too concerned, and for the moment, that was
good enough.

Diamedici cast a careful eye in all directions, but otherwise
wandered with the casual gait of nearly every other man in the
street, though Gabe knew they were in fact steadily creeping
toward Milangino's shop. When they came to a little building with

an oval placard of etched brass that read Il Milan, Gabe sighed with relief. In the lower corner of the sign was a little symbol, a chisel and hammer forming an X. The mark of the Sculptor's Guild.

Gabe's stomach was growling like there was a tiger in his belly. He wanted food.

"I'm hungry," he announced.

"Not now," Hadyn said tersely. Apparently, he didn't understand. Gabe wanted food.

"*Really* hungry."

"Hush!" Hadyn said, his eyes on Diamedici. Gabe dropped his head, slumped his shoulders. An all-too-common feeling gripped him. *Just because I'm the youngest doesn't mean I don't matter.*

He reached for the doorknob, but Diamedici shook his head. The prince, usually boisterous, motioned solemnly. Together, they slipped around the side of the shop into another alley. Gabe decided he was sick of alleys.

At the back door, the prince knocked twice. Paused. Then once again. Then three more times. A piece of wood slid open at eye level, revealing a roving eyeball that scanned them up and down through the crack. The wood slid back into place. There were sounds of movement, bolt and bar. The door swung open.

Two hands reached out, pulling them into a back room filled with large sections of tree stumps that had been debarked and stacked along one wall. Balsa, limewood, pear. The room smelled strongly of pine resin and hemlock fir. It was dimly lit, with no windows, many candles. A half dozen roughly face-shaped or human-shaped carvings in various stages of progress were mounted on pedestals here and there. In the stern, flickering shadows, their sightless eyes all seemed cast upon Gabe, piercing inside, through him. Freaky enough to make his skin crawl. He turned away, but their blind gaze on his neck stayed with him. Instead, he chose to focus on the two men who stood opposite them, arms crossed in silence. One, a little older than Diamedici, was covered in wood chips. He held a hammer and chisel in his hand. The other, cool and distant, was older again by half, graying at the temples, with countless frown lines curving down from the corners of his mouth. His attire was upper class, possibly a courtier or lesser nobleman.

"Milangino, my friend," the prince said with obvious warmth, finally removing his hood as he addressed the sculptor. The two men clasped forearms.

"How goes your road?" Milangino asked cautiously, appraising something in Diamedici's eyes. He glanced at the boys.

"We're alive, let's leave it at that," Diamedici replied.

The older gentleman drew attention to himself with a polite cough. He was clearly perturbed, yet there was something else in his eyes. A glint of amusement, perhaps?

"So . . . the carving is a ruse," he observed, not bothering to make eye contact with anyone. He stood at a stiff distance, still stuck in his pose. Beside him, a chunk of wood bore the beginnings of a remarkable likeness to his visage. Gabe again found himself staring into the blind, unfocused eyes, as if the carving might come alive and speak—tell him what was going on. Strange as that would have been, it would have been nice to know.

"Lord Rosalier, please forgive my poor contrivances," Diamedici said, pausing to study the chiseled wood block and compare the results. "I am the one who secretly ordered your likeness, which, I must say, is shaping up quite handsomely."

Lord Rosalier sniffed with contempt. "How lovely that you think so, my lord prince. Am I sufficiently the butt of your joke, then? Or should I dance a jig, as well?"

"I've seen you dance, my lord. Thank you, no. But you misjudge. Tell me, would you have come otherwise, with no contrivance?"

"Absolutely not." Shucking the pose, he gathered his robes to leave.

"Yet the times press upon us, so we must all take risks," the prince said hastily. "Getting you here was my risk. Staying is yours."

Rosalier stopped at the door.

Diamedici continued more slowly. "I've come with two Outlanders, my good lord. You've heard of them, I know. Hadyn and Gabe. Alethes sends them as ambassadors of the abbey, with news for Uncle. It is news he may not wish to hear, but he must. And he will never hear it unless *you* take it to him. We both know this is true."

The room was still. Gabe and Hadyn shifted uncomfortably on their feet. Lifting his chin, Rosalier drew a long, begrudging breath.

"Ill advised, perhaps, but clever," he said. "Even needful in these troubled times. I'll allow you that much."

Ever so slightly, Diamedici inclined his head, bowing from the waist. No gloating.

"Then you will help?" he said. "My noble friend, you are the only man at court I trust."

"Bah! You I hardly trust at all, Diamedici di Etrascus! You are impetuous and vain. Always have been." He sighed. "Yet I suppose, in this struggle, we are allies of sorts. At the very least, I know you love my land, even more than you love yourself . . . if that is possible."

Milangino broke in softly. "There is much to strengthen, to reform. The military is in shambles. The fair vine is rotting to the root."

"We must change our ways," Diamedici added, taking a half step forward. "Ally with those we can no longer afford to keep as enemies. We must be bold. For the good of Vineland."

Highlanders, Gabe realized in a flash.

Rosalier tilted a wary eye. He seemed careful. "Not too bold, I think."

"Wisdom in all things, of course. Care in all things. But make no mistake, it must be bold. Nothing less will do."

Things were slowly becoming clearer. Gabe knew from Va'nya the two dominions were eternal enemies. Always had been, ever since Aion forbade shapeshifting to an ancient clan of the Wild South and, on those terms, welcomed their forefather Gil into Karac Tor. Though thousands of years had passed, there was still much bad blood. To the refined and noble Vinelanders, Bird Men were primitive barbarians. Apparently the prince thought to change things.

Rosalier stepped forward, knotting his fingers together. Shadows played on his face.

"For the good of Vineland," he mumbled. It was political suicide to entertain such talk. The cost of the enterprise made his voice quiver. He glanced disparagingly toward Hadyn.

"Outlanders, eh? Yes, we have all heard the rumors. They say you have power with words, boy. Is that true?"

Hadyn didn't answer, fidgeting with the hilt of his sword. He looked between the two Rosaliers, from the living, agitated human to the image in wood. Tentatively reaching out, he grazed the chiseled shape with his fingertips, eyes closed. He held for a long time, then ever so slowly, withdrew his touch, filling his lungs. Stepped back. Formed a word on his lips. Loosed it. A strange, earthy word, unknown to him except that he heard the sound of it when he listened to the wood. He was getting faster at finding, hearing the names, speaking accurately what he heard, but was better with simple woven things—fiber, fabric, rope. Metal, water, and fire eluded him. Also, nothing living.

Though mastery was slow, wood had recently come within reach. With a dull, grinding sound, the sculpture of Rosalier shredded, peeling like a dried onion, layer by papery layer. A hundred splintered chunks fell to the ground in a cloud of sawdust.

The old man remained expressionless for a long time. Slowly, he began to chuckle. The sound turned sharp and bitter, then became a belly laugh. "Looks like the joke is on you now, Milangino. My thanks, boy. I didn't much care for it anyway." He grabbed a fistful of sawdust, dropped the fine powder into the air, watched it settle. "We are all but dust, I think. So say the priests. Dust, with choices to make. I don't know how you have come to be here, Outlander. But I shall carry your message. Tell it to me."

Diamedici grinned fiercely. "Go on, Hadyn. Tell him. For the good of Vineland."

Two down, two more to go, Gabe thought.

Hadyn drew a breath to speak, pulling a second copy of Alethes's gilded letter out of the small leather pouch at his waist. Just as he was about to begin reading, a loud thump rattled the iron lock on the door in the next room. Gabe grinned at the ironic tone of the muffled voice.

"What kind of sculptor locks their front door? Milangino, it is Cruedwyn Creed! Let me in!"

CHAPTER 6

Jackal Raids

Quiet! Stay down!" Har Hallas whispered hoarsely. "The first to make those jackals scatter will never kiss a woman again, cause I'll rip your lips off. Now wait for my mark! And stuff your ears or we'll all be dead."

Ewan tensed, feeling the enormous pressure Har had laid upon him with this test. It hung from his shoulders like a heavy woolen mantle, but also brought a thrilling jolt of importance. In a few moments, the command would come, not for his silence, but his song. Har was hushing the men in preparation for the attack, keeping them low to the ground on the ridge overlooking the broad plain below. The entire raiding party, some twenty strong, was practically holding their breath. Ewan figured the only way he could get lower to the ground was if he magically turned into soil.

Pressed flat in the dry, knee-high grass, he gave Sorge an irritated look, the kind that said, *what more does he want?*

The monk kept his focus over the low ridge, but the corners of his eyes creased with humor. Big, barrel-chested Har. Nobody messed with the Earl of Midlands. Below, their prey crept slowly through the arid grassland—fangs with four legs, black tongues flopping. Three of the larger jackals constantly snarled and snapped at one another. Fights broke out, clawing, yelping. The smaller ones wisely kept their noses pressed to the ground, but every scent they caught drove them to a state of near frenzy. Ewan saw their hunched spines, spiked with gray and black fur. Huge, foul beasts—even the puny ones. He remembered all too well that short, terror-filled sprint along the fringes of Redthorn toward a ratty rope bridge.

The raiding party was perched on a low rise just north of the White Abbey and south of the small, high-walled outpost city of Stobnotter. They were lying in the grass, in their sweat, faces toward a mild, humid breeze that felt like a gloved hand smothering them. Below and to the east, the torrid plains stretched toward the black rash of Redthorn in the distance.

Har had a problem. Not a new problem, but a problem that was getting worse each month. Jackals were getting braver, roaming farther. Especially troubling were the packs, like this one, ranging west of Goldfoam River. The river had always formed a natural barrier, limiting most jackal activity to the eastern shore. Without it, the attacks on Stobnotter would be routine and bloody.

"At my signal, crossbows fire one volley. I don't want to waste bolts, so confirm your targets. We gut the rest." Har lifted his head slightly. "That is, if your boy can handle his part. What do you say, monk?"

"In a half span we'll know. That's what I say."

The whole thing had been Sorge's idea, sort of. He had brought it up mostly in jest, then Har had run with it. Ewan wasn't sure whether to thank the monk or kick him. Har grunted.

"Let's hope it works."

"Ewan," Sorge whispered, pressing two little balls of soft wax into his ears. "There will be other raids. If you aren't ready . . ."

He let his question drift away. Ewan pulled out his whistle. From Ireland, to America, to another world. Here, now. He took a swig of water from his flask.

"No. Let's do it."

Of the twenty soldiers, six carried crossbows. They had already put bolt to string and cocked. The others held swords at ready. All the men were lightly armored, dressed for speed and agility more than defense. All had similar wads of candle wax stuffed in their ears. Sorge had his staff beside him, a bow and quiver in his hands. Previously it had been slung across his back. For emergencies only, he had said. Basic longbow, borrowed from Har's armory. Probably wouldn't ever use it. Grim-faced, the monk now notched an arrow.

Ewan counted twenty-nine jackals below. He was nervous. His very first raid. His first real test. Alethes had protested the whole affair. Why risk the safety and mission of the Outlander for a whiff of magic? True, the high priest had been forced to consider some new things of late, but Whites were natural pessimists of all things esoteric. It was their part in the Order of Aion to trust the faith's objective tenets and defend them. He was probably saying prayers back at base camp. Sorge, while also torn, decided the need was greater than the risk, not only for the problem of jackals, but also to determine the limits and possibilities of the power of Ewan's song. Over the last few weeks, Ewan had been practicing—a lot. *Practice* might be the wrong word, since he wasn't taking lessons and didn't know exactly what he was doing. His method was simple. Whenever he strongly felt a certain mood or had a burst of inspiration or heard a phrase of melody in his head, he developed it and found notes to put it to music. Some were songs, some were just bursts of noise. Some were terrible.

Regardless, strange things happened whenever he played.

One day last week, engulfed with thoughts of both homesickness and anguish for his dad, he had played a deeply melancholy tune, so simple and spare as to be pointless, only to witness a nearby tree suddenly drop all its leaves in rhythm to the melody. It had been green and hale one minute, then stripped for winter the next. Two days later, during another random surge of emotion, a cup of dirty water turned clear right under his nose. Rather, his flute.

But most strange of all was the night he, Sorge, and Alethes first set out to meet with Har, during the Midlands earl's annual summer raids. Every ruler born to the seat of Brimshane was guaranteed two border problems: Fey to the north and jackals to the south, and this year was shaping up to be a doozy on both fronts. Sitting around the campfire—what, three nights ago?—Ewan had played a simple, peaceful song inspired by the dancing flames. As the fire spit and hissed and the melody unraveled in the burning coals, Sorge became ensnared in a vision. The trance was deep and vivid, lasting nearly twenty minutes. Likewise, Alethes was overcome with sleep and did not wake for *eleven* hours. When Sorge eventually came to his senses, he was so disturbed by the vision that he would not speak. More comically, neither he nor the high priest remembered Ewan playing, and both forbade him to play the song again. Ewan complied, until they joined Har's company and he played the tune again, after Sorge wandered outside the camp that evening. Once more, the effect was remarkable. Har's men passed out, right where they were. Eating, walking, they just dropped. The song was like a powerful drug. Their eyes grew heavy; their mouths grew slack, right in the middle of lifting their forks. Even Har's hounds dropped cold. Which, upon his return, gave Sorge an idea. How might it affect other creatures?

Thus, the test.

Har had been impressed. He had been able to resist—he was a strong old bear—but knew the feel of deep magic. So today, after the first wave of killing with crossbows, the plan was for Ewan to play his sleepy little tune and see what happened. If it worked, there would be a great slaughter of jackals.

If it didn't . . . well, that part got a little tricky. The number of jackals in the pack was greater than anticipated. If it was going to be a fight, they should have brought more men.

"Make me proud, boy," Har said. And Ewan, for some reason, wanted to.

The earl motioned three fingers forward. His captain echoed the motion. Up and down the line, men nodded, watching for the signal. Har raised his fist just a few inches, held it. Then pulled down, as if cranking a lever.

Six bolts tore through the air, struck their targets, ripping throats, bellies, hides. Six jackals fell, their gray fur splattered with red. For a halting moment, the entire pack froze. One jackal immediately leapt upon the nearest carcass and began devouring it. But when the lead jackal raised his head and howled, the others pricked their ears, began scanning the land. They were mad, but cunning.

Suddenly, they started running. Toward the rise. Toward the raiding party.

Ewan froze.

"How'd they know?" he said. "The wind is against us. How'd they know?"

"Hush! Stand and play." Sorge shoved Ewan to his feet, moving his hands, pushing the flute to the boy's lips. "Play!"

The jackals bellowed with rage at the sight of a single human, alone on the ridge. But he was not alone for long. As one, Har's men stood, steel flashing in the sun. Four men formed a barrier between Ewan and the jackals, bracing for impact. The jackals climbed the hill with frightening speed, leaping, snarling. Ewan felt the blood drain from his face, his hands. Felt music drain from his memory. All of a sudden he couldn't recall any song, ever.

Har bellowed for another volley. Six more bolts fired. Only two jackals fell. They would be upon them soon.

Ewan took a deep breath, put the whistle to his lips. Blew. Too soft against the wind. He played louder. Finally, the melody rolled out clean and smooth, like the movement of flame on seasoned wood when the night is thick. It poured from his flute, flowing down the hill toward the jackals. The first beast leaped. The second and third were right behind. Har's men plunged their blades toward the flesh of the beasts. One of the men in front of Ewan was knocked over by the weight of a leaping beast. There were too many. Ewan saw their mangled fur, their yellow teeth. He smelled the nauseous stench. They would be overrun. The test was a mistake.

Har bellowed something. Ewan kept playing, unable to hear. All he knew was a rasping, rabid wave of noise and hunger, of snapping teeth and padded feet. The men in front of him cried out, lashing with their swords. He repeated the tune a third time as loud as he could.

Music and beast collided. The first jackal slumped as if his legs no longer worked. No struggle or whimper. Two more lost consciousness mid-leap, landing in a heap. On the perimeter of the music, other jackals began to stagger drunkenly or slink to the ground. Their malevolence turned to a cold stupor. To the rear, the remaining beasts yelped and fled. Har bellowed again. Crossbows snapped. Swords plunged. Near and far, the jackals died. The dry brown grass turned slick with blood. Twenty-nine jackals, dead.

Ewan was panting, still playing. He didn't realize his shoulders were being shaken by Sorge, that he was being hoisted by the men. They were cheering. Har laughed.

A good slaughter that day.

CHAPTER 7

Sorge's Mission

Back at camp, as the sun slid low and the leaves on the scattered trees burned with light, Ewan was still basking in the thrill of victory, in the pleasure of his gift. His music was more than melody and rhythm. It was power, rising from a deep place within him, like a wild bird leaping free into the air. From his soul, from his flute. *His* flute.

The men of the raiding party kept the tale moving, repeating it again and again. Har rewarded them with ale, and the more they drank, the grander the story became. They showed the men who stayed behind the little scraps of wax that protected their ears, their bloody swords, the head of a jackal brought back as a trophy, fangs bared. They pointed to Ewan, smiling, giving him a thumbs-up until he finally entered Har's great, lantern-lit tent along with Sorge and Alethes. The earl sloshed a mug of ale and pounded the table, bursting with a fatherly sort of pride. A ring of froth seemed perpetually fixed to his beard.

"Now just craft me a tune to keep the Fey in Elkwood, boy, and I'll build you the finest home you've ever seen, right on Plumwater. You can even charge a handsome toll—a silver shil for every barge and boat that passes by. How about that?" He grinned, then shook his head ruefully. "Ah, what a chore. Curse the Fey folk—the whole lot of 'em. That was real fine out there today, boy. Take this. You've earned it."

He slid a long object wrapped in cloth across the table. Ewan unfolded the fabric and found a short sword wrapped inside. He touched the blade carefully, almost lovingly, looking first to Sorge, then Har. "Thank you," he whispered.

Har smiled. "Good Yrgavien steel, that. It'll cut when you need it to."

Alethes had listened carefully to the whole tale more than once, adding nothing. He was still quite skeptical of mystic songs and true names and other sundry supernatural events, but to his credit, he had done something rather rare in the last two weeks. More listening. Less talking.

Sorge joined the revelry, but only halfheartedly. He chewed a piece of bread in silence, full of other burdens. Hardly any time had passed since receiving news of Eldoran's death. The Gray Abbey, in uproar and mourning, had called for Sorge to return for the Last Requiem. It was the duty of all elders. Sorge had agonized for a day and a half before finally refusing the summons. His mission, he declared, was now with the Outlanders. Ewan knew it wasn't easy. Eldoran had been the most stabilizing presence in Sorge's mostly troubled life. He had been the one who nursed the warrior-turned-monk through his darkest days of grief and guilt over Nemesia, over Corus. He had led him down a path of spiritual awakening, to Aion's Way. Most important of all, he had been a friend, as had Melanor.

Har noticed Sorge's quietness. Big and rough, but not without discernment, he toned down his boisterous laughter, laid his mug on the table. Silence, more timid than the rising moon, gathered around each person. Outside the great tent, soldiers continued to chuckle and eat. Some sang softly. Many had already faded for the night. The camp would pick up tomorrow and move north toward Stobnotter, continuing to hunt jackals. After another week, it would be time for a few short days at Brimshane, resting and restocking. Then the patrols would fan out along Elkwood, seeking Fey.

It was a gift—possibly a curse—of the bloodline of Midlands earls to be attuned to that invisible world. Some few previous earls had been able to see Fey with their eyes, as Ewan could. Most felt the Fey folk as a passing breeze grazing their skin, a gathering of mischief. In the movings and churnings of some deeper instinct, an earl could tell if a spoiled well was merely bad water or Fey doings. By grace and breeding, he then mustered the will to push them back. The urge was primitive—a part of their connection to the land they governed. And it passed to their sons. With each generation the land heir, upon his father's death, would feel a sudden, rising tide of protective intuitions, along with a tingling, foreign awareness. And the next round of raids would commence. Har Hallas was considered among the greats in this respect, fierce and unyielding. But he had no sons, no one to whom he could pass the gift.

Once he had three. All were dead many years past, for various reasons. Ewan had heard the tale of his grieving wife, the Lady Madwyn, who had retreated from life, who wandered her gardens alone.

So much pain in the world, he thought, *every world.*

"They say Jonas has disappeared," the earl announced abruptly. "Archibald maintains he sent him away on a diplomatic errand. I don't believe it."

"A strange man," Alethes agreed. "I have met him at court. He's a fairly recent advisor to Archibald and, for the most part, seemed reasonable to me. But for some reason, I do not like him."

"You're being too kind—"

As if his chair had burst into flames, Sorge suddenly stood. He seemed agitated when he announced, "I have decided to go north. In search of Corus. I believe he may still be alive."

Alethes spilled his cup of alm tea. Har slowly leaned forward, resting on his elbows. Neither high priest nor earl spoke. Ewan lifted his head.

Sorge pressed his thumb against the grain of the wooden table, drawing words from memory. "Before Nemesia fell, she said something to me. 'Find Corus,' she said. 'Find him. Tell him Nemesia stayed true.'" He shook his head. "I cannot get it out of my mind. 'Find him . . .' as if he were still alive. I think she knew something we don't."

His voice faltered, but Alethes was compassionless. "You absolutely cannot trust the tellings of a witch, Elder Sorge. Isgurd's shore, man! Whatever she told you, the words are lies."

All of Sorge's strength seemed to drain into the dirt beneath his feet. He lifted one hand to his face, began wiping downward, rubbing his forehead, eyes, and chin. "Three days ago, I had a vision of terrible darkness. Darkness which no eye could penetrate. Blinding darkness. Corus was there, barely alive, in chains. Somehow, in the darkness, I saw his eyes." The monk turned to hide his face. His voice was barely more than a whisper. "They haunt me. I have never had such a vision. It was more real than this moment."

"A witch's word and visions?" Alethes scoffed. "You chase a *vision?*"

Sorge's shoulders sagged. Ewan wanted to help, but he didn't know what to say.

"I do not expect anyone here to have faith for this," Sorge said. "It is my burden, which I have pondered for three nights and three days. We have seen a measure of the Ravna's riddle already come true: four names, one blood." He motioned to Ewan as proof. "Next, she says there is a *great one* who has fallen low. The riddle says he rises new."

Alethes curled his face, as if he had been handed a bowl of smelly, rancid meat. With a brittleness he made no attempt to hide, he said, "Have you considered, Elder Sorge, that the Ravna could also be saying an *ancient foe* will rise anew . . . not the fallen one?"

His words lingered in the air like a gift no one wanted to open. Ewan felt an icy chill spread across his skin at the mere suggestion. Har rumbled impenetrably. Alethes clipped his words as if they were snapping twigs. "I will grant you, the riddle seems fulfilled. In part. That does *not* mean we can start predicting the future with it. Or take it too literally."

"I have the witness of three: Nemesia, the vision, the riddle. That is enough for me."

Har, rough and tender, said "Sorge, my friend, it's been twenty long years. Not twenty days. *Years.*"

"I know it's foolish. But this is Corus. You know what that means to me. Perhaps to the whole kingdom." He trailed off into something nearer to despair than hope. His gaze fell to the dirt floor, then lifted again. "If he *could* be brought back . . ."

"He's dead, son," Har said. "He's dead."

In the firelight, Sorge's eyes gleamed. "Har, I cannot risk Ewan coming. Will you take care of him until I return?"

Ewan started. He leapt to his feet, ready to protest. But when Sorge laid a heavy hand on his shoulder, something in that act of quiet resignation caused him to hold his tongue.

"I don't even know where I'm going, Ewan. I don't know where to start or where to end. It's too dangerous. And that's final." Sorge turned to Har. Both men studied one another. The Midlands ruler seemed ready to say more, but in the end only inclined his head once.

Alethes swept to his feet in a show of disgust, pushing outward on the flap of the tent. He crisply announced, "I find myself surrounded by madness and superstition. Thus I shall return to the White Abbey tomorrow and consult the Book of Law, as I do on all things. I bid you good evening, Lord Earl, Elder Sorge." He hesitated, seeming to struggle within himself. Ewan watched with a wary eye, trying to figure a way to wiggle out of the new arrangement. He laid his sword on the table, as if lightening his load would help. Alethes, straight as an arrow, having announced his departure, still remained.

"There is a former White," he said at length, reedy and bitter. "A Master Wordsman. Worthy fellow, once. He had a rare and forgotten gift among the Whites, the power of Trulight, from which even Hel itself cannot hide. He might have been high priest instead of me, save his pursuit of strange theories, much as you have now chosen. He belongs now to a band of wanderers and fools—the *Remnant* they're called. Last I heard, he was casting about amidst the Ruins of Lotsley, looking for clues to the end of the world. If you wish my opinion, Sorge, it would be to abandon this folly. But if you want the guidance of one fool to another, he may be able to help you. His name is Barsonici."

With that, he was gone into the night, and the flap fell. Alethes was always in a twitter, always upset about something, it seemed. But Sorge had made his choice and nothing could be done for it. Har looked at Ewan with a certain gentle pride.

"Don't worry lad, I'll take care of you. By Auginn's eyes, I'll watch over you as if you were my own son."

CHAPTER 8

Toward the Ruins

L ate in the dark night, with the moon creeping through the turbid clouds and a gentle noise of wind in the grass outside his tent, Ewan awoke. At first, heavy with sleep, he had no idea why he had stirred. He rolled over on the soft palette, grumbling for more sleep. Something light and feathery prickled his skin. One eye crept half open.

Shimmering and silvery with light, he saw her. Though the air inside was still, her hair twirled about her face like spun flax, as if caught in a breeze. She floated just off the ground, watching him with wide, curious eyes—eyes that changed color like shades of opal, from innocent pearl to cool platinum. As he watched her, they became like sapphire, deep and timeless blue. Ewan blinked. A waking dream, he thought. But he sat up just the same.

"Please tell me your name," he said softly. His mouth was dry. "Please."

The pixie blinked. He could not see her wings, only the milky swathe of air, the hint of glitter where they fluttered behind her.

"Names are power," Elysabel said. "It is not my wish to give you power over me. Your bloodkin has this power. Perhaps you will, too. Maybe?"

Ewan wiped sleep from his eyes. He didn't really expect that to be true, but sighed. "Okay. But will you stay this time? Can we talk? You're always rushing off."

"I go here and there as I desire. But I continue to watch you. It is the wish of my queen. And . . . it pleases me."

It sounded like a confession. Ewan felt like he should reciprocate.

"I'm glad too," he said. "You're so beautiful."

In spite of his compliment, Elysabel's expression remained strangely blank, but the color of her eyes and hair changed, flushing deep red. She studied him. "Strange mortal, kept safe by your youth. Your heart is still innocent. It will not last."

Ewan wondered what she meant. He had never told any girl she was beautiful. Even now, it wasn't a statement of desire, but fascination, like standing in front of the *Mona Lisa*, feeling smitten by her smile. He knew there was more to it. She was Fey. Magic.

Anna had been beautiful, too. His mom was the clearest image of beauty he could imagine, until seeing *her*, whatever her name was. Suddenly awake, hearing his own words, he wondered if he should be embarrassed. But no, the Fey creature was, in fact, beautiful.

"We have no time to talk. You must gather your things. The dark one, the monk, has left you."

Ewan stood up. "Now? Tonight?"

"He tries to leave before you awake."

Ewan spun around, and began frantically gathering his things. Baseball cap, Har's sword, his whistle. "I thought he was leaving tomorrow!" he said, sounding hurt. "Why are you telling me this?"

"Because he is your friend. Because I know you wish to keep his company."

Ewan quickly laced his britches, shirt, and jerkin, and pulled up his boots.

"Thank you," he said. To nothing, for she was already gone.

He crawled between the night sentries as they warmed their backsides on the embers of a fading fire, holding spears, fighting sleep. He passed the largest tent of all, Har's. Heard the old bear snoring. Felt guilty, a little. Come morning, Har would worry. But he had left him a note. He hoped that would be enough to keep them from chasing after him.

Once amongst the scrub brush and tall, patchy grass outside the perimeter of camp, he sprinted into the dark night, toward a faint blue light nearly lost in the distance. The monk was already a long way off, walking alone. Ewan might have lost him were it not for the dim color of Sorge's glowstone. Huffing and puffing, he came upon Sorge so suddenly that the startled monk nearly brought his staff down upon Ewan's head.

"Ewan!" he exclaimed. His grip remained tense. "Swords and blood, why are you here? Go back!"

Ewan began a casual, determined stride. With a crook in his mouth, he asked, "So, Sorge, my friend, how goes your road?"

"Crowded."

"Better than lonely."

They argued. Sorge insisted that Ewan return. Ewan refused. They argued more, but Ewan was determined and didn't mind being stubborn one bit. For a moment, he feared the monk might take him by the ear and drag him back to camp. The thirteen-year-old had no backup plan for that. Luckily, after snorting and threatening and tossing his head like a wild stallion, Sorge relented. He chewed a few more mumbled words like a cow chews cud, then spat them on the ground and marched away.

"If we are separated and you are lost, if you die a horrible death . . . if the Fey catch you and haul you away forever, don't blame me."

Ewan followed one submissive step behind, smiling.

They traveled north for another couple of hours, then laid upon the barely damp grass wrapped in thin blankets and slept until sunrise. Dawn spread wide to the east, shaking with color like feathers on a peacock. To the west, still blue with night, spears of light glanced off Mount Bourne's snow-capped summit, arising from the plains in sudden, solitary majesty. As morning bloomed, the high snows seemed to melt with the new glint of fire.

Sorge awoke quietly, rose in stealth, only to find Ewan sitting on his haunches, staring at him. A small fire of dry grass and twigs was beginning to crackle beside him.

"Not gonna sneak away again, are you?" Ewan said, grinning.

"If I was a Black seer, I would have left you sleeping," Sorge murmured. "But I do not know that magic."

"C'mon, Sorge, cheer up! We work good together. I'll help you find this guy."

"He is no *guy*. He is the Champion, Corus. My friend. And I do not know if it is even possible to find him."

Ewan waited an extra beat. "I meant the guy Alethes told us about. In the ruins. Barsonici."

Sorge acted put upon. Ewan knew better. The monk would cool down soon enough, and then be glad for his company. They ate a hurried breakfast of nuts and tea. When it was time to leave, Sorge found a smooth, round pebble. He took his knife and scratched something upon the surface, then held the stone to his mouth, cupped his hands, and breathed—a word, a gust of air. He poured a bit of water on the dry, packed earth, waiting for it to slowly soak in, then punched a hole in the dirt with the bottom of his staff. After dropping the stone into the hole and pressing dirt around it with the heel of his sandal, he seemed satisfied.

"It is a lodestone," he said. "There are many kinds. Flogg will be able to find us now."

Unlike Sorge, Flogg had returned to the Gray Abbey to pay his last respects to Eldoran, but his plan was to rejoin them as soon as possible. By now he was likely on the road south, headed toward the White Abbey. Ewan had missed the gnome. It would be good to have the old gang back together.

"How long?" he asked. He knew Sorge had determined to aim for the northern leg of the Goldfoam, then follow the river toward Portaferry. From there, to the ruins.

"Flogg will find us long before we reach the ruins," Sorge answered.

The days were bright, hot, dry. The Midlands were favored with none of the rains drowning Vineland and it showed, especially the farther north they traveled. Fields were shriveled, farmlands cracked. Clouds of dust speckled with pollen and seed husks scuttled over broken stalks of cotton-grass when the wind stirred. Everywhere, corn was burnt on the stalk and livestock looked thin and weak. Fear rimmed the haggard faces of people drifting by on the road, pulling half-empty carts of meager vegetables. Some begged Sorge for a blessing. Others cursed him under their breath, his gray robe representing all their hopes and fears. He tried to show them kindness, but had little time for ministry. Passing through two smaller villages, Kildane and Elbridge, Ewan felt the oppression among the huts and hovels. It was getting bad. More than one Nameless-looking youth wandered the streets. Though their countenances were no longer dark, they held the slavish residue of Nemesia's spell—aimless and glassy-eyed.

"Their minds are no longer captive," Sorge mused quietly, "but it will take time to truly be free. So much was stolen."

They reached the quaint little hamlet of Fornburg, notable as the birthplace of Abbot Abernathy the Sublime, founder of the Bernithic Order, dead five hundred years. One youngster, idling time near a cobbler's shop, took note as they passed. His eyes, mean and wild, slowly dawned with recognition.

"You realize some of the Lost may not like us too much?" Ewan whispered.

Sorge gripped his staff with disgust. "I do not fear the Lost, but poppets and witchery. Look, there." He pointed. Small scoops of grain and a few shriveled cobs of shucked corn were laid on thin copper plates outside a few homes and businesses. Others had dried twigs of ivy, or circles of iron above their doors. "That's for the Fey. Either to keep them happy or keep them away. Very common in the Midlands. But there—" He pointed again. Ewan looked, saw smudges of charcoal on the walls, shaped like a giant black bird. On the roofs of those homes was a spike, and on the spike, thrust into the open sky, were skewered all manner of small rodents, mostly rats or mice. But there was a raccoon, too. And the carcass of a cat. "Offerings for Watchers. Soon we'll see pinning wheels and bones in wells. The sacrifices will get bigger."

Ewan swallowed, knowing now why the air smelled like rotting flesh.

"Bigger?"

"Eventually, humans. Even their own children." Sorge paused to stare at the spikes. "These are all freshly killed, to gather Watchers in this region to the blood. We must make haste. The open country will be more safe."

Ewan shuddered.

They maintained a steady pace across the land, filling their flasks in the villages they passed, moving hurriedly from stream to stream outside the towns, locating water as Sorge was able. The monk never once seemed lost or confused; Ewan had to remind himself that Sorge had spent most of his adult life as Master Bowman to Corus on far-flung journeys, during which time he came to know the Five Dominions as intimately as an aging woman knows the wrinkles on her face. But a monk cannot summon water, and a warrior cannot find it, if it's not there to find. Most streams were hardpan clay veined with spider lines, cutting like bony spines through the land. Others were barely more than pools of fetid water crawling with mosquito larvae. Upon these, Ewan found that if he played the cleansing song he had created, all but the worst water became drinkable.

"Even the springs of Harthing are hard pressed these days, I'd wager," Sorge said in a raspy voice. "It is a curse if the Pool of Silon runs dry."

Ewan wiped sweat from his brow. "Hold on, don't tell me. *Ayr Taine*, right? But you said none of the Taines have been performed in a long time."

Sorge took the last swig of water from their flask and kept marching. Near an outcropping of stone and oak amidst the heather, Ewan spotted a tree festooned with strange little figures. He motioned with his head. Sorge wearily explained, "A poppet tree. Only a matter of time."

Ewan looked closer. Little dolls carved of gnarled roots, potatoes, or formed wax dangled from the branches. Some were frayed burlap scraps stuffed with old hay or wild herbs.

"They are tokens of the souls of those who wish to gain power and favor with Watchers. It is called *Maleficantis*. The path to the craft of Watchers, opposite the mirrorling way."

Ewan dawned with insight. "Watchcraft. Witchcraft. I get it."

Sorge nodded grimly. Ewan felt both sobered and amazed, "You know, a lot about our two worlds seems to connect."

"Nine Worlds spring from the same divine mind. How could they not?"

They continued across the heathland. Behind them, the soaring, singular peak of Mount Bourne grew hazy and small in the distance. Night and day came and went thrice. On the fourth day, late afternoon, a shrill sound split the sky. Something large and black soared high overhead. The noise it made was like a nest of screaming cats.

Sorge immediately dropped into the tall grass, taking Ewan with him. The shadows were long and harsh, a gift of the light. "We're lucky. It hasn't seen us yet."

Ewan pressed himself behind a thicket of bracken and crow-berry. "How do you know?"

Sorge didn't reply, but the look on his face made Ewan think the answer must be obvious. Of course, they were *alive*—that's how Sorge knew. Ewan peeked upward, saw a dark smudge in the parched air. A rush of wings filled his mind as he remembered the hateful cries on the Isle of Apaté, when Watchers had tried to silence his song.

"I could try my sleep song. Worked on the jackals."

"Too much risk, especially with no blessed water. Watchers are spirits."

"But this one is flesh now, right? Otherwise, we couldn't see it."

"Maybe, maybe not. It is a process. Many will have found blood by now, even small animals in the forest. Any dead flesh helps them cross over. The villagers offer blood gifts to keep the Watchers content, or so they think. But spirit or flesh, they can call others to us. Remember, Ewan. What saved you at Apaté? Aion's song did nothing."

Ewan did remember. "Asandra's prayers. That's what held him back."

"Exactly. You have brought something new to our world. But what if your songs don't work the same every time? What if this power proves unpredictable?"

The Watcher drew nearer in great, slow arcs, like a vulture. Its faraway cry sent shivers down Ewan's spine. He drew the small sword Har had given him, wondering almost with embarrassment what he intended to do with it. Most of what Creed had taught him he had already forgotten.

"The small village of Chumley lies beneath the Watcher's path over there. It flies near to torment them. Midlanders are especially superstitious, spooked by myth and Fey. They will worship whatever stirs strong emotion, and fear is the strongest of all. They've probably got an altar outside the village, in a grove of trees. More poppets, more offerings," he sighed.

"It's getting closer, Sorge. What do we do?"

The monk scanned left, right, searching. "No cover. No choice."

Ewan tensed. His face was glossy with sweat. Something tickled his leg, and the grass behind him unexpectedly began to rustle. He twisted suddenly, clenching his sword, only to find a stunted, unlovely gnome face peering through the brown grass. Ewan exhaled deep and slow, grinning. Flogg crawled forward on his elbows.

"Perfect timing," Sorge mused. "Now you can die with us."

Flogg stared into the cloudless sky. Framed in bright red hair, his other features disappeared into the folds of his leather frown. "Piles of trials! Darkwing have eyes soon."

"So that's why I'm lying here?" Ewan teased. "And I was just about to take a nice nap."

Flogg regarded him with a wooden expression. The two had gained a lot of ground over the past few weeks—trust, friendship. One thing hadn't changed. Gnomes had no sense of humor.

The Watcher screeched a different sort of sound, blood-chilling, with lust and recognition. The lazy circling had stopped. The flight of the black shape became an arrow heading straight toward them.

No point hiding. Sorge leaped to his feet. The Watcher bellowed.

"What about the rats and mice?" Ewan cried. "Why us?"

"Not *us*," Sorge said flatly. "Flogg, small bag and strapping."

The gnome tore open his new satchel, grabbing a pouch of tightly packed black powder the size of a golf ball.

"Short fuse," Sorge instructed, whisking an arrow from his quiver. Flogg cut the fuse.

The Watcher's speed was frightening as it tucked back its wings, blurring through the sky. Ewan imagined its gaping beak lined with teeth, and claws puncturing his flesh, lifting him away. The mental image paralyzed him. Not so long ago, another Watcher had set its many eyes upon him. Raving and murderous, trapped in glass by Asandra. Later, released to the water for a slow, cold journey back to Hel. Now a strange thought gripped him. Nemesia had freed thousands of Auginn's kin, damned for countless eons in the frozen, fleshless realm of Undrwol. Could this one be the very same as that day, in the Gray Abbey?

A flicker of movement drew his attention. Sorge had taken the strapping from Flogg and was tying the pouch to the steel tip of his arrow, binding it fast, while the fuse dangled free.

"Too much weight," he murmured. "I'll have to wait until the last possible moment." He notched the arrow, pulled the string back to his cheek. The wood creaked under the strain.

"Ewan, we have a small chance," he said tightly, "if the Watcher does not veer. That means you must bait him. Do you understand?"

Ewan nodded. He forced himself to move in front of Sorge, where nothing stood between him and the Watcher. The beast shrieked even louder to see its prey so vulnerable. It swooped in, ready to tear flesh, to feast. Ewan felt utterly exposed.

He closed his eyes, said a prayer of one word. "Sorge . . ."

"Light it, Flogg!"

The Watcher's razor beak clicked madly before gaping lustfully wide. Two more seconds and its claws would tear his heart from his chest.

"Fly true," Sorge whispered behind him.

Ewan heard the arrow split the air just over his head, heard the sizzle of the burning fuse. Saw it strike the back of the great bird's throat. The Watcher wheeled in panic, slashing, chomping at the arrow's shaft. Ewan dove to one side, screaming as a talon raked across his back. Sorge and Flogg fell back. A dull, muffled explosion sent the Watcher arching in one great spasm of crippled wings, landing near Flogg with a thud. Full of eyes and malice, it labored to breath. Even in death, it focused on Ewan. A gurgling noise of blood came from its throat. Wincing, Ewan rose, pain striping his back.

The monk wiped his mouth on his sleeve, asked for Ewan's sword. He spoke softly to the bird. "You shall not return to Hel. You shall depart, forever."

With one stroke, he severed the head. Black, slimy fluid gushed out. The stench was terrible.

Sorge was sweating. The fleshy circle on his forehead flushed pink in the failing light. He wiped Ewan's blade on the grass.

"Forever," he said again.

CHAPTER 9

The Legend
of Lotsley

It took another day to reach the Goldfoam where it angled
north past Fornburg, two more to Little Wixey, a village
famous for apples and sweet pears, and a third, still following
the waterway, to reach the small, flat-bottomed barges outside Portaferry that would carry them across the river. The Goldfoam was
the widest, deepest river in Karac Tor, stretching from massive Lake
Bakathram in the southern province of Quil through Redthorn to
Champion Bay. Seafaring ships could maneuver its entire length
with room for two abreast, though barges large and small were
more common as merchants preferred shiploads to caravans for
exotic Quilian goods. Since they followed the river now, the merchant's road gradually clotted with more and more carts and foot

traffic, peddlers and donkeys. As the level of wealth increased, the desperation of the villagers decreased. Ewan hobbled along, moving slower and slower. The gash on his back had begun to fester. Fever was setting in. He complained of pain and fatigue.

"The talons had poison, or disease," Sorge noted with worry. He and Flogg gathered what few herbs they could find in the open field, too few to really help. As the wound steadily reddened, veins of yellow and black began creeping outward from the inflamed skin. Ewan had begun to shiver. He didn't speak; he burned. He hurt. Sorge had to carry him on his back the last mile to the ferry.

With the city in sight to the west, Flogg sat with Ewan in a thin stand of trees while Sorge journeyed to Portaferry for better medicines. Even at this distance, bleary-eyed, Ewan could glimpse the brightly colored pennants on the upper decks of the Cirque coliseum and the burnished reflections of the high, copper-crowned bell tower. After a few hours, toward nightfall, the monk returned with a vial of liquid, a bag of freshly cut leaves, and food. By now, Ewan felt truly awful. Sorge drew a shard of thin crystal from the folds of his robe, sharp as a razor. Pinched between his fingers, it began to burn blue and clean, without heat. While Flogg pinned Ewan to the ground, belly down, Sorge drew the crystal in a swift, steady motion along the newly formed scab. Ewan cried out and shook as hot yellow pus squirted from the wound. The monk squeezed the length of the sore, inch by inch, also along the lines creeping outward from the wound, until only watery blood remained. He washed the wound with clean water, dried it, then poured half the contents of the vial into the open flesh. Ewan screamed. The pain was blinding. He felt light-headed.

"Strength, manling," Flogg said, bearing down on Ewan's wrists. "Purgings not kind."

Sorge crushed the green leaves, fashioned a poultice from a heavy strip of cloth, then wrapped a sash around Ewan's body to hold it in place. He propped Ewan's head up to drink. "You must swallow the rest of the vial. It will not taste good, but don't spit it out."

Ewan felt cold all over. His clothes were soaked with sweat. Sorge's voice came to him from far away and nothing made sense. When something touched his lips, he opened his mouth like a child being spoonfed. The liquid was bitter. Pepper, or flowers mixed with fire. It burned in his throat. A hand clamped his mouth.

"No spittings!"

His vision began to fade in and out. "He's grown . . . pale," the faraway voice said. Sorge. A Gray monk. "We need . . . across the river . . . rest." Ewan grinned and frowned at the same time. It sounded like a question. He didn't know the answer, but nodded deliriously. Yes, let's. After that, the only things he knew were shapeless dreams, without purpose, save that he never seemed to have enough air to breathe. As if he were drowning. Or burning alive. Or both.

When he awoke, Flogg's ox-hide face blotted the sun like a solar eclipse, filling his vision. The gnome leaned over him with, if possible, new lines of worry creasing his skin.

"Fevers and shivers, all night, the manling," Flogg said. "Today new day."

His words would prove prescient soon enough. Ewan did feel much better, though chilled and wet from the fever breaking. Testing his lungs with a timid breath, he tried to go deeper, but couldn't without effort. The air smelled of smoke and river water. He focused on Flogg's face, dimpling a weak smile. Five minutes later, he was asleep again. When he woke next, he sat up and looked around. The river wasn't where he expected. It took him a while to realize that Sorge and Flogg had hauled him across on a ferry while he slept. Was that last night? Times and events jumbled in his head. He ached.

Flogg prepared meals cooked over a fire for breakfast and dinner, rather than dried journeyman fare. Ewan slept most of the afternoon, awoke for dinner, then drifted back into a long, dreamless night. He stirred a couple of times to Sorge and Flogg conversing in low voices. They spoke of Eldoran, Melanor, matters of the abbey. Soon, Flogg said, they would choose a new Father. Sorge couldn't be there—said he wasn't sure he could be a Gray anymore. Ewan didn't get that, fog-brained as he was, yet Flogg had also resigned as head chef, it seemed. Ewan heard all this as if under water. Come morning, it seemed like just another dream.

They broke camp the next day. By late afternoon, they were climbing the dusty hill toward the Ruins of Lotsley, a queen city from a bygone age, still glorious and decadent in her ruins, home now only to foxes, jackrabbits, sparrows and memory. A path of worn, uneven cobblestones led from the Goldfoam toward the city's ancient gates. Many stones were missing or fragmented or strewn along the ground. Weeds clawed through the cracks, tangling around Ewan's feet. He stumbled more than once, feeling weaker and more winded with every step. The surrounding terrain, hilly and overgrown, seemed to push against the three travelers, warning them off with a wall of windless silence. In the distance were fallen towers and crumbling buildings, stripped of name and life. There was not a soul in sight.

Near the moldering remains of the city gate, they crossed a large open plaza, where stood a broken fountain and a statue of a proud, noble-looking man, his visage now darkened with age. A sword was raised in his right hand, while his left rested on the shoulder of a boy, presumably his son. The features of both figures were chipped and marred by time. The upper half of the man's sword was broken. Part of his leg was missing. Even so, the boy's face looked up with a smile toward his father, and past him to the open sky.

"Leonid of Lotsley, founder of the city, and his second son, Lahns," Sorge said. "It is one of our great legends. A rather sad tale. The boy disappeared on the outskirts of Elkwood on a hunting trip with his father when he was only fourteen. Search parties were launched, to no avail. The Fey were blamed, probably rightly so. Others had been snatched just as they entered manhood. But Lahns was different. Much to everyone's surprise, he returned many years later, haggard and gray, with tales of another world. Tales . . . and a curse for the sons he was yet to sire. He was never the same man. Weary and broken with secret grief, he took a wife. She bore him three sons. Thus, the curse."

"Of the second born?" Ewan asked, perking up. *He* was a second born. Staring into the face of the boy was like a window opening into the misty past. A bit creepy.

"So you *have* been paying attention," Sorge said, mildly amused. "Yes, the curse of the second born. Now, if you've really been listening, you will remember that Corus is a faraway descendant of Lahns. Second son of a second son. And so on. The last of the line."

"If he's still alive."

"If indeed."

"So you're saying the curse continues all the way to now? It's really real?"

"Curses and blessings? Aion's beard, of course! What do they teach you in your world? The influence of a curse continues, either until its aim is accomplished or a greater blessing prevails. Or blood intervenes. That is why Aion gave the Three Taines to the Black Abbey, to bring blessing wherever a curse blights the land. Corus always bore his curse like a fire in his blood. It was a great burden. No matter what he was doing, one thought, one possibility, ever compelled him."

Ewan studied the lichen-riddled face of the boy that would become the man of legend. He was caught up in the tale. But he had one rather obvious question.

"To find the king!" a strange voice bellowed, seemingly reading his mind. Ewan sought to locate the voice.

"'Tis the curse of the second-born sons of Lotsley: *to find the king*."

Picking his way over the rubble of the fallen gate, an old man approached, wearing tattered clothes, mumbling to himself. His face was stern, bright-eyed; his hair and face were unkempt, with a wispy beard that wrapped along his jaw but left his cheeks mostly clean, and no mustache. As he drew near, Ewan nearly gagged. The old man smelled as if he hadn't bathed in years. He shook a stick in Sorge's face, like an irritated master instructing his negligent disciple.

"I work alone. Speak your business, quick!"

"Barsonici?" Sorge exclaimed, puzzled and relieved at the same time. "Are you Barsonici?"

The stick lowered. The crinkled eyes narrowed, surmising monk, boy, gnome. "There's a crazy old man around here goes by that name. So?"

"The man I seek is a member of an Aionic cult called the Remnant. We are—"

The old man cut him off with hoarse, sudden laughter. "Aionic cult? Who put that thought into your head, eh? Har? That old bloodhound knows better, or at least he should." He hacked, coughed, and spat, slowly collecting himself. "No, no, someone else has your ear, I'd wager. Probably His Greatness, Alethes. That's simple math. But that doesn't explain you, Gray. Are you henchmen for the Whites now? For shame! Eldoran must have gone soft and senile to let that happen. You've normal been more reasonable folk."

He paused, unsmiling. Tapped his stick in his palm irritably.

"You came here to find me. Get on with it."

CHAPTER 10

Barsonici

S till feeling weak, Ewan barely managed to hide his surprise. Barsonici was not at all the type of man he was expecting. But really, what should one expect from an old hermit who lived in the ruins of a city now forsaken for hundreds of years? After a moment of awkwardness, a settling of dust and light, Sorge spoke. The low slant of the sun bathed all their faces in molten glory.

"You're Barsonici? The one skilled in Trulight?"

Almost as an apology for the doubt in his voice, Sorge made the sign of the circle to the old man. Barsonici did not return the gesture.

"We've come a long way," he added hastily. "I am Sorge. Corus of Lotsley, the Champion, was once my master in arms." He pulled up his sleeve, revealing a simple tattoo that wrapped around his muscled upper arm. "We bore the Mark of Twine together, the covenant of brotherhood. Twenty years ago, I betrayed him. I traded him to the Fey. All these years, I thought him dead or lost. Now I have reason to believe he lives. I was told you could help me find him."

Barsonici squinted into the light. "You seek . . . yet you betrayed him?"

"I was young and foolish."

The old man seemed confused. His eyes began darting across the ground as if he had lost something. "All these years trapped in these ruins, for a doltish Gray? But I've wondered, I've wondered."

He continued to ramble semi-coherently, glaring beneath a pair of bushy gray brows. Watching him rant, Ewan felt a measure of pity. Barsonici seemed like a relic of the ruins, trapped in the past. He realized he felt trapped, too. He was weak and sore. The adventure part had certainly dimmed over the last few days. In a strange, unsettling flashbulb thought, Ewan pictured himself as a young Barsonici, lost and searching for answers. Ever since arriving in Karac Tor, it had been right in front of him, shoved deep, screwed down tight. But now as the screws twisted a quarter turn too far, stripping bare, questions screamed for attention in his brain.

How can this be real? Why am I here? Home was a bright-burning, far-distant star—one he wished on every night. Yet every night, never fading, the light of it felt colder, more and more unreachable. It made his heart ache to think about it. Dad, home, a soft, warm bed, orange juice, weekend trips to grandma . . .

Can't give up. Find a way. Fulfill the mission.

He knew he was here for a reason. He kept telling himself it was for Sorge, for the land. For the Lost. For Aion, who had called them. But what did that mean, really? He had discovered a flame in his soul for melody and music. At home those had been matters of passive interest. In Karac Tor, music had become fierce, joyful, liberating. *Urgent.* Here, music stirred within him, almost viciously, collecting like fog or honey or light—or a shout inside—demanding to be shaped into tunes of sorrow and flitting wonder. Here, to his constant surprise, his fingers found the notes on the flute with ease. Here, his bones vibrated with sound, the whistle becoming the means to access and extend that deep place inside which always swam in song. He could never go back to hearing music secondhand. In coming to the Hidden Lands, he had realized, if nothing else, that he was born to *make* music.

Nevertheless, his longing for home was nonnegotiable. He and Hadyn had made a deal with Sorge and Alethes. The terms were very clear. They would do their part—whatever that was—as long as everyone involved kept focused on finding a way home for them. They would go out as ambassadors, whatever. They would form alliances. They would serve the need. Not as Champions, but brothers. Maybe, along the way, someone would have a clue, or another portal would be found. And they could go home.

Frankly, it wasn't a great plan. But no one had a better idea.

Somehow, standing amongst the ruins, listening to Barsonici mutter his castigations, Ewan felt simultaneously closer to his purpose and farther from home than ever before. The old man might have gone on forever, or at least until dark. And Sorge might have weathered his quiet tirade for an equally long time, out of politeness or stoic guilt. But Ewan broke the chain.

"Mr. Barsonici, sir . . . if wrong has been done, we've come to undo it."

The simple gesture seemed to release Sorge from his self-imposed silence.

"*My* wrongs," he corrected. "My sins. And I am sorry if they have cost you. In fact, they have cost us all. But I have dreamed of late. I have spoken to the fallen Black, Nemesia. I have reason to believe Corus is alive, no longer with the Fey—"

"Of course he's not with the Fey!" Barsonici snapped, astounding everyone. "Hasn't been for years!"

Sorge's voice dropped off, dry as bones in a bucket. He didn't bother to close his mouth, just stood there, gaping. A mild breeze carried Barsonici's rank odor to where they stood. Did the old man know he smelled like a hog pen?

"King's teeth, man! Am I the only one with brains?" Barsonici said disgustedly.

Sorge slowly turned to Flogg, dumbfounded. Ewan leaned wearily against a large stone slab.

"The Remnant has heard what the trees tell," said Barsonici. "Seven years ago there was a fluttering among the Fey. Corus was taken from them. A deal was made. So say the winds and leaves."

Sorge's dark skin paled. "This cannot be. Seven years?"

Barsonici snorted, glancing toward Flogg. "Does Huldáfolk listen to the earth and not hear the story it tells?"

"Not Huldá," Flogg sniffed. "My kin, Alfólk."

"Yet for all folk, creation groans. You know that much, right? Watchers clot the sky and mares won't foal. The Midlands have no rain; Vineland weeps. Archibald the Arse sits on a throne of compromise. Hel trembles. We have no king. How is it that you do not know?"

Sorge composed himself. "You know things we do not, to our shame. Will you help us?"

His show of humility did little to impress Barsonici. "Bah! It doesn't matter anymore. Whatever will be has been. And whatever has been will be again."

"Yet the War of Swords is coming," Sorge countered. "When Aion sets it right. Until then, our hearts must not fail."

"Yes, yes. So I believed, once." Barsonici waved the thought away as if swatting a fly. His lips pursed with a riddle. "But really, if it's coming, and if all is set right, then why should I bother with all this? Eh? I used to think I could *make* the War of Swords happen. You know, help Aion out a bit, speed up the process. I was young . . . younger, at least. So I came here to do my little part and have now spent a decade amongst the ghosts of Lotsley, creeping through the shadows, finding hidden places. Big things, little things, forgotten lives. Shrines, coins, and cups. Scraps of books, faded scrolls. Old iron keys that open nothing anymore. Here on the borders of Elkwood, I completed my practice of Trulight alone. Hour upon hour, day after day. In cold and snow. I sought clues to the Wild Water, that I might glimpse the Fey and find the Sleeping King, if perhaps *he* might be our salvation. I have come so close . . . for naught. The doom of Lotsley has passed beyond memory, unfulfilled, and with him, our last hope of ever finding a king." His shoulders sagged. "I stay now because there is nothing left for me to do. This is all just habit, the tired labors of an old man waiting to die."

The warmth of the air turned the silence to lead. Ewan's knees felt weak, his head still a little woozy. He had been on his feet too long without a break.

"You won't find him, Sorge the Gray," Barsonici said almost sadly. "Even if he's alive, you won't find him. Go back to the abbey. Take the boy, the gnome. Tell Eldoran you came seeking truth but found none. Tell him whatever you want. But leave me alone."

"Eldoran is dead," Sorge announced, resting his chin on the crown of his staff. Barsonici had already turned away, climbing back over the rubble, past the fallen stone columns of the old gate and the rotting timbers of long dead trees.

"He was old, like me," Barsonici mused aloud, barely hearable. "Now he is at peace."

Flogg growled. "Killings and chillings never peaceful."

The old man hesitated in his climb. For a moment, he seemed unsure. "All men come to an end, gnome. Eldoran walks with Olfadr now, on Isgurd's blue shores. I envy him."

"No, you hide!" Sorge said so forcefully Ewan flinched. The monk flung his arms wide as if to encompass the ruins. "This isn't a habit, it's an escape! Don't blame the years, the disappointments. They are not in vain, Barsonici. I believe Corus is alive. Maybe he walks Isgurd's blue shores, but maybe *not*. And if he is alive, we must find him. Aion wills it!"

Barsonici cackled like a madman, brief and fierce, then done, as if someone had flicked a switch. His lips pursed. "Do not think to teach *me* the will of Aion!"

Something had shifted in the conversation. There was a new edge, a desperation in the grip of Sorge's hand on his staff, the way his feet stood upon the paved earth. Barsonici by now stood atop a section of crumbling wall, his tattered cloak billowing loosely in the warm western wind.

Sorge stood taller, set his jaw. His tone became more accusing. "You forget your vow, Master Wordsman. Your duty is to those written in the Book of Names. It is a vow for life."

Barsonici nearly shook with rage. "How dare you! Is this the new courtesy of the Grays? Throwing words like stones at old men, who have served Aion longer than you have been alive?"

Ewan saw the veins in Sorge's neck begin to bulge. He watched through blurry eyes. He felt so tired. He just wanted to lie down. Sleep. Barsonici smiled a rotten smile.

"Ibsla," the old man declared grandly, jarring Ewan awake again. "Daughter of a gnome witch, born deaf. When her mother, Grina, realized the defect, she howled, cursing her daughter with forty-nine curses for bringing shame on their clan. Being deaf, Ibsla could not hear her mother's wretched words and was thereby saved. Made free of her mother's evil spells, she received her hearing, blessed her mother, and departed."

Flogg grunted with recognition of the tale. "Ibsla. Grina."

Ewan grunted, too, mainly because he was lost. But Sorge understood. He pounded the earth with his staff. "Don't blame me for telling you the truth! I come to beg your aid and you say it is a curse. Why are you here if there is no hope? Why bother searching at all?"

"Because there is nothing left for me out *there*!" Barsonici shouted, pointing south, beyond the river. "Bah! I don't expect you to understand, but there's nothing there, because there's nothing *here*. I've spent years searching for answers. I had a quest. A quest built on riddles and scraps of old books. Legends, told with a wink, because every sane person knows they're merely fables. Still, I wondered, what if? They laughed at me. I didn't care.

"So I came here. Surely, here, I could do my part. The Remnant blessed it. For Aion, they said! I was going to change things." Barsonici spat again. "Almost, almost, it seemed it would work. That's when I heard the rumors. Corus, with the Fey, now gone. I thought I could find him at first. Then, failing that, I could do his part for him. Seek what the Champion would seek if he were alive. He once spent time here, looking through these ruins for clues to his own life. So I took upon myself the curse of the second son's blood." Barsonici almost staggered back under the weight of the thoughts flooding in.

"Such a fool! To think I could force the hand of history and time, of Aion himself! The Sleeping King cannot be found without a true son of Lotsley—and maybe not even *with*. Fey magic is too strong. So whether Corus, the last of the line, is enslaved or dead, what good am I? Only the Fey Queen knows whether he lives or lies cold in the ground and she will not tell, and I do not have the eyes to see. Trulight is for darkness, not magic. It does no good in Elkwood, woven with sorcery, hidden from the eyes of men . . . as I prefer to be. Curse the lot of you. Go away."

He ended with a sigh. Ewan could barely stand. He had mustered all his focus to get through that speech, but his fragile strength was spent. He was hungry. Dinner and another long night of rest—that was what he needed. He was hot.

"I cannot go to Elkwood," Sorge said, shaking his head. "There must be another way."

"Are you deaf? Who said anything about going to Elkwood? There is *no* way! Not this way. Not any other way. The riddle has no answer. No one knows where the Sleeping King lies. And certainly, no one sees Fey or bargains with them. Those were the deeds of Tal Yssen. Now please, leave me alone. Let me piece useless old pottery together and grow my herbs and practice Trulight, for all it matters."

Ewan found himself chiming in. He smacked his lips, said, "I see Fey."

Actually, he felt surprised to hear his own voice speaking. Fueled by his simple confession, he was even more surprised at the song that unexpectedly burst open inside him. The suddenness was like a melon splattering on the ground. He giggled. It was a funny thought. He listened to the sloppy, delicious mess of it, shaping it in his mind, getting sticky with the juice. At the moment he was a mess for many reasons. Still, spent as he was, he felt inspired by the beauty and largeness of the thought behind the song: *Vision*, to see what is hidden, and believe. Fairies weren't real on his world, were they? Maybe he just needed the eyes for it. The melody swirled briefly inside his belly then slowly began to fade. He hoped he could remember when he woke next. As his knees buckled, he felt almost panicked to play it before sleeping, afraid it would drift like sand through his fingers and never return. But that was a silly thought. He couldn't play anything. He was about to pass out.

"Sorge, I'm really tired again," he said, slumping forward. From a long way off, Barsonici spoke in a pale, nervous whisper. Ewan could tell the difference. Not a whiff of cynicism remained. If anything, the foul-smelling man sounded fascinated.

"Did that boy just say he sees Fey?"

CHAPTER 11

Five Tenets

Yes, he did see Fey, thank you very much. And yes, Barsonici was fascinated.

But seeing Fey didn't keep one from collapsing from exhaustion. Sorge didn't respond fast enough, and Ewan hit hard. Another bruise. His last thought was that he was getting tired of falling, bumping his head, feeling sick, getting attacked.

Thankfully, the next day he felt *much* better. Nice to finally get a break.

As for Fey's eyes? Strangely enough, after all his fatalistic ranting, Ewan's declaration settled the matter for Barsonici. It was either a glowing case of redemption, or textbook schizophrenia. Equally strange, for Sorge, the new swirl of excitement seemed more like a death sentence. While Ewan slept, the two monks exchanged more heated words, this time for entirely different reasons. Eventually,

Sorge had to yield the point: there were no other alternatives. Ewan woke the next day to Sorge sitting in sullen silence.

They set off with Barsonici's donkey and a mangy, mixed-breed wolf he had raised since it was a pup. The donkey was so old and tired its belly nearly dragged the ground. Both would be of little use on the journey to Elkwood. Sorge said so quite irritably. Barsonici insisted they come along.

"And salt," he said. "Though hopefully we won't need it."

"Feybane, always," Flogg grunted, patting his satchel. "Spicing for eats."

The wolf-dog, Ruel, seemed all too happy to get far away from the ruins, loping playfully across the tall grass. The donkey was a more ill-tempered, methodical beast. For the most part it kept a steady pace, albeit slow. But the first afternoon, after resting in the shade of three lone trees, it simply refused to budge, planting its feet and braying for an hour. Barsonici tugged on its rope, loudly disparaging the beast's lineage. He wouldn't look at Sorge. When it finally relented and began clumping along again, Ewan just laughed. The journey resumed.

Hours dragged on in a haze of thick, muggy air, dusty boots and bland, warm drink. Mosquitoes nipped at their sweaty skin in the bright sun to the point of madness. Before long, Ewan was covered with itching welts. He tried to recall the melody of the song, the one that had come so suddenly at the ruins. The Fey song. Perhaps it had merely been the fever, but something was missing, some burst of revelation. Secretly, he couldn't help but wonder when he would see the pixie next. In the forest? Maybe then his song would be complete.

Hoping to fill the silence and get his mind off the mosquitoes, he said aloud, "So what's the big deal about Trulight? Is it like a special torch or something?"

He chuckled at himself. Barsonici either didn't hear or didn't care to answer.

"Some say it is a birth gift—" Sorge began.

"Hush!" Barsonici snapped. "The boy obviously has no care for the answer. Let him wait."

Okay, so lighthearted he was not. Were all old people so temperamental? Ewan decided to swallow his pride. "I'm sorry. *Please* tell me about Trulight."

Barsonici ambled along, apparently unconvinced of his sincerity, so the task fell back to Sorge. "Part of the vow for Whites is to penetrate darkness, to unbind minds. Thus their devotion to the law. The study of the Doctrine of Trulight is part of that."

Barsonici scoffed. "You obviously haven't been among the Whites in a long time, Gray. Alethes has grown soft. But who can blame him? In a lifetime, a strong wordsman might master one or two progressions. Some three, if they are very disciplined."

Ewan's curiosity was piqued. "And there are . . . ?"

"Five," Barsonici said, jabbing his walking stick like a chef might poke a cooked pig to see if it was done. Every time he flapped his arms, the whiff of ripeness nearly gagged Ewan. "Five Progressions, or Five Tenets if you like." He seemed torn between his irritation and the pride of his craft. "It's very simple, really:

Light is Truth.
Truth is Knowledge.
Knowledge is Hope.
Hope is Vision.
Vision is Light.

"And then it all starts over again, back at the beginning, only deeper each time."

Ewan looked at Sorge, puzzled. "I'm sorry. I don't get it."

Barsonici licked his lips, searching for words. "It's not about rote memory, that's a trifle. Trulight is the clean, clear direction—the process, if you will—of actuality. Light is truth! You must begin here, knowing that truth exists, that it is possible, and from whence it comes. Of course, there is more to it. After that, you move on to the Secondary Maxims and the seven Tertiary Insights. But if you manage to keep your wits, and let it unfold from within, you may just begin to understand certain things: That darkness cannot comprehend truth. That even if the mind is divided, light remains single; it cannot be hidden. Light reveals, invades. The mind is full of darkness, but light brings freedom. These are more than mortal conceptions, more than poetry and verse. They are pathways for the soul." His voice resonated with awe.

"But it takes time," Sorge added carefully.

"A long, long . . . *long* time."

"And then what? You start to glow or something?" After all, Sorge made rocks glow.

"Nonsense!" Barsonici huffed. "Is your head full of drivel? Sorge, I will not speak to this one anymore."

"Ewan, Trulight is revelation," Sorge said gently. "Don't think *shining*. Think *seeing*."

Barsonici couldn't help himself, thundering with indignation. "There are lights that the mind sees which the eyes cannot!"

He's going to have a coronary, Ewan thought. Why the drama? He rolled his eyes. Crazy old man.

They kept on. With his booted feet, Flogg crushed more than one copperhead slithering through the grass hunting field mice. By the second day, Ruel's bounding and chasing had turned to trotting and panting, dragging along like everyone else. The endless brown palette of the earth seemed to steal even the memory of green. Thankfully, as they plowed farther and farther north, Ewan caught the first faint scents of autumn in the wind, of smoky things, orange leaves and long nights. Cool breezes brought occasional relief with the promise of more to come. The faraway peaks of the Frostmarch could be dimly glimpsed from time to time, appearing through mist and cloud as faded blue crags on the horizon, blushing with snow. By the evening of the second day, Elkwood was in sight, and the mountains were lost again behind the woods.

"Beast needs drink," Flogg said, patting the donkey's hindquarters. "Flogg find."

For maybe the fifth time, Sorge grumbled under his breath about the pack animal coming along. Even Ewan was getting weary of his complaints. What was the big deal? But then he began to realize that Sorge had been on edge almost the entire time since leaving Har to search for Corus. Ewan didn't get it. Isn't this what he came for, was determined to do? Something was off-kilter. Sorge seemed to dread the forest, but why?

"The mule will panic," Sorge said flatly, out of the blue. "Once it feels them, it won't put one hoof in the forest. Send it away now, Barsonici. The farther we go, the less likely it can survive. Let it go back to the ruins and wait for you there."

Barsonici made a sound in his throat. "Hmmph. And just who would carry my books?"

Ewan couldn't help but smile. Since they collectively owned next to nothing, and carried even less, the donkey hardly qualified as a serious beast of burden. Ewan kept his only two possessions with him at all times—baseball cap and flute. They had two nearly empty flasks of water. Two blankets. Flogg carried his satchel. Yet, the donkey did carry heavy items. Of all things, Barsonici had brought a sack of books! Books, paper, quills . . . and not a bar of lye to be found. Ewan was beginning to think the man never bathed.

He was right. When they came to a pool at the base of a clean running stream later that afternoon, his suspicions were confirmed. He, Sorge, and Flogg joyfully stripped to nothing and took a refreshing plunge. The cool water made them all gasp. Ewan laughed, splashing Sorge, trying to dunk him. It was his first fully normal day since the Watcher attack, and his back was finally starting to heal. Sorge's mood lightened enough to play a bit. After a long time under, Flogg came up with pearl drops glistening in his red beard and a wiggling crawfish pinched between his fingers. He popped the creature into his mouth, chomping and smacking his lips.

"Tasty prawn snacking," he grinned, licking his fingers. "Good water."

"It's called Bunhalley Creek," Barsonici called out hoarsely in reply, but he offered the information with a tone of disapproval. He stared at them from a distance, frowning.

"Come join us," Ewan said. *And please bring soap!*

"I will not," Barsonici replied flatly. After which, he said no more.

CHAPTER 12

Into the Woods

On they went. For whatever reason, the mood brightened by half, at least for Barsonici. The nearer they drew to the fabled woods, the more eager he became.

Flogg became more serious. "Tricksters, Fey. Not helping holy men. Not White Woods, to Aelfheim."

"We have no choice, friend," Sorge said. "I don't like it either."

Barsonici licked his lips like a child licks a honey stick. His eyes widened with delight. "No choice, no sovereign will? Does the gray monk follow the weak-minded, blaming fate, yielding to despair? What about faith and action?" He was obviously enjoying himself. "Isn't that basically what you told me in the ruins?"

Sorge, fuming, said nothing.

Dismissing him with a wave of his hand, Barsonici turned to Ewan with an eager, childlike glee. "Ah, I wish I had your eyes, boy. I have been a fletcher, a baker's apprentice, a holy verseman, a seeker of secrets. I am a follower of Aion. But I have always wanted to see Fey!" He sighed. "I will tell you a tale, eh? The famous riddle of the Tower of Dreams." He cleared his throat. Then in brooding tones, like a sail catching wind, slowly began to unfurl his tale.

"Once there was a noble prince who in the course of time became bewitched by a lovely Fey. The Fey would visit him at night, unseen, and sing to him in his dreams. Sleep soon became both sweetness and torment to the young man's soul, for he could only hear her voice, never see her. He became spellbound. One day, the thought came into his head to build a tower to catch and hold her. They would wed, he thought—a fool's notion, but he became obsessed with the idea. Inspired by her songs, the prince began building a mysterious tower, carved with the Fey shapes he saw in his dreams—a windowless, doorless tower. Once caught, she could never escape, or so the prince thought. But as the tower neared completion, he was not satisfied. He became obsessed with his need to *see* his Fey enchantress, not merely possess her. And so he braved realms of danger and madness where men should not tread. With powerful incantations, he sought to see farther than human eyes are allowed to see. Then one day, it happened! Sight was granted. He beheld a vision, but not of Fey. Instead he saw his father's death, surrounded by great darkness. Driven nearly insane by the thought of losing his beloved father, the prince imprisoned his sire in the very same tower he had intended to capture his lady. He did this to protect his father from harm. But that very night, the Fey enchantress abandoned him in his dreams, never to return." Barsonici's voice became melancholy. "It was as if she drove him to build it for her own fame. The prince sought her the rest of his days, forsaking all land and title and wealth. He left his father and sought her with many bitter tears. But never found her."

The story ended, leaving only the sound of their feet, softly crunching pebbles and grass. Ewan found himself strangely moved. Barsonici might be a loon, but he could sure tell a story.

"What about the dad?"

The old man gave a wan smile. "He died, lost and forgotten in the tower. Surrounded by darkness, just as the prince had foreseen. It is there still, on the coast of Bitterland."

"And doorless, as you say," Sorge groused, "but hardly windowless. I could tell you three other folktales about that tower, all very different. Its twisted seashell shape, with slots, sockets, and pipes, moaning in the cold winds sweeping down from Yrgavien—"

"—for the prince's tears, over losing his Lady Fey, and his father," Barsonici said meaningfully, unwilling to shed the spell of his own story.

Flogg broke in. "Alfólk say . . . barrow. Fey shapings."

"Oh, indeed! Most likely, those carvings of strange creatures along the base. Yes, Flogg, good. Some say they aren't etchings, but Fey, gone there to die."

Ewan tried to picture it in his mind. Sorge, speaking confidentially, put a hand on the boy's shoulder, as if shielding him from lies. "Nobody really knows what it's for."

"A pox on your blinkered ways, Gray," Barsonici huffed. "It doesn't matter whether the story is true if it *tells* the truth!"

"A pox on your heresy, White. *Everything* about truth matters."

"So what, we tell only the stories with no magic, stripped clean of mystery...is that it? Tell me monk, do we starve the soul with too many dreams, or too few?" He turned to Ewan. "*That's* the point, lad, the power of our own stories, even history itself. In Lotsley, I was able to glimpse the ambition of earlier times and learn from it. I saw other men's dreams, and was reminded that nothing is built that is not first imagined. And this—this!—is what it means to be faithful, so that future generations gain our wisdom by what endures, or humility and warning by what crumbles to dust." He stooped, grabbed a fistful of grass and dry earth, let it slip between his fingers and blow away in front of Ewan's face. "Do not be so shallow, boy, as to think the world is built of what you can see and touch. It is built of dreams, not stone. Vision! Vision, I say! You see Fey, Ewan Barlow...and I envy you for that. But what else might your eyes perceive, if only you thought to look?"

Ewan felt scolded, though he knew he wasn't meant to. Still, something gnawed at his gut. "What about the fact that the prince went too far? Isn't vision a two-edged sword?"

Beside him, a quiet, satisfied smile tugged at Sorge's lips. Barsonici was unfazed. "There are risks. There are *always* risks."

But a new realization gripped Ewan. "Hold it, back up. I thought Fey were immortal."

For a moment, Barsonici seemed to deflate, as if all his wisdom had been cast aside. But the Fey obviously fascinated him. He adjusted quickly. "Does immortal mean undying? The old ones tell us Fey will turn to stone when they are weary of the world, from shame or despair." His voice drifted. "Anyway, as Sorge has astutely noted, some say the tower was the source of Hhyss One-Eye's power, long ago. That's what I believe. Others hold forth that it hides the Pillar Map till the time of the end."

Sorge took a deep breath. "I do not wish to strive with you, Barsonici, I truly don't. But the Pillar Map is a dangerous myth.

Corus thought he found it once, and it was ruinous. Any claims have all been forgeries."

"And what does a forgery prove?" Barsonici countered. "Follow your own logic, monk. Isn't witchery but a perversion of the Nine? Or do you not recall Tal Yssen's Maxim of Inverse Demonstration, a proposition for quantifying—"

"Enough!" Ewan snapped. "You're both right in different ways, so quit arguing. Sheesh, worse than me and Hadyn." He found himself walking faster, harder. "There's nothing easy about figuring out what's real. We have legends and secret maps on my world, too. Stuff like Merlin. I've always thought he was made up. Now it turns out he and Tal Yssen are the same dude. Why can't you both just admit you don't know?"

Both men grew quiet. "Tal Yssen traveled between worlds. He trafficked with Fey," Sorge said thoughtfully. "He had eyes like you—a man of legend on two worlds. How many others might there be?"

Barsonici wrung his hands together. "Ewan, you must promise me. If you *do* see the Fey, as we hope, you must inquire as to the Pillar Map. At least ask."

"No," Sorge said flatly. "I'm sorry, Ewan, it's not worth it."

Barsonici seemed pained. "How can it not be worth uncovering our most sacred story?"

"The story is spiritual," Sorge replied, "not geographical."

Ewan sighed. "Are we talking about Yhü Hoder? When Aion died?"

"Chained and struck dead, yes, but no one knows the place," the old man said emphatically. "The Pillar Stone is lost. How can this be? Mockers say the story cannot be real or we would know the place, while the devout seek pilgrimage. I am of the Remnant,

and we want the riddle solved. If you are given the chance, you
must ask."

They took a break. The forest loomed ahead. Sorge drew a map
for Ewan in the dirt. Ewan was surprised at the length of the woods
and their size on the crude map. Elkwood was like the profile of
a large, fat, one-legged man, with his lone appendage stretching
south all the way to Mount Bourne. They were not on that path.
They were heading into the belly, up the forest's throat, to its brain,
Fey Haven. It felt spooky to think about. Ewan tried to sidetrack
himself. Didn't work. The thought of seeing the pixie again excited
him. If all Fey were like her, it would surely be a wonderland.

"It is called the White Woods," Sorge mused, pointing to the
dirt map with his finger. "You'll know why when you see it."

Barsonici wandered over, mouth open, spilling chunks of food.
Juice dripped down his chin. "Elkwood is a marvel, lad," he said.
"The natural land boundary for Karac Tor to the west, all the way
to Lake Avl, here," he took a stick, pointed. "Finally joining ancient
Fealy Forest, here."

"What's over there?" asked Ewan, pointing to the empty space
west of the forest.

"Disputed territories, impoverished land. Farther west, the bar-
barian empire Quil."

After a few more minutes orienting Ewan to the local terrain,
Barsonici wandered away to stretch his legs, while Flogg put his
fingers to the ground to listen. Sorge used the opportunity to draw
his charge aside. His voice was tentative. "If there was any other
way, you must believe me . . ."

Ewan waited for Sorge to finish. He never did, just letting his
voice trail away, dropping his gaze. Having seen the monk at his
best, and lately at his worst, Ewan was puzzled. Sorge was obviously

afraid. What took longer to comprehend was why. Sorge was afraid for *him*.

"I would do this for you if I could," the monk said, as if pleading forgiveness in advance of a crime. Ewan frowned, but Sorge continued. "Humans don't enter Fey Haven willingly. They are coerced, or drugged, or succumb to magic. It's a place of great danger." His guilty eyes stayed on the ground. "I would go with you all the way to Hel and back. You know that don't you? I have pledged myself to two things: finding Corus and, above all, keeping you safe. But this is different. I'm useless in there. You see them. I don't."

Comprehension began to dawn. "Ahh, so I'm going by myself . . ."

Sorge nodded. "Mind you, no one's making you. You don't have to go at all. Maybe Barsonici will accompany. Maybe Flogg." He took a lump of dried clay, smearing the dirt between his hands, then trying to wipe it clean, as if it were his soul. "The older you grow, the more you will understand that some sins leave their mark forever. I have known a traitor, been a traitor—here, at these woods. If this is our only hope of finding Corus and I enter again . . ." His voice trailed away. "I simply can't."

"What? What will happen?"

He wouldn't say.

They ate a quick meal. Ewan had little appetite. What he knew from his encounters with the Fey gave him no cause to fear, but Sorge's dread was contagious. In spite of all the energy expended— Ewan had probably walked more in the last three months than in his whole life—when they made camp that evening not a one of them was hungry. Too much heat and sweat and dust in their pasty mouths to feel pangs in their belly. Flogg, having listened to the earth once with his fingers yesterday, and again today, had nothing to report. The two monks bickered a little, conversed a little. When dawn broke, they plodded on in moody silence.

Ewan didn't ask any more questions, mainly because he didn't want to hear the answers.

Finally they drew near the bulk of trees—vast acres of beech and white birch, a few grand oaks—laid like miles of rumpled blankets on the high plains. Far beyond sight, Sorge said, the woods began their slow ascent along pine- and fir-covered slopes toward the Frostmarch.

For no clear reason, their pace slowed. Ewan found himself holding his breath, feeling as if he were somehow outside his own body, anxiously looking on. He took long, slow breaths, reminding himself to be calm. After all, there was nothing to fear, certainly nothing to compare with Redthorn. Elkwood wasn't overgrown or ragged or sickening to look upon. It was the opposite, beautiful and enchanting, like a gathering of tall, thin angels. Birches, draped in cool mist, rose like pearled knives from the forest floor, shining with an inner glow, leaves the honey color of the sun. Tufts of milkweed and brown puff seeds floated in the air, defying gravity. A cluster of bright blue butterflies twirled in a circle. Larks and thrushes wove a spell of song.

The day had passed quickly. Surprising. Light, failing. Soon, evening. Perhaps not the best time to enter an enchanted wood. But why not? Ewan's thoughts grew sluggish in reply.

Magical and serene. Nothing to fear at all. Yet as they drew closer, Ruel began to whimper and tuck his tail. He turned in confused semicircles, head low to the ground, haunches quivering. The donkey began slowly backing away, pulling against Barsonici's grip. The old man tried to calm the pack animal with soothing words. It rolled its eyes, snorted, brayed. With one quick snap of the head, it finally jerked free. Galloped away. Blankets bounced off its back, along with one of Barsonici's books. It kept on. Ruel, begging softly, stayed.

"Cursed beast!" Barsonici shouted. "Dumb ass!"

Ewan was staring into the woods, at the dancing motes of dust and seed, the whirling eddy of butterflies, like sparks rising from a fire. The pale woods. He heard music in his head, a song of sweetness. His eyes grew heavy.

"Sorge," he breathed, feeling a dull sense of panic.

Beside him, the monk was statuesque. Barsonici, too, had grown still. Flogg watched, arms folded. The air between the trees shimmered and the dappled sun turned to shadow on the leaves. The woods grew simultaneously darker and more luminescent as twilight came. Flecks of light darted about, pirouetting with the seed tufts, rising and falling, never landing, floating. The air teemed.

"Sorge," Ewan repeated. "I see them. Dozens, hundreds. Coming toward us."

Sorge's answer came in a slow, strained voice. "I don't see anything, but . . . my skin tingles. My legs are so heavy. Aion preserve us, I thought we would be safe this far out." He gripped his staff. Barsonici thrust out his hands toward the woods and made the sign of the circle. He did not seem so eager now. A wild sort of fear carved new lines into his face.

With great effort, Sorge said, "By—the Nines—has it grown cold?" He did not move, could not move. Barsonici was also transfixed, hands upraised. Flogg's hand was in his pouch, stuck there. All he could do was snarl and strain.

Something new, a rumbling. Ewan felt the earth tremble with the sound of hooves pounding the dirt, swords being drawn. Har Hallas. Brimshane was not far away. Ewan was never so glad to see someone as he was to see the earl at that moment. He felt a fresh wave of guilt for sneaking away. No time. Outside the woods and in, there was movement, color.

Many things happened at once. He heard Har shouting. Heard his men. Saw figures moving. He saw the Fey take form with clarity at the edge of the woods, forming a wall many hundreds, maybe thousands, thick. Male and female, if those were the proper terms. Strangely neither. Flitting spirits of severe beauty, swimming in the liquid air, gliding above the ground. They had stern, exquisite features, eyes of silver and gold. They stood in formation, watching Ewan, watching Har, as if they were the only two that mattered. Sorge, Barsonici, Har's men, they might as well not have existed.

Har hurled imprecations at the silent trees. He could not behold them, as did Ewan, but knew their quality. He raged. Cursed Fey! Having arrived in Brimshane, he had felt their gathering and come like thunder to punish them for their impudence.

He did not expect to see Ewan or the monks.

Ewan felt awe. He saw, physically *saw*, a wall of power released from the earl's voice. A wall of the earl's will, magnified, expressed as a weapon, rippling like water through the air, pushing back against the Fey. Authority. Ewan saw Fey faces grow strained, angry, determined. Saw them lift their hands with effort, open their mouths. A sound came out. The entire image of the still woods became a spoon dipped in brown molasses, turned thick and slow. To the eyes of others, he knew, nothing had changed. The woods were white with trees, empty, quiet.

But there was war.

Sorge fell to the ground. Barsonici fell. Ewan saw and heard Har's men hitting the dirt, one after another, crumpling like sacks of grain. They lay unconscious, eyes open, as dead men.

He stood. Har stood. Flogg stood. But neither Har nor the gnome moved any longer.

Light flared, emitting from the Fey, enveloping them all. No one could see it. But it was there. Ewan saw. He heard Flogg and Har, growling with strain.

When the light faded, everything had changed.

CHAPTER 13

Magic and Melody

Y ou see us so easily," Queen Marielle told him in flat,
ambiguous tones. Her statement was neither threatening, nor matter-of-fact, nor amused; somehow all of
those and none. She was taller than most of the other Fey, arrayed
in a flowing dress of glittering, gossamer green that billowed constantly like churning water, though there was no breeze. Her feet
grazed the mossy forest floor in what seemed a mostly perfunctory
connection. Her hair, iridescent purple the dark color of eggplant,
had whorls of green. There was frost on her eyes, her eyelashes. She
was magnificent and dreadful.

"Why do you think . . . *you* can see, Outlander?" she said
after an interminable pause, during which Ewan dared not speak.

Hundreds, perhaps thousands, of Fey crowded close into the inner sanctum of Fey Haven. Here all was green; all was spring. There were hanging vines and a deep, plush carpet of sod and flowers. The evening air was rich and velvety, with pools of moonlight pouring through the canopy of leaves high overhead like fresh cream spilled from a milk pail. Everywhere there were lights, winking like fireflies. Like a drizzle of silver rain. Larger lights, like torches, were scattered here and there, though they did not burn, nor were made of flame. A slow and steady drumbeat filled the air.

Ewan found himself instinctively taking on a formal tone for his reply. "My lady, I only know that I see you, not how—though I am grateful for the chance to look upon your loveliness, which is surely beyond compare."

Honestly, he didn't know how he managed such graceful speech. Thing was, he felt sincere, which made it almost embarrassing. The crowd of Fey twittered and laughed and gasped. This had not happened for a long time. A human, with eyes, who entered free of their spell? Four humans, actually! Plus a cursed gnome, the mongrel. Behind Ewan, reposed on the ground and bathed in radiance, lay Sorge and Barsonici. Their arms were folded peacefully across their chests. Ruel, who refused to leave Barsonici's side, whined and trembled next to his master. Nearby, Flogg was a pillar of stone with bright red hair. He had no satchel. It was gone. Sorge had no bow, no arrows. Iron and salt, forbidden. Bound with rope and power, blindfolded, the gnome could only manage to growl. Ewan heard the whispers of the Fey.

"*Despicable creature . . . warthog . . . Queen should turn him into a goat.*"

"*Ah, but the Gray monk is a fine one. He's a fine catch.*"

"Nothing but trouble, I say. They are not worthy of Aelfheim."

"Yes, but will he do it? Will the music play?"

Their voices collided like foamy waves washing ashore. All fine, but where was Har? Where were his men? Ewan remembered the struggle at the edge of the woods, the flash of light. He remembered Har crying out. Then, dreamlike, he had found himself moving with great speed, as if carried through the woods. To this place. The air had blurred and buzzed with thin, filmy wings, as it did now. Enormous trees shook their leaves of green and silver.

Marielle smiled a smile like falling snow. All voices fell silent in anticipation. It almost seemed as if the many white trunks of the bower, gnarled and peeling, now bulged with strangely human shapes of mouths, noses, eyes. Watching. Ewan tried to clear his mind of cobwebs. Fey magic apparently didn't work on him, but he still felt a bit thick in the head.

"The Midlands brute. The one called Har. He will not let us roam free as Fey should. He fights us. Today we have shown our power. He pushed too far."

"I'm sorry, my lady. He says you connive against his butter, crops, and wells. The people fear you."

The queen seemed pleased to hear this. Her ivory skin was nearly translucent. A wreath of holly and mistletoe in her hair shone like jewels. There was a long pause.

Ewan dug his fingers into his pockets, fingering his flute nervously. "Begging your pardon, ma'am. Why are we here?"

"Because I willed it." Marielle answered curtly, rising from the ground, blooming with light. "Because I am Queen Marielle, and you are nothing."

She softened quickly, her voice turning to silk, drawing near on fluttering feet and silver wings, inhaling the night air as if it were wine. Her body swayed and danced; her lips smiled. Ewan blinked. She stood before him.

"You are a young one," she said, lightly clicking her teeth. "Otherwise you would weep to see me. Or beg."

Her expression shifted from imperious to alluring. She drifted toward where Sorge lay, letting her gaze slide toward his recumbent, robed form. Her eyes had become hard-cut sapphire.

"This one," she said, arching a thin brow, "this one I will keep. He is late in coming. I am not pleased. But at last, the circle shall be made complete."

"I'm sorry, did you say keep?"

"I am due. He bears the mark on his arm. Thus, it is my right. A mark of covenant between two brothers, pledging their lives for one another."

Ewan frowned. The queen laughed lightly.

"Do not be so foolish as to think you can prevent me, Outlander. There are limits to your power in this place. There are no limits to mine."

Probably true. But Ewan wasn't altogether sure what that meant. Since mortal and Fey didn't mix, what could the Fey really do? It might just be posturing. Yet Sorge had been truly afraid, right? Ewan decided he didn't want to find out why. He was beginning to understand other things as well. In the Mark of Twine, Sorge had pledged himself to Corus, *for* Corus, and likewise, Corus for him. It was not uncommon among master soldiers and their finest students. Ewan realized this in an instant and therefore what the queen intended. He had to scramble.

"I must begin by saying thank you, my lady."

The queen let slip a guarded smile. Ewan continued. "We weren't sure if we could find you, so I'm glad you brought us. Thank you."

"You were searching for me?" the queen said, bemused.

"Oh, yes. Otherwise we would not have risked coming so near to Elkwood. We were coming to ask you a question. About Corus."

The word instantly sent shudders up and down the ranks of Fey, causing them all to buzz their wings excitedly. Whispering, like rustling leaves.

"Corus! Did he say Corus? The prize of the queen?"

"A brave mortal, give him that."

"No, a fool. The queen was forced to release him. She was humiliated. She will strike him down for his impertinence."

"Even as she claims another in his stead?"

On and on it went. Ewan shifted his weight nervously. He heard the whispers and knew it was risky, but the ploy had maybe served to turn the tables a little. He made sure to appear innocent and wide-eyed.

"The mortal named Corus was here, once," the queen said. "My captive. My prize, so beautiful. A great Champion to your people, I know. This one"—she pointed accusingly at Sorge—"gave him to me."

Ewan summoned his courage. "Pardon me, my lady. I don't know the right way to do this—don't know how to be proper with royalty. But, if I could kindly ask, do you know where Corus is now?"

A hush fell upon Fey Haven. Sounds of birds and bugs, the noise of wings—all settled to nervous stillness. Ewan fought to hold his composure. He hoped he hadn't blown it.

Lifting her chin ever so slightly, the queen looked down upon Ewan with narrow, calculating eyes. She floated upward, seeming to grow more splendid, more imposing. Sprinkles of light trailed the space beneath her. The air smelled like a gathering storm.

"I have wishes too. I wish to hear your music," the queen said in a commanding tone, dismissing his request altogether. "I wish to hear the gift you carry."

The request caught Ewan off guard. He stepped back, confused. "My lady?"

"The music you play. Elysabel tells me it is a rare gift. I wish to hear for myself."

Ewan didn't move. *Elysabel. That's her name.*

"Play for me!" Marielle cried. "I command it!"

Ewan jerked into motion, pulling his flute from his pocket, putting it to his lips. Play what? Sweat formed on his brow in the cool night. He felt a drop trickling down his scalp, as gravity seemed to gather beneath his feet. What was that tune from the ruins, when he had his fever? Scraps of melody that rose unbidden whenever he spoke of the Fey or thought of them, hardly more than fragments in his head. He had yet to weave the pieces together. Yet with the Fey Queen bearing down upon him, finding a way to play that song seemed the only thing that mattered. He took a deep breath, held it in his lungs until they burned. Time, like nectar, grew sweet and slow.

Ewan let loose with a long, slow note. A low note, like the roots of the trees in the forest around him, clawing deep into the earth. A note of heartache, of searching for unseen things and wishing they could be true. In his mind's eye, flickering from shadows to light, he caught a glimpse of his mom. The freshness of the memory made his heart hurt, feel ashamed, realizing with shock how long it had been since he had last thought of her. But there she was now, inside, bright and clean.

Something hot formed in his eyes, as he blew and blew that one note, becoming like the roots himself, searching through the dark soil for the scent of something. Searching for the melody the way roots search for water. And then, in the coldness of the earth, one solitary root of his soul broke through to some underground spring. The song soared. Ewan took flight as a flood of memories came. He was caught in visions. His fingers danced along the slender metal shaft of the flute. His mind sped down streets lined with color. He thought of Hadyn, somewhere far away, and Gabe. And Garret, lost, with Taliesin. Merlin. In the Hidden Lands. Right there, in the midst of his song, Ewan played a prayer of music over all his brothers, over Sorge and Barsonici, and the dangerous game they played with the Fey. He didn't know where the melody came from for any of it. Only that it came.

Then it was gone. He stopped short, breathing hard. His face was streaked with tears.

Not a single Fey moved, except as they swayed to the rhythm of the faint, trailing echo. All their hair burned orange, like flame, rising from their heads like bubbles in water. A quiet, holy hush lay upon Aelfheim.

"This is more than music," said the queen at last, with awe. "It is the very breath of Aion."

Ewan didn't know what to say. Really, he just wanted to be alone. The music had found its mark inside him, releasing emotions that were now difficult to contain in public. Eyes closed, he tried to hold on to the sweetness.

"I must have your music," Marielle whispered. "You must give it to me."

Ewan opened his eyes. The Fey Queen was staring hard into his face, waiting.

"I'm sorry?"

She folded her arms. "I wish to have your music. Therefore, you will give it to me."

CHAPTER 14

Gain and Loss

I don't understand," Ewan said, shrinking away. "Do you want me to play something else?"

"Not play—I want it all! I want *essence* and gift, all of it." Marielle flung wide her arms, as if taking the green hollow of the woods to her bosom. She rose in a cascade of light, darting left, right, all around, settling again before Ewan with a wild, dangerous look in her eyes. "I will take your song and let it ring in my green halls for all time. The Fey shall dance and sway to hear it. It is of our kind, immortal. It is magic."

Ewan turned instinctively toward Sorge for help. Both he and Barsonici lay asleep on the grass, covered with the dew of night. Ewan saw the ring of Fey faces gradually breaking free of his spell over them, becoming a spray of color again.

"Flogg, can you hear me?" Ewan whispered. "Can you help?"

The gnome stood captive beside him, useless, silent.

"The rat creature cannot help you. You are alone, mortal."

And so he was, an island in a teeming sea of strange life. He looked for Elysabel, couldn't find her. Loneliness engulfed him.

"I do not know how to give you my song," he said, shaking his head. "Please let us leave now."

He couldn't be sure, but he thought he noticed a glimmer of strain in the queen's face—carefully masked by her natural grace and air of authority. It may have been there all along. He pondered, coming to a burst of realization. Ever since his arrival, the queen had been exerting her will against him to no avail. Over the other humans present in Fey Haven, certainly over the Fey, her power might be absolute. But not over him. She could force him to do nothing. For whatever reason, he was immune.

And the queen knew it.

"I want to take my friends and go," he said, shedding the innocence, gaining confidence in his tone.

"With no news of Corus?" she mocked. "Would you depart with no more knowledge than you came?"

The strain was barely visible in her hardened face, but Ewan perceived it with naked clarity. He shrugged. "If you were going to tell me, you would have by now. I can't force you."

"True, indeed, mortal. I am Queen Marielle the Fey. My mother was Queen Morgiona. I will have your song, or you will not leave at all. It is only by my good grace that you stand, rather than sleep—"

"No," Ewan countered, letting his voice rise in challenge. "I stand because you have tried to lay me down and cannot. I tell you now, release my friends. Let us go."

Chittering amongst themselves, the closed ranks of Fey began to fan apart like dandelion seeds torn loose in the wind. It was obvious enough. Nobody spoke to the queen this way. Their faces grew both fearful and indignant. Fascinated, too. Humans were strange creatures. Weaker and more powerful, both. Strange, beastly lumps of earth—to be avoided at all costs, unless safely made captive. But this one would not obey. He would not lay down and rest.

"Fine, mortal," Marielle said slyly, smiling. "I will make you a bargain. A good bargain, if you are not a fool. I will tell you where Corus is if you give me your music."

"I don't even know what that means, 'give me your music'!" Ewan cried in frustration. "Here, take my flute. Is that what you want?"

The flute. His mother's gift to him, no small gesture. But he offered it freely, sensing the level of danger ratcheting up, knowing they needed to escape. All of them. Quickly.

"I don't need your flute. I can craft thousands of wood and stone, much finer than your silly trifle! No, I want the *song*. The music inside you, from your soul. If we bargain, I would seek *that* from you."

"Not my voice. I can still talk and play . . . but you take the music somehow?"

"Indeed. You can still blow or strum. Sing whatever you want. But! The magic of the song will have passed from you to me. If you give me your song, from this day forward, you will no longer possess the innate revelation of melody you carry. You might still choose to make music, but the beauty and grace will be mine."

Ewan blinked. "Permanently?"

Marielle nodded. "Pity not! Your music will live forever, here, with us! An audience of immortals, worthy of your gift. Far better, don't you think?"

As the nature of her request sank in, Ewan felt as if he had been struck in the gut. He had been awakened in this land—to music, by music. *For* music. It was all so new and strange and wonderful he barely understood what that meant. Back home, he had played his flute as mere diversion, but here in Karac Tor, melodies had come alive, and he had come alive with them. The gift was beyond reckoning. His fingers knew what to do, skillfully bringing forth sweetness and undeniable power; he had barely begun to explore its full range. How could he forget, go back? He lowered his head.

And just what might the Fey Queen try to do with this power?

Marielle smiled. The tides had shifted. She had the upper hand now.

Ewan took a long, deep breath. Another. Breathing was all he knew to do. How could he say yes? How could he say no? Why did it seem that everything he loved kept getting taken from him? He glanced at Sorge, motionless on the ground. Some things were lost forever. Anna was gone. He couldn't change that. But he could protect his friends.

"I'll do it," he said.

Marielle leered, said nothing.

"But!" Ewan demanded in a flash of hot anger. "You must first tell me what happened to Corus. The truth and only the truth, and all of the truth you know. And you must remember, beautiful queen: I see Fey. I know their mischief. I will know a lie if you tell it. Try to trick me and I will keep my gift."

Marielle hesitated, eyes narrowing. She nodded once.

"Done."

Ewan set his jaw. "You will also release whatever claim on Sorge you have ever had, from this day forward and evermore. My human friends shall be free to leave in safety. Again, no tricks."

The Fey began darting about, angry and powerless. How dare this impostor challenge their queen so rudely! Ewan felt their minds pressing against him, their magic and malice. They were no longer curious and pleased. None smiled. Only one did not radiate contempt. Far off, by a tall tree, he glimpsed a familiar face. Elysabel. Watching quietly, shivering, her hair grown pale blue, she was not stirred to anger like the rest. She seemed sorrowful.

"Be careful, mortal," the queen said, sliding her tongue along rows of fine-boned teeth. "Do not trifle with me—"

"Swear it!" Ewan shouted recklessly, holding up his flute as if it were the scepter of a king. "In front of all your subjects! Do you swear it, Queen Marielle? Give me both of these requests, or I will walk from these woods and you will never hear my song again. Once outside your realm, I will never give you another thought."

"I could kill you!" Marielle hissed. "Strike you blind. Or deaf."

Ewan held his ground. Bluffing. No, *she* was bluffing. Wasn't she?

"Do it," he said, trembling, "if you can."

"I will!"

The Fey Queen's hair became the dark, roiling color of storm clouds and lightning, as sounds within the haven swirled to a high, careening wail. Thousands of Fey shrieked, their voices rising in crescendo. Ewan flinched. Now it would fall. Now it was—

Nothing.

Opening his eyes, he saw night and grass, trees and stillness. Most of the Fey had fled. Elysabel remained, distant, moving no

closer. Wide-eyed, she watched along with a few of the queen's clos-
est courtiers who stayed behind, who understood why such things
happened. The other Fey, perhaps, could not bear the thought of
their queen yielding to a child, a mortal child at that. Pent-up air
slowly bled through Ewan's nose. He prayed his knees wouldn't
buckle. The queen became two figures, one veneered with calm,
the other churning like boiling oil, full of quiet fury and shame.
She sank back to the earth, slumping ever so slightly forward. Her
eyes no longer flashed with fire. Her hair no longer swam in the air.

"I must have your song!" she wailed. Pointing at Sorge with a
long-nailed, slender finger, she said, "He will not leave this place
unless you give it to me."

Courage and adrenaline surged in Ewan's veins. He had challenged the Fey Queen and lived to tell it. Recalling Barsonici's
request, he said, "My queen, you have gambled and lost. I pledged
in faith, only to have you threaten my life with a lie. So I will give
my song, but now you shall pay double. Now I want all that I asked
prior . . . *and* the Pillar Map."

The queen lifted her head, lips quivering. Before she could
speak, Ewan cut her off.

"I remind you, I did not come seeking trouble, my lady. I came
to ask a question and depart in peace. You overcame my friends,
took us by force, threatened to kill me. You lied. I came as a friend,
and you treated me like an enemy. Even now, I give you my song.
But if you press any further, I will display your weakness to all the
haven." Ewan stood taller. "You have seen my power. I am Ewan
Barlow. I will go from here of my own will, not with peace, but
releasing songs of destruction all through these woods. Songs you
cannot stop. Songs that will overpower you. I was more reasonable
at first. I am less reasonable now. You should gladly accept my current offer before I raise it again."

Marielle sniffed. "Or what?"

Ewan knew better than to answer. Let her guess at the repercussions. He would be the head, not the tail. Marielle motioned with her hand. One of the Fey brought a small box of ivory and pearl and laid it before the queen. She opened it, reached inside, her wings fluttering gently.

"Song for a song, riddle for a riddle," she said, extending a thin, slotted tube toward Ewan. The shape was made of polished quartz, blue and gray like the sky. "Find the answer, find the Pillar Map."

"Answer to what?"

Marielle grinned wickedly.

"Music unlocked, lock without door,
Not crypt, not prison, not metal, but sword."

"And Corus?" Ewan said, taking the strangely shaped key from her hand. It was thicker than his whistle but half the length, with strange grooves and indentations. Solid, not hollow, and cold to the touch. He was tired of riddles and games.

"Seven years ago, the dark one came. He wandered undetected through my web of magic, entering the woods as a stag. The Horned Lord bargained with me for the life of Corus. I could not refuse him. He took him north, to Helheim. Corus is a prisoner there still."

"And?"

"That is all I know."

A disquieting smile slowly crept over Marielle's face. Ewan took a step back. Somewhere deep in the woods, Fey drums began playing.

"Now for my song," she said hungrily.

CHAPTER 15

Second Son

I n the blue twilight of that night, Ewan could not hear Corus screaming. Nor did Corus hear the anguished gasp of surprise that caught in Ewan's throat as his song unraveled from the binding of his soul. It happened at almost the same instant. Ewan, on his knees in moon-bathed Fey Haven, felt the last fluid note slip away like an icicle through wet fingers, as if no part of the song had ever been his. And Corus, hundreds of miles to the north, strung up between chains in a whipping ritual of blinding pain. The lash of the Horned Lord bit his skin with the familiar, fleshy sound of a willow switch striking a bag of sand. He no longer bothered to writhe away.

His pain was a terrible contradiction. On the one hand, he remembered so little of how all this had begun. Past and present had become indistinguishably smudged together in his mind. Each day was like the last: more suffering, more loneliness. More terror among the beasts below. More bland, rancid food forced down his throat to keep him alive. Forgetfulness taunted him with sweet promise, while memory was a paradox without relief. For twenty years he had nurtured and protected his memories—secret, dangerous luxuries he should not allow, and they were barbed claws he could not pry loose with a thousand tears. Much like the snap of the whip on his skin, memory kept his hate alive, kept him alive with it. Blessing and curse, memory. Hard, tiny seeds, stuck between the gums and teeth of his mind. A delicious obsession, though he would chew his face off to be rid of them.

Many years ago, the Horned Lord had come to where he lay amongst the Fey, entranced. Fey magic produced a state of suspension rather than sleep; deeply restful, lacking volition, yet somehow aware. For thirteen years. He remembered ethereal melodies lasting all through the night. Noises of the haven. Wings and birdsongs by day. The constant music of drum and flute. He remembered the queen, growing wrathful at pixies and sprites, screaming with rage, or doling out favors like sweet butter-drops. More vividly, he remembered Marielle's graceful shape, her unearthly allure. Her laughter, like a waterfall. Effortlessly, she made Corus covet her, and then, laughing, left him in a stupor of hopeless longing. It was not enough to gaze upon her. She drove him mad, made him want to utterly possess her. The effect was benumbing and liberating, enchanting and complete. And all this while he slept.

He was a plaything, he knew. A prize, but he didn't care. Fey were like children, consumed with their own pleasure, caring nothing for the pain or feelings of others. So when Marielle would awaken him every now and then, donned in robes of white, adorned with flowers, he would feel intensely self-aware, burdened with the need to hold forth his human dignity. But then, when crowns of budding mistletoe were placed on his head, when nymphs and brownies brought him cups of nectar and the juice of rare mountain flowers, his pride would melt, and he would revel in the glories of his slavery. In those waking moments, he would be given a throne of woven vine, made to sit beside the queen for her pleasure, as consort and king. It was a jest, humiliation masked as honor. He was prize and slave. And exile. But oh, how he loved those moments! Be they flickers of time or years, he knew only their rich intoxications. Crowned fool and lord, he gladly despaired of the outside world—if only that he might awaken again to see the silver queen with her dancing Fey, reveling in music and song and the ageless wonder of the haven.

They would bow to him, and she would kiss his lips, dance before him, drive him mad with desire. Eventually he would give in. Knowing it would fell him, still overcome, he would kiss her in return, deeply. Every time, at that moment, she would smile and, without a word, put him to sleep again. Sometimes for weeks, sometimes for months. One time he slept a whole year, was allowed to awaken for a day and a half, and then, weakened by her beauty, reaching for her, was put to sleep for another long spell.

Thus passed thirteen years.

In the realm of the Fey, where time curled upon itself in the strangest of ways, thirteen years seemed at once an eternity and the passing of a single hour.

But no, that was not the real reason for the knot in his belly, the one that drove him to hate, and by the strength of hate, to live. He had had a friend once, a warrior-at-arms. A student of warcraft, excellent with the bow and skilled with a blade. If memory was a hard rock inside, it bore a name: Sorge. Not Marielle, who mocked, nor even Kr'Nunos in all his cruel sport of pain. No, it was *Sorge*. While captive to the Fey, drowning in pleasure, he had forgotten Sorge. But then, Kr'Nunos came. Even now, the name was more bitter than hemlock in his mouth. How many long hours had Corus spent chewing his own teeth, biting his lips till they bled, plotting revenge? How many times had he clawed his fingers against the rock and wept, dug deep into the dark places of a quiet moment, imagining the day he might somehow escape and hunt down his old friend, extracting justice with a blade across the throat?

He and Sorge had taken the ritual of blood and brotherhood, marking their own bodies as a symbol of their covenant together. A mark, wrapped around the arm. A holy circle, symbol of Olfadr, who neither begins nor ends, whose very name began with a circle. It was a pledge that nothing would befall one while breath continued in the other. That any triumph would be equally shared and any defeat equally mourned. The mark meant one stood in the place of another to fulfill any debt or oath, even should the debtor pass beyond life to the peace of Isgurd.

Sorge had been more than a friend. He had been a brother.

Then came Nemesia. Love and bitterness. The two were torn apart. He could have killed Sorge if he had wanted. They battled for her heart, though it was utterly superfluous by then. Sorge knew, but could not abide the truth: Nemesia had already given her heart to Corus, not him. Being the master, Corus bested his student, but he didn't kill him. He took pity. Did Sorge care, bend the knee, submit? Was the sparing of his own life ever noted with gratitude? No. He was blinded by jealousy. Shamed, he had fled, afraid Corus and Nemesia were devising plans of greatness for the kingdom that did not include him. Partly true. Corus had spent much time in the ruins, searching for his destiny. He had found a great treasure there. Nemesia would know what to do with it, of course. She had power. And he, of course, was a Champion. Together, they would have brought order and goodness back to a tattered world—by force of reason, by moral right. He was the second son of an illustrious, almost mystic lineage. His forefather had traveled between worlds, the Champion of another king who now slept under the water and stone of Karac Tor. Corus was meant to find him, wake him. All these plans, cut short. Sorge had lured Corus away by deception and trickery. In a secret encounter with his old friend near the borders of Elkwood, the trap was sprung. He was ensnared, abandoned to Marielle.

Erased from history.

Then came the day like any other when he woke from his long sleep among the Fey, ready to be dressed in mistletoe, tempted as always. But a new and strange presence had entered Fey Haven in a swirl of shadows. Kr'Nunos had come with a claim upon him. Or had it been merely power and threats that the Fey Queen could not resist? He could not remember. Only that Marielle finally relented. Corus awoke to chains, to the Horned Lord leading him on a sled on the long journey to the Black Gates, past Angwyn and the Chamber of Keepings, where Kr'Nunos held many treasures of Karac Tor. He was brought to his cell, brought to life again. And the beatings began.

There was more to the story, of course, inconsequential matters he never cared to ponder, rats and roaches in the darkness of caves and the solitude of thoughts. Always there, hiding from the light. The facts were plain enough. Sorge had betrayed him, snuffed out his lamp, stolen his future. He, Corus, son of Cordun, was justified with righteous anger, was he not?

Drool ran down his cheek. *Justified. Innocent. Sorge, the betrayer.*

For seven years, he had known the lash, the gruel, the torment. For seven years he had wasted away in the frozen north, forgotten by all. Kept alive by Kr'Nunos, whom he learned with pain and blood to be real, and not mere legend. Kr'Nunos had disguised himself as an old lord of the northern passes, a tyrant and murderer named Baron von Gulag, long thought dead. The baron was a legend in his own right. Very clever, to assume his guise.

Yet in the end, it was not Kr'Nunos who kept him alive, either, though he forced him to eat after beating him, and restored him whenever flu or pneumonia took his lungs. No, not the Horned Lord, nor tooth-and-nail visions of retribution upon Sorge kept Corus safe from the cold comfort of the grave. Deeper forces compelled the son of Lotsley, scarred and chained, tasting the whip, defying the pain, and this, he cursed with more vitriol than he cursed Sorge. Though he longed to lay in the dust and never rise again, the claims of his lineage forced him to each next breath. He didn't understand until the ruins, but now, what did it matter? Living or dead, hope had rotted in his soul. The Horned Lord was all.

Rising before him now, tall and dreadful, Kr'Nunos blew hard, frothy air from his lungs. He had a vicious smile on his bearded face that was wildly human, but his rack of horns, glistening with ice, and the pelt of fur on his torso and legs, smelled of decay and beastly things not meant for men. He was naked, like an animal, except for a purple cloak, snapping in the wind.

"Why do you not rise to deliver the land you were sworn to protect?" Kr'Nunos jeered. For the moment, at least, he was done whipping the former Champion. Maybe for a day. A month. Maybe only for a few minutes. They stood in a sheltered cave upon the precipice of Mount Agasag, fifteen thousand feet in the air, looking out across the frozen tundra, south, beyond the reach of mortal eyes. "All you know shall fall in fire and darkness, Corus, if you do not arise. I tell you, arise, man! An entire generation of youth—mighty ones who might have taken your place to resist me—are now rendered powerless, with no name, no inner resolve, no source of will. They are ruined. It will take years to overcome and by then, it will be too late. My triumph will already be complete."

He waited for a response. Corus gave none.

"Do you not care, oh great and mighty Champion? If I brought the Severing Blade from my treasury below—if I put it in your hands and gave you your freedom—would you stride forth as did the dread lords of old?"

Corus hung his head low. His back and chest were brightly striped with fresh lines of blood. He could not move a half inch without throbbing pain. Trails of red ran down his loincloth, down his legs, dripping from his bent knees onto the shelf of granite jutting out from the mountain face to overlook the whole of Bitterland. Far below, lost in the snow and ice, lay the doorway to Helheim. A high wind whistled through the mountains, cutting his skin like ice. His teeth chattered beyond his control. The mountains, if he dared look at them, were terrible and beautiful and cold. A vast stretch of granite peaks. Snow dusted the northern flatlands beneath Agasag, the first signs of a hard, early autumn.

Corus groaned—unable to help it—trying to focus above the pain. The Devourer was amassing strength every day, he knew. Of late, it had reached the point where his power actually swirled around his presence physically. Dark, visible energy. When he was not shape-changed, not actively restraining his raw substance, the force of his power had begun to leak through like Yrgavien tar pits bubbling up through the earth.

Kr'Nunos spoke in a low rumble, as thunder that rolled across the Midlands plains. "You have seen my army of Goths, many thousand strong already. Tens of thousands more to come. Soon, I shall launch a force against Röckval to test the will of men. The city will fall, which is the beginning of woes. Archibald is weak, and with him, the land. A king is meant for strength, but Karac Tor has no king nor champion, and the men in the cities have grown soft. So while you lie here like a gelding, I will bring back blood. Yes! I will put their heads on pikes, here on this precipice, for you to look upon and despair. After you have witnessed the fall of Röckval, on that day, I think it may please me to kill you, with your heart emptied of all that is bright. I shall show your dead body to the earls and dukes, and all of Karac Tor will crumble in a day. Their last hope, dead."

He took Corus's once-chiseled jaw in his hairy fingers, lifted the chin. The eyes were slack. Corus's face drooped.

"Son of Lotsley. You are not the first man I have whipped. You remind me of pitiful Aion, long ago, hung high upon his stone gallows. Yhü wept when he realized my deception, but I laughed."

Corus barely heard. His own name rang in his ears. *Son of Cordun. Son of Lotsley.*

He heard it in all its bitter reckoning. Corus of Lotsley, once an illustrious family from a bejeweled city. Both now lay in ruins, relics fit for history books and children's songs, and the curious ponderings of old men. He often imagined himself rid of the legacy, delivered of its singular compulsion. Trapped in the mountains, forsaken—why carry the burden any longer? He could not bring the legends to pass any more than he could turn into a bird and fly away.

More than once, he had profaned his father's fathers all the way back to Lahns. But this time, as the Horned Lord boasted and

mocked, he pushed too far, beyond brokenness, to the unquench-
able fire. There in the darkness of the setting sun, something more
irrepressible than Hel gasped for air inside Corus. For at the end of
the day, neither hate nor memory, but *purpose*, kept him alive. For
the first time in months, he remembered.

"You will not kill me," he whispered, his eyes as cold and hard
as the stone at his feet.

Kr'Nunos turned, hunger in his beastly eyes. "Why? Tell me
why."

He punctuated his question with a glancing blow to Corus's
cheek. Then his stomach.

"You will not kill me," Corus repeated, gasping for air. "Not
now, not later."

The Devourer bent near his victim's sagging head. "You are
wrong. I will kill you at my leisure, as and when I please," he said.
"I am a god. You are a man."

Corus coughed. Blood came up. He licked his lips, could barely
feel them, numb and swollen. Tilting his head just enough to meet
his tormenter, he managed a weak, idiot's grin, the expression of a
man with nothing to lose for all his madness.

"A god, you say?" He laughed bitterly. "Perhaps, but you will
not kill me. For all your power, you are not greater than my curse,
and I am the last. No more sons."

"That's it, son of Lotsley," the Devourer agreed, almost as if
he were feeding Corus spoonfuls of his own hate. "Destiny must
repay its debt of service to the Sleeping King. And yet, here you are,
trapped in chains. Abused. Emasculated. Enfeebled. Why don't you
just die?"

Corus clenched his teeth. "Because I am a frayed patch in the
garment of your glorious plan. My chains mean you fear my doom

may be true, that I may one day stand beside a king, and the land unite. And you will fall. So you labor to prevent this king from ever arising. If I am captive, he never appears. But kept alive, you can still seek him out, perhaps destroy him."

His voice echoed, feeling like triumph. He had spent many hours in the darkness, thinking. He knew he spoke the truth.

"Such a great Champion, such a small mind," Kr'Nunos mocked. "You miss the point entirely. I don't *have* to kill you, only hold you. The heat in your blood will drive you mad long before I am done with you. Once you are gone, the Sleeping King never awakes."

Corus refused to look at him. More lies. Even if it were true, it was still a lie.

"But there is another way," Kr'Nunos panted in the cold. "Of course, I've given you seven years to consider it, but you are too dull." He leaned closer. "There is one thing, only one, that could truly set you free. Imagine if the Sleeping King were to *die*"—he shuddered, and a sound come from his throat, a low, grumbling threat like a lion makes before it roars—"then the doom in your blood would be done. At last you would have your freedom . . . from me *and* the curse."

Corus stared blankly at the walls of his living tomb. For once, Kr'Nunos had spoken truly: he had never thought of it. A million times, he had considered ripping his own heart out of his chest, blotting his own name from the book. But never of somehow sub-verting the prophecy.

"Ah, so now we talk as men," Kr'Nunos said with sweet delight. "Because if I must confess it, I do fear you, in that as long as you live, a king remains, and kings are dangerous things for me. It's a small thing, but I wish to leave no weakness in my plans. So I sought you. I found you with the Fey and kept you here all these years." He lightly smacked the whip against the back of his own hairy knuckles. "You see, I left the youth of this realm to Nemesia's spells, but my purpose with you is no less, slowly stripping you of your name, leaving nothing to chance. I've given you my highest attentions . . . and I can be very persuasive, wouldn't you agree?" He laughed again. "But there is a problem. You won't let me take it from you. I've tried pain, forgetfulness. I've tried scorn and depriva-tion. Yet you hold dear this notion of destiny, even as you despise it. You whisper to yourself, alone in the dark, racked with pain, that, no, destiny holds you."

Corus lifted his head, reeling at the Horned Lord's suggestion. Could he actually escape his own doom, or was it just another mind game? He didn't know. But it reverberated in his soul.

The Devourer laughed until the walls shook. "I see it in your eyes, the dim flicker of new intelligence. For the first time, you realize you don't have to dwell here forever, under my lash. And yet, we both know you *choose* to. Your name may keep you alive, but it is your shame that keeps you my prisoner. What will you do?"

He paused, waiting for rebuke, retaliation, defiance. Corus gave none.

"If I set you free, would you go?" he asked. Still, Corus said nothing. The Horned Lord blew out deep air, as if defeated. "As I thought. And since I will only set you free to find the king and kill him before he wakes, you leave me no choice but to discipline you with more pain."

The Devourer strode to the wall, took in hand a second leather whip. Corus grit his teeth.

It would be a long night.

CHAPTER 16

The Arch of Time

My king," Tal Yssen said with deep reverence, bowing from the waist.

Lying before him, bloody and torn on a makeshift bier, the man he called king fought for air. Leather armor and chain mail clung to his wounds in a tattered mess of metal and viscous red fluid. His belly was slit open. He had a deep slash down his neck. Bone and muscle were exposed. His peppery hair was matted with dirt and sweat and blood.

"No more, Merlin, my old friend," the dying man said, struggling to open his eyes. His skin was a pasty, ashen gray. "No more a king. I am a dead man now. *Cursum perficio. Ecce homo.*"

"You are king forever," Tal Yssen answered gently. "Once and evermore. Never just a man."

"No future . . . except the grave, no kingdom save *infernus*. My queen is not mine. My champion is my foe. And my enemy is my son. My sins shall follow me to the cold earth when you bury me at Gigantum. Thus I shall pass into memory. *Ad astra per aspera*."

He shivered, and someone hurried to cover his legs with a blanket. It was early morning. Two armies had fought through the night and the battlefield was littered with thousands of dead from both sides. Ghostly fingers of fog stretched across the tall green grass, extending from the river Cam as if groping, searching for the dead. Garret could hear the river's watery passing nearby—the very same river that had brought Tal Yssen and him to this place. So strange. Yet not so strange as seeing a field covered with dead men. Garret felt nauseous at the sight, felt numb with shock. He tried to hide his eyes, but there was no way to cover the other five senses. The air stank of mud, lifeless flesh. Thick mist, rising from the earth, mingling with the fog, muted all sound. A sacred, shadowless hush covered all.

The man on the bier spoke a mix of thick accents. Garret hadn't understood a word so far, though he desperately wanted to. (Later, Tal would tell him it was a mix of Welsh, Saxon, Latin.) As he strained to make sense of the words, a thought, like a butterfly, came into his mind.

I will help you, said the thought. *I will help you hear. This moment is too costly to miss.*

Garret nearly jumped out of his skin.

Is that you? he thought silently, glancing up in alarm at the old man beside him. Just when he thought it couldn't get any weirder.

Tal Yssen remained fixed on the king.

Eyes forward, lad. Yes, it is me. You will need this skill. Get used to it. Just so, I taught the man before you. Many, many years ago.

Garret felt foolish for not understanding sooner. Lying on his deathbed was Arthur, King of the Bretons. Artorius, he had been called by the monks at Ynys-Witrin. Dazed and humbled, the boy stepped back, feeling somehow wrong to be here, as if he were desecrating something sacred. He didn't truly *belong*. He was an intruder. But his heart pounded just the same, and he couldn't take his eyes off the legends before him, so very real. Alive, in *their* time. And the greatest was dying. Garret watched in silent fascination as the two men before him clasped hands.

"I have no strength to heal you, my king," Tal Yssen said. "But perhaps I can save you, give you what you need most: time to heal. A great soul like yours is meant for more than you have yet achieved. But you need sleep. You need a long, long rest, hidden away, until you are strong again."

With great effort, Arthur shook his head. No. The look in his eyes told Garret he just wanted to go, to be released. He was done. His chest rose and fell.

Tal gently challenged him. "I have foreseen. In all Nine Worlds, men of great heart are needed. Your courage and leadership will be required again."

"*Credo quia absurdum*," Arthur answered, smiling faintly.

Tal Yssen, also smiling, shook his head. "*Credo ut intelligam*."

It was a moment beyond Garret's understanding, of master and pupil in one alignment, sovereign and servant the other. Tender friendship above all. He understood the words now, or most of them. Not all. The process was disruptive, listening to foreign words in all their strangeness, while the butterfly in his mind spoke words that made sense—in a voice other than his own. It was hard to concentrate. But it worked.

"What of my son?" Arthur whispered. Thick, dark blood trailed his cheek, stained his teeth. His eyes stared toward the sky. "Does he live?"

"Medraut is dead, my king. I'm sorry."

Arthur did not blink, showed no emotion at all. "He hired Picts. Too many."

As he spoke, Garret could see Arthur's breath in the cool morning air, coming in shallow gasps. Saw past him, to more men in disheveled, bloody armor, ambling about the battlefield with local peasants, searching the fallen. Monks wearing dark brown robes and holding crosses before them checked for movement or puffs of breath, dragging the wounded and maimed toward tents where they could be given care, drawn back to life or given last rites. Countless prayers for the dead were uttered that day.

Three knights, battered and filthy, knelt in the mud beside Arthur's bier, leaning against their swords, driven into the earth. Splintered shields lay around them. Quietly, they wept to look upon their king. He lay with one hand on his chest, gripping the haft of his sword.

"The spring rains have come," Tal said. "It is not far to the tor by boat. Morgiona and two of her kin have sworn an oath to me. They will carry you. Care for you."

For a moment, Arthur's eyes brightened, though Garret couldn't tell if the look was one of fear or wonder. He strained to form words, gripping his sword even tighter.

"To . . . Avalon?"

"My lord, through the gate at the tor. The Fey have power to revive you. Keep you in a place of sacred water. There you will sleep until the world needs a king again. But it will take a long, long time. Your wounds are deep."

The king's eyes suddenly fell on Garret for the first time. The young Barlow felt a shiver to look into those eyes. Clear and blue, lined with crow's-feet from laughter, weathered by wind and sun. A face of clarity and pain. The force of Arthur's presence engulfed him.

"Who is . . . the boy?"

"A friend, my lord. His fate is woven with yours. Look at him well, and remember."

Arthur held Garret's eyes for a moment longer. Garret was transfixed, breathless.

"*Eram quod es, eris quod sum,*" the king said.

He lifted his gaze back to Merlin. Garret exhaled, as if released from a spell.

"I know why you are here, Merlin, but it is too late," the king said, as if confessing to a priest. A faraway expression gathered in his eyes as he told his secret. "I have already cursed my champion. Cursed him for his treachery, for destroying us all. Second son of a second son."

He fell into a fit of coughing, his face contorted in pain. The knights kneeling beside him flinched, reached out their hands protectively. But they had no skill or aid to give. They could only watch.

Arthur's face hardened. "He shall never know a moment's rest, nor his sons to come, until they have paid their debt to me. Wherever I am, they must find me. Until restitution is made . . . with blood if needed."

"Save your strength, my king," said one of the knights.

Arthur rolled his head to look at the three who kneeled before him. With surprising, sudden force, he said, "You must not touch him! I forbid it . . . no harm! He is my greatest champion and always shall be. But he must make amends. He must live with his sins as I must live and die with mine. And you with yours. Swear it, or I shall curse all of you alike."

Two of the men nodded. "We swear."

One did not.

"Gawyn. Nephew. Swear."

Gawyn pressed his lips together bitterly. "No, my lord."

"Swear!"

Gawyn looked away, his face streaked with tears. In agony, he said, "On my life! I will do him no harm! But only for you, my king. Otherwise, by sunset, he would be for the worms."

Arthur sternly held the gaze of all three knights a moment longer. Then closed his eyes, satisfied. His face relaxed, so much Garret wondered if he might have passed on, especially when a monk approached, murmuring prayers. Garret felt himself tensing, clenching his fist. He felt caught up in the emotion, yearning for something, anything. A miracle. He had been in this place before, in a hospital room, watching someone die. Someone he loved like summer loves the sun. Wishing for a miracle.

Help him! he cried, not knowing the cry was a message sent.

I wish I could, came the reply. From Tal. *God moves in circles, lad. The completion of one rotation is the beginning of another, yet never the same. Everything changes. Nothing changes. Sometimes we get dizzy from the spin.*

He was looking toward the crown of a hill not far away. Garret followed his eyes. Three women in flowing white dresses stood in the morning light, seeming almost to glow. The lady in the center, tall and slender, did not move except to tilt her head in a gesture of recognition. In response, Tal Yssen bowed his head ever so slightly. With visible effort, perhaps even regret, he roused himself, broke his connection with Arthur, began barking orders at the men kneeling in the mud.

"Fools! Enough pity and tears! Get another man!" he commanded. "Take your king! Now, before it is too late. To the river, to the ladies who wait. Pray there is enough time."

The knights rose stiffly, ashamed. One of them hurried to fetch another soldier. Together, the four grabbed the corner poles, gently lifting the bier. Startled awake, Artorius's grip on his sword slipped. For just a moment, Garret saw the razored lines, the silver etching wiped clean of blood and mud. He saw the yellow-swirled amber peeking like eyes above a handle of curved teeth.

The man they called Merlin spoke sternly. "Bedwyr, wait until the lady bids you return the blade. It is hers, and she will want it back. But only as and when she commands, however strange the request may seem to you."

"Yes, my lord."

Tal Yssen clutched Arthur's hand a final time.

"Farewell, my king," he said. *Aeternum vale.*"

Arthur, in spite of his pain, seemed surprised. *"Aeternum?"*

Tal Yssen nodded. "Yes, my friend. *Forever.*"

The king's hand slipped from Merlin's grip, deathly pale. Slowly, the four knights strode away, bearing their king between them.

Tal watched for a few moments. The world seemed to have caved upon him. Presently, summoning his strength, he said to Garret, "We must away to the tor, lad. You must rejoin your brothers. The matter of Breton is done."

They began walking toward a stand of trees curving along the river. A small, two-man coracle with a crude sail was pulled ashore not far ahead. Three days had passed since they departed the abbey through the arch on the hill. Tal Yssen explained that in passing through, they had gone backward in time nearly five months. Now they must return to the portal again. He could travel many places, Tal said, and through many times, but only from door to door, of which precious few were scattered on earth. In old places. One had to know where to look.

"What did he say to me," Garret asked, still full of wonder and sadness. "What did it mean?"

"He spoke a puzzle. A truth: *I was what you are; you will be what I am.* Death comes to all, lad. We live once, and then pass into judgment. With the help of the Fey, I shall delay death for Arthur until his destiny is complete. But then he too shall die. Small and great are the same under that curse."

Garret took a deep breath. "I just can't believe this is happening. I can't believe you're *really* Merlin. I can't believe I just saw Arthur. *The* King Arthur!"

"Lad, I have learned many things in my travels. I have learned the future will always think lightly of the past. I have learned that the truths of one age will become the smirk and wink of more enlightened ages to come. 'Tis a pity, really. Men are such proud creatures— always thinking the world begins and ends with them. Remember this well, because your eyes have been opened to see beyond the lie. Let today humble you, and live carefully with the gift."

They walked faster, picking their way over driftwood and rocks. Garret glanced one last time over his shoulder toward the four men, made small with distance, slowly carrying their king to three ladies, waiting in stillness. He heard soft music coming from their direction. Strange, otherworldly singing. A beckoning. The sound drew Tal, as well. Both man and boy had to force themselves to turn away. The music cast a spell.

Garret began pushing the coracle into the water, chewing on a question. For some reason, he felt embarrassed to ask it. To actually witness famous events many centuries old, celebrated in movies and books far into the future, then forget how the story went, made him feel like a poor student. Garret was the kind of kid that tried hard to do everything right. He was a pleaser. He did not like being a poor student. "I feel silly; I know I should know this." He fumbled for words. "Hadyn would probably know . . ."

Tal was obviously in no mood for conversation. Still haunted by his conversation with Arthur, he stepped into the boat, motioning impatiently for Garret to follow. He pulled his hood over his face as he pushed against the shore with an oar, then against the shallow mud of the riverbed. Soon, tugged by the swirling fingers of the current, they were caught away.

Garret tried to form the question again in his head. *What was his name?*

He really should know the legend better. How embarrassing.

"Lahns," Tal answered, speaking to the awkward silence. "Or have you already forgotten that I can hear your thoughts? He is a man from my world—the king's best knight and dearest friend. One time when I crossed over, he snuck through one of my portals against my will and without my knowledge. Not much older than you at the time. He became enmeshed in your world, a part of its history. As did I." Garret's face must have registered surprise, because Tal Yssen began chiding him. "By the Nines, lad, do you really think others have not crossed before? From your world to mine, mine to yours? Is it so strange to think other dimensions would lie beyond what your eyes can see?"

Garret licked his lips, had no words.

The mirling sighed. "Lahns is an excellent swordsman—the best on any of the Nine worlds, really. And a decent man, for all his faults. He was a spoiled brat on Karac Tor, but found rebirth in this world, making a name for himself of honor, chivalry, courage, and skill. Right now he is fleeing for his life, ignorant of the curse that is about to overtake him. He will seek to see the queen one more time, to repent, but she will not allow it, leaving him doomed to wander in both grief and guilt for many years. For a time, he will be a reckless mercenary, then a brother in brown, seeking penance. One day, spent and broken, he will come to his senses. He will return to Karac Tor, the land of his youth, with gray hair and a broken heart. He will father three sons in his old age. The curse will pass to the second. On and on . . . and on."

Tal stroked his chin, his eyes faraway, toward a lady on a river barge and a king not quite dead but not truly alive. He spoke softly, "The tragedy that happened here is worthy of the memory the world has given it. Pity the day it ever grows dim."

The shadowed visage of the mirling seemed to demand a response from the boy who was busy scrunching his face, still trying furiously to remember. It was one of those frustrating blind spots, where the thing was right in front of him, on the tip of his tongue.

Arthur, Merlin, Excalibur . . .

"It should be quite obvious to you by now," Tal said. "Names have a way of changing over time. Like mine. And yet the truth is always there. *Lahns of Lotsley.*"

Garret blushed, furious with himself. Then he knew. All at once, he knew.

"Lancelot," he whispered.

CHAPTER 17

A Gift of Wind

Well done, Tal answered within his thoughts, sad but satisfied. *Lancelot.*

"It was in your head all along, lad. Like a lame horse, you were bound to get there sooner or later. Now take heed for a moment. Pay attention. You've seen things historians will wonder about for hundreds of years to come. All of Angleand will lay claim to that man you just saw, my king. They'll say he was here or there, borrowing on his name. This round table in Wynchster, the real thing! This old fort was Camlyt! No, this one over here! They'll argue and fuss, because they don't know. But you have seen the man with your own two eyes. 'Tis a rare gift I've given. Hold on to it."

The older man patiently stroked the water with his oar as he spoke, using it as a rudder to nudge the vessel left and right through the steady current. Garret sat anxiously in the front. He wasn't a great swimmer. The coracle, made of woven willow rods, horse hide, and tar, was barely big enough for both of them. Even so, it was quite nimble.

Again, the voice in his head spoke. Gently this time.

If you hear this, raise two fingers on your right hand.

Garret giggled, raised two fingers on his right hand.

Now hoot like an owl.

"Hootie-hoot! Hootie-hoot!" Garret called out.

"Very well done," laughed Tal. "I tell you the truth, Arthur was not so skilled as you when he began."

Garret beamed. Morning had come, not yet enough to burn off the fog, but warming the gray chill so he no longer shivered and chattered his teeth. He sat with a cloak wrapped around him. Underneath that he was dressed in drab garb Tal had procured from one of the villages they passed on their way here from the tor.

Garret said, "Will Arthur make it? Will the king live?"

The old wizard didn't answer, handing him an apple, a crumb of bread, and a wedge of sharp, yellow cheese, instead. They ate in the boat, not talking much. The flood of events, of emotion, had left both spent. Tal retreated into his own inner world, pushing with the oar, wordless.

Garret wanted to sleep but couldn't. Not enough space. He might tip the boat. Letting his thoughts drift along with the water, he recalled a schoolbook he read last year, with a section on "Folk Tales and Legends." Arthur was there. Camelot. Beyond that, he could only remember one movie—a Disney cartoon of all things. But Tal Yssen was nothing like the pointy-hatted wizard of that tale, and Arthur was nothing like a gangly little boy pulling a sword from a rock. No, this was very different. Brutal and cold and beautiful. He didn't know to use those words, but he felt them. The story behind the story.

Smoke and fire, his dad always said. *Where there's one, there's the other.*

True enough, and Garret was right in the middle of the blaze. It was Dad's job as a professor to find those fires, to piece together clues from history and try to make sense of the pale shadows left by the passing of time. It had been Mom's job too. Before Hadyn, Ewan, and the twins, she had been here, had traveled the rolling hills, the green forests, the misty shores of the British Isles. Garret knew in his gut: He was right in the middle of everything his parents loved about their life together. Right in the soil and rocks, the bones of memory, drawing history's dusty air into his lungs. Things others must be content to read and speculate about, he was *living.* Carried along by a man named Tal Yssen. Who was really the legendary Merlin. And really, that was all just a misunderstanding, a slow deterioration in name and remembrance. *Crazy!*

It was like somehow visiting your parents on their first date, only weirder. Long before Reggie and Anna Barlow were born, or their grandparents or great-grandparents, this place, this river, this period of time was putting in motion the very events that would eventually attract those two people toward one another. He shook his head with the slow unfolding of the epiphany. If it had not been for the likes of Arthur, he might not have existed at all.

When she was alive, he recalled how Mom and Dad were always swapping old stories around the dinner table. He wondered if she had been to this very place on one of her digs. How would it have looked different to her eyes? What might have changed? What future trees hung as acorns in the branches above him, living and dying twice before his mom and dad would even be born? Hadn't she brought him a piece of rock one time from a dig outside some Roman fortification in ancient England? He recalled now. So many pictures of all these places, so many stories lying around the house. He had never really cared, never really listened. Now, of course, he wished he had. Too late.

He closed his eyes, and the day passed. They paused for lunch, ate on the shore, then kept winding along the river. For a while, Tal didn't bother to row. He sat carefully at the back of the boat with his small black leather-bound book. That and a small quill pen were with him at all times, along with a corked inkwell tucked safely in the folds of his robe. A travel journal, he said. The river was slow going. Although Tal had indicated they were in a hurry, he no longer seemed to care. In spite of the somber mood, when a pair of kestrels flew overhead in the mating dance of spring, Garret brightened. Ancient Breton was greening. The air smelled sweet and clean.

Their course was a series of waterways, beginning with the Cam, then connecting to others on their way to and through the more petulant waves of the bay—tossing their little boat, forcing them close to shore—then against the current of the river Brue toward the tor at Ynys-Witrin. They would have to travel upstream, which was nothing. By now Garret knew there would be wind.

Tal Yssen soon began regaling Garret with tales of other places and times. Also of this place, this time: the Cymri's northern mountains, enchanted old Cadir Idris, glorious sheets of lavender blossoms running along the heather-covered uplands and heaths. Farther inland a few leagues—they had not time to go—there on the rolling chalk plains, he said, lay the giganteum, the ring of giant bluestones for stars and kings, rising from the earth.

"And no matter what anyone tells you," he said with a wink, "those were here long, long before I ever came."

"But I still don't *get* it," Garret complained. "How have you traveled so much? You're telling me about Greece and Rome and Egypt. Incans and Asians." He blinked, feeling helpless. "How?"

"Lad, don't trouble yourself. You are young and bright, but it is different for you. You are trained to new things, the cold logic of machines. Not the ways of spirit. You live in a different kind of world."

"But I *want* to learn."

"And that's a fine start. Fine, indeed. But I can't undo in a day all you've learned."

"Okay, then just tell me this. If we're the ones with all the cool stuff, why aren't people in the future, my time, doing this sort of thing? Time travel and stuff?"

"Because all that *cool stuff,* as you say, shrivels your brains. You think you are greater, more advanced, and there is a certain brilliance. But you are also less, because you limit your faith only to what you can measure or touch. Nothing more. Lad, there are whole worlds of more!"

Garret sighed. "Do you ever make sense?"

"Nothing could make more sense! Men of your age look in the mirror and think they are the summation of history and culture, while everything around them is artificial. Ideas are devised, rationalized, labeled as true, whether or not they have any connection to what is really *real.* You have a word, a substance, what is it—*plastic*? You live in a plastic time. Plastic people." He smacked his lips distastefully. "Tell me boy, from whence comes the corn bread you eat for supper? I have visited your time. I have seen your food. From where does your father gather the meat he serves?"

Garret shrugged. "Grocery store?"

"No! It comes from a growing thing in the fields of the earth, tended by a man with dirt on his fingers. It comes from a cow or a pig or a chicken, fed grain, led to slaughter. You think it comes from a tin cup? It comes from life and death! Growing, feeding, rain, harvest, then starting over again. How can it be called progress to forget those things?"

Tal laid his oar in the boat, left it dripping. Untended, the boat drew near to the river's grassy banks. With his sharp nose and silver beard, the old wizard resembled a blue hawk swooping across the water. He might as well have been a screeching bird or a barking dog for all Garret understood.

Noticing his charge's blank expression, the man with the ageless eyes sank back, brooding inwardly. After some time, he drew forth a poem of liquid words.

In a dark vision, I glimpsed the high skies,
When Lucifarnus fell, to ocean and rock below.

I carried the banner before great Alexandros,
Naming every star north to south.

I watched in the fields when Absalom was slain.
Behind Magdalene I stood at the bloody tree and wept.

With whip and words, I warned Romulus and Remus of pride,
For I too was once deceived, as foreman to Nimrod's spire.

Elias tutored me in the school of the prophets,
And my spear was bloody in service of Troy.

I was in Llys Don before the birth of Gwydion.
I received the muse from Ceridwen's cauldron.

I have gone hungry for the Righteous One,
In stocks and fetters for a year and a day.

I was at the White Mount in the court of Cynfelyn.
I was harping bard to my liege, to Deon of Lochlin.

Tal fell silent, took the oar again, began nudging the vessel back into the current. Garret hadn't been listening for the last five minutes. Why did adults and old people have to make everything so big and heavy? Besides, he wasn't quite ready to plunge headlong into the new world Tal Yssen was offering. It seemed dangerous. He began to think he needed to get home. Quickly.

Days passed. Nights passed.

As expected, approaching the river Brue, the current began to fight them. Tal touched his fingers to his neck, spoke a word. The earth inhaled, exhaled, catching in the sail like water in a cup. The coracle pushed upstream. Garret watched, fascinated. He had seen it twice already, but it still amazed.

"Not so plastic, that, eh?" Tal said. "Some might even call it a mystery."

It was said chidingly. Garret felt as if he were in trouble on someone else's behalf.

"Don't worry, lad," the mirling said. "I will teach you the ways of wind. Would you like that?"

He was nine years old—eager, but unsure. Tal reached for the clasp of his necklace, opened it, handed it to Garret.

"Lesson one. Put this on."

"What is it?"

"Something I hardly need anymore. It is yours. It is called *Aeolo,* Wind Bringer."

Garret held the necklace in his palm, staring in wonder. It was simple-looking, a circle quartered by two lines with an empty spot in the center, a fitting for a stone. The braided leather strap of the necklace felt fairly new.

Tal said, "A blue stone goes there. That will come later. The stone is where the power lies, at least when you're starting out."

Garret raised his hands above his head, as if he were master of all elements. He shook the boat. "You mean I can control the wind now? Cool! When's my lesson start?"

Tal frowned playfully. "When we need more wind. And after you have the stone. At first I needed the necklace too, but not anymore. Now settle down or you'll topple us."

They sailed along in peace, Garret beaming and pretending all the way. The wind kept its focus right on them, pushing them deeper inland. Soon, the abbey and the tor came into view, rising from the plain like a green wart on the flat cheek of the earth. When they couldn't go any farther, the two disembarked. They greeted the abbot, the monks, shared a meal together. They spoke of the passing of Artorius in somber tones.

Tal gave firm instructions. "Three ladies will arrive by tomorrow's eve. They will be greeted by six more atop Ynys-Witrin. Do nothing to hinder them and everything to aid them should they require it. Arthur will pass into the womb of time, there to be held until his wounds are healed. Offer many prayers. And believe. One day, the king *shall* return."

The monks nodded, fearful and tearful for the loss of their king.

"Where," the oldest monk asked timidly, "shall he return?"

He was the same old monk from before, though Garret still didn't know his name. All of a sudden, it hit him. He shuddered to realize these men did not remember their coming before, atop the tor. That was in the future, not the past. It was yet to happen. From that initial time, he and Tal Yssen had gone back five months, to be here now. Guinevere was not yet come.

Tal answered him gravely, "To one of the Nine, though I know not which. Wherever he is needed most. Wherever the people believe."

After eating, resting, they climbed the tor into a day raging with light and hope. Garret clutched his necklace with joy and awe.

"Where do we go now?" he asked, fingering the gift as it hung around his neck.

"To Karac Tor. To my world."

Garret braced himself for conflict. During the last five minutes of the hike, he had expected Tal Yssen might say as much, but had come to a different conclusion for himself. He couldn't make that journey. Not yet. Not until he did something first. He hoped Tal would understand.

"Can you please take me back?" he said. "This has been fun . . . and weird. But I need to ask my Dad before I do anything else. He's probably not going to be very happy."

Tal Yssen paused. "No doubt, destiny is best when blessed, lad. But it doesn't always wait for permission."

"Maybe not destiny, but I do. I'm his son. I need him to know." Garret's eyes began to well with tears. "I've tried to be brave, Merlin, but I'm scared. I want to see my dad again. At least let him know where I am."

Tal heaved his chest, making unpleasant noises deep in his throat.

"This isn't so easy, you know," he grumbled. "I don't wave a magic wand and go poof! The currents of time are fluid, much like the river we just traveled. They move in unruly layers—top water, undercurrent, different speeds—generally past to future, but not always. Inside the portals, I am able to channel an additional force, like our little wind, to allow us to skim the surface in an opposing direction. But it is more art than science. I never know until I step into the portal how the water will feel, how fast the current is flowing. I make decisions in the moment." He sighed. "Sometimes, Garret, to open a door, one must become the door. That is all I know to say."

Garret blinked, without comprehension.

"Do we have to rush? Can't we take some time to think about it?" He looked at his watch, as if it might answer that question. The faceplate logo of the Kansas City Chiefs looked wildly disparate on the soil of ancient Britain. Noting Garret's small, unconscious gesture out of the corner of his eye, the old wizard croaked. He grabbed Garret's wrist, fingering the timepiece.

"Indeed. Let's take some time."

CHAPTER 18

Portents for the Future

All became blinding white. Into the portal they went, feeling water and whiteness, if white can be felt. Suddenly, it *could* be felt. Cold, crystal snow crunching under Garret's feet. A strong, bitter wind sliced his face, leaving him blue-skinned and chattering. Fortunately (he couldn't believe he was actually thinking these thoughts), he was draped in a thick wolf pelt given to him by the chief of a thousand-year-old village in some remote, highly unpronounceable wasteland called Xiongnu; or something like that. Land of the Huns, wherever that was. A miserable place. One day, Tal informed him, it would be called Mongolia.

That was Asia, three days ago. Before that, they had visited a sweltering, crowded city on the Yucatan peninsula with another unpronounceable name, where an old Mayan with a sharpened, needle-thin bone stuck through his cheek greeted Tal as if he were a long lost member of the tribe. Tal switched to the man's language as easily as changing a pair of socks. The two spoke urgently for half the day. When they served Garret a bowl of wet cornmeal and beans, he felt hungry, and thankful. When they added fresh armadillo flesh and a mash of avocado and papaya, he was ready to leave. Tal made him eat. All of it. Garret thought he was going to retch.

About midday they took their leave, journeying deep into the forest with an escort of mostly naked warriors carrying spears. It was a long hike, several miles removed from the stepped pyramid temple at the heart of the Mayan city. Garret was terrified every step of the way, but it was also becoming strangely normal. He was learning to cope with unfamiliarity and high stress. The natives seemed friendly enough to Tal, even with their fierce, painted faces, but they kept looking at *him* with expressions Garret felt were uncomfortably . . . hungry. If they ever decided to do it, he knew he could be gutted in a heartbeat. One quick spear thrust, a twist of the wrist. Done. Half expecting it to happen, he tried to avoid eye contact, tried to breathe normal, act normal as they walked, even though he hated this. If their journeys had ever been fun, they no longer were. Arthur and England were a million miles away. Home was farther still. He was going to be in big trouble whenever Dad found out, and Tal didn't seem to care.

Ugh! The butter-thick air kept his clothes clinging and wet with sweat. It was utterly miserable. When they finally came upon the arch of cut stone hidden in the leafy foliage, standing three times as tall as the arch in Newland, Garret sighed with relief. The surface, carved with square images of faces and animals—eagles and leopards and snakes—might as well have glowed like bright neon tubes. *Escape route! Exit here!*

Let's go, he urged Tal with his thoughts. He was getting better at the mind thing.

Soon. Patience.

Tal embraced his Mayan friend, said something in their language. Probably farewell. He waved his hand with a flourish.

Off again. Into darkness. Wetness. Light.

Each jump took them a little closer, Tal said, though he wouldn't say to what. He maintained his claim even when the opposite seemed to be happening, like trekking up mountains or crossing bleak terrain just to find the next portal. Garret learned that portals weren't all arches, nor all stone, though most were both. Each was somehow nearer to the mark the wizard sought, though, again, Tal Yssen would never quite admit to what that mark was.

When Garret asked, he would simply grunt, "Being creative" or "Getting permission."

I just want to go home, he thought, feeling more and more heavy of heart, as if it might never happen. How long had he been gone now? It was getting harder to sleep at night, harder to quit worrying.

He wasn't like Gabe. Gabe didn't feel guilt so easily. Gabe immersed himself in the moment. Garret, on the other hand, was a pleaser, always wanting to see the permission slip with a signature at the bottom before he plunged into a new venture. Of all the brothers, Garret was most concerned with doing the right thing. Color inside the lines. Be careful.

More than once he had overheard his dad bragging about his good behavior to someone else, seen the polite smiles of disbelief on the other parents' faces. But that was okay. He was proud of his obedience, perhaps a bit self-righteous because of it. But, truth be told, he was working on that, too.

Now here he was, gallivanting across the seven continents without so much as a by-your-leave. It was unsettling in the extreme. More than a little thrilling, secretly, if he allowed himself to go that far, but he wasn't sure his stomach could handle much more thrill.

They kept going. Tal tried to explain how he anticipated the ebb and flow of time within any portal at any particular moment. Like everything else the mirling said, it didn't make sense. Had he forgotten Garret was only nine?

"Through a glass darkly," Tal explained. Great, riddle number fourteen thousand! Anyway, it seemed the mirling could never fully predict what was going to happen until they actually entered a portal, at which point he had to make a choice. *Where* was easy. Portal to portal. Fixed points. *When* was the hard thing. From time to time Tal consulted his journal, though Garret couldn't imagine what in there could possibly help.

Still he was learning, slowly getting used to the strangeness of those two variables and the slithering journeys between them. Point A to point B, no problem—geographies were certain. Time, being fluid, was not. Thus, Tal's frustration with the attempt to return Garret to his father, rather than stay the course. Apparently the attempt could potentially trap him there.

"Too much for you to do," he said rather tersely. "No time to get stuck."

He elaborated on his river analogy. Time was the river, moving at varying speeds and in slightly variant directions, so it was *never* a perfectly straight shot. The shoreline on either side was the start and end points, with time passing unevenly between them. Two shores, two portals. Put in those terms, it wasn't hard to understand why the fluctuations in the river could make for an unpredictable landing on either side. In fact, Tal liked the word picture so much he wearily scrawled it in his journal.

"For all my skill, the Fey are much better at this than I am," he said, closing the book, tucking it away. "I learned from them, of course. But they travel with much greater precision, anywhere, anytime, as they desire. For me, it takes much more concentration than I am able to muster repeatedly. Not without rest."

"We can take a break. A day or two," Garret offered. "You look tired."

"A nice thought. But no, I'm afraid not."

They kept on. Garret said, "So how did you get all these powers?"

"Ah," Tal said. He sounded pleased, as if he had been expecting the question for some time. "First, I will tell you the folktale, as some would claim it. How about that?" He put his hand on Garret's shoulder as they walked. "You see, there once was a magical brew that was stirred for a year and a day. This brew produced the legendary three drops of Inspiration. As a young boy, I supposedly found the cauldron in which the brew was made. I stole those three drops from a Fey named Ceridwen. After this, many strange things supposedly happen that always make me laugh when I think about it. The way the truth gets distorted over time."

"Which is?"

"That I was Called, much like yourself. By Aion himself. The Call led me to Ceridwen, and she gave me drink." He shook his head. "The Fey punished her severely for it."

Garret felt timid but could not resist. "Is there more?"

"That will have to do for now."

And so at last, on their fourth jump in seven days, they came to the blinding white snows of southern Norway. Nóreegr in the ancient tongue. The year, Tal informed him, was AD 1024. Rock and snow scuttled together in a race toward the barren coast of the fjord a few hundred feet away. Garret saw broken plates of ice crowding together, drifting like white rafts. Farther inland, cold gray mountains clawed the sky. A white-tailed bird soared high in lonely flight. Garret felt for him, that he should fly so high in the cold air, alone. In his wolf fur, he was looking more and more primitive, a young caveman. Strange or not, he was thankful. But he felt very lonely, too.

It was a clear day. The glare of the sun on the fresh snow was like a welder's arc. Shielding his eyes, the young Barlow was able to make out thin trails of smoke rising over the next rough crown of ice in the direction they were moving. Tromping through the deep snow, sinking six inches every step, they came upon a band of Danes, dressed for war, crouched around a fire, belching and chewing chunks of flaky white fish. There were numerous animal hide tents, fires, swords stuck into the ground, piles of wood. Clay pots circled the fire, melting snow into drinking water. In the distance, at the bay, two longships were tethered to rocks on shore.

As they crested the hill, the rowdy noises of the men died away as one of the Danes, spotting them, mumbled to his companions and pointed. As one, they leapt to their feet, reaching for swords from scabbards and cold earth. One man had black hair. The rest were blonds or redheads. Most were burly, though a couple were smaller than the rest—thick beards, dirty faces, scars, and fur. They wore metal skullcaps. Even though none had the proverbial horns, Garret knew what they were: Vikings.

"Finally, this is where we need to be," Tal said softly, so only Garret could hear. "Don't be afraid. But don't speak. Not one word. Your language will confuse them, and that's not what we want."

"Gwion?" one of the men called out, his voice hoarse and suspicious. He eyed the old man and the boy beside him with open fear, squinting against the glare. "Gwion den Vardlokkur?"

"How many names do you have?" Garret whispered.

"Hush, not another word," Tal warned, scowling.

Tal Yssen held up a hand, palm out. For the first time, Garret noticed a white scar on his palm, as if it had been branded with a hot iron long ago. The mark was in the shape of a circle, drawn into four quarters by two lines crossing through the center.

"Gwion!" the other men exclaimed, shuffling back so fast they nearly tripped over one another. Alone among the men, the one who had addressed Tal held his ground. He was tall and thin, with long, greasy blond hair. A fleshy pink scar stretched from his temple down across his jaw. He did not smile.

Tal maintained a steady, silent pace. He was building fear. Garret knew it was also weariness. About ten feet away, he stopped, stared at the man soberly, arms folded in front of his chest. A high keening wind whistled through the valley of ice.

"Rögnvaldr den Uí Ímhair," Tal Yssen addressed him at last in a low, ominous voice.

Swallowing, the other man's fingers twitched on his sword. He and Tal began to converse in words completely unintelligible

to Garret, though they bit like teeth in meat. Tal did no transla-
tion in his head, and that was fine with him. He thought he made
out a couple of names. Maybe . . . Edmund? Ivar? The two men
talked at length. Tal did most of the speaking in a friendly, tutorly
manner, Rögnvaldr glancing occasionally toward Garret and giving
short, grunting replies. At one point, all the men closed their eyes,
and it almost seemed Tal was praying with them. The peace didn't
last. Shocked by something Tal had said, Rögnvaldr became louder,
more strident. His face reddened. Tal responded with thundering
impatience, railing against him, causing the Viking captain to
shrink back in silence. The old wizard pulled a small roll of hide
from his boot and handed it to the Viking leader.

Rögnvaldr took it, studied it. Garret saw glimpses of a map
and route lines. The man shrugged, turning the gesture into a
question.

"Vineland," Tal Yssen answered softly.

The men went white. Then began roaring in anger.

"*Skraeling?* Vineland *skraeling!*"

Soon all of them were shaking their fists and bellowing in protest. Garret felt himself stepping back, moving behind Tal, out of
harm's way. He was done. Done with adventure. The Vikings had
swords and anger and muscles. He and Tal had nothing.

Tal calmly stretched out both arms, commanding the skies
with a word. The men fell silent, glancing upward. Every screaming
wind grew still as a hush fell upon them all. No one knew what to
think until it hit—a blast of wind funneling down from the clouds
above. The torrent of frozen air poured upon the very place where
they were standing. Waterfalls of wind. Snow shot up from the
ground as if the rock beneath it had exploded, whipping away in
white streamers. Snakes of flame hissed in the fire pits before being

sucked away in the updraft, leaving behind great, belching plumes of smoke. Garret was nearly toppled by the blast. He widened his stance, clutching the back of Tal's leather vest. The Vikings fell back, moaning and wide-eyed.

"*Miskunn! Miskunn*, Gwion den Vardlokkur!"

The wind slowly died away, but a storm remained knotted in Tal Yssen's silver brows. This time, when he spoke to the men, Garret didn't have to understand the words. He understood the tone. No negotiating. The Vikings had been chastised with power. They had been given instructions and were expected to carry them out. Rögnvaldr was sullen but penitent. His men huddled behind him.

"Give me your time device," Tal said to Garret, glancing over his shoulder. "On your wrist. Give it to me now."

Garret didn't hesitate. He stripped off his watch, handed it to Tal, who took it, and with it a small stone from a pouch at his side. The stone was flat, about the size of a quarter. Using the sharp point of his dagger, Tal carved a mark on the surface of the stone. He took the watch and the stone, took the map from Rögnvaldr's trembling hands, wrapped them up together, and tied them with leather straps. The final bundle he placed back in the Viking's hands.

"Do!" the mirling said. He turned and tromped away, nudging Garret ahead of him. They never looked back.

When they were a safe distance away, Tal said, "It was all I knew to do, but it will be enough. The Uí Ímhair are the descendants of Ivar, called the Boneless, who once ruled parts of Daneland and the Geats. About 150 years before this time, Ivar and his brother invaded east Angleand, where Edmund, king of East Anglia, ruled. Edmund refused to renounce Christ the Lord, nor would he surrender to be the vassal of a pagan. So Ivar had him tied to a tree and shot full of arrows. A blood curse has rested on the Uí Ímhair ever since, much like Arthur placed on Lancelot. I gave Rögnvaldr a chance to be free of it, to deliver his children from the generational curse. I prayed with him to break the curse, then challenged him to be faithful. It is a hard task he has been given, but in it he will find penance . . . and peace." Tal sighed, laid his hand on Garret's shoulder. "This is all I can do, lad. We cannot go to your father. But rest assured, he will know what has happened. You have to trust me."

"Why? Because a bunch of Vikings go to Vineland?"

"Indeed," Tal said. "Or, as the world will come to know it, America. You call it home."

Garret's mouth dropped. "The Vikings went to *America*?"

Tal chuckled. "You thought Columbus the discoverer, eh? And Vikings were not the only ones. What have I been telling you, boy?"

"I know, I know. Men are proud. They believe what they want, not what is true."

More laughter. "Ah, miracle of miracles. A student who listens!"

"Okay, so we've been all over," Garret said with all the gravity and melodrama he could muster. "I've had my brain busted about you and Lancelot. Vineland and America. What other surprises do you have for me? Let's get to it."

Merlin grinned. "Curiosity for the truth. A reluctant, budding adventurer. Ah, that's the spirit! You will need all your powers, my boy, because now, with your permission, we really must be going. Somewhere in the Hidden Lands, a king will soon rise in search of his champion. He will reach for a sword with yellow dragon eyes. A blade lost for ages, called in the old Welsh, *Caledfwlch*, bearing another name in Latin, *Chalybsure*, which means 'burning steel.' Arthur chose the name in anger, feeling cursed by it at first. But he grew older, wiser. After many years with the sword it became *Ex Calor Libera*. You know the name well."

Garret didn't blink. One more surprise. But this time he knew. An awesome thought, burning steel.

Excalibur!

CHAPTER 19

Assassin's Creed

Moonlight dripped like melted pearl down the length of the blade's polished steel edge to the finely wrought handle. Yellow amber. Dragon's teeth curving around the haft under Cruedwyn's closed fist. Hadyn held his sword at the ready too. Not nearly so magnificent a blade, but good enough in a fight to kill. Or be killed.

How had it come to this? he couldn't help but wonder. One day he'd been sitting at home, Googling for clues to ancient runes on a rock outside his house. Eating peanut butter and jelly sandwiches. Hating life, trying to adjust to bone-deep loneliness, mad at the world. Next thing he's saying silent prayers, thankful for the asylum afforded by murky shadows and three squatty oak trees a few paces off the main road more than halfway between Slegling and

175

Tinuviel, just north of Gelding. With a sword. Desperately trying to stay alive.

Thankful, too, for a thin crescent moon and wispy clouds that might, just might, swallow a few stars.

Thankful for a friend named Cruedwyn Creed.

Hadyn tried to gather his breath, slow his heart rate. *Stop panting so loud!*

Once more, he and Cruedwyn were on the run. In truth, they had been running ever since parting with Gabe and Va'nya back in Faielyn. How many weeks was that now? Three? He had lost count. It was a complicated matter, to be sure. After delivering their message to Rosalier in Milangino's shop, it was decided (thankfully, with neither Diamedici nor Va'nya present, as they had removed themselves for their own private conversation) that Gabe should return to Alethes with a message: Vineland and the Highlands were in secret treaty. To what end? No one knew. But Hadyn and Cruedwyn agreed. Something was up. It seemed of little use informing Archibald, and besides, Hadyn wouldn't consider sending Gabe that far without him. The White Abbey was near enough. *Somebody* should know. Alethes was a good place to start.

"I'll wager it's a bad omen for the Duke of Greenland," Cruedwyn said the night before the four split, two east, two west. "I'll double the wager to say that's why Giovanni has exiled the prince. His spies have told him the royal nephew is arming for a coup, or something like it. Or old Giovanni simply cannot abide the thought of an alliance with the Highlanders."

"But the bigger question is, why?" Hadyn said, frowning. He didn't like it.

Of course, Hadyn didn't like Gabe being out of his sight either. Since coming to Karac Tor, he was always asking himself, *Would I be in trouble with Dad for this?* It was the best barometer he could devise for decision making. But there really was no choice. Va'nya, in whatever role of conspiracy he played with the Vineland prince, in whatever ways he had used his allegiance to Gabe or his commission from the Jute to further those conspiracies, had nonetheless proven himself a loyal defender of the young Barlow twin—almost religiously so. He was fierce, brave. Good in a fight. And, always a plus, he could pull out a pair of wings and fly if needed. If, that is, he could find a high enough spot to launch from. Yet Hadyn's stomach still sank to see Gabe walk away.

But that was only half the story.

As Dinbalo had intimated at the tavern, the League of Assassins had tracked Cruedwyn to Faielyn. Whatever debt it was that he owed them, the Black Hand had come to collect. With Quillian getting closer and closer, the safest route for Gabe was in one direction: away. Hadyn, on the other hand, still had the task of warning the land barons along the coast. Sorge and Alethes had agreed that the will of the rulers must be marshaled and unified, and perhaps a visit from an Outlander might intrigue them enough to halt their squabbling. Hopefully, his encounter with Odessa's captain, Thorlson, at the smithy would serve to complete that task for the Bittermen.

He had given Lord Rosalier the same warning to pass along to Giovanni. *A rising tide of darkness will soon pour across the land like floodwaters breaking levies. We must prepare. Rouse the people. Amass arms. Purify your homes. On this, the abbeys are of one mind. Watchers are loose. Prophecy is being fulfilled. Dark powers are stirring. The land barons need to set aside their differences and unite before it is too late. Be ready. So says Alethes, High Priest of the White Abbey, be ready!* That was the message given him to carry. And carry it he would.

All things in time, though. For now, the warning seemed trivial compared to the far more urgent task of staying alive. The menace of Quillian following behind pressed increasingly upon them. Besting Giovanni's guards in Faielyn had only been the beginning of Cruedwyn's troubles that day. He and Va'nya had spent all their time eluding Quillian, dashing street to street, atop roofs, hiding in empty barrels and storefronts, before finally slipping into Milangino's shop. Diamedici—a hunted man himself—had created a diversion for them before they left, allowing perhaps a full day's lead. But Quillian had proven a ruthless tracker, gaining every day since. After escaping Faielyn in a swift vessel captained by Diamedici's men, it wasn't long before they saw another vessel trailing behind. For two and a half days, they deliberated whether Hadyn's message to the duke in Seabraith was worth the risk.

Deciding they had no choice, they disembarked—and nearly lost their lives for it. The duke wasn't in residence at the moment, thank you very much. He was north, in Tinuviel, directly engaged in a scuffle on the straits between Emryl Isle and the mainland.

Hadyn, meanwhile, inquired hurriedly about Asandra. She was supposed to be in the city on business from Cassock. Maybe she had already come and gone. He mentioned a mirling visitor to the dock hands, surely a rare enough thing to be noticed by some. No luck, though. No one knew her by name or rank, and Hadyn had no time to visit the Black Sanctum on the other side of the city. Seabraith was huge, second only to Stratamore as the largest city in the kingdom. It all took time: traversing the city, finding the royal residence. And time was something they didn't have, not with Quillian on their tail.

By the time they made it back to the docks, Quillian had already arrived, had laid a trap, so getting in was not half so hard as getting out. They barely slipped through, thanks to a loose-lipped, half-drunken sailor. But they had had to fight—even Hadyn. He held his own, mainly because the men he fought were also drunk. Once again, they fled by boat. Diamedici's captain was fierce and loyal, but his crew probably cursed the bard and the boy in private. Seamen didn't want any trouble with the League. No one did.

With a good wind behind them and the assassin's shadow haunting their path, they had set sail for Tinuviel, ancient capital of Greenland, by way of Slegling-by-the-Sea, Cruedwyn's birthplace. He knew the town well, was hailed by all who saw him. Most did so with a smile, some with insults and threats. A few dainty ladies batted their eyes at him and giggled as he passed. One didn't say a word, just strolled up, narrowed her eyes, and slapped him on the face. Hadyn wondered if they might need to visit his family's farm, perhaps find refuge there. But no . . . no time. Not this trip. Not with the Black Hand so close behind. They pressed on.

"Besides, my family is a bit odd," Creed said. "Always talking. Always boasting. A reasonable man can hardly get a word in edgewise."

Hadyn laughed so hard he blew snot from his nose. And on they went, toward Tinuviel.

Tinuviel! Like a crown atop a bed of velvet green, with sweeping eastern views of Emryl Isle and the Wyld Sea, the city grew from the very rock and bones of the Cliffs of Felwyn. It pressed right up to the edge on a massive protrusion of stone, with nothing beyond but a breathtaking thousand-foot plunge to the frothy water below. Utterly unassailable by sea, Tinuviel had long been the kingdom's second and most powerful line of defense against attack from the north. A long time ago, after the bloody Second Battle of Grym Fields, it was Aventhorn Keep, the heart of old Tinuviel, that had stopped the insurgency of Hhyss One-Eye into the deep core of the kingdom.

They had built another decent lead on Quillian from Slegling, passing through two smaller villages along the way, trailing streams, sneaking through leafy woods. The Black Hand might be a master assassin, but Cruedwyn was cunning enough in his own right, and he was now in his home territory. He knew this part of Karac Tor better than any other, like he knew his own sword. And as for that, well, as far as Hadyn could tell, that blasted sword was precisely the reason they were perpetually in harm's way, barely half a step ahead of death.

Quillian wanted it. Cruedwyn wouldn't give it.

Ironically, his devotion to the weapon was beginning to make more sense to Hadyn as he became more attached to his own sword. On top of which, Cruedwyn's *was* magic—though a blade that scorched you whenever you told a lie hardly seemed useful.

Only moments ago, approaching a thin stand of trees with the thought of making camp, Hadyn had thought with relief how nice it was to have *terra firma* under his feet, not rolling sea swells. Pleasantly cool, the early autumn breeze curling over the stone lip of Felwyn's distant ridge had a sweet, clean, salty smell. He didn't mind that. The smell of the sea was nice, just not the feel. Night had come. The grass was tall here, a mix of wild rye and barley, false wheat, burdock, and flowering goldenrod. They had barely unloaded their packs when Cruedwyn abruptly hushed him. Hadyn knew better than to think he was joking. The attentive pause was brief, nerve-racking.

"To the trees!" Creed commanded.

Hadyn moved in gulps and leaps. He had learned not to hesitate. Charging for the trees, he slammed his back against one, Cruedwyn another. Calming himself, he heard the sound Cruedwyn had heard—feet in tall grass, not far from the spot they intended to set up camp. Clinging to the trees, unmoving, neither spoke. Hadyn eventually tried to peek around for a glimpse, but it was too dark. The sky was opaque. Cruedwyn had told him enough stories of Quillian and the League to know meeting an assassin in the dark was a bad idea.

How had it come to this? he couldn't help but wonder.

"I'm tired of running," Cruedwyn whispered irritably beside him, as if he were offended at himself. "I'd just as soon fight the man fair, face to face—"

"Cruedwyn, hush! Not now. Your sword will give us away."

But the blade was silent and still. They waited a few moments more, before Cruedwyn said, "I think we're okay. Must've heard wrong."

"No wait." Hadyn made a suppressing motion in the dark. *Shh.*

Cruedwyn slowly rolled his face around the trunk to get a better visual. Hadyn did the same. Thin waving grass needles were silhouetted against the sky. Wind scraped the stalks. They waited more. Nothing happened. Maybe they had heard wrong. Haydn began to relax. Far in the distance, the pale blush of watch fires could be seen flickering on guard towers.

Tinuviel. And hopefully, Pol Shyne, Duke of Greenland.

Ah, now *there* was a tale worthy of any soap opera, save for the depressingly human squalor of it all. Having lost his wife to a fever after his daughter was born, the grieving duke, in a moment of weakness, got a scullery maid pregnant. The boy, Win, had the character and face of his father right down to the twitch in his nose. Even so, for two decades the duke refused to own him. He had the

scullery maid cast out and forbade the castle staff to speak of her
ever again. Pol Shyne was a complicated man. As a devout patron of
the White Abbey, he lived in stern and rigid conformity to White
dictates regarding a proper, holy life. Sins that led to illegitimate
children were not to be tolerated, not in your own home, certainly
not in yourself. Thus, all must suffer. Since the birth of his son, Pol
had forced him to live on the fringes of bitterness and hope, occu-
pying the space around his father's legacy but never allowed in. It
did little to quell the rumors, yet it allowed Pol to live within his
own carefully constructed shell of integrity.

In terms of leadership, Pol had spent years currying favor with
Archibald the Twelfth by volunteering to patrol the Wyld against
pirates, which notably improved commerce for all Five Dominions.
His efforts had made the shipping lanes safer for all the major
north-south routes. For nearly a decade, he did this at his own
expense, charging Archibald nothing, though the governor ben-
efited immensely from all the goodwill it engendered him among
the merchants of Karac Tor and the provincial land barons. The
favor and political capital was an enormous boon.

Then came fleet increases. Double, nearly triple the warships.
Toll fees.

Almost immediately, the protests began. Outright acts of sedi-
tion soon followed. In fact, merchants had begun turning to the
very pirates they once despised to help them smuggle their goods
because it was cheaper to fund the pirates than pay the tax. Greenland, proud of its new status under Pol, was evenly divided against
itself since Pol taxed his own shipping merchants the same as the
rest. (Fair is fair, he said.) And though it was not voiced loudly,
the common folk sympathized with Win. The young man was
a friend of the people, good-hearted, and ready to help whatever

cause seemed most pressing at the time. A sort of local hero dealt a bad hand.

Then there was Sáranyása, the duke's beautiful, cloistered daughter, held in perpetual vigil and purity by the duke's iron will, though all the land buzzed with the rumor that she and a certain exiled Vineland prince were secretly engaged. Meanwhile, fueled by escalations in merchant gossip and the cost of common goods, the other dominions cursed Greenland for its greed and duplicity. Even an old ally like Har was beginning to grumble.

The onetime perquisite had become a major irritation for Archibald, another headache to complain and wring his hands about. Mince and murmur. Do nothing.

Ironically, if war were coming, Alethes had told Haydn before they parted, Pol's immense fleet might prove to be the greatest gift the kingdom possessed.

And for all his faithful consular travels, Hadyn could not help but wonder. *War from where?* He had seen the great evil Nemesia let loose. He knew the message he had to give and believed in it, if for no other reason than because Sorge believed. But he wondered how effective the message could be, when as yet the substance of his warnings was principally a matter of prophecy, circumstance, and the mandate of a priest. The high priest, to be sure, but still a man of the cloth, in an abbey known more for mediating legal disputes than rousing a nation to war.

"I think it's safe," Cruedwyn said again after a long while, stepping from the deep shadows of the tree into the thin, milky gaze of moon and stars. He motioned for Hadyn.

Out of the corner of his eye, Hadyn imagined a phantom clad entirely in black—cloak, hood, and gloves—materializing from the tall grass like a departed spirit rising from a crypt. Maybe *not* imagination. His throat, suddenly dry as cotton, became incapable of noise, warning.

"Come on," Cruedwyn pressed, oblivious. "Let's set up camp and get some rest. Make it short camp, mind you, nothing but blankets. I'm exhausted. We need to be in Tinuviel first thing in the morning to stay ahead—"

His voice unexpectedly choked. Hadyn blinked, looked away. The shadow. He should have cried out. He should have. Quillian, at last, had come.

CHAPTER 20

The Black Hand

T he blade, *ca'Libre*," a pale voice spoke; a soft, sibilant whisper. "Give it to me. And nothing noble, or you're dead before you hit the ground."

Hadyn, pressed against the tree, tried to stay calm. Was he known? Had he been seen yet? Peeking around, he glimpsed the vague form of two men tangled together. He could not tell if the washed-out metallic glint of the blade at Cruedwyn's neck had already drawn blood. Maybe Creed was already dead? Maybe Hadyn was next.

Quillian called to him in a raspy voice, like a rattlesnake on a warm rock when a fox passes by too closely—soft and sure and tinged with warning.

"Get out from the tree boy, if you want to live," the assassin said. "If you want *him* to live."

Hadyn obeyed almost instantly, in pure reaction. He didn't know what else to do. As he took a faltering halfstep from behind the trunk, feet scraping the ground, a thousand thoughts came together in a moment. For some reason, he stopped. Possibly, it was the contemplation of his own death. Possibly, he thought to retreat back to the tree, take his chances. Or scream, fight.

Regardless, that suspended moment of uncertainty deflected Quillian's gaze by a breath, a blink. The angle of his grip on the knife at Cruedwyn's throat adjusted just a hair. It was all the bard needed. Hadyn saw a blur of shape and form. Cruedwyn, crying out, wrenched away, landed a grinding elbow in Quillian's gut. The assassin groaned. Rolling to his feet, Cruedwyn pawed the ground for his weapon. He tottered back, pressing the palm of his free hand against his neck.

"Go!" he croaked. His words were thick and wet. "It's the sword he wants, not you!"

This time, Hadyn did not hesitate, rushing to his friend with a fearful eye on the dark field. Already, Quillian had lowered himself into the grass, melting away. A snake, slithering off. Assassins did not enjoy straight fights. They worked best on fear, surprise, and dread.

Blasted darkness! Where was the moon when you needed her? Hadyn strained his eyes, but the murky night was nearly impenetrable.

"Don't bother trying to convince me," Hadyn said firmly. "I won't leave you."

"You fool, go!" Cruedwyn roared, but then he put his mouth close to Hadyn's ear. "Tear your shirt and wrap it around my neck," he whispered, "then fall back to the trees. Quickly! And light a torch so we can see. He's got the advantage."

They tumbled over one another until they were behind the three oak trees again. Hadyn groped blindly in their pack for a dagger and one of two small torches they carried.

The Black Hand called out from the tall grass. "The cunning hunter knows. He waits for the right time."

He had moved. The position of his voice was far from where he had first dropped out of sight. It brought a terrible dread to think of playing this game. Every other name assassins were known by came suddenly to his mind: *Widowmakers, Deathlords, Blades.* He knew they had earned them all. Cutters and Gutters, Diamedici had called them.

"It would have gone better for you to give me the sword when you had the chance," Quillian said, mocking and light. "The boy should have just come from the trees. I would have taken the sword and let you both live. Or you could have given it to me in Three-fork. Or Faielyn."

He had moved again. Fast. There was an edge to his voice. A razor-tipped metal star struck the tree trunk near Hadyn's ear. Hadyn jerked to one side, heaving.

"You have proven a worthy adversary, bard. I honor skill such as yours. I find it . . . stimulating."

Without moving his head, Hadyn whispered, "How's your neck?"

"Still bleeding," Cruedwyn muttered. "He's trying to distract, create fear. Keep sharp."

Slicing at the bottom of his shirt, Hadyn tore loose a long, wide strip, then pressed the cloth on Cruedwyn's neck, wrapped twice and tied a loose knot. He could feel the wet blood, even smell it in the darkness.

"Just a little woozy. Not as bad as it looks."

"Oh, right, and how would you know? You don't know what it looks like."

"Would it surprise you to know I don't know what Quillian looks like either?"

"And yet he's still there! Just like that gash on your neck."

Creed sighed. "Clever boy. Such a wit. I'm so thankful we've shared this moment."

Hadyn heard the smile in his voice. Yep, he was fine. Striking flint and tinder to the balled, waxy head, Hadyn lit the torch. Light bloomed outward. Hadyn held the fire high.

"What do you want with the sword?" Cruedwyn yelled. "*Why* do you want it?"

No answer. The leaves of the tree swelled with air and light. The grass waved, but there was no sign of the black-clad man.

"Not good," Hadyn murmured.

"No, it's part of his game. If he wanted to kill us, he would have by now," Cruedwyn said. "No one escapes like I did. No one." He spoke louder. "Isn't that right, Quillian?"

Creed's blood-soaked rag was frightful to look at. He had been lucky. The cut was low, at the base, near the tendon—not the throat, not the jugular. In the dark the rag looked glossy and black.

"Quillian, let me be a friend to you. Listen: She's not worth your trouble! The metal's cursed, by Loki himself, I'd say. Besides, you lost fair and bright as noon. We played a game of bones. I didn't know who you were—just another guy at the table. We were both full of ale. I was out of money. I wagered my sword. You bet high and laid claim to her; I bet higher and won. You said I cheated, but I didn't. Now come on out. Let's be done with this. Perhaps we can make a deal."

Hadyn waited for the sword to prove him a liar, but there were no protests.

"I traded my harp for her, see? She's not yours. She's mine." His voice dropped to that of a timid confession. Hadyn wondered if he was meant to hear it. "She's all I've got."

A voice came from slightly behind them. Or was it an echo? They turned.

"Where . . . the harp? Who did you trade with? Before bones in Threefork."

A jagged metal star cluster hit the tree, grazing Hadyn's cheek.

Hadyn loosed a short explosion of air. "What the—!" He felt his cheek. "I'm all right," he said, regaining his composure. "It's okay; he missed."

"He didn't *miss*," Cruedwyn corrected softly. He raised his voice in reply to the Black Hand. "A trader near Yrgavien offered more for my harp than it was worth. It was old anyway, so I took the money. Next thing, I'm buying me a nice sword from a smithy in Tinuviel. Turns out he was crafting a special gift for the anniversary of the duke's rule when the duke canceled the order. Left him hanging. He needed to be free of the blade, he said."

It was a bald-faced lie and grueling to maintain. The blade quickly heated in reply. Soon, Cruedwyn was shouting just to be heard above the bright, metallic wail. Hadyn couldn't believe Cruedwyn managed to hold the handle, even gloved. It had to be scorching by now.

"Okay, okay!" he raged, flicking the sword from one hand to the other like a game of hot potato with himself. "There was a woman, a Fey. Near Bourne. I dreamed her. She took my harp and gave me the sword. She told me to guard it. When I woke, the dream was real. I had the sword." He spoke angrily to the blade. "That's the truth and you know it! Now cool down!"

Rising from the perimeter of light, Quillian did the unexpected. He stood up. Apparently, he knew what he needed to know. His black-gloved hands held a narrow tube to his lips like a straw. Hadyn felt a mosquito bite on his neck. He slapped at it. Cruedwyn twitched in similar fashion, feeling for a spot on his shoulder. Within seconds, the oldest Barlow was beginning to feel very sleepy.

"Tippers!" Cruedwyn hissed. "Better lean up against the tree; you won't last long. Try to keep the torch alive."

Hadyn mumbled something. He could not comprehend what had just happened. Stumbling backward, he hit the tree with the flat of his back, knocking the air from his lungs. He felt *so* sleepy, as if his arms and legs were turning to gold. What was happening? Tippers? He felt his neck again, found a little nub sticking out of his skin. A chip of wood, maybe, or glass. A dart. His knees, for some reason, no longer felt connected to his body, could not keep him from sliding down the trunk to the ground.

"I don't care to kill you," Quillian explained, stepping forward. He was covered head to toe in black so that only his eyes could be seen through the black wrappings. "They're lorqua-dipped, not fatal. You will both sleep for a long time. I just want the sword."

Cruedwyn, staggering, fought with embarrassing determination for his balance. His sword began to tip forward. His arm began to slump.

"I feel fluffy inside," he said, his words slurring.

Hadyn chortled nonsensically. The two rubbery things he used to think were his lips weren't working so well. Not for Creed either, who stared at Quillian with an odd expression, working hard to form words. "Don't you get *hot* in all that black stuff, Mr.

Ass—Mr. Assassin?" The bard giggled. Behind him, moaning, Hadyn dropped the torch to the ground. It still burned but with less light. Fortunately, the earth was bare and stony near the trees.

Cruedwyn grew more incomprehensible by the moment. "You know I call me the Black Hand. You, silly. Not me. But have we never thought of pink? Think of the possibilities."

"I'm impressed," Quillian said wickedly. "You have a strong constitution. A worthy opponent to the last. I salute you. Now give me my sword."

"*My* sword!" Creed declared loudly, drunkenly, waving his index finger in warning. He wildly brandished his blade once, twice, fighting the phantoms that swirled around him. Maybe pink phantoms for all Hadyn could tell. He heard everything, but couldn't really process anything, couldn't move.

Cruedwyn's wild swinging cost him his balance. He fell to one knee. "You have helped me pee—I mean helped me *not* to pee—to peel—feel! Feel the pain! See, you aren't listening! *That's* what I meant. Cursed sword! It hurts a lot right now." Tears streamed down Cruedwyn's cheeks. "But the burning isn't so bad with your little sleepy stuff in my blood. I thanks you." He sounded pitiful, looked pitiful, nearly cross-eyed. With the last of his strength, Cruedwyn tried to focus his blurred vision on the assassin. Quillian had cautiously crept to within reaching distance.

Cruedwyn shouted, "Hey, I have. An idea! Could you maybe leave some of those prickly things with me for when she gets all mad at me?" He patted his sword. "I don't know why that happens so much. All hot and red. And yet, whoo!" He flopped his hand, gurgling at the numbness. Then spasmed. "Ouch! Okay, I do know why. Blarmey! Easy girl, you are feisty tonight."

Quillian stood directly above him. He held no weapons. He was an amorphous shape of black, cloak billowing slightly in the breeze. He bent over toward where Cruedwyn tilted on the earth, near to falling.

"Maybe I will kill you after all. You are nothing now, are you? Why do you think she chose you to guard the sword? I mean, in the end, what good did it do?"

Cruedwyn grinned stupidly, could no longer even speak. Tears still ran down his face.

"I will tell you something, Cruedwyn Creed. The League has been looking for your little sword for nearly seven hundred years. Few people know it, but the League was founded for that very purpose. To find ca'Libre. The magic Freedom Blade. Now it is found. I, Quillian, have found it . . . and my reward shall be great."

Cruedwyn blinked, drooled. Stared with watery, vacant eyes. All an act.

He sprang.

Catlike and clearheaded, he lunged to his feet, landing an uppercut to the assassin's chin, jaw to skull. In a single, seamless moment, leaving ca'Libre on the ground, he whipped two daggers free from either side of his belt, and in the roundness of his motion brought both to rest simultaneously at Quillian's throat. Before the assassin could even breathe, he was pinned.

"You think you are the first Blade I've ever dealt with?" Cruedwyn snarled, his face pressed up against Quillian's. "I practically drink lorqua for wine. You should have finished me when you had the chance."

Quillian's dark eyes simmered. "If you want an early grave, press on with this folly," he said, his breath bulging the fabric covering his mouth. "Either that, or kill me now. Because I promise, it will not go nearly so well with you next time. I showed you mercy tonight, but we will never stop coming. Not I. Not the League. Is the sword really worth your life?"

Cruedwyn considered the question soberly. "Apparently it is. Hadyn, get up!"

Hadyn groggily stirred, pulled himself to his feet. "Huh?"

"Reach in his bag. He will likely have an antidote. Come on, get up, get up! Clear your brain. Look now, you've started a little grass fire there. Stamp it out quickly; then help me tie up our friend."

They put out the fire, found the vial—a sour-tasting, mint-colored liquid—and stripped Quillian of all his weapons, which were numerous. The slip knife on his wrist was Hadyn's favorite.

"Keep it," Cruedwyn said. "A souvenir."

For his part, the bard kept both knives pressed hard against Quillian's neck—hard enough to mark his skin. He never relaxed in grip or focus. Together they tied the assassin with new rope around one of the oak trees in a posture that left him upright, as if he were hugging the tree.

"All right, Hadyn, this is your thing. Make sure the rope is good and tight."

Hadyn shook himself to jar loose his sluggish brain. He would have a raging headache after this. But he knew what to do. He touched the rope with his hand, his thoughts, stroking the woven, interlocking strands with unfolding awareness. The effect was like water coming to a boil. Gratifyingly soon, a name presented itself, barely different from the name of the rope he had used against Nemesia. Speaking it softly, he saw the word in his mind and, with the tone and substance of that name, began drawing the strands together in the picture he held. As he did, the knots of the rope cinched tighter, tighter still. Far tighter than four strong men could have pulled on their own.

"You will live to regret this—just long enough to die," Quillian said with strain. "I swear it. Nothing will slake my thirst. I will stop at nothing."

"Neither will I!" Cruedwyn grinned maniacally. He began to speak an absurd sequence of bald-faced lies. Quite comical, really. "I am a lovely little girl! I love to dance! The sky is red and cold in the winter, but the snow is a wonderful green. And I've never been to Portaferry in the fall!"

The sword screamed with heat. Cruedwyn continued with more ridiculous statements until the tip of the blade was red hot. Hadyn had never seen it so hot.

"Press his face to the bark!" he commanded Hadyn. "And put your strength into it. Don't let go, no matter what."

Hadyn hesitated. This was weird. He had never seen Cruedwyn so ruthless.

"Do it!" Cruedwyn commanded. Hadyn laid his hands on Quillian's head, pressed his face against the tree trunk. Quillian began to sweat profusely. Using a double-folded blanket as a wrap, the bard took his blazing sword and grazed the burning tip down the assassin's cheek. The air smelled of burnt flesh. Quillian bubbled at the mouth, but refused to cry out. When Creed was finished, the letter V had been seared into the man's flesh. Right through his black face scarf.

For the second time, Cruedwyn put his face against Quillian's. "You know what I have done, don't you? V for vanquished." He grabbed the man's chin, shook him. "Do not *ever* trouble us again. You have the Stygma now. You are scarred. The whole League will rise up against you. It is part of their code of honor, remember? You will never be safe again, anywhere."

Bard and boy gathered their things and strolled off into the night. Hadyn's legs still felt weak underneath him, but the clear night air in his lungs brought hope of a clear head and a better day tomorrow. Aion knows they could use a good, easy day. Maybe they could even catch some sleep for once, for there would be no sleep on this night, that much was certain. Though both were exhausted, they decided to press on, to get far away from the spot where an assassin would be found, scarred for all his days. It was a great risk, but it was worth it.

Perhaps by sunrise they would be at Tinuviel's gate.

CHAPTER 21

Toward Frostmarch

As morning broke, cooler than normal and streaked with green, Sorge awoke to a squinting sun, followed by lancing pain behind his eyes. Light fell upon his face in segments, broken by the shadow of dirty blue clouds, followed by another swath of light. He closed his eyes again. Next thing he knew, something was licking his face, whimpering.

He slowly cracked one eyelid, then the other. Normally, he would already be on his feet, staff in hand, alert. Not this time. Ruel was in his face, baring a fanged grin. Once the monk seemed suitably awake, the wolf-dog barked once with concern, then padded over to Barsonici to lick his cheeks and palms. Both men stirred, feeling cottony between the ears—thick—with bodies made of lead. The heaviness in their limbs persisted as it slowly became clear where they were, what had happened.

"We were there, with her," Barsonici said. "Do you remember? I thought it was a dream. A long, sweet dream."

"Not a dream," Sorge said. He rubbed his neck, trying to massage out the pain. A shock of fear shot through him. "Where's Ewan? How long have we been here?"

He tried to stand too fast, sending a blinding arc of pain from heels to temples. He teetered on his knees. Next thing he knew he was sitting again on the leaf-strewn ground, trying to figure out where he was. For a long time he just sat and stared. Eventually, the oddness of his surroundings made him take note. The long white wall of Elkwood was at his back, but the land he faced was not the rolling hills of the Midlands. Which meant the long barren stretch of land in front of him, heading west, must be the road to Quil. And yes, there, north, of course, the Frostmarch. They were closer than he expected—much closer—dumped far to the north where the forest joined the mountains. Separated from Ewan. How did they get here?

"I almost remember her words. The queen . . . but I can't find them to say," Barsonici murmured as if dreaming still, his eyes lost in the faraway blue of the jagged Frostmarch. "I remember a vision. Many visions, I think. In one, I saw a Fey. A pixie or a sprite. Her wings were being torn. She was weeping."

His voice trailed away.

"I remember a song," Sorge said softly. "A flute, I think. Ewan." Hearing his own words, his heart sank. He said the name again. "Ewan."

"He gave her the song, didn't he?" Barsonici mused aloud, with sadness. "For us. The more we talk, the more I remember."

"He gave more than a song. He gave the gift. Otherwise she would have kept us. She had rights to me, by my mark. I knew it. I did not want to go."

Both fell silent after that, not wanting to speak, possessing no will or strength to move. If Sorge were honest, all he wanted to do was return to that sweet sleep. He remembered the images and emotions the Fey Queen's beauty had stirred inside. Feelings not fit for a monk, that much was sure. He remembered them from years ago, when he had delivered Corus into the Feys' hands. He had never actually seen her then, or now, though she had let him hear her voice. It was a rare gift.

Barsonici petted Ruel, scratching behind the dog's ears, tangling his hands in the thick fur. Ruel panted, his wet pink tongue wagging as he sat contentedly by his master. About midday, without speaking, the two men gathered their things and started walking. Together.

"I go to Bitterland, you know," Sorge warned in a flat, emotionless voice. "Across the mountains, to a land most men would do well to avoid—Hel itself if needed. That's where she said he had been taken. By the Horned Lord."

"I know," Barsonici replied. And that was that.

They walked on, putting one foot in front of the other.

After a long while, Barsonici said, "We will see more Watchers the farther north we go. They will be drawn to their old home."

"They do not want you or me." Sorge stared at the skies. Dimly, he realized he no longer had his bow. Had nothing but his clothes, his staff. "For some reason they know to fear the Outlanders. More than that, they are busy gaining followers. I doubt they will be distracted from their worship."

"Perhaps."

Ruel trailed off every now and then, barking at a rabbit or a bird, but otherwise stayed close at hand. They walked for more than two hours without another word, over steadily climbing ground sprinkled with heather and little orange flowers. As they approached the foothills of the Frostmarch, they began to get winded, especially Barsonici. Slowly, the ground grew stony and dry with blue-and-gray shelf rock. As Elkwood grew distant in the east, the trees turned to short pine and Hoder spruce. Yellow butterflies bobbed in the air, sucking nectar from whatever flowers they could find before the last warm winds faded for the year.

"We should aim for the steeple," Sorge said. His head was beginning to clear, but his muscles still ached. "I haven't been this way in a long time—I need the lay of the land. Carmon's Pass is my first choice. The watchtower will give us a better view."

They plodded along. As the sun sank into the west, melting into the ground like ice on a hot stove, the air grew colder than any Sorge had felt in a long while—enough that he could see the faint wisp of his own breath. Glancing behind, he saw the tops of the trees of Elkwood far below, the land rolling away beneath them like a tumbling river. He needed rest, needed to catch his breath. They both did. They set about gathering sticks and dry wood, turning over and over again all that had transpired—feeling the desperate ache, the dulcet song of the queen coaxing them, her voice draped like gauze and honey over the shape of their weary souls.

When the fire was crackling merrily, Sorge boiled some water and tossed in a few tea leaves. He and Barsonici sat and sipped in silence, staring into the flames.

"I have no idea what happened to Flogg. I have no idea what happened to Ewan. All I know to do now is find Corus. He is there still. I feel it more and more."

Barsonici seemed hesitant to reply. Cautiously, he asked, "Tell me how you know. Is it merely the queen's word? Have you received a prophecy?"

Sorge took a sip of his steaming drink. Moon and stars cantered across the iron sky, bleeding light. Earth and rock and trees were bathed in ghostly, pale blue.

"I usually never have visions, Barsonici. But when Ewan plays, I do. It happened again in the forest. I can't explain it. His music has"—Sorge swallowed hard—"*had* power."

Barsonici nodded. "I too had a revelation while I slept in the haven. Never have I had such an experience! Beautiful and terrible all at once. Clear as the starlight above us now. It is the most precious gift Olfadr has ever given me. In fact, Sorge, no matter what, I *must* go with you. Please do not forbid me. Do not ask me to—"

He fell silent, as if shamed. Sorge perceived in the old man's mix of reverence and finality that he had spoken more than he wished.

"Leave?" he asked. "Is that what you were going to say?"

Barsonici's tone was fatherly. His rough edges seemed to have softened a bit since their first meeting in Lotsley's crumbling ruins. But he was equally blunt. "In Helheim, only Trulight will pierce the darkness. You do not know Trulight."

Light is Truth . . . is Knowledge . . . is Hope . . . is Vision. Vision is Light.

In the darkness, the flickering firelight, Sorge's eyes shone. His bald head reflected the fire. His circle scar burned white.

"What is the Remnant?" he asked.

Barsonici shifted his weight where he sat, as if the question made him uncomfortable. "Not what, but who? A small group with a long history. Laymen and priests from every dominion, from all three abbeys. We stretch back for centuries, believing there is always a truer way, a purer path. More than anything, we are seekers."

Sorge frowned. "But . . . your reputation is poor."

"Oh, undoubtedly," the old man chortled, perhaps more petulantly than he intended. "Tell me Gray, since when have you known any truth to be popular? Eh? Since when have you seen truth revered above all other considerations? Will crowds follow the man of truth, or flee?"

Sorge chewed on the end of a twig of sassafras. "Depends on the truth, I suppose."

"If it is a hard truth, they will flee. The Remnant does not pick and choose. In every age, we labor to be salt on meat, preserving what others no longer value. Not because it is easy or popular, nor because we gain favor in our task. We do it because the truth is worth it. Even the hard truths."

Sorge lay upon his blanket, covered himself with a cloak. His pillow was his pack. Nice words, but in spite of Barsonici's surprisingly gentle tone, they struck him as arrogant. His mood worsened at the odor that hung like a foul cloud over the camp. Sorge scooted farther away, grousing. Why was the old man still tagging along? Really, for what purpose had he come? Barsonici had done nothing to help them find the Fey. Ewan had drawn them, had done the hard work. Ewan had lost the most. Of course, Sorge came up empty-handed in his own complaint, having failed Corus and Ewan, both. In Isgurd's justice, he was probably now stuck with the useless old man as punishment, a test of character. Barsonici would slow his pace, drive him crazy. He knew it. Didn't he understand the rudeness of his own stench? At least Sorge was trying to make things right.

Laid upon the ground, eyes on the stars, he felt his anger rising. Repented. Still angry.

Finally, he slept, dreaming once more of the Fey Queen, whose fragrance mercifully blotted out Barsonici's odor, at least in his dreams.

CHAPTER 22

Dog Fight

he next day, with the haze of Marielle's spell clearing like a drug from their systems, both men felt alert, rested, nearly normal. Unfortunately, Barsonici's normal stank. As fresh, new glimpses of the old man's cantankerous self reemerged, Sorge slowly grew distant and irritable. The thought of Corus alive, suffering, had begun to fray his normally steely composure.

Come first light, they began heading north in silence, climbing steadily higher. The sun followed them, bright in a cloudless sky, a painter's palette of delicious colors laid one upon another in collage: robin's egg sky, foaming white-capped peaks, viridescent evergreens. Gray stone underfoot.

"We will soon be in cold, heavy winds. And neither of us has boots," Sorge observed.

"Neither of us knew this would be our road," Barsonici said. "It will happen as it must."

Sorge thought that an odd response but decided not to comment further. They walked until their legs were worn out, broke for lunch, walked again until evening, then made beds for themselves of springy pine needles on the patchy grass. The air continued to cool, especially at night. High, keening winds swept down from the mountains, moaning across the stone valley.

They slept fitfully, huddling in their cloaks to stay warm. They trusted Ruel to hear for them and guard against any predators, so neither man sat at watch. Sorge lay down secretly wishing for dreams of the Fey Queen, her thorn still lodged in his heart. He said many prayers that night, feeling the reproach of his own conscience, while the rule of the Grays remained muted in his ears. On a night like tonight, in the midst of his own discipline, he was surprised to discover that what reached him most deeply were the Five Tenets.

The mind . . . trapped in darkness. Light is Truth. . . .

Midday of the following, they found a brook of clear, shockingly cold water where they drank deeply and refilled their flasks. The effect was bracing, and both sighed with pleasure. Renewed in strength, they moved on, following the stream upward. The climb began to steepen, gradually leading to a high, lush valley of dense sea-green foliage sprinkled with yellow flowers that tilted toward the sun. Due north the bluffs became less friendly, more sharply defined, turning eventually to mountains looming large in the distance.

Traversing the valley, they soon came upon the ghastly sight of giant bones littering the ground for the couple miles or more. Standing guard like the collapsed walls of an ancient city, the bones were the crumbling skeletons of some herd of enormous beasts of yesteryear. Huge, sun-bleached rib cages and long, curving tusks arced toward the sky, pinching at the fat clouds. Hundreds of toothy, grinning skulls lay strewn upon the ground, overgrown with centuries of grass, weeds, and occasional pines. The bones had become the quiet play land of field mice and birds. The effect was eerie.

"Lindwurm, Valley of Bones," Sorge said softly. "Mammoths and firedrakes."

Ruel did not scamper in delight, as expected. Instead, he crept up to one large, cracked bone, sniffed it warily, whimpering.

Barsonici chuckled. "Ah, boy! Doesn't know whether to be happy or sad at the size of the place. What good are bones so big you can't eat them, right Ruel?"

Sorge did not think Ruel was confused, but nervous. Recalling a line from his studies under Eldoran, he quoted low under his breath, *"What good the blessing that kills?"*

Barsonici nodded. "So you've read the Old Ones?"

"Are you surprised?" Sorge answered. He began to recite, *"What shall be made of the lover who gives his beloved a deadly asp because she has always been fascinated with snakes? Or a parent who gives a child a razor before the child knows the danger of metal? To want a thing and to be ready for a thing, to desire and to comprehend consequence, are different positions indeed. So what to do when the lover cries out for the asp as proof of her beloved's devotion? What to do when the child interprets his father's refusal as unloving—even though it is for love and protection that the father withholds? Weak love too easily grants the blessing that kills. Strong love marries wisdom to the gift. It resists begging until time and maturity prevail."*

He smiled, pleased at his memory, hoping a quote from the philosopher Valusian might serve as a connecting point between him and Barsonici. It did the opposite. Almost immediately, Barsonici grew agitated, began mocking.

"Well-read, I suppose. But what good is it if you're still trapped in your little gray robe? Little gray walls. Duty and prayer to cleanse the soul."

The rebuffing tone caused Sorge's temper to flare. "Cleanse? Are you joking? Do you even know the word?"

A pang of mild regret struck him for his unkind words, but Barsonici seized upon them.

"'Tis true, Gray. I do not bathe and do not care." The wispy fuzz of beard hanging from his jaw trembled. "You want me to smell good? Bah, vanity. This shell is the least of my worries. It is a sign, nothing more—a sign to this wicked generation! They whose souls are darkly stained find me offensive for my filthy clothes, while my heart is pure." He shook his head slowly, as if instructing a child. "Who are *you*, Gray? You have the strength and impatience of a warrior. I see it in your muscles, in the way you grip your staff. You are not a holy man."

Sorge was flabbergasted. "What are you talking about? I have kept my vows!"

"For what? Vows are cowardly for one such as you. Admit the truth, at least to yourself, that you are divided. Purity of heart is to will one thing. This, too, is part of Trulight."

"Are you so righteous, Barsonici? So sure, not even knowing me, that I am bound and blind, while you, hiding in your ruins, are the only true seeker of Aion? Has the pride of Trulight blinded you?"

"Light is tru—"

"Then behold the truth! *A mule is pretty but to itself and its mate!* You imagine yourself so pure and great that you cannot see how foul you've become."

For the first time in many days, Barsonici shed his calmness, grinning madly, as wild and tattered as the first day Sorge had met him in crumbling Lotsley. "Oh, so good! Mules carry great burdens no one else can handle. They are stubborn. Good, Gray, good! Likewise, I am a creature of no size or consequence. Of low reputation, like the mule. Yes, let's play your little game. I will be the river pebble that directs the stream—"

Sorge rolled his eyes. "No you won't! You will be a crazy, smelly old man. Go back to your broken cups and coins, wordsman. For both our sakes, we should part ways now."

"Ha, cups! Better a cup of *wisdom* than a pot of *gold*. You are finally on the right path. But will you listen? No—"

"Better a pot of *water* and a bar of *lye*!" Sorge snapped. He through up his hands, exhausted. "This isn't going to work, Barsonici."

The old man's expression hardened. He didn't budge. Sorge stumped away. Ruel, who had been sniffing around the Valley of Bones, seemed torn, eager to keep exploring with the monk, but not wanting to leave his master. Barsonici soon followed a pace or two behind, though Sorge ignored him. They passed rib cages twice as tall as a man, bleached with age, saw teeth as long as daggers, still sharp enough to draw blood. For several hours, neither spoke. At last, Sorge broke the silence. "Just ahead, look. The Steeple."

At the far end of the Valley of Bones, atop the last of the tall bluffs before the mountains began, what looked like a needle of rock poked into the sky, a remnant of the wars with Quil. Sorge stared at it, offering a silent prayer that Olfadr would somehow guide him to Corus—perhaps even that both could find redemption. It was a bitter, foolish thought, bringing no reply from the skies. Sorge felt a weariness that soaked him to the bone. Glancing ahead to the rocky path, he hesitated. That's all he had, the next step, nothing more. The next step, and a tender hope that it was truly wisdom and not stubborn pride by which he had chosen this path. Because the truth was, some things were better left for dead.

Under other circumstances, he might have rested there to ponder further, but Ruel's low, urgent growl drew his attention. The dog held the snarl deep in his throat, fully tensed, hackles raised. He bared his fangs toward the crest of a low ridge to the east, not far away. Sorge scanned the ridgeline, saw what Ruel saw: two white wolves. No, four. Not twenty paces away. Two were already loping toward them. No time to run.

Sorge braced his staff, ready to swing. Ruel met the first beast midair, yowling. The white wolf was larger, but Ruel was enraged. Their screams were bloodcurdling. Sorge heard bone splinter behind him. Heard a wolf's sharp, shrill cry. He turned in time to see the second wolf staggering on its feet, blood pouring from its skull. A scrap of Barsonici's torn robe and bits of flesh from the old man's leg clung to its yellow fangs. An enraged Barsonici held a heavy red-spattered rock high above his head, brought it crashing down a second time. The beast slumped to the ground, dead.

Clutching his leg, tottering, Barsonici motioned past Sorge. The monk turned in time to see the last two wolves sweeping down the tall grass to join the fray. They moved too fast to see or smell anything but dirt and old blood in the white fur. Sensing Barsonici as the weakest prey, the lead wolf leaped high, paws outstretched. The old man froze.

"Drop!" Sorge bellowed, swinging his staff, missing. The wolf slammed into Barsonici's side, snapping at his neck. Sorge lunged, hoping he wasn't too late. But the weight of the beast that toppled Barsonici also tore him free as the wolf went tumbling over. Scrambling to gain its footing, the wolf bounded once more into the air, but the overshot gave Sorge the time he needed. Crying out, the

Gray monk swung his staff like a fully extended windmill. Man and beast met mid-leap. The heavy rosewood shank crashed down against the wolf's spine with a sickening crunch. The beast yelped, struck the ground like a burlap sack of flour. Back broken, it still crawled forward on two legs, pitiful and determined.

Two more blows to the head stopped it. The beast lay still, dead. But the battle was not done.

"Ruel!" Barsonici cried in pain.

Sorge saw the large first wolf sink its teeth deep into Ruel's hindquarters. Ruel yelped, writhed, somehow ending up with the wolf's bared throat in his jaws. He clamped down hungrily, wrenching his head, tearing fur and flesh, ending it. Blood dripped from the wolf-dog's jaws. He took three limping steps in victory, then fell to the ground, heaving. Barsonici rushed to his side, trailing blood. He stroked the dog's neck and face, rubbing his hands gently over fur matted with blood. Ruel whimpered.

The fourth wolf remained outside the ring of dead bodies, circling wide and wary, licking its chops, studying the lifeless shapes of the other wolves. Sorge took a stand between it and Barsonici, staff in hand. The wolf regarded him with intelligence, showing rows of teeth. It seemed torn by the urge for fresh blood and the loss of its pack.

"Not today," Sorge said, holding out his hand.

Almost as a challenge, in a fit of instinct, the lone wolf lifted its head and let out a primal howl. It was the last sound it ever made. Sorge arced, stretched, crashing the hardened head of his staff down once more. Blood spattered. The howl was cut short.

Sorge rushed over to where Barsonici lay beside Ruel, tears streaming down his face. The dog's breath was labored. He didn't even try to move, except once, to look into the face of his master.

Patches of fur were missing all over his body, and a thin trickle of blood came from his mouth.

"Go away, Gray," the old man whispered, taking the dog's head into his lap.

"Barsonici, we can't stay. That howl has already been heard. Others will come—"

"Go! Leave me! Maybe Ruel can make it if I tend his wounds. We'll catch up to you."

Sorge spoke with soft conviction. "Listen to me. White wolves do not attack humans the way these attacked us—certainly not in such small numbers. Something else has caused this. It is too dangerous to stay, and you will have a hard time walking. The wounds that need tending are yours. Ruel served you well. Don't let him die in vain. We must get to the Steeple."

Sorge touched Barsonici's arm, sliding his hand down to the old man's wrist. He tugged lightly.

"Come."

Ruel's eyes closed, and he gasped for air, his chest rising and falling only with great effort. Barsonici sobbed. "I found him as a pup, lost in the woods! Abandoned. For three years he has been my only friend."

Sorge exhaled, said, "I know . . . come. This is dangerous territory."

Slowly, Barsonici rose.

"Good bye, my friend."

He hobbled off, not looking back, his arm around Sorge's shoulder. Together, he and the Gray elder made their way toward the Steeple.

CHAPTER 23

Desolation

"E wan, wake up lad! Wake up!"

He did. He didn't want to. Not because he was lying facedown in the mud. Not because he was separated from Sorge—he didn't know that yet. Not even because he felt so tired, so disconnected from muscle to bone that he might as well be a giant rag doll.

No, Ewan Barlow didn't want to awaken because he didn't want to remember.

But there was bear-faced Har, rousing him with his big voice, his big, meaty hands shaking him to life. There was the circle of faces gathered around, all Har's men, whispering at the sight of the Outlander who stood against the Fey magic when every other mortal fell. Even Har! He had been swept away, gone three days. Now he was back.

Ewan only wanted to curl up and die. He came to, stared at the sun, the sky, the glittering leaves. He moaned. There were no words.

"We've been searching for days now, boy!" Har said. "What happened in there?"

Ewan's mouth was dry. He saw himself standing in the inner ring of Fey Haven, not knowing what to expect. How could you know what it would feel like to have your soul torn in half? Marielle had given him the information he bargained for. The Pillar Map. Corus. He put his finger in his pocket, feeling the quartz key wobbling inside. Key to a doorless tower. He remembered.

Then came the flood. He squeezed his eyes shut, wishing he could build a wall around his thoughts and never go back to Fey Haven, not even in his mind.

It had been a fast, utterly cold procedure. Standing in the center of the Fey, still spinning, he had caught Elysabel's eyes by chance, feeling unsure. It almost looked like she was crying. Shamed, she had looked away.

After that, everything changed.

The queen made a noise in a strange language, with no warning. It was a beautiful language that nearly made him beg to hear her voice. She was so beautiful. He had been harsh with her, but he had had to be. There was no choice.

Then she began to take his song, and nothing was beautiful again. With outstretched arms, as if coaxing a lover, she pulled it out of him. He felt made of fibers, a poorly stitched blanket. The queen found a loose thread inside, begun pulling strand by strand until nothing was left of him. Each blinding flame of note he had come to possess, to know and believe in, came loose within his soul, octave upon octave. The vision of melody and harmony, the fusion of intimacy and inspiration slipped free of his grasp, his comprehension. He screamed, but he had no breath. He convulsed. Thus passed Ewan's song into the realm of Faerie.

Afterward, silence. The most awful quietness. Hollow and terrible. He had been unwound from himself and did not know who he was any longer.

Slowly—it may have been hours, maybe days later—he realized the silence was only within. All around, laughter and cheering had broken loose. Bathed in moon glow and wild song, Aelfheim erupted with triumph and dancing, imbibing to the point of drunkenness the sorcery of new melodies Ewan's gift had bestowed.

They painted Ewan's face with elderberry juice and draped garlands of flowers around his shoulders, placing a wreath on his head. A banquet was prepared, with roots of silverweeds, stalks of heather, milk from red deer and wild goats, barley meal, mushrooms, honey, and dew. They hailed him and lifted flower cups of dandelion wine in his honor. They did not mock. What a fine mortal, to have given such a song! What a powerful, magical soul! But mortals were so strange. Why was he sad? Why, now that his music would live forever among the Fey?

Ewan had stood in the center, unmoving, unfeeling. He was numb. All he could do was gasp for air, as if his chest were perpetually crushed. That, and cry. He had only felt such desolation one other time in his life. One other terrible, engulfing memory that swallowed him whole and could never be forgotten. Pain upon pain.

He felt Har lift him gently, no longer shouting. Obviously, something was wrong. Ewan just stared, limp and unresisting. The Earl of Midlands carried the boy to his tent. There, Ewan slept. When he startled awake late the next day, Har was there. His tent was camped a mile south of the border of Elkwood.

"I don't know how you did it, boy," Har said, a mixture of awe and concern written in the lines of his face. "I've never had Fey magic bring me down, and I'm stronger than most. And not a one of you with a pinch of salt in your pocket! What was that gnome thinking? Fey and gnome, they hate each other enough; he should know better."

Ewan sat up in the pallet they had made for him. He had no energy to tell Har the whole story, or correct him about the salt. He had cleaned off the mud, but felt weak and ravenously hungry. Har offered him a plate of cold bacon and sweet corn muffins, a cup of alm tea.

"Where is the monk?" Har asked.

Ewan chewed slowly. The food tasted like dry leather in his mouth. Maybe he wasn't hungry after all. "The queen sent Sorge away," he said. "She tricked me. She did what I asked, but not what I meant."

He told Har of the great arch he had been shown, made of two trees curving toward one another, intertwined and laced together with creeping, flowering vines so densely woven as to form patterns and strange shapes on the surface. The Cardinal Gate, they called it—the main portal through which Fey trafficked.

They had frolicked with *his* song for three days before Ewan summoned the strength to use his voice. "I want to go," he said in a voice as strong as he could muster. Though he felt hollow and cold and his voice was barely a whisper, all the haven fell quiet.

"Let me leave. Let my friends leave."

Marielle agreed, uncaring whether the boy stayed or left now. She commanded an escort for him to witness the fulfillment of her pledge. Along with Sorge and Barsonici, floating on beds of air— fast asleep—he was brought before the Cardinal Gate. Flogg and

Ruel were there, too. Though not unconscious, they were entranced. A circle of leafy willows parted as they approached, pulling back the veil of foliage to reveal the great, arched portal of the Fey.

"Take them west, to the far corner," Marielle said. "Then take the boy south. Give the gnome to those who seek him, that he may be judged by his kin."

Ewan lifted his head. "That's not what we agreed."

Marielle laughed. "Of course it is! You said that my claims were forfeit and you would be allowed to depart. I am allowing you to depart . . . separately."

"What are you doing with Flogg?"

"His kin know of the betrayal of the Raven Trail. They have been searching for him. He will face the judgment of the Stone Moot."

"No, please!" Ewan cried. "He did that for me, for my brother."

"He knew the risks. He broke the code of his people. Let him face his kin."

Ewan had no strength to protest further. He could only watch in anguish as Sorge, Barsonici, and Ruel were carried by Fey into the open space of the portal. The leaves of the vines crawling up and down the two curving tree trunks shivered as they passed through. Then they were gone. His heart sank.

Flogg was next, groaning. Ewan knew he understood, but had no power in this place. He was betrayed. And Ewan had caused it.

"Flogg, I'm so sorry," he whispered.

Then Flogg, too, was gone. Ewan was alone.

"Never return here," Marielle warned. "You have the eyes. But you no longer have the power that preserves. Your song is mine. Never return."

And then, in a rush, he was blown forward, as if he were a boat on the water and wind had filled his sails. He did not pass through the portal, but flew through the forest of Elkwood, feet lightly grazing the leafy carpet beneath him. Birch and beech blurred into a frothy foam on either side, while ahead trees bent out of his way, forming a long, unbroken lane for him to pass through. He was a bird, carried on wings. Carried by Fey.

"It is wrong what she did to you," Elysabel whispered in his ear, surprising him. She was one of a dozen Fey rushing him back to the border of Elkwood. Her face looked pained. She whispered so that none of the other Fey could hear.

"I will find you again," she said. "Soon."

Ewan didn't care and had made no effort to reply. He told Har the whole story, the taking of the song, the separation, the betrayal of Flogg. He did not mention the search for Corus, only because he did not think to. He showed Har the key to the doorless tower and asked what it was, but didn't listen to the answer. Instead he stepped outside the tent to stretch his legs, then stared toward the white woods. Then west, at nothing. In the distance, he saw a large dog sitting on its haunches, watching him. For a moment, his heart leaped. Ruel? No, of course not. This dog was silver and had the look of a hound, not a wolf. It was large. For a long time, it stared at him and did not move, which Ewan found strangely unnerving. He cast his eyes to the ground, feeling fresh tears. When he looked up again, the dog was gone. Wiping his eyes one more time, he entered the tent again. Har was still sipping wine from a pewter cup.

"So you cannot hear the music inside anymore? Not at all?"

Ewan felt naked to hear the question put so bluntly. He knew the answer deep in his bones. He shook his head.

"But you have your flute?"

"It's not the flute. It never was. It's me."

Har was a warrior. Fey and the like—the esoteric, the arcane—all were things meant to be subdued, not celebrated. But once he had also been a father. He knew the troubles that afflict a young man's soul, knew the cuts that bleed and the wounds that feel as if they will never heal. He sat in silence, creating space to share the pain as much as the moment allowed.

"Ewan, my boy. I will take care of you until you find your way again," he said in a rough, gravelly voice. "By my blood and breath, you will be safe with me. I pledge it, though Isgurd fall into the sea."

Ewan looked up, found Har's eyes, warm and strong and tender. He did not hurt less. But for the moment, he felt safe at least. Covered.

Har took a blanket, wrapped it around the boy's shoulders.

"Rest, lad. We've got time. I'll take you to my hall in Brimshane if you like, until we know the whereabouts of Sorge. You'll have a fine time there. It'll help you to forget."

Ewan laid his head on the table and wept.

Night Run

The next morning, as the sun climbed above the horizon like a red-shelled crab crawling from the sea, Ewan knew what he wanted to do.

"I want to find my brothers," he said.

"Which brother?" Har asked.

"Any of them. I don't care. Who could help me find them?"

Har considered, stroking his cheek with a thick, dirty fingernail. He was a warrior, not a seer.

"If we listened close enough, the trees would tell us. But I'm not that good of a listener. Which is why that gnome friend of yours would sure be a help right now. No doubt he'd rather be here with us too. A Stone Moot is a bad affair."

Ewan stopped chewing, slowly sat up in his chair. Flogg's betrayal already felt like a lead ball in his stomach, but he had nothing left to give. He just wanted to run far away. He knew he had to try, though. "So where does a Stone Moot happen? Maybe I should try to help. Should I?"

Har shook his head like a dog flinging water from his fur. "Bad idea, that. A Stone Moot is a trial within the clan, attended by all the clan lords, held in a secret place known only to gnomes. I'm telling you, boy, put it right out of your mind. There's nothing you can do."

"So, what should I do?"

Har either didn't hear him or chose to ignore him. "If you want to find one of your kin, I suggest His Holy Stiff-Neck down south."

He offered Ewan a wry, knowing expression, but Ewan didn't get the joke.

"Ah, Ewan. You fit in so well, I forget. We have a saying in the Midlands: *Even when Olfadr smiles, the priest will frown.*" He shook his head ruefully. "Alethes is a good man, mind you. A good, grumpy man. We Midlanders like our song, our drink, our women—too much at times. We bleed the colors of the land we live on, we sing to the sky and return to the earth when we die. For all those reasons, we believe the earth is good. By the Nines, it is *meant* to be enjoyed! We fight for Aion no less, but in our own fashion. Meanwhile, the priests at the White Abbey keep sending us sour young men who spend all their time telling us we are wrong to like anything. We call 'em stiff-necks."

The thought must have amused him, because his chest began to rattle with laughter, perhaps remembering the last sour young man to come along. "They don't last long, believe me. 'Tis of no account, though. Alethe's your best bet for tidings from about."

Ewan wasn't in the mood for chitchat. "How soon can we get started?"

"Whoa, now! I'm still a bit sore from your sneaking out of my camp *last* time without so much as a fare-thee-well. Slow down, lad. That's what I used to tell my own boys, slow—"

"Please," Ewan interrupted softly. "How soon?"

A cry broke from one of the guards outside the tent. A sound of horse hooves pounding the earth. Har rose and Ewan followed, wiping his eyes. A dusty soldier approached on a lathered horse.

"The Lady Madwyn bids you return to Brimshane at once," the soldier said, putting fist to chest in weary salute as other men gathered around. "Much is afoot."

Har growled. "Let's have it, then."

"Disturbing news from the coast, my lord. Concerning Duke Shyne. And news from Lady Odessa." He hesitated, dropped his voice. "Also, the Lady Madwyn wishes you to know . . . another shrine is being raised to the Darkwings. Some of the lost youth have returned from Apaté and are spreading their devotion."

Har's beefy frame slowly expanded under his travel armor. "Where?"

"Toward the abbey, north of Grayvale. At the edge of the forest on the tall hill."

Har stared into the distance as if he might see the shrine with his naked gaze. He seemed lost in his own private thoughts. He looked at Ewan, frowned, unabashed of his concern. "Will you come back with me, Master Ewan?" he said, and his petulance became a gentle, almost fragile smile. Almost hopeful. "It will be good for both of us. I'll promise you that."

Ewan shook his head. "I am honored, my lord. Truly. But I want to find my brothers. Perhaps after that I will come to your fine hall."

Har tried to mask his disappointment. "Of course, your own kin. I would do the same." He saw the short sword at Ewan's side.

"So you still have my blade I guess. I may want you to bring that back to me someday. That's a good reason to visit, eh?"

Ewan nodded. He liked Har.

"Have you ridden before?" the earl asked. He didn't wait for an answer, turning and barking at one of his men. "Fetch the smallest horse we've got. And you, Claran, ride with him. All the way to the Whites, if needed. Understood?"

"Yes, my lord."

Ewan bowed slightly from the waist, and said to Har, "Thank you." He meant it.

"Nonsense," Har said gruffly. Then again, more softly, "I would go with you myself if I could. Be wary on the road." He put his hands on Ewan's shoulders. "May you find peace, my boy. Even greater than the song you lost."

They parted. Har and his men tore down camp with deft effi- ciency, then thundered east toward Brimshane. With decidedly less urgency, Ewan and Claran turned south. Ewan rode a beautiful cream-colored mare, Claran a muscular bay. It would be a long trip. No rush. Ewan was pleased to find he still had the feel for a horse. He had attended a couple of summer horse camps near where his dad's folks lived north of Tulsa, Oklahoma. But when Har offered him a horse, he wondered if he might have forgotten how to ride. The feel of the stirrups, the reins, the canter and rhythm, all came back in no time.

They rode in silence. Claran didn't speak, and Ewan was glad for it. He really just wanted to be alone. Even on the open road, the dangers he knew well enough by now seemed of little consequence.

Later that night by the fire, Claran asked, "Are you sore? Should we go slower?"

"No," Ewan said. That was all. He rolled over in his blanket, feeling the mild air lay on him like dampness on morning grass. He stared at the moon, waiting for the light of the fire to turn to embers, then ash. Soon, Claran was asleep. Ewan was still awake.

He wandered off a bit into the rolling field, flute in hand, sword slung at his side. As he fingered the whistle's cool metal surface, a slow anger began to bubble and boil inside his chest. He had spent hours on horseback trying to summon inspiration from the sights and sounds of the land around him, the feelings of Elkwood and the Fey, his longing for his dad, his brothers. Hours, without melody. No song sprang forth and none would. He had come to this land and found his gift. Now it was gone. Before it was even fully developed, it was taken back. Stolen, actually. He was just Ewan now. Hadyn's little brother. Nothing special.

He took the flute, lifting it up, thinking to crash it down on his knee. Snap it in two and throw it away. Sobbing, he couldn't. It was a gift from Mom. Like her, gone—broken already inside him.

He snuck back into camp, quietly folded his blanket, saddled his horse in the dark.

And rode away.

CHAPTER 25

The Lonely Road

Once he knew he was out of hearing, he rode hard all night. It would have been terrifying but for his state of mind. He rode, awake and dreaming all at once. He wanted to put distance between him and Claran so the man would be forced to give up and return to Har. It wasn't Claran's fault.

It is what it is, Ewan remembered his dad saying.

Somewhere just before dawn, exhausted, he found a small copse of trees silhouetted against the star-spattered night sky and camped there, letting his horse rest. For just a few hours, he slept hard. Morning's harsh light forced him to rise early. Around noon, he stopped to let his horse graze near a mostly dried-up little brook. He wouldn't have to ride so hard today, he figured. He nibbled food from his pack along the way. His course was due south.

He ended up at the Goldfoam a couple miles east of the ruins before he remembered the ferry and had to backtrack. With a couple of coins Sorge had given him, he had enough to pay for him and his horse. Other than the great bridge at Fornburg and the large barge service in Portaferry, the ruins at Lotsley were the only place to cross the northern Goldfoam. On the other side, he camped in the very spot he had spent a delirious night battling the fever of the Watcher's poisoned talons. He felt for the scar on his left shoulder blade. It felt more tender than normal. Or maybe that was all in his head. Instinctively, he glanced toward the sky.

No more Darkwings. Please . . .

He ate, fed his horse at the river, kept pressing on. He tried to avoid the curious gazes of villagers and homesteaders he passed along the way. Fortunately, they were used to seeing lonely, wandering youth. More than one boy or girl his age also wandered along, staring dolefully into his face, as if pleading. Some looked bitter. Some looked lost. One chased him, angrily waving a stick. Ewan's horse was easily able to outrun him. The road could be dangerous. He had to keep his wits.

Another day, another night. He kept to the road running south as it followed the river toward Stobnotter. He figured it would take a week or two to make the whole trip, and he knew he would need to ration his food. He still wasn't hungry anyway. With one eye on the sky for Watchers, the other on the fields ahead for stray jackals or Lost, he rode the better part of every day. Keep going, he thought. He *wanted* to be alone. Sure, the news for Har would be hard, when Claran finally returned to Brimshane. He would likely be reprimanded. Nothing to do for it.

Ewan thought of Hadyn trapped with the Nameless for so long and shuddered. He remembered from the trip to the ruins that at some point he would need to leave the road and aim more toward Mount Bourne. He wanted to avoid traffic on the rutted cartpath to the White Abbey.

That night, he dared to put the flute to his lips. He thought of something simple. *"Mary Had a Little Lamb."* The tune that came out was clumsy and unbeautiful. Not offkey so much as simply pitiful. He felt nothing as he played—a dead tune from dead lips.

He stuffed the flute in his pocket, thinking, *Never again.*

At least Sorge was safe. That helped. He hoped it was worth it.

The sky offered no comfort. Wind from the north chilled his breath, and he wondered if he would need to, or be able to, build a fire. Maybe it hadn't been such a good idea to go tearing off on his own. Too late now. He branched off the road in search of shelter from the wind, found an old abandoned shack not too far away, crumbling with years. The look of it was kind of creepy. Still, it felt safer than sleeping in the open air, and certainly warmer as the nights had become more chilly. His eyelids were heavy. His horse was weary.

Except to care for the horse, he didn't bother to unpack, over-taken by quick, hard sleep, full of dreams. Dreams of Elysabel. The pixie unfolded liquid wings before him in a sparkling cascade of color and light. Her hair and eyes were silvery and clear. Her porcelain skin seemed to glow.

Ewan felt her in his dream even before he saw her, as if she were sneaking up on him. He was in the shack, pouring out his heart to the moon, which had Mom's face, when Elysabel slipped through. His horse whinnied nervously.

"Your song," she whispered. She was shaking. "It is so beautiful, I cannot bear to hear it. Yet all the haven lives in your song now."

Ewan didn't answer. There was nothing to say. For the first time, he didn't even care to see the Fey. Elysabel was behind him; he left her there. All he wanted to do was keep talking to the moon.

"I must be a bad pixie. I should be ashamed," Elysabel continued, sounding both contrite and angry. "But it is not *right* what she did. The queen."

Sparkles of light, like drops of ice, swam in the air, reflecting on the walls. Ewan didn't know where they came from. From Elysabel, somehow.

"I just want to go home," he said to the moon in his dream. "Will you take me, to be with you?"

"She took a great gift from you. A great gift. In five hundred years the Fey have not seen its equal." A pause. Elysabel sounded frightened, determined. "I cannot settle accounts, as I wish. I should not even be here. But no matter, I have decided . . ."

At this point, Ewan turned, seeing her for the first time. Even knowing what she looked like, she still caused his breath to catch in his throat.

"If they took so great a gift from you, then I have decided to give you something great in return. The greatest secret, the greatest treasure of the Fey: the location of the Sleeping King."

Ewan lifted his head. His eyes glistened.

Elysabel continued. "Many hundred years ago, the Sleeping King came to our world on the verge of death, brought by the mirling we once called friend—the one who learned our ways, who built our portals. He had eyes too. He was the first mortal in Fey memory to see us so. The queen's mother, Morgiona, fell in love with him. I know very little of their story together in your world, but Morgiona was driven to rage and jealousy, to the point of becoming the mirling's enemy. Yet when the Earth king nearly died, out of love, she and her kin granted the mirling one last favor and brought him here, promising to keep him safe until the times were fulfilled and he was ready to awaken. She brought this king of Earth back to kingless Karac Tor, and he has been here ever since, healing, waiting for someone to call his name."

Ewan heard each word, took them into his mouth, his ears, like little bites of tasteless porridge or a numbing foreign language. He heard, but the words meant nothing. Elysabel, noting his uncomprehending stare, drifted closer, higher into the air, her wings gauzy and fluttering.

"You must journey to the holy mountain," she said. "Mount Bourne. Where Yhü drank from the forbidden stream. At the golden lake of Avl-on-Bourne, under stone and water, *your* eyes will see what others have missed all these years. And this"—she held out her hand as light poured through her fingers from a round crystal vial—"is Fey powder. Faerie dust, some say. If you find the Sleeping King, this will wake him. The Fey guardians who stand by his side will be forced to honor your possession of such magic. Otherwise, you would forfeit your life."

Ewan reached out in a daze, touched the vial. Light engulfed his hand. His skin tingled on the smooth crystal. Suddenly, he withdrew.

"I don't want any more Fey bargains. I can't bear it."

Elysabel's hair turned from clear silver to orange.

"I am the queen's servant. I am *not* the queen." She placed the vial in his pack and closed it. The twirling lights thickened, faded, overcome with darkness and night. "To prove it, I will lead you to your brother if you wish. I will make things as right as I am able. The little one, Gabe—he is searching for you as you search for him. The White One sent him north two days ago with a guardian, to seek out you and the Gray monk and convince you to return. I will lead you to him if you are willing to follow. Then I must go. The queen must never know these things."

Ewan pursed his lips, refusing to budge. "Take me to Gabe, but someone else can wake the Sleeping King. I'm not interested."

Elysabel floated upward, away. "Follow me tomorrow. Sleep now. In time, you will see."

The dream ended with Ewan searching for the moon again, only to find that it had slipped behind a curtain of clouds, lost to him. He felt a great wave of sadness in his dream. By morning, he had forgotten everything that had passed between him and the beautiful Fey pixie.

Forgotten, that is, until he opened his pack and discovered there a crystal vial filled with fine, shiny dust, like crushed grains of sunlight.

CHAPTER 26

Reunion

Shortly after lunch, Ewan saw her again. Up until that point, he had no idea if he had been dreaming or awake or something in between—whatever that might be. This whole world seemed something in between. All he knew was that he found a vial of faerie dust in his pack. He had stuffed the tiny crystal bottle into his breeches pocket and set off south, following the pixie, just as she had said.

Even so, this time was different. This time, she would not approach. She stayed ahead, within sight, out of reach, floating in the air, rarely looking back. Once she returned to him, to tell him where lay the best place to cross a stream. Ewan felt a strange vibe coming from her.

Girls, he thought.

"The guardian you mentioned," he said aloud. "Is Gabe with Va'nya?"

She hovered near him, frowning, blinked once. Wide-eyed again.

"The Highlander . . . the Bird Man that watches over Gabe," Ewan explained.

"He departed many days ago. I do not know where." Her manners were terse, her tone almost hurt.

"What's wrong?" he said.

She flew away.

Even worse, Fey girls.

His horse—he had decided to call her Peg (short for Pegasus)—was munching contentedly on some leaves, but perked her ears when Ewan called her new name. It had been a lazy morning, cool enough to merit his cloak early on, then gradually warming to become a mild, pleasant day. Off the main road, cutting across the wooded hills, he noted Mount Bourne looming ever larger in the distance. By midday he had already seen half a dozen glassy, self-contained lakes nestled in the valleys between hills—little, still mirrors of peacock blue, rimmed with trees.

And then he saw Gabe.

The youngest Barlow was sitting alone with five different kinds of birds perched on his outstretched arms. He was laughing at nothing. At the birds, maybe. At words no one could hear but him. Nearly choking with relief and emotion, Ewan wanted to run and tackle him. It meant even more than he expected to see one of his brothers. Instead, he checked himself, stopped for a moment to watch. Gabe was alone. In the middle of nowhere. Talking to birds. Ewan didn't know whether to be proud or frightened. What was he doing?

Gabe would say something aloud, and then a bird would fly off and return with something in its mouth. Gabe would laugh again, and as his shoulders shook, his fine silvery hair would flop and bounce. Ewan approached quietly, as quietly as you can on the back of a horse.

"Hello, Ewan!" Gabe called out, even though his back was to Ewan. He hardly seemed surprised.

Ewan dismounted, ran to his brother, held him tight. Gabe returned the hug and didn't try to pull away, even though the commotion had startled all the birds.

"I knew you were coming," he said. "They told me. I'm learning a lot. I can even ask them to do things for me now, and they do it." He held up a grubby worm in his hands, grinning. "That little blue jay just brought me this."

"Yuck. You've been eating about like me, looks like."

Gabe laughed. Like a good big brother, Ewan punched him in the arm. He didn't know what else to say or do, feeling wistful and relieved all at once. Maybe even glad. For the first time in many days, glad. He saw Elysabel out of the corner of his eye, watching. Her expression was unreadable, but the sunlight passing through her wings seemed like spun gold.

"Where's Va'nya?" Ewan asked. "Or anyone for that matter?"

"Va'nya is on a mission. I asked him to go. I just now snuck away from the White dude Alethes sent with me to find you. It's lunchtime, so he's probably still searching for berries and hasn't noticed I'm gone yet. But it's okay, he didn't like the birds anyway. We'll probably bump into him on our way back, and I'll be in trouble." Gabe grinned. "You know how it goes."

Obviously, Ewan did know a bit about such things, but it was odd to hear Gabe speak so matter-of-factly. He sounded older than his age. A strange thought occurred to Ewan. They would all be turning older soon (though in Karac Tor, it was hard to tell what Earth time it really was). For crying out loud, Hadyn might already by sixteen! Just a few weeks after that, Ewan would turn fourteen. He felt twenty and twelve all at once, but not fourteen. Being in this world, fending for himself, had forced him to grow up quickly.

"I'm really glad to see you, Gabe."

"Yeah, me too. Hadyn is somewhere in Greenland by now. Hopefully talking to the duke. He wouldn't let me go with him, so I've been messenger boy back to Alethes . . . now to you. Cruedwyn thinks the Highlanders and Vineland are near a secret treaty. Maybe against the duke. It's a big mess."

That launched a flurry of questions from Ewan. He was thirsty for information, but it also served to keep Gabe from circling around to the inevitable: Where was Sorge? What had happened? Ewan didn't want to talk about it. His strategy worked. After a thorough debriefing and quick lunch, Gabe climbed behind Ewan on Peg's back and they aimed south, with a dozen noisy birds trailing along above and behind them, chirping and croaking nonstop. Crows, finches, hawks, sparrows.

"The buzzards are the weird ones," Gabe said confidentially, as if someone might overhear. "Listening to them gives me the creeps."

They never ran across Gabe's guardian monk from the abbey. Gabe seemed a little concerned about this, but Ewan was grateful. He decided to just keep going, let the monk draw his own conclusions, as Claran had been forced to do. Two days later, the land began a long sweep downward to the Kinsman Vale, many miles of gradual decline and breathtaking views overlooking the Vineland bottoms that formed the throat between the Great Rim and the

Midlands steppes. By nightfall the next day they might make it to the abbey, at least to the river.

Stopping to enjoy thirty miles of visibility, Ewan realized he hadn't seen Elysabel in a while. Engrossed in a playful banter with Gabe for the last couple of hours, he had stopped watching for her. But something was amiss. The birds had begun to chatter more loudly, fly higher. As their conversation died down, Gabe glanced up in alarm.

"What? Where?" he cried out.

But it was too late. A tall, thin boy approached—they didn't see from where—seizing Peg's reins near the bit, clasping them in his fist. Blood was on his hand, both hands, and splotches of blood were on his clothes. Peg jerked her head, but the boy held firm. Not a boy, really. Hadyn's age, maybe older. A young man. Ewan knew him or at least felt he *should* know him. Recognition came all at once. He had been at the grove with Nemesia. One of her captains. Ewan couldn't remember his name. He sat on Peg's back, frozen like stone. Behind him, Gabe was silent.

"You are the one who played the Song of Aion," said the Nameless youth. He had long, unkempt hair and a greenish tattoo that ran across his left cheek, along his jaw, down his neck. The tattoo was new. What looked like smeared dirt on his face, Ewan realized, was blood. His mind raced. Sorge had warned that some Nameless might never recover.

"I am Shameface!" the young man declared. "That is my name, the name I choose. Nothing you say or do will change that, do you hear me?"

Shameface's eyes flashed with anger, his thin smile dripped with disdain. Ewan remembered his dry, haunting voice from the Stone House, so long ago. It was less surreal now, more desperate—but

mostly the same. In his other hand, Shameface held a small wand
trailing darkness. Ewan's eyes widened. The wands had all been
destroyed, hadn't they? Shameface must have hidden his away. The
nearness of sorcery made Peg jittery.

"We don't want any trouble," Ewan said.

Shameface scoffed. "Too late, I'd say. You've caused nothing but
trouble, Outlander."

"Fine. I'm sorry. Please let us go."

"You aren't sorry one bit! Look at you, all high and mighty. You
think you're better than us! Well I was important, too, to Nemesia.
And I still am. You think you killed her? Wrong! She's been working for years. You only delayed her for a while."

Ewan couldn't help himself. "Why do you stay with her, Shameface? Don't you see how she used you? Don't you want to be free?"

"I want revenge! On all the world, for all the pain! On you for
your song." Shameface dropped his eyes. "I remember your song.
I hated it. But we're still here, Outlander. You didn't get rid of us
completely."

Still clutching the reins, the Lost boy thrust the tip of the wand
into Ewan's face. Peg began edging backward, stamping and snorting. Shameface clutched tighter.

"Who's that behind you? He's got the look of kin. Ah!" Shameface grinned wickedly. "You must be the one that White was searching for." He held up his other hand, splayed open his red-stained
fingers. "Don't worry, Outlander. He won't be looking anymore."

"Hold your breath, Gabe," Ewan whispered. "Close your eyes
and hold on tight!"

Ewan's leg was dangling at just the right height. Like a spring-
loaded lever popping loose, he kicked Shameface in the groin as
hard as he could. The boy doubled over, fumbling to keep hold of

the reins, dropping to his knees. Peg reared, jerked hard, tore loose. Ewan clicked his heels in the mare's flank once. That was all she needed. They tore off at full gallop.

Behind him, Shameface began to roar. Ewan fearfully glanced back, saw the boy put his fingers to his lips. Heard a loud, long whistle. A call to battle.

Over the ridge from the direction of Redthorn came hundreds of jackals. Like a wave of gray fur, like boiling water, they swarmed past Shameface at a dead run, howling with bloodlust. Gabe's fingers dug into Ewan's ribs.

"Ewan, do you see?"

"Faster, Peg!" he urged in his steed's ear. The horse's eyes rolled white. "Hyah!"

Foaming and red-eyed, the jackals bounded up the southern and eastern slopes, cutting off their path to the abbey. Ewan edged the reins lightly, increasing his angle, spurring Peg on. Maybe, just maybe, he could make it. A little more speed. Wind whipped his hair. Ground and sky shook around him. He felt Gabe's arms wrapped tight around his waist. Pegasus galloped fast and smooth—not fast enough. Ewan knew he had to do something else. He tried to think, *What would Sorge do?*

The answer was clear enough. His path was blocked east and south. Change course.

"Hyah!" Ewan cried again, digging in his heels as the ground blurred underneath them, brown grass and weathered stone smearing together, turning gradually into moss and woods and hills. Behind, four-legged devils. Howling fiends, snapping at one another. Hundreds of them.

Ahead, a looming, quiet shadow. They were headed west.

To Mount Bourne.

CHAPTER 27

The Wind Bringer

Garret emerged from the portal, from the cold and snow of old Daneland into the warm darkness of an unknown room. He was alone. The journey had taken mere seconds—a blink of time. His arms were folded tight over the tokens he carried, tucked into the inside breast pocket of his leather vest. Gifts from Gwenhwyfar. Tal Yssen had placed them in his hands before bidding him farewell: the folded note sealed with red wax, a silver ring. The ring, shaped like two snakes entwined together, had rubies for eyes. Garret's mission was simple, Tal said. Meet the Old One, follow the instructions, rejoin his brothers.

The wet feeling of motion, the fluidity of time and space, passed quickly, absorbing into his skin like salty waves into sand. Garret was accustomed to it by now, but he was nervous, nonetheless. He was finally entering Karac Tor. He had learned a great deal from many conversations with Tal, but now the old wizard was gone. He was on his own. In his young life, he had never been on his own before, and he wasn't too sure he liked it. He had begged the old wizard not to leave. Yet for reasons beyond his understanding, Tal would not stay. With every passing day, he had seemed weaker, more feeble. The constant travel had taken its toll.

As the darkness faded, shapes emerged. Odors of oiled wood, paper, and lambskin filled his nostrils. The darkness became walls, the walls a room, a library. For some reason, he was standing on the ledge of one of two great, arched windows recessed into a cut stone wall.

Clever, he thought. *They made it a window.*

Lining the tall shelves were rows and rows of books, scrolls, fragments of parchment, stone tablets, and small clay steles. Three long wooden tables ran down the middle of the room. Behind him, he sensed a vast, blue nothing. He didn't want to look but felt compelled. Sea and sky lightly kissed at the horizon. The view left him clinging to the curved stone frame of the window. The entire room seemed to be floating in midair, a library on the edge of a cliff plunging to the water below. Mouth dry, he backed away.

"Hate heights," he said, hopping down to the tiled floor a few feet below.

He landed in sync with the loud thump of a book hitting the same floor. The sound startled him, brought him whirling around. Sounds of shuffling paper came from around the corner. He crept forward, angling toward the back of the library. Beyond the easy reach of light pouring in through the windows, a figure sat at a small table, engrossed in many books at once, awash in the soft glow of a rock sitting on his table. He was a man of average height, robed in dark gray, with a pale, circular scar on his forehead. The man seemed agitated as he leaned against the table, matting his fingers in his long woolen hair. He was muttering to himself, over and over again: "Follow the white crow, wherever it may go. Follow the white crow, wherever it may go. Swords and blood!"

He pounded the table. Garret jumped. Startled, the man looked up.

"Who are you?" he demanded. "How did you enter this place? Every door is locked."

He had a stern, unwelcoming face and a scruffy beard. Both of them breathed hard from the rush of surprise. Garret knew what he had to do. Library. Monk. He had practiced and practiced until Tal had been satisfied. It was just as he was told it would be.

"You are Soriah," Garret began nervously, speaking into the still, dusty air. Beams of red light snagged on the motes, turned them to flame. He closed his eyes, slipping into recitation mode, like when he had to memorize poems for school. He said, "You study the writings of the great mirlings of old, searching for clues. Yesterday you found a blue stone and a second stone with the mark of Tal Yssen. The blue stone will match this necklace." He withdrew his necklace, displayed the quartered circle with an empty fitting in the center. "I need it. I tell you these things so you will know to help me and to do what you must. In years to come, you will become more than a Gray. You will be a prophet to the kingdom. In the message you speak, they will say Aion has come for the seventh time. On the ninth comes the War of Swords."

Garret stopped, took a deep breath. He had done it. He figured Tal would be proud. Meanwhile, the man in gray had turned pale. Slowly, he rose from his seat.

"Follow the white crow," he murmured again, staring at Garret, but also through him. Being pale and blond, clothed in white fur,

Garret could not help but wonder if Soriah thought he were the white crow, whatever that was. "Who are you?"

"My name is Garret. I bring the gift of wind back to Karac Tor."

"The necklace."

Garret nodded. "But I need the stone."

Soriah stepped forward to the table where he had been reading. He lifted what looked like a small, smooth pebble of glass from between the pages of an old, cracked tome. There were two small stones, actually. The other was rough-edged with writing on it. Soriah held the blue crystal in his hands, held it up to the light of the windows. Something seemed to swirl in the middle, like smoke, barely visible. A moment of doubt overtook him.

"You have been with Tal Yssen?"

Now it was Garret's turn to be surprised. He had not mentioned traveling with Tal.

"Through many arches, to many places," he replied shakily. "All in my world. I've come to the Hidden Lands for the first time. I need to find my brothers."

"You have come from the world Tal Yssen visited? The Fourth World?"

"Earth."

"Earth?"

Garret nodded.

"If I give you the stone, what can you do with it?"

"I don't know. I practiced as I was taught, but it's all useless without the stone."

Garret cupped the necklace again, as if in proof. Soriah studied him with an intensity that made the younger Barlow uncomfortable, though he had nothing to hide. Everything he had said was true. Soriah pressed the stone into the center of the necklace. It snapped into place, fit tight.

Garret draped the chain around his neck.

"Try something. Show me," demanded the Gray monk.

"Now?"

"Now."

Garret licked his lips. "Tell me what you are reading," he said, stalling.

Soriah hesitantly picked up the leather-bound book where the stone had been. It was small, had an open metal clasp. "I spend much of my time looking through old manuscripts, seeking the wisdom of old. I am an Elder among the Grays and a Seer with the Blacks. I travel far and wide, as far as the Wild South, even Quil. I have read the prophets, the Venerable Fleec. But this . . ." His voice trailed away. He shook his head, grasping for words. "The second diary of Tal Yssen has been lost for many years. It is a rare treasure. I found it here in the keep of all places. Right under my nose. Then yesterday . . ." He raised a quizzical eyebrow. "Or do you already know what I read?"

Garret shook his head, no.

Soriah slowly began to read.

"I am sought out, hunted. They want Aeolo. I have no choice but to hide it, as far from my own eyes and mind as possible, and certainly from the eyes of others. To that end, I will divide necklace from stone. A day shall come when a boy shall take it from my hand, a boy from the Fourth World. I have foreseen it. But I must first let it pass into memory, to safeguard it. Besides, I do not need it any longer. The boy will travel to Karac Tor. He shall learn its power. I will try to help secure this as I learn more. Some things are hidden from me at present. Is there one boy? Or two? Maybe even four? Odd. I do not understand.

I do know three more portals must be built before my task is complete. I will rest now, gather my strength. Morgiona will care for me. Though she thinks herself affronted, she loves me still."

"There is more," he said, moving forward until he stood directly in front of Garret. "But I will say nothing else, because I am troubled by your appearing. So *try*. Make wind."

His guarded tone bordered on threatening. Garret nervously touched the necklace. He tried to remember everything Tal Yssen had taught him. To let his thoughts flow, to sense the lightness, the nothingness of empty air, to find the secret hidden inside its currents. But he hadn't had the stone then, could never really practice. He lifted the stone, stared into its center, until he saw the eddies swirling within. Tal Yssen didn't need Aeolo Wind Bringer anymore. Garret did. But he needed the old man even more.

"I'm afraid," he said.

"So am I," Soriah murmured, trembling with the truth of his own words. For a moment he did not seem so scary. "More than you know."

The monk considered his dilemma for a moment, then reached back to the table, put the other stone in his pocket. He picked up another book—different, smaller. Black leather. Garret recognized it with surprise. Soriah's expression remained troubled as he began to walk.

"Follow me," he demanded.

He marched to the far end of the library. Garret followed. On the third shelf, Soriah pulled the spine of a slim, red-bound volume. The wall behind the shelf made a clicking sound. Soriah pushed against the shelf. A section rotated inward, revealing a small, dark passageway.

"Come," he said.

On the inner wall, there was a lever and a torch. He lit the torch with a touch of his finger, pushed the lever with his palm. The secret door closed to the heavy clank of a hidden metal bolt locking tight. They followed a winding path through the orange glow, the smoky shadows. In a couple of places they had to hunch, but the passage was roomy enough for the most part. The walls were rough. Eventually they came to a dead end. Soriah put his ear to the stone, listening, then pulled a lever on the right side. Again, a section of the rock wall swung wide. They slipped quickly through. Garret's heart was pounding. Tal Yssen had said to trust the Gray monk. Do what he said. It wasn't easy. *None* of this came easily to him.

On the other side, Soriah cranked on one of several brass wall sconces—forward half, back half. Again, hidden gears ground together. The door closed, forming a perfect, seamless joint on the other side. Garret had little time to be amazed. They were in a small antechamber with three hallways leading off into various other parts of what must be an old castle. In the center of the floor there was a railing with stairs leading down. Soriah hurried down the winding stairs, increasing his pace. His cloak billowed behind him. Garret nearly had to run to follow.

They moved down into a small central alcove with cave-like entrances to four iron-barred prison cells facing north, south, east, west. Garret gulped. Was it a trap? He couldn't flee. Soriah caught him by the arm.

"This is the private dungeon of the keep, where the duke holds the more noble, more *dangerous* guests. It has not been used for years. You are safe to try your wind here."

Garret let out a huge sigh, almost bursting into tears. It was a test lab.

"I can't promise anything," he said weakly.

It took several moments to calm his beating heart. Closing his eyes, he felt Soriah's steady, patient appraisal. It made him self-conscious. Edging away from the wavering circle of torchlight, he imagined noises coming from the dark cells, their iron bars swung wide. The damp stone felt creepy, but anonymous, which was good. He tried to block everything out.

Everything but Aeolo. Focus. Summer storm. Night breeze. Breath of Aion.

Folding his fingers over the circle-shaped pendant, he let the palm of his hand lay against the blue stone. Felt a tingling, as the room became still. There were no windows, no doors, no draft, yet he called for wind just the same. At his beckoning, with surprising ease, a quick gust of air scuttled along the ground, stirring up dust, causing Soriah's cloak to flutter slightly. The monk made a soft, low noise in reply. Garret smiled inside. *Wind!* He tried to make it stronger, blow in one direction, couldn't.

"I'm not good enough," he said apologetically. "Tal said I'll get better."

Soriah nervously guided Garret into one of the four dungeon holes, as if he wanted even more privacy. Handing Garret the torch, he began thumbing through the pages of the black book.

"In the library, I read to you the second diary of Tal Yssen. This . . . this is his third. His last." He flipped a few more pages, eyes sparkling with torch fire. "The date he gives is nearly forty years after what I read before. Here, listen."

"I have recently shared many adventures with a young boy from the Fourth World. He is the boy of my vision from many years ago, I'm sure of it. We have journeyed far and wide. Not only does he have a place in the future of Karac Tor, but I am beginning to understand the larger purpose for my portals these many years. At my bidding, Danes

have gone ahead to prepare the way for him and his brothers. I must return to hallow the stone, but this will not be required for many more centuries. I just released him to the Gray Elder that will do so much for the cause of Aion in his time. As for me, my time is near to ending. My king is safe. I have done all I could, with all my strength. I am weary of traveling. One more journey is left, to Isgurd's sun-drenched shores."

To hear Tal speak so fondly of their time together made Garret smile and ache. He remembered the wizard's scribbling, could not dwell on it now. There was a final thing to say.

He recited the last of his memorized lines. "You are that Gray Elder, Soriah. You think that I have come simply to receive the Wind Bringer? I have come to give you something. You must never veer, never grow tired. Never stop. You must search for the Pillar Map until people believe you have found it; then you must hide it in Lotsley, before the city comes to ruins."

"What?" Soriah blurted out. "I don't have the Pillar Map, that's crazy! What ruins?"

"The days of Lotsley's thriving are numbered. The ground will shake. Listen! You must make a forgery of the map. Seek *nasmith*, seek *orn*. So says Tal Yssen. Now place the lodestone in my hand. Our time is done."

He handed the torch back to Soriah, feeling strangely calm, full of purpose. He held out his open palm expectantly. Soriah looked upon the nine-year-old as if he were a sage of old. He reached into his pocket, took out the lodestone.

He placed it in Garret's hand.

CHAPTER 28

Of Swords and Spies

*L*ongtooth. That's what Hadyn had finally named his sword. He thought it clever enough. Not too ostentatious for a first sword, not too boastful, but meaty. It had bite. Longtooth!

"Drop it! Lay it down now!"

He had grown unusually fond of the blade over the last few months, practicing daily—morning, noon, and night—to the point that he could now hold his own in mock battles with the bard. Cruedwyn could best him easily if he wanted, but praised Hadyn's quick study, said it was no small thing how Hadyn had held his nerves against Quillian. The oldest Barlow had, in fact, bonded with his steel, as a warrior should, the net effect being a certain metallic quality forming at his core . . .

"I ain't jokin', kid. And you, bard. In the dirt!"

. . . which meant he wasn't just going to lay his weapon down, no matter how many men surrounded him—as they did now— or how loudly they demanded that he drop his sword. It was like another variation of the same bad dream he and Cruedwyn seemed fated for: badly outnumbered, bigger men, all wearing the uniform of the keep, with bigger swords.

But it wasn't so easy, to just let go.

Cruedwyn, of course, *talked* to his sword. Doted on it and despised it, all in the same breath. Once it had all seemed so irrational to Hadyn. So amusing and juvenile. A silly quirk for a magic blade. Now he understood. Nobody touches a man's sword.

"Cruedwyn?" he said low under his breath. They stood back-to-back, turning slow circles together, blades drawn. Fifteen guards against two. Nice odds. They had woken up to dirt being kicked in their faces, surrounded, just outside the city walls. They had let their guard down after disarming Quillian, but—merciful Aion!— how did people always seem to know where they were? Every court kept elaborate spy networks, but were they really *that* good? Cruedwyn had warned him that Pol Shyne was known for ruthless security measures.

"Cruedwyn?" Hadyn whispered again, speaking the name like a code. Properly rephrased it was, *What the heck are we doing?*

"Don't make me conk you on the head or fetch the nets!" the captain leered, a bulky, big-bellied man with a flat nose and a flatter face. "Just surrender, the both of you, and come along. The duke is asking for you."

On cue, Cruedwyn dropped his sword to the ground, stood up straight.

"The duke? Blarmey, man! Why didn't you say so in the first place? He's an old family friend! Come along, Hadyn."

Thus, Hadyn learned there *was* a time to drop your sword. Having never seen Cruedwyn willingly release ca'Libre, he watched in stunned silence as the bard handed his sword over. Together, they had faced a professional assassin to keep it. Now Cruedwyn just let it go. Odd.

"A calculated risk," the bard explained quietly. "I'll get it back. He has no eye for the rarity of the blade. Best to be agreeable." He kept muttering to himself, things perhaps not even meant for Hadyn's ears. "But if this is the duke's way of calling for us . . . might not go so well."

The captain was more astute than Cruedwyn gave him credit for. He picked up both ca'Libre and Longtooth, fingered Cruedwyn's carefully, studying the craftsmanship of the haft with an appreciative eye.

He grunted, studying Cruedwyn as if making silent calculations. "Move along."

Thus Hadyn entered Tinuviel, a stunning city, jutting out over the lower Cliffs of Felwyn on a gigantic shelf of rock, so precarious it seemed it might tumble into the sea. The austere section that overhung the Wyld was the old city, Aventhorn Keep. The new city, blooming inland, was less fortress, more metropolis, with cosmopolitan excess and decadence to match its well-storied past. Much of Greenland's money and prestige made Tinuviel their home. It was a district of wealth and power, boasting summer homes from across the Five Dominions, rivaling even Stratamore, though much smaller in size. As such, it merited a small stone wall for an outer defense. But the real bulwark of the city was inside, at the keep.

As the guards hastened their prisoners through the streets, only a few residents took notice. Most continued about their business, especially the old gaffers, flicking their tongues across toothless gums and swatting flies with lazy hands. Catching the yeasty aroma of fresh twistbread, Hadyn felt ravenously hungry all of a sudden. Putting his hand to his side, he felt for Longtooth. It was instinct. The sword, of course, was not there. A strange feeling.

"Can I get something to eat?" he asked.

The leader of the guards didn't even glance back. "Shut yer jaw and walk," he said. So much for hospitality.

"Be mindful of my sword, captain," Cruedwyn said, a bit possessively. "She's a live one, that's for sure. I'll want her back in good shape."

The captain pretended not to hear. It was a long walk on a cloudy day. Wind curled up the cliff, gusting through the city streets, sending small pieces of trash skittering along like mice. Hadyn licked his lips, tasting salt and sea spray. In the distance, he could hear the slow, steady roar of the waves crashing among the rocks far below.

As they approached the keep, the landscape of the city began to change to something grayer, harder, more primitive. The mud brick and carved rock, the newly thatched roofs and cobblestone streets, the carved limestone fountains with glittering spurts of clear water and marble colonnades quickly morphed into granite, concrete, and huge old timbers slowly crumbling to dust. The allotment of the keep was obvious, as it had once been not just the old city, but the only city, perched atop the cliff. On the landward side it was guarded by a massive outer curtain wall with high parapets, guard towers, even the vestigial hints of breastwork from the time before Tinuviel attached itself to the keep and overtook it. Strolling through Tinuviel, past the last row of shops and homes, one came suddenly upon a city within a city, tucked away at the back like a secret room in a mansion, still furnished by the owner and left undisturbed for centuries. Passing through to the inner ward, they glimpsed archers in bright uniforms with bows in hand, standing on the rooftops, yawning, pretending to guard ramparts and tower tops.

"They're not even soldiers anymore," Cruedwyn said, nudging Hadyn, glancing upward. "It's all just part of the show now. Part of the history of the place."

"So this is all just one big tourist trap?" Hadyn mused. "Is that what you're saying?"

"Sounds about right." Cruedwyn grinned affably. He explained how the wealthy and nostalgic would make pilgrimages to see legendary Aventhorn, pining away for the old days of Tiernon and Soriah the Gray and all their conquests. The treachery and beauty of Raquel, Tiernon's wife, who was secretly a witch. The twenty-one day battle of Falafel and Vigmoth.

"What about the League?" Hadyn whispered. "Are they in Tinuviel?"

"Not so much anymore. I mean, yes, they're everywhere, but Pol has worked hard to rid Greenland of them. He's a stickler for outside influences. Besides, we don't have to worry about Quillian anymore."

Hadyn grinned. "It's gotta be rare to beat a Cutter at his own game."

"Bah! It hardly matters," Cruedwyn said, relishing the praise. "I've lost count, really. Don't know why everyone's so frightened by them, I'm certainly not."

The swagger and pomp rolled off his lips like an easy lie. Not so easy for the captain ahead of them, bearing ca'Libre in his bare hand. The man suddenly jerked as if he were a stringed puppet, dropping the sword to the ground.

"Swords and blood!" he burst out, gingerly rubbing his fingers.

Hadyn pressed his mouth into his sleeve to hide his grin. The captain picked up the blade again, holding the haft with a kerchief from his pocket, staring curiously at the metal.

"Sun ain't *that* hot today," he murmured, wrapping Cruedwyn's sword in his cloak.

Cruedwyn was pleased. Quietly, he said, "I'll let you in on a secret if you promise not to tell. I got lucky with Quillian. Court politics and all make dosing lorqua a part of the job for hired swords—at least the smart ones. Quillian should have thought of that. Of course, there aren't many smart, hired swords out there anymore. Just mercenaries. Killers. It's like my pap always used to say, 'A Creed would rather be lucky than good.'"

"Hush!" the captain ordered. "Straighten your clothes. The duke will see you now."

They crossed the massive drawbridge, which was permanently lowered by chain over a deep, pike-lined gully. Hadyn had never been much outside Missouri, except to his grandparents' house in Oklahoma, and Oklahoma didn't have castles. It looked like every castle he had ever imagined from Mom's and Dad's many stories. Camelot and all that. As he passed over the bridge, a sweet stirring of memories took wing in his chest like moths fluttering toward the moon. For the first time in a long time, the feel of the memory was more good than bad.

Guard boots clattered on the stone, as they were ushered into a small chamber decorated with shields, crossed spears, and banners bearing the crests of Greenland's many noble families. A large tapestry on the far wall depicted a man on a mountain slope, drinking water from a rushing stream while lightning gathered in the clouds above. Yhü on Mount Bourne, Hadyn guessed. He knew more of Karac Tor's history than he realized.

"My lord, the men you requested," said the guard. "Found outside the city gates."

An old, oil-rubbed round table filled most of the floor space of the chamber. The man seated at the table was lean and hard, with a shock of peppery hair crowning a face that looked like an ivory dagger, sharp and ready for battle. His eyes were narrow, and he wore armor. He did not look pleased to see them. Nevertheless, he pushed a platter of food toward them. Smoked meat, cheese, bread. Hadyn eagerly set to. Cruedwyn showed more restraint.

"Wait for us outside," the man commanded the guards, who smartly saluted and left. The next words spoken caused Hadyn to choke on the dry crust of bread. "I am Pol Shyne, Duke of Greenland. You are under my arrest."

CHAPTER 29

Prisoners

A t first, Cruedywn smiled warily. "Surely you jest, my lord! I am one of your own, a Greenland man from a Greenland clan. Cruedwyn ap Fergisfencreed, your humble serv—"

"Save it," Pol snapped. "I know who you are. And let me tell you, Creeds have never been humble about anything. Your father, Creyloch, sang in my father's hall before me. He fought with swift steel and a stout heart in the Raider Wars at Lismoych. But he had a bad voice and a foul temper, and was too quick by half with his mouth. He was good for war and tale-telling. But humble?" Pol rolled his eyes. "He's dead now, I think, yes?"

Cruedwyn lowered his head. "Four years now. Five of his sons still live. I'm the babe."

"Indeed. Which leads me to the obvious question: Are you true?"

A common saying in Greenland, it carried a tone of challenge. Pol narrowed his eyes to pinpricks of light.

Cruedwyn stood taller. There was no hint of irony in his reply. "Proud to be a Greenland man, my lord." He sounded utterly sincere, perhaps even a little wounded.

"Then why are you consorting with my enemies?" the duke smacked the table with his gloved fist. Hadyn jumped. This was not the plan. He had assumed their escort, though a little rough, had mostly been for their safety, their swords taken as a formality. Beside him, Cruedwyn waited for the echoes to absorb into the walls.

"Whatever your spies have told you, they are misinformed," he said calmly.

"Ware your words, Creed, they will sink you. I *know* you carried a message to Giovanni!"

Cruedwyn did not back down. "Then you must also know it was delivered in great peril. In fact, in the end, it had to be delivered by another messenger, not us. Why? Because we were not welcome in Vineland, any more than we are proving to be welcome in Greenland. Hardly the way of consorts, my lord. The high priest, Alethes, has sent my charge to all the dominions, bearing news of war and trouble. He is one of the Outlanders."

"Yes, yes, I know the game. Alethes sends him in person to somehow prove the point. Give me your message, boy. Whoever you are."

"My name is Hadyn, sir."

Pol raised an eyebrow. "Watch your cocksure tone with me, boy. By the Nines, you might just be an Outlander, or you would surely know the peril in which you stand. You're a spy until I say otherwise. Do you see that? The High Priest is keeper of the Books, not my court." He faced Cruedwyn once more. "I've got four warships in the Emryl Straights right now—and one on the bottom of the sea—because the merchant fleets have begun paying armed pirates to help them get through without paying my toll. A week ago I caught one of these ships, a Bittermen vessel from Yrgavien, sailing south with a hold full of gorse. It's the third ship we've intercepted, and I know others have gotten through. Then yesterday, traders coming from the Gray Abbey tell my stable master that they've seen large herds of gorse being moved south *through the Shimlings*. Now why would so many gorse be moving south, as if in secret? Tell me, Outlander?"

Wisely, Hadyn kept silent.

The edge in Pol's voice increased with every word. "Here's another one. Why is a Creed dragging the League onto *my* soil, when he knows I hate the League? The Black Hand, no less? Found tied so tight to a tree he could hardly breathe. And *marked*. Kill him and bury the body if you want, but marked? With the Stygma of all things? Fine for you, but what of the honor toll they'll require of my house now? Did you think of that, Fergisfencreed?"

Pol cut off the bard's answer by standing, leaning forward, knuckles pressed against the wood table. The sternness of his gaze made clear he wasn't interested in further conversation.

"Guards!" he barked.

The guards entered, swords drawn.

"Take them until I decide what to do with spies. The old detention cells, out of sight."

As they shuffled off, Cruedwyn muttered, "Black gates! Tell me again why I chose to be your friend?"

Hadyn failed to see the humor.

By the morning of the third day in the dungeon, the oldest Barlow was nearly beside himself, stomping back and forth across the floor as if he might grind the rock to dust and thus be free. He prowled, feeling more angry, more afraid, with each passing day. Why were they constantly opposed? Nobody even gave them a chance. Didn't they understand he was trying to help! He balled his fist.

I didn't have to come! he shouted in his head. *I was called . . . but I don't have to be here!*

It was only half true, he knew. He hadn't found a way home yet. But that wasn't the point, was it? He had chosen to help this bunch of ingrates, and for what? Pacing, fuming, he tried to go against the grain, think positively, but there was too much of his grandpa's dour Lutheranism for roses and sunshine and the theme song from *Annie*. Not now. Sunshine didn't exist in a dank cell beneath Aventhorn Keep, not today, not tomorrow. Nope, Murphy's Law was the only thing that made any sense in situations like this. If it could go wrong, it probably already had. Wait! He grimaced, realizing the irony of his own thoughts. Situations like *this*? Throw out the rule book, he had *never been in prison before*! In Fairy Tale Land! He shook his head at the double irony. In a sense, since arriving, prison was almost all he'd experienced.

"Creed," he said, trying to keep his voice from breaking. "I can't stay here. I'll go crazy. This is worse than the boat with the Lost. Worse than Nemesia."

It was a lie. The numbness of Nemesia was far worse than the terror of this cell. He didn't care. Biting his lip, he gripped the iron bars. He just wanted, needed, to get *out*.

Cruedwyn was sitting in the corner on a shelf of damp, dirty stone, one leg propped up and an arm draped casually across it. He didn't bother to answer. What could he say? Not only was there no sunlight, there was also no bed, blankets, or fresh water. The walls were rough. There were rats and rotten straw and roaches, and cobwebs in the corners with spiders, which Hadyn avoided at all cost. He had been as strong as he could. How many times did he have to be held captive and abused?

Two guards sat just beyond the iron bars through a curved opening in the stone. Their post was a central alcove with four cells connecting to a hallway with perhaps a dozen more. Stairs led back up into the keep, where it sounded like one of the guards was snoring. The other fiddled with a loop of keys hanging from his belt. Some of the torchlight from the alcove spilled into their cell. The smell of smoke and oil mingled with hundreds of years of odor from the dirty, unwashed bodies that had been imprisoned here. The odor clung to the walls, nearly causing Hadyn to wretch.

"I can't take this," he said, squeezing the bars harder, wondering how many other people before him had said the same thing. They might have deserved their confinement. He did not.

Pol Shyne thought otherwise. To him, the presumption was guilt.

Longtooth and ca'Libre were tantalizingly close, yet impossibly far away. They lay discarded in the corner beyond the cell bars, against the wall that separated the two rooms, in a small trough of old straw supposedly used for bedding. Even stretching his grasp as far as he could, Hadyn still fell a good three feet short. Anyway, what use would swords be behind bars?

"I didn't even give Pol the message," he said aloud, struck by the thought. "We went through all of that in Faielyn, at Seabraith, with Quillian, just to reach the duke. And for what?"

"Look on the bright side," Cruedwyn said. "We've got these lovely accommodations, for free. Good food. Cheer up, Hadyn. We put in our time, and then we get out. Never forget there is justice in the world."

"Sometimes I wonder," Hadyn grumbled.

"Wondering or whining? 'Tis a weakness, friend."

"As is lying, but you don't hear me rubbing it in," Hadyn shot back. He hung his head.

Cruedwyn was unfazed. "In point of fact, you just did. Besides, I would challenge the notion that a Creed lies. We simply tell stories to the fullest extent imaginable."

Tiny vibrations tickled Hadyn's feet through the floor as the sword began a low, familiar hum. Hadyn rolled his eyes. *Perfect*. The conversation trailed away to nothing. He felt ashamed, didn't know how to say he was sorry. He wasn't good at sorry. After a few moments, the odor of something burning wafted his way. Hadyn sniffed the air. Sniffed again. His eyes widened.

"Cruedwyn, I have an idea."

The bard grunted. "And I have a question," he said. "What's that?"

"You smell it too?"

"No, I see it. Right behind you."

Hadyn spun. In the middle of the dark cell he saw what Cruedwyn saw, a vaporous figure taking shape in the darkness. It looked like steam rising from a pot, or a ghost stepping out of shadows into the light. The dry air had ceased being dry, had become watery and moist. Something was emerging from the wetness, holding out its hand. Hadyn could hardly believe his eyes. He knew that shape.

"Merciful Aion," he whispered.

The Steeple

They were almost there, almost to the needle of rock used eons ago as the northernmost watchtower alerting Karac Tor to any surprise attack from the pagan hordes of Quil. At the foot of Mount Junta, where the grassless, pine-covered hills turned to sharp, grinding stone, there was a platter of solid rock and, rising from the plateau, a narrow, square tower of cut stone and chipped, failing mortar. It was nearly a hundred and fifty feet tall, with a thin, winding staircase accessible from inside the broad base. Sorge remembered; he had been here before. The Steeple was a good defensive location for one to hold out against many. It was their only hope.

His muscles ached. He was out of breath. Below and not far away, rising from Lindwurm, a small cloud of white teeth and fur was in pursuit. Burly men in bearskins had joined the white wolves since the previous battle in the valley below. He and Barsonici had a good lead, but the old hermit was in poor shape and limping badly. By contrast, the wolves were *not* tired, *not* wounded. They were hungry for blood, and Barsonici had left a fresh trail to follow. Sorge cursed himself for not taking the time to bandage the wound properly.

"Who are the men?" Barsonici panted as Sorge hauled him up the next cold lip of rock, using his staff as a pole for Barsonici to grip.

"Outcasts of Bitterland," Sorge said. "A clan of murderers. The Bittermen call them Vargs. They are not part of the three kithlands. It will not be pleasant if we are captured."

It would be getting dark soon. The sun was already passing low behind a dense bank of clouds. The temperature was dropping as night came on in the shadow of the mountains. If the blood they left was not trail enough, the relentless baying of the winds kept gushing their scent right down upon the wolves. It was a race to the Steeple.

And then what? Sorge wondered. Even if they made it? Sorge couldn't believe what a fool he had been. Arrogant. Stubborn. He had not taken the time to think of the best path. He had just set off, full of his own need for justice and redemption. He stopped to catch his breath.

"I got us into this mess," he said angrily. "I was a fool."

Barsonici gasped for air. "No time for remorse. We must go until we can go no more."

Sorge stared at the man's bloody ankle, at the torn, bruised flesh, the thin scabs made black by the dust and dirt of the climb. He had to be in enormous pain, yet he had not complained once.

"Can you make it?"

Barsonici grimaced, glancing at his foot. When he brought his eyes back up, his gaze was meaningful and heavy.

"No," Sorge said, refusing. "We go together."

A howl rose from the pack below—no, not a howl, a long, high blast from a gorse horn, followed by two shorter blasts—sending shivers through the air. A smaller, faster wolf tore loose from the pack as the horn sounded, leaping and bounding closer along a different path. Sorge's heart sank. They would have to fight it, which was guaranteed to slow them enough to allow the rest of the pack to overtake them.

Capture by Vargs. Sorge had heard the stories. He grit his teeth.

Barsonici was talking. Sorge had asked him a question. *Can you make it?*

"Even if my strength fails, Olfadr will provide," the old man said through labored breaths. He was a strange bird. Cantankerous and bitter one moment, the paragon of serenity the next. He touched Sorge's shoulder. "Come, my boy."

My boy? Who was taking care of whom now?

The steepness of the last slope would slow the men a little, the wolves less. Sorge could only hope that when they reached the Steeple other Vargs would not be there waiting for them, drawn by the horns and howls. He could barely see the platform cresting above the hill. From a distance, the tower looked lanky and pinched. So far to go.

Using his knees and interlocking his hands, he hoisted Barsonici by his good foot to the next ledge of stone. Barsonici held onto the end of Sorge's staff while he pulled them both along. Thorny plants and thistles grew through cracks in the rocks, tearing at their robes. The overcast sky was slate-colored, gloomy. It was chilly. Barsonici held the staff with one hand, held his chest with the other, shivering. He was nearly spent.

Sorge tried to think ahead. Somewhere along this path, there were . . . *stairs.*

He glanced down to the west, bursting with memory, had to jerk back his head as an arrow whistled past his face. The Vargs also knew of the stone-carved stairs. Their bows were notched and launching. Wolves were sprinting up the incline. The stairs would lead them straight to the Steeple's base.

Sorge hugged the stone, edging around its contours so that he increased the angle of difficulty for the bowmen.

"Keep low," the monk said, shoving Barsonici in front of him. "Move, old man! Hurry! We're almost there!"

The breakaway wolf was struggling up a sheet of gray, pimpled stone, made slippery with pebbles and bits of shale. It had positioned itself on their other side, as if herding sheep, forcing Sorge and Barsonici to advance *toward* the pack, not allowing them to steer away. Sorge took a stone, big as his fist, and hurled it at the wolf below. It missed, but the wolf got the point, beginning to creep along with greater stealth. Sorge could hear it growling over the pounding of his heart. He threw another stone and another. The fourth hit the beast in the hindquarters, making a dull thud. It yelped and hunkered lower.

Sorge turned back to his climb, saw Barsonici reaching down with his hand. It was only a short sprint to the base of the Steeple from here. Arrows whizzed overhead. The angle had shifted again. The Vargs were also near the top.

"Forget me!" Sorge hissed. "To the tower!"

The old man obediently rose. The wolves howled. Sorge saw a hail of arrows arcing up and over.

"Stay low, Barsonici!" he yelled, though he couldn't even see the man anymore.

Then he was up and over. Hunching low, running. Behind and to the right, the wolves crowned the last scoop of rock, tongues wagging. They began a dead sprint for Sorge. Perhaps six, no, ten. More coming up behind. If they caught their prey, they would get meat tonight. They wanted meat.

Sorge heard the Vargs yelling brutish, unspeakable words. Another arrow hissed by, clattering off the stone. The crumbling mortar of the tower base did little to reassure him of the worthiness of this escape plan. The Steeple had been abandoned for decades. Inside it was tight, perhaps four arm spans wide. Winding stairs cramped the space further. The door was made of splintered, spongy timbers fastened with rusting iron brackets. Sorge heard a snarl, saw the nearest wolf leap just as he slammed the door shut. The jolt of the beast knocked him backward, but the door held. While Barsonici leaned against the wood, Sorge braced it, sliding his staff through iron mountings attached to the stone on either side. Darkness thickened in the tower, save for twilight lancets leaking through gaps in the mortar. As his eyes adjusted, Sorge noticed the rough-hewn shape of the stairs—a hundred and fifty feet of stairs.

Barsonici clutched his chest.

"I have no breath. I can't go."

"You must," Sorge insisted, taking the man by the arm and pulling.

"What about your staff?"

"There is no magic in it. I'll make another."

The Varg men arrived, bellowing and pounding on the door like battering rams. It would not last long. Sorge shoved Barsonici onto the stairs.

"Climb! There used to be a door at the very top. A metal plate. Perhaps we can outlast them."

"What then?" Barsonici replied doubtfully, huffing, putting one foot wearily ahead of the next. "They wait. We don't have the stores to outlast them."

"True, but they cannot burn us out. We take our chances. Climb!"

The pounding continued below, echoing up and down the dark, damp walls. They had made perhaps three full rotations of the circle climbing upward when the first sound of splintering wood hit their ears. One of the Vargs from the rear must have brought his axe. It would not be long now.

"Keep climbing!" Sorge commanded harshly. "I'm going to try something."

He squatted low, turned to the step behind where he stood. Feeling the stone surface with the palms of his hands, he began uttering quiet, prayer-like words. His thought was simple: deplete the stone, weaken its commitment to the mortar and to itself. He had neither the time nor the talent to scoop enough material away to matter. But perhaps its inner strength could be compromised enough to collapse under weight—create a gap large enough the wolves would not leap across. The stairway was not quite wide enough for two people. He could hold his ground against the Vargs. Keep them at bay until Barsonici finally reached the top. Then sprint for it.

No! He swore, realizing it would be a poor fight without his staff.

Below, the door shattered. He had weakened four steps. It was all he could do. On, up . . .

Vargs and wolves came thundering through. The sound of snapping teeth and shouting voices filled the enclosed space. Sorge and Barsonici were perhaps a third of the way up. There was no railing. Fifty feet was a long way to fall to a hard floor. A quick death. Not so bad to contemplate right about now, Sorge decided.

Within moments, he heard a frantic, bitter squeal. Then another. His trap was sprung. Distant sounds of crumbling stone hitting the floor brought him grim, quiet satisfaction. Next came a sickening thud, doubled, as the first two wolves fell to their death. A piece of debris must have struck a Varg at the base, for he suddenly began to curse and rage.

Suddenly, a wolf was snapping at Sorge's heels. The lead wolf, light and fast. It must have passed over his trap but triggered the collapse for those behind it. The monk wheeled, dropped low, kicking outward with a powerful thrust of his feet. The wolf lunged, made it through his barricade of legs. Sorge grabbed the wolf's ear and a leg, rolling his torso just enough to force the weight of the beast to shift over the lip of the stairs. It fell. More cursing below.

Sorge was breathing hard, but the soft, determined padding of footsteps rising from the darkness spurred him on. The collapse of the stairs had only stopped the advance of the wolves, not the Vargs. He rose, climbed. Halfway. Three-quarters of the way. Three or four turns ahead of the Vargs. Then only two rotations of the stairs ahead. Barsonici was barely climbing now. They were near the top. One rotation's lead. It was getting close. The tower had narrowed considerably to an almost constant turn, only one person wide.

"Almost there, Barsonici," Sorge urged in a whisper. "The platform is wider on top. You can rest there. Go!"

With that, the monk turned and rushed *down* the stairs as quietly, as quickly, as he could. The Vargs were too close. No choice. Making a sound like a wild ox, he barreled into the chest of the first man, caught him unawares, head down. Sorge's bellowing yawp ricocheted off the walls in the dark, tight space. The Varg never saw the monk's black skin, or his dark gray robe. He toppled backward into the man behind, and again into the next behind them. It sounded as if one might have pitched off the stairs, was hanging suspended, begging fearfully for help. It gave Sorge the time he needed. Barsonici should have made it to the top by now. If the metal top hatch was still there, they should be able to secure it. Then rest. And figure out what to do next.

He emerged, slammed the door shut, bolted it with iron. Yes, good. The hinged lid was flaking and crusted with rust, but solid. Underneath, the Vargs would soon begin to pound, but there was only space for one man to strike at a time. And strong metal. They would weary of it. From the mild light of evening, a moon of promise rose in the east, robed with a thousand stars. Compared to the darkness inside the tower, the gray color of the sky was nearly bright. Bright enough to see a strange sight. There. On top of the tower. Sorge swallowed, stunned.

"Sorge?" Barsonici said guardedly. The monk had no reply.

Four muscled figures with great artificial wings spreading from their backs stood in the twilight at the top of the Steeple.

Sorge stared, dumbfounded.

"A fortnight ago," one said in a thick Highland accent. "The L'ka had a vision. He sent us to a high place, where the winds are strong for our wings. We have flown many days to reach this tower. To find you. It is just as he said. Come, Elder Sorge."

Sorge absorbed it all in an instant. A fortnight? How long had they lain outside the forest, drugged unconscious by the Fey Queen.

"Va'nya? Is that you?"

CHAPTER 31

Shame

Standing as a man-stag, breathing hoary frost into the air, Kr'Nunos looked across the deep, black heart of Angwyn with a murderous mix of lust and pride. Row upon row upon row of earthy creatures stood slumped over, awaiting whatever semblance of consciousness he would soon bestow upon them. They would not truly draw breath nor come alive. They would not feel pain nor speak. Yet they would move as a man might and kill without mercy any who stood in their way. They were skeletal, crude, brutishly strong—formed in the great cauldron of Angwyn's death and rebirth, of stones and bones, copper and iron, mud and sawdust. One after the other, the Goths had emerged from the pit as thick, lumbering, skinless creatures with no thought save one. Theirs would be a mindless, unyielding compulsion to return to their soil of origin. The location could be anywhere. Whatever dirt—whatever region or city or forest of Karac Tor—was laid in the cauldron, this became the living fury of the Goths, their reason for being. To return to *that* place. To go home.

In this case, home was Röckval, the citadel and capital city of the northland-dwelling Bittermen. Home was inside the city walls, in High Röckval, where the river Witemeld flowed. The reborn earth creatures would stop at nothing to get there. Three thousand strong, stretching down the corridors of Helheim, unwearied and unfeeling, even those that languished outside the entrance in the snow and bitter cold, awaiting their release to follow the urge that would compel them to Röckval at all cost. It was all part of Kr'Nunos's carefully calculated plan. A trial army, to test the will of men.

The Horned Lord licked his lips with pleasure. It would be a short, easy test. Röckval was a symbol. Once known for their strength, the viks had grown soft and weak and fractured. As had all of Karac Tor.

Spies inside the city had given him the soil he needed, though they didn't know who they were dealing with at the time, in his disguise. All they cared for was the gold. Gold was easy. Treachery was hard. Inside Helheim, the S'Qoth brutes had served his purpose well. Now it was time to release the Goths. It would take weeks for them to make the journey to Röckval.

Kr'Nunos motioned his henchman, Oruuwn, who gave a signal with one gloved fist. Oruuwn was a beastly man, with dark skin markings and ritual scars covering his arms, his naked chest, his face. He was shaved bald and wore a necklace of bear teeth. At the raising of his fist, every S'Qoth slave hastily moved out of the way of the opening to Hel. Two groups of muscled S'Qoth pushed against the poles of two large gears connected to chains. As they turned, the massive, black iron gates slowly swung wide. Nothing blocked the exit leading to the frigid landscape of ice outside. The S'Qoth had learned, with many deaths and severed limbs: do not stand in the path of the Goths.

Kr'Nunos filled his lungs, released a command. A word. The echo of the word rolled like a wave across a shore. Three thousand Goths shuddered, straightened their backs, lifted their sightless faces to the wind and began to sigh with longing. The noise they made was dry and cold and anguished, like a piece of old wood rubbed against rock. Mountain wind. The hiss of a cat.

They began to move toward the blinding white. They did not look left or right, except as they passed by the Horned Lord, and then their gaping maw would widen to acknowledge him as their liege and the source of their suffering. Kr'Nunos smiled.

"Now to mighty Corus," he said. "For the final breaking."

The last Champion sat in darkness on a bench of rough stone worn smooth by years of bearing his own weight. The darkness around him was a living thing, inky and opaque, malevolent as the grave. It shrouded his eyes and mind in a blind stupor, so that Corus could not remember himself, not what he looked like, nor where he was. As the crushing immensity of Mount Agasag bore down upon him, swallowing him whole, he felt nothingness clinging to his naked skin like wet silk. All other realities muddled together in his brain, making it seem very real and very possible that there was nothing in the world but darkness.

Here, magic had no power. Common flame could not penetrate this world. Only death. Only despair. Such was the nature of Hel.

He heard a rattling of chains, footsteps coming from a long way off. Laughter. He knew the cruelty of that laugh. He heard the sounds of other beasts crying out, sounds of madness and desolation. They, too, knew who strode the chambers of Hel.

A key tumbling in a metal bolt. A creaking of rusty iron. A voice of doom and dread.

"My armies ride forth. I go in the shape of a crow to spy ahead. I will return in half a fortnight. In a month, two at most, High Röckval will fall."

The voice became as velvety as the smothering blackness.

"Before I go, I give you your freedom, Champion."

Something clattered on the ground. Something metal. It rang brightly, vibrating. Corus didn't move, didn't know what trick the Horned Lord was plotting, only that he refused to take part. He could still do that, couldn't he? Refuse, even with shredded will? Besides, what was freedom, when Kr'Nunos knew his ribs were bruised from the last beating? If Corus even tried to rise, his newly scabbed back would split wide open. Freedom was a cruel gibe.

"I give you the Severing Blade. You know its power. Cut your chains with it. Find your way to the Black Gates, or climb down the mountain. You are my prisoner no more."

"Liar. You lie."

"Yes," Kr'Nunos said, pleased. "But in this moment, the offer is true."

Corus shook his head in the darkness. "You will unleash beasts upon me. Your hirelings will gut me. You offer pain."

"Or death. Isn't that what you want?"

Shame and disbelief deepened the silence within his cell.

At length, Kr'Nunos spoke again. A more sinister tone crept into his voice.

"Ah, and so at last, the darkness reveals all. Who is the liar now?"

A long, accusing pause followed. Corus didn't speak, could hardly stand to breathe. The air had begun to close around him. His head hung low.

"Prove me wrong, coward! Take your life or take your freedom! The blade offers both."

There was motion in the darkness, a movement of air. Corus felt the cold Severing Blade pressed into his hand. His finger grazed the blade, instantly drawing blood.

"Do it *now!*" Kr'Nunos roared.

Corus clenched the haft, lifting his head. He could only feel, not see, the voice before him, shaped of blackness. He dropped the knife, let it clatter on the stone. The curse in his blood would not let him take his own life, and pride would never let him face men again.

Kr'Nunos purred, "Ah, to stand here on the day of your reckoning, as the layers of deception peel away to the core of mortal guilt. Have you truly wanted freedom, begging for it seven years now? Or was it simply to convince yourself, to satisfy the illusion of innocence?" A low, mocking rumble bubbled up from deep in the Horned Lord's throat. "Did you think I did not listen, Corus? That I did not know? When I left you alone in your blood, in the beginning, how you wept like a child? It pleased me greatly to hear you beg the darkness. Did you know that? You asked the walls to hear you and rise up. When you thought I was gone, you would scream and ask the beasts deep in Hel to kill your brother. Because he betrayed you, no? The last kiss of a friend."

There was a dreadful pause.

"But there was another reason, too—a reason you could hardly admit to yourself. For here, in my dwelling, you could pretend to be the noble victim. But he knew the truth, didn't he? He knew, as I do. Now freedom is a word you praise, but not a gift you truly want. Because you know, deep inside, the bowman was right to mistrust you. You were going to give it to her. Blinded by love to what Nemesia had truly become: *mine*."

Kr'Nunos's laughter roared through Hel.

"Seven years chained in the iron of your own lies! Hel itself, your unholy sanctuary, keeping your legend safe from shame. Better thought dead than disgraced. Pitiful, mighty, *faithful* Corus."

In the darkness, Corus felt a wicked smile. "You should thank me, that I found you among the Fey. She might have released you one day."

Corus wished for rage or the gift of *dynamis* to overtake him. He wished for Agasag to quake and collapse upon them both. He wished for the heart he once knew, red and bloody with passion, fire, and the will to fight—for that part to rise in defiance. But there was nothing left. *Stripped to the core,* Kr'Nunos had said, and truly. He slumped, feeling numb. His mind mirrored the darkness around him, a thick vice of despair. Wishing was futile, save for the dim chance that the darkness might finally finish feeding upon him and let him pass into memory.

He did not know he had been struck until his neck snapped backward in the darkness, rattling his brain, sending lines of white light shooting across his mind's eye. Then came the searing pain. He felt a trail of blood trickling down his back, freshly broken open. One more blow came, just for fun, followed by the deep-throated sound of a wild stag baying at the moon.

The Devourer's voice boomed across Helheim. "I grow stronger every day! Soon I will pass the forbidden barrier to Undrwol. I will drag you down into the depths and let the Watchers and trolls and daemons and drakes devour your living flesh for a thousand years. I shall give you the penance you seek with every whipping, and make each day another seven years of torment."

He turned, swept away. Corus heard the croaking of a raven, the fluttering of wings. Then nothing. The door to his cage never clanged shut. The Severing Blade remained on the ground beside him. A thin echo of the Horned Lord's voice trailed back to his cell from a distance, sounding like poisoned wine. "Or . . . do my bidding, Corus! Embrace what you have become here. Escape and find the king who sleeps. Destroy him. Your curse will be satisfied. You can pass into memory then. End your pain forever. Use the Severing Blade to kill the Sleeping King. Who knows? You could even return to your fame among men. No one would ever have to know."

As the voice faded into the fog of his mind, Corus knew the truth of the Horned Lord's words. Bereft of his last vestiges of dignity, chains weren't even needed anymore. Kr'Nunos had dismantled his soul. He would not draw sword again, nor ever truly leave, never be free, nor kill himself. Curses were the messengers of Hel, and no destiny could escape. Unless . . .

Unless he killed the king. *No one would have to know.*

For the first time in years, Corus wept.

In the wall of darkness, he saw his fate in a new light. A new path. After hours of weeping, his heart hardened like a fist. *No one would have to know.*

CHAPTER 32

Bird Men

They flew all night, then all day and night again. They did not stop to eat or sleep for risk of losing their winds or having no manageable high place from which to launch. With empty bellies they sailed past mountains draped in skirts of snow and clotted with pine trees, through flurries of snowflakes cutting the air like knives, through bitter winds. They did not sleep and had nothing to keep them warm but the clothes they wore. It was brutal, frigid, and desperate.

They had already defied many odds, having eaten and slept only twice in two weeks. It had been necessary to make the journey to the Steeple with speed. They could not risk losing height or wind. Their first leg was from the Rim to north of Mount Bourne, along the cliffs of the Normont Front near Stapling, then to the Great Bell Tower of Telmon in Portaferry, each time without stopping, an arduous feat. Then from Portaferry to the Steeple. At both previous resting points, they ate only a little, caught a few hours sleep. Then on again. It was a matchless feat, nearly as great as the Long Flight of Gil, their ancient forefather, who as a boy led his people out of the pagan cruelties of their kin in the Wild South. In keeping with their traditions, Highland boys were groomed for hardship from a young age. It was considered high honor to endure affliction. Before they became men, boys were sent into the wilderness alone, left without food or water for a week. Similar rituals continued into manhood. Highland men knew and practiced deprivation as a spiritual act, a fact of survival in a harsh land. In doing so, they at once embraced the severity of their home and defied it.

Now they flew at great speed. *P'tlu'Ha*, it was called. A rare thing. The Over Wind. A sign of favor from Aion. It had carried them far.

In the ages to come, the journey of Sorge and the Bird Men would become the stuff of legend and song, sung by descendants of the Creed clan, warriors, kings, and fathers; sung in mead halls and around campfires; and every time it was told young boys would take their blankets and stretch them out as wings and pretend to fly. Never before had such a journey been made from one end of the kingdom to the other, hundreds of miles. Never before had Bird Men carried others so far, nor faced such desperate hardship in the howling winds of a foreign land.

In the songs, they would call it The Great Flight.

The Raid on Hel.

Four Highlanders, accustomed to warmer climes all their lives, and two monks, both of whom were very near to losing faith. Lost among the forsaken peaks of Bitterland.

They flew in the blinding snow over the far western outpost of Quorn, with their beards frozen and their skin grown blue and numb. They had torn their thin blankets into wrappings for their feet and hands and faces. They had no boots. They lofted high and low, fighting for control in the gusting crosswinds. They flew because the L'ka told them to fly, from a vision birthed the very night his brother gave all he had: his song.

Ewan's song.

The power of the song and the sacrifice drove them on. They flew, and Barsonici and Sorge found themselves asking, desperately pleading, for the mercy of Aion.

After the first screaming plunge from the Steeple's heights, Barsonici had vomited into the open air. Sorge's stomach had soured in his belly. Soaring was a strange sensation. Sorge did not think it could be done. Were the winds less, it might not have been possible. Va'nya and another carried him, while the other two clung to Barsonici. Bird Men's wings were guarded secrets, able to fold up into a pack they carried on their back, springing open as huge wind catchers. They were fashioned of a strong, thin wicker mesh and filmy sheets of leather and hemp, secured to leather vests and harnesses wrapped around the Highlanders' chest, waist, and legs. Sorge and Barsonici were given similar vests, and the Bird Men were fastened to their human cargo with thick leather strapping. The wings for this journey were specially made, Va'nya said, spread much broader than normal, to bear the extra weight. But difficult to fly.

They worried about Watchers, flying high, keeping an eye on the mountain passes. But Watchers sought the praise of men, and there were few in these parts to seduce. In the failing light of the first day, before the dizzying leap from the Steeple, they had looked out from the watchtower and spied Carmon's Pass. Once through the pass, the worst of the cutting winds would likely die down. They would have a measure of warmth from the sun, at least during daylight. Nights would be hard no matter what. No sleep. No sun.

The flight was excruciating, dragging hour upon hour. It was a torment that seemed to have no end. Sorge wondered if they would lose fingers and toes to frostbite. Only a miracle would prevent it. He tried to wiggle, move his extremities. Keep blood flowing. The blankets helped, but only a little. Finally he gave up. He was just too cold.

He worried for the Bird Men. All the strain was upon them, and they were more poorly dressed than he and Barsonici. They could not risk the weight of heavy clothes. He glanced over and behind, shouting something encouraging to Barsonici. The old man was slumped over in his harness, unmoving. He looked dead but stirred enough for Sorge to know otherwise.

And still they flew. After coming through Carmon's Pass, the winds shifted, just as expected. But a bank of low clouds turned all the world gray. Sorge could no longer feel his toes, lips, or face. His bald head felt like a ball of ice, his ponytail a frozen stick of wood. He could not imagine how the Bird Men had done it, how they had made it this far. It hurt to think, to breathe, so much that he found himself taking shallow breaths just to avoid greatly expanding his chest.

When all seemed lost, when the hope of finding Mount Agasag seemed as elusive as catching handfuls of the fog around them, they broke through to a clearing of sky and sun and a wind slightly more mild. Sorge even felt a welcome hint of warmth graze his face.

Mountains loomed before him in a long line, stretching east. Another line trailed immediately below and leftward, forming a granite wall heading north to south. They had come to the corner

of the Hödurspikes, where the leg turned. Ahead towered the terrible dark bulk of Mount Agasag, angry and awesome, a hulk of
bitter stone scraping the sky. The pockmarked south face was all
gaping hollows and caves, like dark, drooping eyes. Two giant rows
of barbed stone—one high, one low—formed a crooked pattern of
bared fangs that swept across the mountain. Ridges and ledges jutted out at odd angles, as if the stone had erupted from within in all
directions at once. The peak was a crater blown open by spewing
lava thousands of years ago. Nothing living or growing was visible.
Sorge almost recoiled to look at it. Yet he had come of his own free
will, for good or ill.

Another half day passed. Far below, the land was speckled with
tiny green dots, pines and cedars, thin, winding streams, huts. Ants
on the distant earth. No word or signal was exchanged between
any of the six men, but they would all be dead soon if they did not
find a landing. As the mass of Agasag drew near, Va'nya slowed
his approach, spying a place with good footing to descend. Sorge
pointed to a ledge, but the Bird Man had already seen it. Slowly,
they glided in.

Passing over the scarred channels of stone far below, Sorge
thought he spied the enormous arched gateway to Hel, iron gates as
thick and black as night. Skulls were strung on wire and skeletons
impaled on pikes. Bones littered the ground. It was a landscape of
nightmares, with a deep, impassable gorge at the base of the mountain and steam and fire rising from its depths. A long stone bridge
spanned the gap. Helheim, realm of terror.

The closer they got to the ledge the more fierce the crosswinds
became. They bucked and heaved.

"Not . . . make it!" Va'nya cried, his voice torn away by the
wind. "Hold!"

Like rag dolls on a string, Sorge and Barsonici flailed beneath the two human birds above them. When one of the Highlanders cried out, Sorge felt, heard, the snap of a leather strap. Part of his weight lurched. The effect sent them careening wildly toward the target ledge. Both his carriers desperately tried to fan their oversized wings to slow their descent, but overshot, slamming into the rock some twenty feet above the ledge before tumbling down the snow to the cave entrance. All three landed in a tangled heap of wings and harnesses on the hard stone. Sorge couldn't breathe, could only writhe about, begging for air. In a great, thirsty gasp, he finally gained relief. The taste of blood was on his lips. He felt a sharp pain at his side—probably a cracked rib.

Barsonici's trio swooped in next, a better landing, but dangerously near to the edge. The old man hardly made a sound as he landed with a searing crunch on his wounded ankle that even Sorge could hear. Dazed, he rolled away from the pain toward the lip of the cave. Sorge could tell he had no bearings, no thought for the limits of the stone, numb with cramps and cold. Crawling on his elbows, Sorge caught the verseman in a fist of tattered robe just as he was about to pitch into the open air below. It wasn't much, but it was enough to steady him. Tears streamed down Barsonici's face, but the pain helped awaken his groggy mind. As he gained his balance, he slowly seemed to realize where he was.

"Agasag?" he mumbled. Sorge nodded grimly.

Exhausted, the six men lay still for several minutes. One at a time, as they finally collected their breath, they began crawling deeper into the darkness of the cave. No one spoke. Two of the Bird Men had black, deadened fingers. Their spiked hair was thick with fronds of ice. All but one of Barsonici's toes on his wounded foot looked ruined. His whole ankle was purple and swollen from the landing. They shivered beyond control.

"Gu'mo," Va'nya managed, teeth chattering. "You are not . . . well."

Gu'mo held his side, doubled over. It was he who hit the face of the mountain hardest on landing. He pulled his hands away, revealing a bloody puncture midway down his rib cage.

"I—will be fine," he said.

They huddled together for warmth, letting each other's breath create a respite from the cold, while the cave sheltered them from the worst of the winds. Eventually, Sorge laid his hands upon the stone underneath him and began to pray. His black skin looked unnaturally pale. He could barely mutter soft words aloud, but he continued to pray, almost deliriously. Slowly, almost imperceptibly, heat began to spread outward under the surface of the stone he touched. The men moaned to feel it. Sorge prayed more.

"You—may lose those," he warned, eyeing the blackened fingers and toes around him. "But if you warm them slowly you may not. Help one another. Warm a good hand. Then place it on the damaged skin. Be gentle."

He continued to put heat into the stone, letting it course through the rock, pushing back the cold. It was dark. The cave continued into deeper darkness. The six of them stayed, unmoving, for nearly an hour, hoping for more warmth from the stone. Sorge did not stop softly interceding the entire time. Ice melted off their hands and feet where they touched the stone. Each man took a turn pressing his cheeks and ears and lips to the warmth, each laid flat upon his back and belly until his bones began to thaw. By the time Sorge was done, the rock was hot enough to radiate, like a fire.

Va'nya pulled food from his pack, passed it around. Dried meat. Stale bread. The men devoured it. They crammed snow and icicles from the cave entrance into an organ flask, laid it upon the hot rock until it melted, then drank.

Everyone was exhausted. Two of the Bird Men with Va'nya looked younger than he, one older. They were lean, muscled young men, with fear and grim determination in their faces. Sorge felt the same.

The monk rose, feeling stiff protest in his muscles. "We need light," he said.

He felt in the darkness for a loose stone. Holding it aloft in his hands, he blessed it. The stone began to glow. Slowly, the rear of the cave blossomed in the gentle light, bringing a dim glint of metal into contrast with the flat stone. Instruments of iron lay on the ground. Not weapons, but devices of cruelty. Waiting for his eyes to adjust, Sorge's heart sank.

In the center of the cave not far back, two thick beams were planted in the stone a few feet apart. Iron shackles hung loosely from each, at a perfect height and distance to stretch the arms tight and spread the shoulder blades. A truss for whipping. Pools of some dark liquid had dried on the floor in the center between the posts. Blood, likely. The dark stains were spattered on the chains, the beams, the ground, everywhere.

Sorge rushed forward, touching the blood, smelling it.

"Merciful Aion," he breathed, lowering his face to the ground. The blood was cold, but recent. "This is what I've done. Corus lives."

CHAPTER 33

Raid on Hel

They scoured the cave for charred remains of old fires, put husks of rotted wood, old pine needles, shredded cloth, and frayed bits of rope around the base of the beams. Va'nya struck his flint rock many times, but the kindling wouldn't catch. Sorge insisted he keep trying. They needed the heat to recover enough to make the escape, once Corus was found—*if* he were found. Even more, Sorge wanted every vestige of the beams destroyed. The discovery of the whipping posts put a new determination, an almost sovereign sense of purpose, into each of them. Corus *would* be found. The cave must be cleansed. While the Highlanders tried to light the fire, he explored the back of the cave. Barsonici came with him, hobbling and wincing every step.

"This is the final stage. We've come this far, but the true test is yet to come," the old man said soberly. "Find us a way down there, Sorge. And quickly. I am weak."

Sorge shook his head. "First, we need rest. We need another meal. Fire and warmth. You cannot take another journey so soon. None of us can. At least a few hours' worth."

"And if the wood won't burn?" Barsonici objected. "Can't you—"

"Light it? That's what Grays do, right? Don't you think I would have, if I were able?"

Barsonici's reply was ironic. "So you can burn *stone*, but not wood?"

Sorge could only murmur, "Better with stone . . . water. Not very good at any of it."

The old versemen fell silent. The deeper they went into the cave, the more foul the smell. Gradually, the shape of their surroundings morphed, becoming a tall, narrow tunnel with carved steps leading down into the black depths of the mountain. Sorge followed the steps, treading lightly, intentionally keeping the glow of his stone to a minimum. The narrow stairs grew steep quickly, curving with the shape of the rock, down, down, until they came to a wide landing with a railing of metal poles and a platform with a large, empty cage. The platform was part of a shelf of stone that wrapped a quarter of the way around a massive vertical shaft, like a giant throat by which the mountain swallowed air. The shaft snaked left and right into countless smaller ducts, all of them coated with a yellow crystalline mineral that caught Sorge's light and glimmered dully. The stench of sulfur became overwhelming. Thick, heavy rope was bound to the top of the cage, knotted and lashed with copper wire. From there it curved up and over a large pulley, wrapping through a series of gears, before plunging into the depths of the giant hole, which quickly became an inky, fathomless pool of black.

"That is where we must go," Barsonici said, pointing below. "I don't have time to thaw. *We* don't have time. It will grow warmer the deeper we go."

"Let us get the fire going, then I will go."

"Elder, think! Listen! Your light is no good down there. It will only serve to reveal us to others. I will be the eyes. You will be the strength."

"We don't know if Trulight will work," Sorge whispered hoarsely. "You haven't used it in years, certainly never in Hel."

"And yet it is our only hope. Why else have I come?"

Sorge shook his head. "No."

He was prepared for a battle, so when Barsonici softened, it caught him off guard. "If the Horned Lord has truly returned . . . if he is building power again in this mountain, we do not dare stay a moment longer than we must. Let me help you find your friend."

Sorge pursed his lips. "It should be my risk, not yours. Come what may."

"Sorge, listen to me." There was no challenge left in Barsonici's voice, only a quiet sort of acceptance. He smiled sadly. "The risk is already over for me. I have come, but I will never leave this place. In the vision I had many nights ago—the vision given by the boy's song—I saw this moment, this day. This very cave. One of us will have to stay behind. Let me do this. Let me complete the purpose of my life. For years I have sought to release the Sleeping King . . ."

His voice trailed away. Sorge shook his head. "Then find him with us. Do not talk of dying."

"Only Corus can find him. And then the Sleeping King will need his Champion. And the Champion will need his friend. You are a warrior, Sorge. Be who you are."

Sorge set his lip. "Fine, but we stick together. We leave together."

Barsonici raised his brows like a teacher scolding his pupil. "Count, Sorge. Four Bird Men, with *three* men to carry. Three. It cannot happen. One of us must stay behind."

Sorge straightened his back. In the rush and terror of the flight, he had simply not thought past *getting* here. Now they were here. And one could not leave. It was so shockingly true he grew angry.

"We will figure something out. Wait here." He spun, strode up the steps, instructed the Bird Men, returned. "They have found some dry straw, and the fire is near to catching. I told them if we have not returned in two hours to fly. You are right. We have no more time. Let's go."

Sorge was already opening the door to the lift, stepping inside. The cage was large and heavy enough to carry ten men. The old man followed quietly behind. They closed the door. Below the open grating, the deep pit yawned like a hungry beast, waiting to devour them. Sorge reached—barely reached—the lever on the gears of the platform. Pushed. Cranking loudly, the gears began to unwind. Somewhere on a gigantic spool high above, the rope tensed. The cage dropped beneath them, leaving their hearts behind.

They descended into Hel.

It was like drowning, not from lack of air, but lack of light—a swirling descent into an ocean named Despair. Sorge did not extinguish the light from his stone. He did not need to. It was consumed. By the time the lift came to a stop, they had spent more than thirty minutes hurtling into the abyss. In the last few seconds, counterweights and brakes suddenly slowed their descent, but the impact was still jarring. The sound of the metal cage crashing on rock reverberated loudly through the honeycomb caverns of Helheim. The two men crouched, waiting for the clanging echoes to fade into the abyss. It was stiflingly hot.

"Hush now," Barsonici panted. "Let me be."

Sorge waited. He could feel the old Master Verseman battling for stillness, peace, sanity.

"Light is Truth, Truth is Knowledge," he murmured, as if defying the darkness to take those words from him. A few restless moments passed. He continued meditating softly, below Sorge's threshold of hearing. The warrior monk waited impatiently, feeling the darkness press heavily against his mind. It was a malevolent force, the darkness. He had never imagined anything like it. Pangs of doubt crept in. He realized that in Hel there was nothing but doubt. Unless Barsonici pierced the darkness, there was no way they would ever find Corus. And then what? Could they even find their way back? Or make the lift rise again to take them back to the world of light?

Barsonici's voice brought him back to the moment. The old man sounded surprised, almost pleased. "I am beginning . . . yes, there . . . I see! We are at the bottom of a great chamber. There is only one way to go. Hold to my robe."

They moved forward. Barsonici winced at the pain of his crippled foot. Sorge felt utterly blind. He gripped the slack in Barsonici's loose-fitting robe and held tight. His heart fluttered.

"Light is Truth; darkness cannot comprehend Truth," he heard Barsonici whispering, barely above the scrape of his sandals on the grit of the stone.

The darkness was like tar, sticky and warm. The air was hot and dry. When something cool and slimy brushed Sorge's cheek, the suddenness of it made him jerk away.

"Easy, brother," Barsonici said. "There are things flying through the air for which I have no name. Only they are not *real*, at least in the sense of living. You feel them as we pass through their bodies. Oh, do not worry for your head. The walls are tall. Close your eyes. It may help."

Sorge closed his eyes, only to discover that some flying things were real. A fluttering rush of hundreds of wings swooshed overhead. He felt them, heard them screeching all at once.

"Bats," Barsonici said softly. "All over the walls and ceiling. Millions."

So that's why the ground underneath was soft and mushy. Slime and wetness continued to brush his skin, though it remained dry to the touch. The air closed in around them, as if passing from a wide space into a tighter passageway, then became suddenly spacious again. Likewise, the atmosphere shifted to something strangling and violent. The sensation thickened in the air like blood clotting in a wound. With every step, Barsonici winced softly and limped. Noises stirred, sleepy sounds, moaning, as of souls in torment or animals in pain. Or things not of this world, meant to lay trapped in the deep places of dreams and forgetfulness.

"Merciful Aion, protect us."

"What?" Sorge clutched at Barsonici. He whispered louder. He was trembling. "What do you see?"

Barsonici could barely form words. "We have . . . we have entered a great chamber. Bigger than the coliseum in Portaferry . . . much bigger." They stopped. Barsonici turned a slow circle. Sorge felt him favoring his wounded leg. The thick, noxious air made it hard to breathe. "Cages everywhere. Everywhere! So many. High and low, thousands of cages. And vile beasts. I have never seen the like. We must leave here quickly. But I do not see . . ."

"Look in the cages. Is he in one of them? Look closely!"

"I can't, I can't. There are too many to see. It's so hard to focus."

Sorge shook him violently. "Barsonici! Look!"

The old man's voice grew dull. "Tunnels, all directions. I see nothing."

Low, sinuous snarls began to follow them as they crept forward. The voices slowly grew to a mad, cacophonous chorus. The spacious cavern echoed with the thrashing of wings, teeth scraping, iron bars clanging and ringing. There were roars, howls, and screeches. It was a tumult fit for one thing: madness. Shrieks and high-pitched wails—like a last breath given up in death, cursing every generation yet to come—every outburst made Sorge flinch. Rage. Breath- and life-stealing rage. His heart fled in panic. He felt in himself a drowning fear. The stench of sulfur was overwhelming. He wanted to gag.

Hel, clearly, was not meant for humans.

Run, a voice cried inside. *Run!*

No, another voice said, calm and determined. *Finish this.*

This was the test. The Gray monk had faced death before. Faced pain as a warrior, as a holy man. Once he had abandoned his friend to Hel. Never again.

He closed his eyes, breathing hard, deep, forcing himself to focus. The Tenets rose like bubbles in his watery thoughts. Like mercy. *If the mind is divided, Light remains single. Knowledge is Hope. Knowledge is Hope.*"

"There!" Barsonici whispered, as if it were his last breath. Sorge had to strain to hear him above the riotous noise. "There."

"What?"

"A man in a cage . . . but I don't understand."

"What?"

"The door is open."

The cries of hidden beasts turned to shrieks.

"Are there any guards?" Sorge panted.

Barsonici shook his head. "No." He stumbled, near to collapse. The noise was deafening.

"Get me to him! Don't stop now, Barsonici!"

He tucked his shoulders under the old man's arm, supported him.

"A bit left . . . easy now. Ground drops a bit. Now just ahead," Barsonici guided. "Almost there. This is it."

The cage reeked of fetid human odors. Feces, urine, sweat. Dried blood. Both Sorge and Barsonici covered their mouths and noses.

"Merciful Aion," Barsonici said for the second time, his voice breaking with compassion. Gently, he spoke a name.

"Corus. Corus of Lotsley. We have come to deliver you."

Corus didn't move.

CHAPTER 34

Escape

The Champion lay sprawled on the floor of his prison cell in a threadbare tunic, with bloody strips of cloth wrapped around his feet for shoes.

Barsonici gave Sorge a quick, whispered description of the scene before him. The Champion looked half dead. An ornamental dagger in his hands. Shackles, chained to the floor, were strangely broken. Stranger still, maybe severed.

"Corus, it's me, Sorge," Sorge called out tenderly, wishing he could see. He felt shame at the sound of his own name. Corus didn't move, didn't respond. Barsonici fell to his knees by the man's battered body.

If the mind is full of darkness, Light brings freedom. Hope is Vision. Vision is Light.

Carefully, tenderly, he laid his hands on the Champion's head, began to hum softly. The humming never grew in strength, never changed much or became complicated. It was nearly monotone, but clear. It was Trulight. Sorge, hearing the hum, felt his mind strengthen.

Corus groaned, stirred, just a little. He tried to sit up.

Sorge had heard all he needed. Like a father scooping up his son, or a friend on the battlefield, he began to gather Corus in his arms. He felt bones, thin skin. He tried to be gentle.

"Corus, I'm so sorry. I failed you. Failed, but never again. We're taking you home, my friend."

Behind, a strange clicking, jabbering sound grew to a sudden roar.

"No!" Barsonici croaked. Sorge released Corus.

Unseen in the blackness, a burly Quil sentry fell upon him, slashing downward with his curved scimitar. Instinctively, Sorge ducked to one side, spinning low to the ground with one leg extended, catching the S'Qoth's legs, sending him crashing into the wall headfirst.

"Barsonici! Where?" he cried, still blind.

"Ahead, left! Be careful; *he* can see."

The unmistakable, bright, sharp tone of a whistle rang out. The guard had recovered enough to fetch his whistle, was blowing with all his might. It might as well have been a trumpet. The alarm was the smartest thing the guard could have done, and the most foolish. In the darkness, the sound became a marker—all Sorge needed. With all his might, he slammed his elbow toward the noise. The sentry's nose shattered. In a fluid, well-rehearsed move from days of old, Sorge had his arms locked on the man's head, twisting until he heard the snap. The guard's lifeless body toppled to the floor.

Sorge no longer hesitated. He scrambled along the floor to where Corus lay, hoisting the Champion onto his shoulder, horrified to feel his lightness. *So thin!* Fresh blood ran down the Champion's skin, dripping onto Sorge's arm and cheek. Yet Corus did not even cry out. He gasped a little at the sudden movement, but did not resist. Just lay there. If he could, Sorge would have stopped the world, right there, and wept for days. He could not.

"Barsonici, take my hand. Lead me. Go as fast as you possibly can."

Surging with a new strength, the old man grabbed Sorge's outstretched hand and—hobbled though he was—nearly ran ahead. Corus made painful, groaning noises as he bounced on Sorge's shoulder, but the monk held him with a steady grip. They fled out of the chamber of cages, into the narrow passage, past the bats and unseen slimy things flying through the air.

More whistles began to ring out in the darkness. More of the jabbering noises. The sound of boots clapping on the stone.

Sentries were coming.

"A S'Qoth with no eyes in his sockets," Barsonici huffed as they ran. "The Horned Lord has used sorcery. He has given them vision."

The chamber of the great shaft leading back to the cave was enormous. The sound of the guards grew closer. Sorge felt an arrow whistle past his ear, heard it strike the rock ahead of him. More arrows. One struck Barsonici in the shoulder. The old man stifled a cry.

"Quickly, in the cage," he said, shoving Sorge forward. In the blackness, Sorge heard the gate slam shut.

"Are you hurt?" he asked. "Where is the lever? I can't see it."

Barsonici's voice grew soft. Steady. Satisfied. He was panting with effort, but calm.

"I have lived the life Aion gave me," he said in the darkness.

For a moment, Sorge was confused. Barsonici's voice was not in the cage. It was moving away. What? Then he knew.

"No, Barsonici! Don't!"

"*This* is the vision of my end, Sorge. The lever is on the other side. There is no way you can make it unless I go. Be at peace, friend. One of us must remain. I told you this."

"No!" Sorge screamed.

He heard another arrow. Instinctively, he dropped to the cage floor and huddled into the shape of a ball to shield Corus with his body.

Thwip. Thwip-thwip.

In the quiet, Barsonici gasped. Sorge heard the old man shuffling, then crawling away. Suddenly, the boots were upon them. Swords were being drawn. There were cries of anger. One of the guards leaped upon the cage, thrashing with his sword, jabbing it between the iron bars. Sorge kicked the air in vain, blind rage. *Barsonici!*

Many feet away, a sound. *Click.*

For just a moment, time froze. Sorge barely heard the sound of his liberation. Only a moment. Then he was shooting up into the blackness, cradling Corus. The last thing he heard from below was a faint, desperate cry: "Tell him, Sorge! Find the king!"

Then silence.

At the top, carrying Corus like a child up the stairs to the cave of his torture, Sorge saw the glow of a fire. Before he even saw the Bird Men, he was shouting.

"Mount up! We must fly!"

The two beams were ablaze. The Bird Men were awash in light and flame. Shadows danced.

"Enough rest! Guards have sounded the alarm. S'Qoth are coming and who knows what else. Listen to me. Corus cannot survive alone in the cold as Barsonici did. He is too weak. You must lash him to me so that I may cover him with my cloak and keep him warm with my body. The four of you must carry us both together."

Va'nya's eyes widened. "Elder, two could barely fly one. The strain of the winds pushing us in different directions is too—"

"I don't care how you do it!" Sorge said. "We have no choice!"

Va'nya looked at the man in his arms—haggard, frail, emaciated. He turned to his comrades.

"We are *Lo'kotar*, are we not?" he challenged them—the name of Bird Men in the Highland tongue. Feathers of God. It was all he needed to say. Not one of them looked as well or strong as when they first departed the Highlands, leaping from the Rim into a moonless night because the winds were good, because the L'ka had spoken his vision. Not nearly so well or strong, but no less proud. As one, they began reconfiguring their harnesses and rigging, pulling knots in the wet leather, testing it for fit and length.

It almost seemed they would make it.

Then came a cry from outside the cave. Sorge lifted his head. The Bird Men stopped, looked, each feeling weary beyond words. No one spoke. A Watcher streaked past the window of the cave mouth, circling left and right, lofting in the freezing winds. Its huge, vulture-like wings pounded the air, searching for them.

Wings of flesh, Sorge noted grimly. Laying Corus near the smoldering beams for warmth, he said, "I swear you will never have to endure this place again."

He rose then, stiffly, clenching his fist. Something hard and dangerous formed in his gut. There, he found strength.

The creature of Hel must have been dispatched by the guards. Find, seek, attack. As it circled the mountain, craning its neck and bulging its many eyes, it spied them. They didn't even try to hide. It was just a matter of time. Easy prey, trapped in a cave.

The Watcher dove toward the opening.

Va'nya spoke something in his native Highland tongue to the other three Bird Men, then moved closer to the cave entrance and drew his two jirqs from the holster strapped to his ankle. He adopted a wide battle stance, extending his weapons left and right, ready to strike. The Watcher snaked fast through the air, talons forward. Just as they were about to collide, Va'nya rolled onto his back, backward, using the motion to push against the floor with his shoulders and arms, thrusting upward with his legs. The spring action connected with the belly of the Watcher, shoving it against the roof of the cave. It crash landed. Sorge grabbed a large stone.

"Prepare Corus to fly!" he commanded the Bird Men. "Both of us, together!"

He dove toward the dark creature's head, but *mismyri* were more than just large birds. They were putrid, winged nightmares, full of strength. Having dodged Sorge's stone, the Watcher slashed back with a claw, narrowly missing slicing the gray monk's belly wide open. As it flailed, it knocked him backward. Va'nya used the wall as a springboard, leaping high in an airborne summersault. He thought to land on the neck of the bird and end it with his jirqs. But the Watcher reared its head backward, slamming the Bird Man into the wall, pinned and gasping.

It could have—should have—ended right there, with Va'nya crushed and Sorge gutted. But when the Watcher turned its eyes toward the frail man being carefully maneuvered onto a hastily woven leather bed, it screeched. *That's* who it wanted. The Champion.

It lunged toward the three Highlanders. Sorge met it, smashing his stone into one of the Watcher's eyes. The bird shrieked. Instinctively, it tried to spread its wings, lift off the ground. Va'nya, no longer pinned, rolled under its belly and made two quick upward thrusts with both blades. He did not wait for the perfect stroke, just plunged deep, burying both fists into the feathered flesh. As quickly as he struck, he rolled away. The Watcher made a sound like shattered glass. It began to writhe and claw the stone. At the edge of the cliff, it tried to spread its wings; instead, it slipped, tumbled off the side, and vanished into the cloudy depths.

No time. No breath. One of the other Bird Men jabbed his finger toward the darkness behind them.

"Footsteps! From the cave!"

Sorge didn't even look. He scrambled, tore off his cloak, lying down upon his back in the leather webbing. All but Va'nya had their wings on, and Va'nya fitted himself in twenty seconds. Corus was laid hurriedly atop Sorge, back to chest. The monk's cloak was laid over both of them, then tied with extra leather straps. It was not a good fit. Not a good plan.

They would never make it, never fly. After all this, what did it matter?

As the whipping posts burned and smoked, the Bird Men scooted to the edge, dragging the leather cot, the two men. Positioned themselves as best they could. Bird Men flew alone. There was a reason for that.

S'Qoth sentries burst into the upper cave, bawling and waving swords.

Sometimes plans could not be made perfect. Sometimes all you had was the moment you were given, and a ledge from which to leap.

At Va'nya's signal, like a hawk screeching, the Bird Men leapt.

CHAPTER 35

The Storm

Their flight—a frenzied, panicked tear through the dales and wrinkled foothills of Mount Bourne—should have been doomed from the start, except for one thing: a horse named Pegasus simply wouldn't quit. Ewan barely knew the milk-white mare, had only ridden her for a few days. But she carried the Barlows as if she carried a prize, as if the only reason she had lived up until this point was to bear two brothers safely away from certain death. At first she pounded the ground in blind fear. Hundreds strong at the start, the jackal swarm slowly thinned the farther they ran. Soon, Peg lengthened her stride, smoothed her gait. She was born to run. When they got ahead enough, Ewan let her canter and trot as she was able, even rest once. But when he heard the howls grow close again, Peg surged ahead.

As the day wore on, the bright sun was swallowed by increasingly angry storm clouds. Scrub brush and bracken turned muted and gray. Rain was coming to the region surrounding Mount Bourne in a silver haze. If they could just make it into the rain, they might elude the jackals, discourage them. Get far enough ahead that Peg's scent could drown in the wetness.

Behind Ewan, clutching his brother's chest, was Gabe. Nine years old—or ten?—Gabe had grown surprisingly quiet in the midst of all the panic and fear, and jackals nipping at their heels. Oh sure, he had screamed relentlessly at the first jolt of speed, but slowly, through the tears, seemed to match his mood to Peg's steady pace. Now, Ewan thought he heard Gabe mumbling something. Praying, maybe? Like a bird under its mother's wing, his brother's eyes were closed as he nestled in and held tight. Only a few of the fastest and strongest of the pack remained. Perhaps thirty, Ewan guessed. Unfortunately, they weren't slowing down. Once again, Peg was forced to break into a gallop. He wondered how much longer she could go on before her heart gave out.

They had found a footpath winding over the stubbly hills— probably a trail for sheep or goats on their way to green meadows, though no animals, no shepherds were anywhere in sight. The footpath gave Peg the help she needed by limiting the number of jackals that could keep up with her. Many still flung themselves over the rougher terrain on either side, but they soon fell behind.

Even so, the mare was beginning to slow—only a little at first. Ewan could feel her straining to keep pace, but the ground was too uneven. She stumbled more and more. More jackals fell away, leaving a pack of twenty or so in pursuit. Ewan wished bitterly for his song. He could have played. Put them to sleep, maybe. But no, that part of him was gone.

A gnashing jackal suddenly leaped at Peg's hindquarters. Ewan made a wild backhanded slash with Har's blade, striking the beast across its shoulders. As it fell back, he dimly contemplated the possibility of actually dying in Karac Tor. A surreal thought. Out of the corner of his eye, he saw another jackal sweeping up an embankment to their right, mirroring their path at a dead sprint from above. At the high point, it leaped, hit Peg's rump and bounced off. The mare rolled her eyes, terrified. She was near the end of her strength. Ahead, their path led to a steep hill covered with loose stone. It would be a slow, difficult climb. No other trails.

"Hold on," Gabe said softly behind him, strangely calm. The sound of his voice surprised Ewan. "Maybe this can work." He made a strange chittering noise that Ewan couldn't understand.

"What's that?" Ewan asked. Ahead, a wall of clouds full of sleet and rain scraped against Mount Bourne's high, unending snowcap. The foothills turned sudden and steep.

And then there were birds.

Out of nowhere, dozens and dozens of wings filled the air. The birds made a loud, angry racket, swarming like honeybees, diving, pecking, and scratching at the jackals. Birds of all shapes: hawks, kestrels, sparrows, blue jays, warblers, thrashers, even owls. They struck eyes and skulls, they tore at fur. The jackals yelped, snapping their jaws at the birds. They caught some, devoured them. The birds did not strike the Barlows and Peg was unharmed. Against the jackals, they were relentless.

Ewan turned in disbelief, smiling. Saw Gabe, grinning.

"Thank you," his little brother whispered. Not to him, but the birds.

It worked. The jackals began to scatter, and soon Peg left them behind. When it seemed safe enough, Ewan tugged lightly on the reins, slowing her to a canter. Her coat was lathered in foam and sweat and her breath came in large, almost desperate snorts. But though he felt sorry for Peg, they could not stop. Not yet. The footpath, deepening to a wide groove cutting through the hills and trees, offered no good alternate routes. Straight ahead. That was the choice. Or back to the jackals. The sky darkened.

Then came rain.

They were in dry, thick air one moment, a torrent the next. Like a man casting off his cloak, Bourne cast off the heavy gray mantle of clouds, full of lightning and clapping thunder. Storms in this region were legendary for their intensity and fickle nature. In no time Ewan and Gabe were drenched. The path became a slippery, muddy mess. Darkness unrolled in the sky. Fat drops formed rivulets in the rock and clay.

Gabe moaned. His teeth began to chatter. "I'm so cold."

"Can't stop yet," Ewan warned. He had to shout above the sound of the pounding rain and wind. "We need to keep going. Get farther from the jackals."

"You don't even know where we are!" Gabe cried. "Do you really think the jackals are going to find us in this? What we need is some cover."

It was probably true—certainly true that Ewan had no idea where they were, except that the mountain was dead ahead. He tried to keep pressing Peg, but she had reached her limit. Either from fear or stubbornness or exhaustion, she just stopped, began skittishly turning circles.

"C'mon, girl!" Ewan urged, digging his heels in. Peg hopped, tossed her head. Stayed.

A bolt of lightning struck just ahead, near enough to blind Ewan. Peg reared. The brothers tumbled into the mud. Before Ewan could grab the reins, the horse had dashed away.

"Well, this is just great!" Gabe said sullenly, slapping his hands in the muck and pushing himself to his knees. "You didn't have to push her so hard, you know. We were already safe."

He didn't mean it the way it sounded. Really, it was just bad timing. But something snapped inside Ewan just the same. What about how hard *he* had been pushed? There in the mud and raging storm, Ewan spewed forth the disappointment of his life, stolen by the Fey Queen.

"You don't even get it! *Nothing* is safe in this world!" he shouted, shoving his brother down again, turning his face to the raging sky. "You think you could do any better, Gabe?! What do you want from me? I don't have anything else to give!"

He kicked, splattering Gabe with more rocks and mud, then held up a warning finger.

"Not one word!" he ordered. He turned circles, looking for something to strike, feeling drawn all of a sudden to the lightning and thunder on wild display. He wanted to fly to the sky, become a streak of power shooting down to earth, shattering rock and striking fear in the hearts of people everywhere. He didn't want to be taken advantage of, ever again.

But the earth was a black hole of loneliness. There was only his little brother, lying in the mud with tears in his eyes. Ewan stomped off into the rain.

"I had something!" he shouted, clenching his fists. "A purpose. I was going to *be* somebody! Now what? *Still* no way home. Soaking wet. Nearly killed more than once. Why am I even here?"

He turned. In a burst of electric light, he saw Gabe, following behind like a lost puppy, moppy haired and shivering in his wet clothes. Looking at his brother, Ewan felt hollow and spent.

"Hurry up!" he commanded. "I have no idea where I'm going. But heaven forbid you get lost!"

Shelter? There was no good place for shelter. Frankly, Ewan didn't care. All their blankets and supplies were with Peg. She was gone, and he couldn't blame her. He wished he could just run away too.

He couldn't see anything on the path or off it. The word *path* was far too generous. Scattered trees obscured every view. All directions looked the same. Lightning passed into the distance, flickering like a lightbulb with a loose wire. As the storm moved away, it left a more pervasive, complicated darkness in its wake. The rain slowed to a gentle, steady haze. They kept climbing higher and higher, slipping, falling. Gabe skinned his knees, tried not to cry. Ewan didn't bother to comfort him. No one had ever bothered to comfort him in this whole mess. What did it matter?

Smaller creeks formed by the intersecting slopes of land were gushing with water. In the distance, Ewan began to hear a great roar. He wasn't an outdoorsman, but it sounded like a swollen river echoing in a canyon. They fumbled along. Gabe finally crept up beside him, quietly slipped his small hand in Ewan's bigger hand. At first, Ewan wanted to push him away. But he consented. It wasn't Gabe's fault his life stank.

"I told Hadyn he had to want his life," Ewan said. "I didn't know how hard that can be sometimes."

Gabe didn't try to figure it out, or answer, just squeezed Ewan's hand. They plunged through thick ferns and bristly bushes, past the flat sprays of cedars slapping them in the face and prickly juniper needles poking their skin. The uneven forest floor was squishy with a thick carpet of old pine needles. At times, they were literally crawling through mud, then over hardscrabble rock. Then sliding down again, over shale and loose stone. Up and down, with the roar of water always getting louder and louder, and the barest of light to see. Holly, hemlock, and jack pine cluttered their path, and huge boulders were strewn about, as if a giant had once played marbles here. Most of this was invisible to them, except as obstacles in their path. They had no sense of direction or progress. Ewan felt driven to walk. If he stopped and sat with his own thoughts, he might go crazy. But he couldn't drive Gabe on like a slave. He was nine. He had put up with a lot already. He was nearly worn out.

"I'll find a place to rest," he said. "Maybe there's a cave or something. I have no idea how we're going to make it back to the abbey."

He shouldn't have said the last part. He could feel Gabe's hand tensing in his grip. He didn't try to fix it. That would only make it worse. They just needed sleep. Morning and light would help.

Light is what he got, as the rain finally stopped altogether. The clouds began to disperse, letting the full moon peek through, bathing the mountain slope in blue cream. Ewan realized with surprise—they were *on* Mount Bourne, right now. At its base. As they crowned a mantelpiece of stone, the roar of water that had been steadily growing overtook them, like opening the door to a symphony hall and being blasted by the noise of trumpets and kettle Also I am told Poplar Springs Baptist Church still needs drums. He was on a ridge, with a small canyon beneath him, a cliff high above, and a waterfall connecting the two. Below and to his right, down a sharp, slippery decline, Ewan made out a path—perhaps even rough-hewn stairs—leading to the middle of the torrent of falling water. Above and across the plunge, in the near distance, the waterfall spilled over the cliff edge in slow, thunderous descent, crashing into the slender canyon a hundred feet below. Ewan could feel the pounding noise of the water like a bass guitar in his muscles, bones, and chest, could feel the spray on his face as the misty drafts curled up the cliff wall. It was so loud it almost numbed the skin.

He did not know where he was. Had no idea, except to say, on Bourne. He had not studied the maps well enough. If Sorge had been with him, the monk would have told him that he was gazing upon the headwaters of the Kinsman River. Above, unseen, was the famous reclusive lake, Avl-on-Bourne, which never went dry, being ever fed by the melting snows of Aion's sacred mountain.

"Whoa," Gabe breathed, his hand falling suddenly limp in Ewan's grip. Even Ewan, for the moment at least, felt his anger melt away. Wide gaps in the clouds, like holes in a burlap sack, let the moon pour from heaven to earth much like the waterfall poured into the canyon.

"Whoa," Ewan agreed. The whole scene, washed clean by the rain and glittering with moon drops, as if the stars in the sky had fallen into the canyon, now lay glimmering with wakefulness for the brothers' private reflection. The night was ocean blue, serene. The storm had passed.

New rain. And a full moon.

Perfect for seeing Fey.

CHAPTER 36

The King Who Sleeps

Do you see that?" Ewan said. "Down there, by the waterfall. Is that Elysabel?"

Gabe studied where Ewan was pointing and shook his head.

"Who? Come on, Ewan," he pleaded. His clothes were still dripping wet and clinging to his skin. "Let's build a fire and get dry. I'm freezing. And hungry and tired."

"What are we going to build a fire with?" Ewan said, voice rising. "The wood's all soaking wet, like us. We don't have an axe. We don't have flint or matches."

"Well let's at least *eat*."

"No food, either. Peg took it all."

Gabe moaned. He was on the verge of becoming a fountain. Ewan almost felt pity for him, but was too distracted by what he saw below. "Hold on. I *do* see lights. Down there. Like fireflies, only bigger. Let's go take a look."

They wandered down the path, hugging the side, careful with their steps. The stairs were wide and steep, stomach-churning for anyone with a thing about heights. The path made a wide curve around the open space of the gorge, with the cliff wall to the right and empty air to the left. Moonlight filled the bowl of the canyon, splashed the steps, scattering its soft mix of shadow and light. About halfway down the waterfall's great height, the stairs abruptly leveled, flattening to a smooth, passable stone ledge, maybe three people wide.

"Wait, where's the sparkles?" Ewan murmured, turning around. "They were right here."

Pine trees jutting off the cliff rose like phantoms toward the silver moon. A squeamish feeling grew in the pit of Ewan's stomach. He couldn't shake it. Something about this place felt secretive, almost forbidden. The ledge continued across and behind the waterfall, where the cliff angled back. Thundering columns of lake water tumbled over the open space, leaving enough room to easily cross to the other side. Light from the moon catching on the falling water cast faint, vague reflections on the cliff wall. The noise was deafening.

"There!" Ewan said. "No, wait. Do you see that?" He scooted under the waterfall. "That section of stone, it looks like it's melting or covered with gel or something. You see it, Gabe? Do you see the glow?" He looked around, raising his chin as if listening. "Elysabel? Are you here?"

Gabe shifted on his feet, sniffling. "Quit it, Ewan. You're scaring me."

"Are you telling me you don't see this?" Ewan pointed to the stone, letting his hand sweep across the surface. "This archway, carved into the rock, just like back home? And this strange pattern of light inside it? It's coming from the moon. Don't you see? Passing through the waterfall?" He motioned again with his hands. "See the outline?"

Gabe shook his head.

"I'm serious, Gabe, do you see it or not?"

Gabe shook his head. Ewan let out a long slow breath. He saw it. Plain as day.

He put his hand on the rock, tracing the outline of the light. But the stone was not stone, it was more like water. Not hard, but slushy, pulpy. His hands passed through, as if through air. Instead of jerking backward, Ewan stepped forward.

To Gabe's eyes, through solid rock.

For a few moments he felt dizzy, like when he was little and his dad took all the boys to the park and spun them on the merry-go-round till they begged to get off. Slowly, the spinning feeling subsided. The room came into focus. He was in an enormous, vaulted chamber that glowed from the light of the petals of a tree rising from the hard granite floor. The petals were white and yellow. They would shine for a while, then flare and pass away, dropping to the ground, only to be replaced by others just as lovely, just as bright. The floor was carpeted with fallen petals, each looking as fresh as the last and full of color, though no longer infused with light. Four columns crawling with lush green vines supported the high ceiling. Water dripped every now and then from above, making tinkling sounds that echoed off the walls. The chamber felt frozen in time. It smelled of spring rains, ever new.

But, catching his breath, Ewan saw that was only the scenery, the props, and backdrop of the play. Six Fey much like Elysabel formed a circle around the outer wall. They all faced inward, toward the tree; more importantly, toward the vessel of wood hanging from its branches. In the center, suspended on ropes from the two largest boughs, was a boat, floating quietly on air. In the boat, laid upon his back, eyes closed, was a man. A man with a crown.

A king. Asleep.

At each end of the boat stood three taller, more noble figures— more beautiful by far than those standing about the outer wall. Breathtakingly beautiful. Almost terrible in their beauty. Together, the nine stood as sentinels, with flickering wings and focused eyes. They did not flitter or dart about. They did not speak. They did not sing.

As one, they all turned toward Ewan.

"Who dares enter the hidden chamber of the Future King?" said the lady in the center, turning diamond-hard eyes upon Ewan, lifting her head so that she stood even more tall and regal than the others. She looked like Marielle, Ewan realized. Almost exactly so.

"Ewan Barlow," he blurted out. "I'm a kid. From Earth."

"Earth," the Fey replied. Her tone was flat, unsurprised. "You are a traveler then, using Fey magic. I spent many years on your world."

"Really? I didn't mean to—"

"Be here? No, of course not. And yet here you are, where you cannot be. Where it is not permitted."

"Yes, ma'am. I'll leave right now."

"No, it will not do. You have eyes and others must never know. You must be destroyed."

She spoke without animosity. Her tone was matter-of-fact. Her beauty was timeless—a mixture of everything delicate and severe one's imagination could conjure. Her hair was long and golden. Her eyes were like opals set in silver.

Ewan grit his teeth. *You've already destroyed me,* he thought.

"Chances are, I taught the man who showed you the way," the lordly Fey said, taking a step forward. Behind her, luminous drops fell from the tree in a cascade of soft color. The cavern continued to flicker gently with tender lights. The boat seemed to be floating. "I loved him once, that man. Then I grew to hate him. He took my secrets, my power, and became great on your world. I followed him there. I discovered passions on your world, feelings that I despised, yet craved more and more. I tried to ruin him, ruin all his plans. But it went further than I ever imagined. So much was shattered, so much lost. Yet he did not hate me, as I knew he would. He forgave. I promised I would make it right, no matter how long it took." She smiled bitterly. Shadows of memory played in her eyes. "I loved him so, and am ruined for it. Thus, I am here, tending to his king all these years. Slowly healing, bit by bit, the fatal wounds. Keeping him in my secret chamber beneath Avl-on-Bourne, filled with the magic of the sacred mountain, where time has no sway. I am the Lady of the Lake, Ewan Barlow. You have come here at great peril. You shall not leave alive."

Ewan hated her. Despite the enchantment of her beauty, he was no longer muzzy-headed, he was free. What was he supposed to say? *Thank you, ma'am, proud to die for such a lovely thing?* No, he was wet, cold, and sick to death of Fey and their meddling. He returned to the haven quietly in his mind, where for a moment he had been more powerful than any human in that place, yet still was powerless to stop the queen from wrenching away his song. Merciless creatures, he understood Har's contempt. He wanted no part of their world. If he could have somehow done them harm, he might have tried. But he was tired, and while his dad's warnings against impertinence might be wise, they meant nothing here. So he just said what he felt.

"My lady, I will leave as I have come . . . with or without your permission."

Inside, he groaned. He hadn't meant to be brash, though, to be honest, it felt good to say.

The Lady of the Lake laughed, a sound of glittering contempt before the coming storm. Suddenly, she was in front of Ewan, baring her teeth in a fit of rage. Her hair and eyes turned black as night, and the skin on her face grew tight. The petals on the tree burned bloodred like flame. Before Ewan could see the blur of her movement, her thin fingers were at his throat, clamping down like a vice, choking his breath away.

"Brave, foolish words, mortal," she said menacingly. "You are a trifle to me. But I must know one thing: How is it that you see? How is it that you pass through stone marked solid with our thoughts? Tell me, and I shall let you die quickly."

Ewan gasped for air. Either the Lady of the Lake was even more powerful than Marielle, or Ewan, lacking his song, was stripped of other protective strengths. He felt naked. The distinction hardly mattered. Either way, he couldn't breathe.

"I shall fulfill my oath to Taliesin," said the Lady of the Lake. "Though another thousand years should pass, none shall enter here. Till he gives the command or the Sleeping King rises."

He should have been afraid, wasn't. In her eyes, Ewan saw the immortal depths of all Fey, fathomless as night, drenched with color. Elysabel had those eyes. A pang of longing stabbed his heart. He remembered the sleepy dream, with Anna and the moon. Elysabel had given him something. A vial, which he carried still in his pocket.

If you find the king, this will wake him.

In a rush, he knew what to do, fumbling with his free hand for the small crystal bottle filled with magic. When his fingers found it, he thrust it into the lady's face, clenched in his fist. She froze, keeping him in her grip, narrowing her eyes.

"Humans do not carry our dust. Give it to me."

The Fey guardians will be forced to honor it. Otherwise, you would forfeit your life.

"Release me," Ewan croaked. He pressed the vial against her until it touched her skin. She let him go, gliding backwards, straining through a smile of relentless ill will. The other Fey watched quietly, their eyes sharp as daggers.

"Humans—do not carry—*our* dust," she repeated, not so matter-of-factly this time. Now with dread, with fear. Now with hunger.

"You're wrong," Ewan said. He made no pretense at politeness. *Never again with Fey*, he told himself. No more games, no more bowing to their beauty.

"Who gave it to you?" the lady demanded.

"I'm not your slave, and I'm done answering your questions. I'm done with you, period. Now move out of my way."

He stepped toward the center, holding the vial aloft like a torch in a dark cave. Toward the tree and the vessel hanging from the ropes. He had come this far—he had to see. The wooden bier swung in an unseen breeze. Inside, the man had his hands folded across his chest as if gripping a sword, but he held no weapon. He had thick, gray-flecked hair and a thin crown of beaten gold. His face was strong, firm—not peaceful. In fact, he looked troubled, as if haunted by burdens of unfinished business. Ewan saw no blood, no wounds. The king looked neither alive nor dead. Sleeping. Suspended somewhere between life and death.

Suddenly overcome, for reasons even he did not fully understand, Ewan found himself sobbing, leaning against the side of the boat. He laid his head against the wood, releasing pent-up emotions packed tighter than the particles of dust in his vial. He was completely unaware of the nine Fey as they gathered around him—unaffected by the malice of their will, waiting for his grasp to slip, the vial to fall. He felt none of their confusion, to see a human so overcome with grief at the sight of the king on the bier, held safe outside time. Ewan did not know why the dust kept them away, nor why it mattered. Fey stuff, not for him. All he knew was a deep, engulfing sorrow. The look on the king's face was the expression of his soul: of tasks not accomplished, gifts undeveloped. Songs unsung. Of destiny, stuck in neutral, taken as a plaything by others.

He felt overcome to the point of recklessness. He simply didn't care . . . about anything. About himself, the vial, even the Sleeping King. In a fit of rage and despair, he flung the crystal bottle toward the ceiling, watched it shatter there, saw the soft explosion of golden flakes drifting through the air, twinkling with light. He continued to sob as the shower of faerie dust floated slowly to the floor, coming to settle on the tree, the boat, the not-quite-dead man in the bier. It lay upon the king's skin, fine as ash, collecting more and more. A thin coat of fine gold.

On himself, too. A dusting of Fey magic.

Gasping, the Fey stepped back, leaving Ewan alone where he stood, as Arthur, King of the Bretons, took his first waking breath in a long, long time.

Asleep no more.

Arthur's first reaction was unexpected. He sneezed rather loudly, as if the gold flakes were a spray of pepper. But then his fingers twitched, his eyes opened. He lay there for many long moments, looking up at the leaves of the tree overhead, at the petals falling softly all around, twinkling with fading light. Color returned to his cheeks. His eyes enlivened.

He sat up in the boat, felt his neck. Put his hands to his belly in surprise. He stretched his muscles as if to rid himself of the stiffness of a long nap, and looked around. He saw Ewan. The Fey. There was no tiredness in his face—not anymore. His jaw was set. With a voice like a lion roused from sleep, he asked one question. It was a demand.

"Where is my sword?"

CHAPTER 37

The Burning Sword

"Garret?" Hadyn said in hushed tones.

He sounded incredulous. But as his younger brother solidified out of nowhere right in front of him, his brain and eyes were forced to come to terms with the impossible. Within seconds, the ghostly form of a nine-year-old boy had taken shape in the shadows of the cell. "What in the world? How—?"

Garret was holding a small pebble in his open hand, grimacing slightly. When his eyes adjusted enough to see Hadyn, his first expression was surprise, then relief. He fell into his brother's arms without a word, sobbing.

"Hey, hey, what's all that about?" Hadyn said, bending to one knee. He looked nervously over his shoulder. "Are you hurt? Keep it to a whisper or the guards will hear. How did you get in here? Where have you been? We've all been worried."

Garret was trembling. For several moments, he couldn't speak. "It doesn't matter," he finally said. "Now I'm with you." But then, strangely, he perked his ears, as if listening. "Is Gabe here?"

"No, Gabe's not here. Shh."

"He's not? Because I hear him." He spun around in the darkness of the dungeon. "I wasn't expecting to be here," he said. "It's older, but still the same. Makes sense, I guess. Hadyn, you've got to listen to me—"

His voice trailed away.

Cruedwyn, who continued to lie on the ledge of rock that served as his bed, seemed remarkably nonplussed by the appearance of a human being out of thin air. "So this is the fourth Barlow? The other twin. Nice."

"Help me think, Cruedwyn. He can't be seen and it's almost supper. When the guards come next, we've got to hide him." Hadyn turned a circle, thinking. "Give me your cloak. Garret, cover yourself with this. Stand in the shadows. Don't make a sound."

"Gabe, is that you?" Garret murmured, a puzzled look on his face.

"Not now! Gabe's not here. Neither are Dad and Ewan. It's just us."

Garret shook his head, as if casting off a dream. "Hadyn, look. I know what we need—"

"Not now I said! Hush. You're in another world. You have no idea about anything. I don't want the guards to hear you."

Together, they shuffled Garret to the back, draping him in Cruedwyn's cloak. Hadyn whispered in his brother's ear. "You're confused, Garret. *I'm* the one that's here. You're with me and I'll take care of you. We'll get out of this together. Just hold tight. I've got an idea." He moved toward the front of the cell and put his hands on the bars. He knew what he had to do. Right before Garret had appeared, the idea had come to him. Why hadn't he thought of it before?

"Cruedwyn," he said, summoning a wistful voice as bait for the hook. "Tell me your grandest tale, your bravest moment. Tell me quickly. Don't leave anything out."

"My bravest, now?" Cruedwyn said, surprised, but obviously delighted. "I mean, this hardly seems the time." He paused, suggesting modesty. It only lasted half a second. "There's so many, but I *do* remember this one particular moment, now that you mention it. Might as well swap tales, eh? Good thinking, Hadyn." He leaned against the rough stone, propped up his foot, smiling. "As I recall, I was in Befjorg just as winter was coming on. Blarmey! It was colder than a Yrgavien well-digger's boots. Of course, Creeds are nearly impervious to weather, so I was fine. But I spotted this fetching lass selling sweet bread from her father's bread cart, shivering in the cold. She was being accosted by two, no, five . . . no, *twelve* men. Maybe even more. Ah yes, I remember it clearly. Of course, I wasn't even hungry. But it troubled me that they would think to cheat the poor girl. Did I mention she was a lovely thing?"

A high-pitched whine began ringing brightly off the walls. Hadyn smiled. Ca'Libre's painful warbling had never sounded so good. The bard continued.

"I approached the men and informed them in the most diplomatic of tones that the lass should either be given a fair price for her
sweet bread or left alone. Without further provocation, one of them
took a swipe at me with his rapier. Foolish thing to do, of course."

Hadyn watched as a thin trail of acrid smoke began to curl up
from where the sword lay on the pile of bedding straw heaped in
the corner. But it wasn't enough yet.

"Keep going," he whispered. "What happened next?"

Cruedwyn hesitated, sniffing the air. He joined Hadyn at the
iron bars as a small corkscrew of smoke rose near the blade. Recognition dawned on his face. He spoke louder, more cocksure. In the
corner, Garret peeked out from under the cloak. A droning metallic
hum began to echo off the stone walls.

"I didn't start the fight, believe me!" Creed fairly bellowed.
"I was innocent in every way, felling four men before the others
had even taken a single bite of their confiscatory crumpets. Since
a Creed never lies, I don't mind telling you the city guards got
involved. Why, before long, I was fighting more than twenty men,
maybe thirty! All by myself! Without any hope of reward except for
the gentle kiss of that poor bread maker's daughter."

Glass might have shattered if there had been any windows. The
sword wailed and the straw belched smoke, but there was no flame.
Still, it was enough that two guards from the alcove came rushing
in.

One exclaimed, "Fergus, fetch a bucket of water!"

The man named Fergus seemed a bit slow. He nodded nervously and dashed up the winding stairs. The other guard began
stamping the straw with his boot.

No! Hadyn thought. *Not yet. We need fire!*

Cruedwyn talked louder, more urgently. The heat of the sword increased, but not enough to ignite the hay. Smoke began to sting their eyes. Cruedwyn leaned out from the bars with grasping fingers, ready to strike. If only the remaining guard would take two more steps back.

From nowhere came a gentle burst of air, like a tumbleweed rolling along the floor. A kiss of wind, the missing ingredient. A small cloud of dust, smoke, and straw formed, as the breeze moved over the heated metal. Instantly, the dried stalks burst into flame.

"Fergus!" the man shouted again, more nervously, stumbling backward from the blaze into Cruedwyn's waiting grasp. The bard snatched the guard's mail vest, jerked him backward as hard as he could. The man's head smacked the iron with a dull thump of bone on metal and the guard slumped to the floor. Hadyn dropped to his knees, fumbling for the loop of keys dangling from the guard's belt. After three tries, he found the right key.

"Any day now!" Cruedwyn said testily.

The lock clicked. Cruedwyn shoved the heavy door open. Garret dashed out. Hadyn grabbed Longtooth, while Creed carefully wrapped the burning sword in the cloak Garret had left behind. They sprinted up the stairs to the landing on top. Aged brass wall sconces circled the antechamber, and three passages led off in various directions. The far wall was nothing but smooth stone.

"Where?" Hadyn cried, spinning around.

"That way!" Garret said, surprising both men with his boldness. But he pointed where there was no path.

"Hold it!" Hadyn stopped him cold. "Creed, which way? Come on, man!"

"What—how should I know?"

From the middle passage, they heard voices. Fergus returning. With others, by the sound of it. At the same time, the guard
from below began crawling up the stairs, yelling, rubbing his head.
Hadyn felt Garret touch his hand.

"*Trust me,*" his little brother urged. "I've been here before. Turn
that torch holder thingy on the wall. Turn it halfway, then back
again."

No time. "You two, go!" Hadyn cried, sprinting toward the
stairs, sword drawn. "Do it."

He dove upon the guard with a fierce overhand swing. Longtooth came crashing down on the other man's weapon. They began
to thrust and block, but the other man was too dazed to put up
much of a fight. Hadyn landed a quick two-handed blow that
rattled the man's blade out of his hand, leaving him stunned all
over again. Hadyn sent him toppling down the stairs with a foot to
his sternum. He landed with a thud at the bottom and did not rise
again. The oldest Barlow dashed back up. Time was short.

"Nice form," Cruedwyn remarked, winking. "You must have
an excellent teacher."

The bard was turning the sconce per Garret's instructions. As
he did, a perfectly sculpted door pivoted outward from the cut
stone. Hadyn's mouth dropped.

"*What* have you been doing?" he breathed, turning wide eyes
to Garret.

"Kid appears out of thin air, and you're impressed with this?"
Cruedwyn smirked.

The three dashed into the tunnel. Silken webs formed thick
latticeworks of age. Mice and roaches scurried from the light. The
air in the passage smelled like a crypt. Garret pointed to the handle
on the left wall. Creed pulled. The door slowly closed, and with

it, the light vanished. In the panting silence, dulled by stone, they made out the sound of many boots thumping on the other side of the wall. Buckets of sloshing water. Hadyn heard his own heart pumping blood.

"I'm getting creeped out," he whispered. "Let's get going. Garret, you brought us this far. Where now?"

"Just put your hand on the wall and follow it. It'll wind around a bit, but there's only one way."

They did as instructed, following the curve of the wall. Hadyn walked in front, waving his sword blindly ahead to clear any loose cobwebs. They moved as fast as their fear would allow, stumbling over cracks in the floor. Cruedwyn hit his head once, letting loose a mild volley of curses in response. Presently, they came to a dead end.

"On this side, there's another lever. Pull it."

Cruedwyn fumbled in the darkness until he found it. Gears cranked. To Hadyn's surprise, another door swung wide. The blackness in the secret passage transitioned to the starlit gray of a long-forgotten library. It was evening. Shelves, tables, and hanging banners were all coated with decades of fine powdered dust. Whatever colors could be discerned, plus the sum of odors—papery smells of wood and books—all carried the dull tint of age. Garret made a low noise.

"So much has changed," he said softly. He almost sounded sad, staring off toward one corner, toward a crumbling desk and a chair. He started to explain, how entire rows of books were missing; much of the furniture had changed, or was tender and rotting. Spiderwebs and rats were everywhere. The room had an eerie, sacred quality, as if by their presence they were desecrating a grave or a Chantry.

"I was *just* here," he murmured in disbelief. "But it must have been hundreds of years ago. It was so different. Just before I came to be with you. Today."

"I want to hear it all," Hadyn said, awestruck. "But after we're good and gone."

Cruedwyn stared out the windows. "A turn of luck, friends. We have the cover of night."

They shuffled quietly over to the main entrance, leaving soft trails in the dust like footprints in snow. The door was barred from the inside with heavy boards running through the scooped brass handles. When Cruedwyn tried to move them, the boards simply disintegrated. He barely opened one great door, just enough to peer out. The old hinges groaned quietly.

"I think I know where we are," he said. "Sort of. This whole wing has been abandoned for many years. I never even knew this library existed. But the kitchen isn't far from here, and I think it has an exit that leads straight from old Aventhorn to the market in Tinuviel. That secret passage must cut across several rooms from one battlement to another. The streets should be empty this time of night, but if you see someone, act normal. *Calm* is the word. Stay calm."

He put out his hand in a serious gesture, then spat and sneezed and flailed his arms as a fluttering spiderweb grazed his cheek. Then composed himself. Took a deep breath.

"Calm!" he insisted, straightening his shirt. He donned his cloak, sheathed his sword. They stepped out of the old library. Garret looked upon it one more time.

Then, with all the speed and coolness, and calmness, they could muster, they fled.

CHAPTER 38

The Twins

S hivering, Gabe slowly gave in to the tears. He sat slumped on the ledge in clothes still chilly and damp but drying. A thick sheet of water rained down in front of him in perpetual motion—ever falling, never falling away. Occasionally, a big spray would mist his face. There was a light breeze, the smell of pine, but the sound of the falls drowned all other noises. He sat folded in half, arms hugging his knees, refusing to budge. Ewan had gone through the rock, through *solid* stone. Just walked right through it as if it weren't even there. Gabe had pushed on the granite where he entered, then pounded it until his fists hurt. He had screamed Ewan's name. Then, defeated, he sat down to fight the rising panic. He didn't know what else to do, except think of birds for as long as he could until it seemed he couldn't take it anymore.

The storm clouds were long past; the moon was full. The night was a purple haze.

Gabe? a voice said. Gabe spun around. It sounded like Garret. *I thought that was you.*

"Garret?" he said, slowly rising. "Where are you?"

Gabe? I can barely hear you. Concentrate.

The voice was in his head.

"Who is this?" he answered out loud. Redirecting energy to thought, he repeated himself inside his head. *Who is this?*

Duh, like you don't even know your own brother? came the reply.

Gabe closed his eyes, feeling a wave of relief. He had never been without Garret this long in his life. *Garret! Where are you? How are we doing this?*

I know, it's cool. I'm with Hadyn and a funny guy named Cruedwyn. We've just escaped some castle, and we're trying to get out of the city. And get this: I've been traveling all over time with Merlin! Can you believe it? The *Merlin. He taught me how to do this mind thing, but I wasn't having much luck. It's a whole lot easier with you.*

Oh yeah? Gabe said. *Well, I can talk to birds! They tell me what's happening and then do whatever I ask.*

Awesome. Have you tried other animals?

Gabe's wide-mouthed grin turned to blankness. The thought had never occurred to him. He started to answer, then decided to give it a go right now. What could he talk to? With birds at least, it helped to be able to see them. Not an easy thing to do at night. He looked around. There would only be little creatures around here, scampering for their holes or bedded up for the night.

Garret? he thought.

Yeah? Even in his thoughts, Garret sounded as if he were running.

I've missed you, Gabe said.

If Garret replied, Gabe didn't catch it. Movement at the wall drew his attention away. So quickly it startled him, Gabe saw Ewan lunge through the stone, followed by another man. The man was older than his dad and wore a crown. But not grandpa's age. He moved very, very slowly, stepping through the curtain of stone as if he were an actor entering stage left. He carried a torch, writhing with fire. The light was instantly so warm and inviting in the long darkness that Gabe moved unconsciously toward it. The king seemed very stiff in his movements. Gabe could hardly make out any of his shadowed face, except that he seemed very serious.

Ewan said, "Gabe, sorry. I didn't know that was going to happen. The whole disappearing thing."

"Right. Sure."

Almost embarrassed, Ewan said, "Um, this is Artorius. The king. King Arthur, I think, actually."

Arthur took a deep breath. The warm air from his lungs turned to frost under his nose. He swung around to see who Ewan was talking to, stuck the firelight between him and Gabe, bent down. Gabe heard leather stretching, the quiet scrape of metal on metal— the king was still arrayed in his battle armor. His hair and beard were a mix of iron gray, black, and silver. His jaw was hard, his eyes harder. An ugly scar ran down his neck, but in the light of the torch, his ghostly face came fiercely alive. He pondered Gabe quietly, memory swirling in his eyes.

"I know you," he said.

Gabe glanced nervously toward Ewan, then back to Arthur. "Um, I don't think so. Sir. Your Highness."

"Yes, I know you. I remember. It's been a long, long time. It feels like an age has come and gone, maybe two. My head is thick." He looked at Ewan. "How long have the Fey had me?"

"Several . . . hundred years, they said," Ewan replied, tripping over the thought.

"Yes, yes. It's coming. We were at Camlann. A bloody, brutal war. And then she came. They came. I remember floating. And then . . ." He trailed away, refocused on Gabe. "You were there. I *remember* you. With Merlin. Is he here too?"

"No, sir," Gabe answered. "I don't think so."

Arthur rose stiffly, groaning. He stared at the wall of water, at the two boys, with a troubled expression—a force of will that seemed to require everything around him to explain itself. For Gabe, the sounds of the world seemed to drain away. Arthur strolled several paces up the ledge, toward the stone steps which led back to the woods and out of the canyon. Above, the sky was a nest of stars that drew Arthur's lonely gaze. His hand rested uneasily at his side. Every now and then it would reflexively grasp at something. An empty space where his sword should be.

"I do not recognize these sky patterns," he said. "Where am I?"

Ewan said, "Not Earth. Not England, either . . . or Britain, if that's a better name."

"You know of my country?"

Ewan found Gabe's eyes. Something private passed between them.

"My parents have been there many times," he said. "Studying you, sort of. We're from the same world as you, but a different time . . . a lot later. You're very famous. There are many stories." He held up his hands, held the night between them. "*This* place is called Karac Tor. We came here by accident."

Stroking his beard, Arthur withdrew inside himself.

"*Credo ut intelligam*," he murmured.

"What's that mean?"

"I must believe," he sighed, "in order that I might understand. Such is life sometimes."

Something clicked inside Gabe, bringing revelation. Merlin! And Arthur, thinking he had met Gabe before. But it wasn't Gabe. It was . . .

"Garret!" he said, more loudly than he meant. "Not me! But I think you may have met my brother—my twin. He just told me he's been with Merlin a lot."

"What?" Ewan gushed. "When did you talk to Garret?"

Gabe nodded proudly. "Just now in my mind. For real; I mean it. He's here now. Not *here* here. But here. Finally in Karac Tor."

Arthur continued to quietly survey the land, though what he saw under the pale moon Gabe could not fathom. "Taliesin the Merlin would sometimes speak to me of other worlds. I didn't understand then. He said he came from a hidden place."

"That's what they call this place. The Hidden Lands."

Arthur took another deep breath, as if the weight of the ages suddenly pressed upon him. "Young squires, if I am here, I am here for a reason. Merlin would not have sustained me so long unless it were to serve a purpose, of that I am sure. I beseech you, take me to the king of this land."

Ewan shuffled his feet. It made him almost sad to have to tell Arthur the truth. "Your Highness . . . Karac Tor has no king."

Arthur did it again, gathered the whole world into his eyes.

"It does now," he growled.

CHAPTER 39

Son of Shyne

"Can't we just stop now?" Garret moaned. He was so
tired he could barely walk. Not so much because of
physical weariness, but lack of sleep. It bothered him
that he hadn't heard any more from Gabe too. Fleeing Tinuviel,
he had formed the initial bond across the miles. In fact, from the
very first second he entered the present of Karac Tor, he had sensed
Gabe's thoughts in his own. It took concentration and time to reach
out, connect. The conversation had been strange and wonderful,
then cut short. Only silence now in his thoughts.

"If they were going to chase us, they would have already, right?
But we didn't see a soul. So can't we just stop?"

The moon was a full bowl of cream, spilled across the open sky.
Silhouettes of old, lonely trees blocked the stars here and there, left

and right, having no pattern. The three escapees had no path, no direction but forward.

"Just a bit farther," Cruedwyn said hopefully, dragging his feet through the tall grass. His shoulders were slumped. It had been a very long night. "There, see the light? Somebody's got a fire going. They're up as late as us. We may even get some scraps of dinner. Folk around here are pretty friendly."

Hadyn made a loud, sarcastic sneezing sound. "Have we been on the same trip? Should I thank the good duke or Giovanni for their hospitality?"

"Detours. Minor trivialities. Pol just wanted to scare us, I tell you."

"Well, it worked."

Cruedwyn dismissed him with a wave. "We're alive and breathing, aren't we? And such a beautiful night. Crisp, clear."

"Cold," Hadyn corrected, shivering. "Have you ever noticed we travel a *lot* at night, Cruedwyn? When we should be sleeping . . . you know, in a bed? Not chased by assassins or land barons or who knows what else? What will it be tonight, you think? Watchers?"

"Watchers?" Garret piped up. "What's a Watcher?"

"Never mind, we'll be fine."

"Tomorrow," Cruedwyn announced, steering the conversation in a new direction. "We shall finally resume your studies, my young swordsman. Riposte, I think. You were strong with the guard, but cumbersome. A quick clip to the chin with the haft while he was wide open, and you could have finished him two strokes sooner." He clapped Hadyn on the shoulder. "I must say, on the whole, not bad."

"All due to my excellent teacher," Hadyn teased. "Or so I've been told. More than once."

"Of course," Cruedwyn agreed. He wasn't teasing at all.

As they approached the edge of the firelight, they hunched down in the tall grass. They were about two miles west of the city. Cruedwyn held a finger to his lips. Inside the swath of light, a single man sat on a cut log before the fire, smoking a long, thin pipe.

Cruedwyn whispered, "Blarmey my soul. Another bit of luck." He stood. "Win?"

Garret couldn't help but feel nervous all over again. The man in the center shaded his eyes from the fire to study the darkness in their direction. Creed stepped into the ring of light.

"Is that the son of Creyloch I see, all bedraggled in the dead of night?" the slender man asked.

Cruedwyn bowed low. "Wooer of Women. Master Verseman. Tormenter of Evil."

"Bastion of Justice, yes, I know."

"At your service, my lord Shyne."

Win Shyne's eyes quickly moved from Creed to his two companions.

"Boys, what causes you to keep company with a ruffian like Cruedwyn Creed?" he said seriously. "Where are your parents?"

Win was a willow reed of a man: dark-haired, fine-featured. He wore a patch over one eye and spoke with restraint. Hadyn didn't even attempt to answer his question, nor did Garret, but the serious expression on Win's face quickly became a wry smile.

"Best join me by the fire and have a bite, friends. You're likely to catch your death out here. Course you may catch your death with me, too." He chuckled at the irony.

Cruedwyn exhaled with visible relief and pulled the Barlows with him toward the fire. "We're no more welcome in the good duke's house than you, my friend. Just escaped his dungeon this very night. For some reason, your father does not like us very much."

"Reason?" sneered Win, staring into the flames. Cruedwyn sat on the ground, began warming his hands. Garret quickly followed his example. Win said, "When a noble lord and devotee of the White Abbey has a son with the milk maid, the only official response is denial. Thus, my lot in life. A father who will not own me."

"Give us some dinner, and we'll own you." Creed winked.

Win laughed. "If you can't have true family, buy false friends, is that it?"

"That's the spirit!"

The two men chuckled together. Garret wasn't sure how he should act.

Win lifted a spit, slid the meat to the end of the stick, and began passing it around. Cruedwyn tore the flesh and handed chunks to the boys, who immediately devoured their portion. Neither brother asked or cared what it was. Win pulled some bread from his pack. He passed it around, with bruised apples. For the first time, Garret noticed a horse tied to a tree outside the firelight.

"I'm two miles from a home I've never been able to enter," Win observed. "Yet I serve my father faithfully every day. To show his thanks, he no longer tries to kill me. I guess that counts for something."

Cruedwyn munched quietly. "A bad father is a long torment. I had a lousy one, and then he died. But we must keep our chin up, right, my lord? Mustn't be the man who goes blind at night and remembers only the dark."

"True enough, I don't want to stay stuck in the past." He shook his head, as if clearing it of cobwebs. "Tell me boys, what are your names? I have my guess of who you are. You're practically famous, you know? Tales of four brothers, all Outlanders. But my ears heard of only one traveling with Cruedwyn Creed."

"Got me a second one," Creed said. "In prison. I have yet to learn the story of this one," he pointed to Garret. "Tell us, Garret. Don't be afraid. You can trust Win Shyne. I daresay there is not a man in the kingdom you could trust more."

Garret glanced at Hadyn for guidance. His brother nodded.

So Garret told his tale. All of it, from entering the arch to his travels with Tal Yssen, meeting Artorius as he lay dying in ancient Breton, to Soriah, to now. For some reason, he deleted the Wind Bringer hanging around his neck and the items from Gwenhwyfar. He would inform Hadyn, in private, later. He didn't know Cruedwyn or Win at all, certainly not well enough to trust them with everything. But Hadyn trusted Creed, that much was obvious. And Creed trusted Win. By the time he was finished, the gentle laughter around the fire had turned to wonderment. No one spoke a word, least of all Hadyn, who stared back at Garret with new appreciation.

"Nice job, Garret," he finally said in a low voice. But he seemed troubled.

The fire crackled, dying down to nothing. Chunks of charred wood collapsed on themselves, sending showers of sparks into the air. Cruedwyn, for once, was speechless.

"I have not heard of deeds like this in many generations," Win said soberly. "These are important tidings. And yet hopeful. I am not sure what to make of it."

Cruedwyn shook his head. "Do you really think the legend of the Sleeping King could be true? Artorius and Tal Yssen? On two worlds . . ." For some reason, he sounded irritated.

Hadyn said, "Garret, show me the lodestone. It's like a portal in your palm, is that what Merlin said?"

"Pretty much. They take a lot of energy and skill. They fix a place and a time, but only work once. One-way tickets. It turned to dust in my hand after joining you guys in the dungeon."

"Soriah? You're sure?" Win said.

Garret nodded.

"It's hard to wrap my brain around," Hadyn said. "Even with everything I've seen. I mean, I grew up reading about King Arthur. But I know Garret; he doesn't make stuff like this up. I can't explain it. I can't explain how I'm here, either. But I am."

If he had wanted to, Garret might have taken offense at the undercurrent of doubt. At the moment, he was too sleepy to care. All he wanted to do was lie down, close his eyes. So he did, right there on the grass, no blanket, nothing. The rest of the story, the questions, could wait until morning. With the heat of the fire wrapping around him like a blanket, tired as he was, he didn't fall right to sleep. Cruedwyn and Win were discussing the implications of the news. Apparently, Win had just returned from talking to a guy named Har Hallas, from somewhere named Brimshane. Win had sailed the great lake, to Lismoych—from there to Tinuviel. There was news of Ewan that wasn't good. And the guy Hadyn talked about, Sorge, was missing. Garret didn't understand any of it.

"There's more, still," Win said. "I have friends at Lady Odessa's court. They tell me rumors from fur trappers in the northern reaches. The trappers have abandoned their winter hunts. They've gone nearly mad, babbling of strange creatures killing elk and wild gorse, even gutting one of the trappers' kin. Terrible faceless monsters with no eyes, just bone and rock and wood all pressed together. It almost sounds like a tale made up to frighten children." He paused, puffing on his pipe, letting the smoke curl around his lips. "I was headed to Tinuviel to tell my father, wrapped up in his naval blockades. He will refuse to meet with me, as usual. But for this, I knew I had to try again. Now"—he puffed—"I think I should journey to Röckval instead."

Garret heard Cruedwyn ask why, didn't catch the reason. He tried hard to listen; had so much to learn. More than anything, he was glad to be with Hadyn again. Later, he would learn what he needed to. At the moment, sleep was like lead on his eyes and brain. His last, fleeting thought was of his dad. What would he think about all this?

Almost in response, there came a familiar voice inside his head.

Garret, are you there?

Garret lay still. The voices of the men continued, but he had his own little private conversation, like a secret. *Yes. But I'm sleepy.*

Well, wake up. You won't believe who I'm with.

Who?

Guess.

Gabe, I'm tired. I figured you weren't talking because you were asleep. Why aren't you asleep?

Because I'm with someone. Me and Ewan. We're still wet from the rain, but we're building a fire with him right now so we can dry off and sleep. But it's crazy, Garret. Crazy like you with Merlin.

Garret sighed. *Who, Gabe? Just tell me.*

Gabe sounded breathless. *King Arthur! They call him Artorius. He's alive, right here with us. Been asleep with fairy creatures for a buncha' years. I don't get it all, but Ewan says it's a big deal. He said Hadyn's going to freak. Did Merlin mention any of this to you?*

Garret sat up so swiftly he did not notice the hush that fell upon the other three as they watched the startled little boy they thought was asleep.

Yes, he said cautiously, to his brother, across the miles.

Well, he's back. We've made a fire. We're camping for the night. Where are you?

Outside a city called Tinuviel. At a campsite.

Ewan said you need to tell Cruedwyn and Hadyn. He says to tell them that Sorge has gone north to look for a guy named Corus. Too much to tell, but—

Wait! Garret interrupted. *Slow down. I can't remember all this.*

C'mon, I don't have all day! Gabe sounded like he was rolling his eyes. *Corus the Champion! He's some big thing, and everyone was thinking he was dead. Now they think he's alive again. But somebody took him from the . . . Fey? . . . in a forest, and Sorge was going to rescue him.*

Where?

From Hel, Ewan said. *I don't know, just tell Hadyn: We've found King Arthur, and maybe Corus is alive. Ewan was nervous about telling Arthur this stuff, so he may decide to wait. I guess Corus may know Arthur or something, but I don't get that, either.*

Garret's mind reeled. He had begun breathing fast. Tal Yssen had said to find the Sleeping King, wake him. Ewan and Gabe had done it.

So much to learn.

Good night, Gabe, he thought.

In his mind, Gabe's reply was bright, like the clear tone of a bell. *Good night!*

He felt hands on his shoulders. Hadyn had scooted closer, knelt in front of him. He felt himself being gently shaken.

"Garret! Garret, what's going on? Stop it, you're freaking me out."

Garret blinked, focused. Saw his brother. Saw Creed and Win studying him. Hadyn looked alarmed. The other two looked confused.

"The Sleeping King has been awakened," he said. "Arthur—King Arthur, from our world—he's alive. Remember, I can talk to Gabe? He just told me. They woke Arthur from his sleep or something. And Sorge has gone to Hel to find Corus. The Champion may be alive."

There, he had said it. He couldn't do anything else about it and didn't want to listen to any more conversation. It was time for bed.

CHAPTER 40

To Save a Champion

They nearly made it to Röckval. Nearly.

Four Bird Men—one badly wounded, another weakened with frostbite—had lofted on weary wings, with a makeshift net to carry their cargo. They had flown valiantly, keeping to the central plains where the sun was noticeably warmer, and low, where the winds were not so fierce. It was a calculated risk. They *needed* wind. Yet Sorge feared Corus could not endure the worst of the cold for long. It was all such a ridiculous gamble. A crazy, foolhardy, impossible feat.

And yet . . .

They might make it. It might kill them all in the end, but

monk and Bird Men had already accepted the likelihood of their fate. They might die. So be it. This was not about them.

It was about Corus.

So they flew with no stops or food during the day, and only a small ration of water, which Sorge nursed into Corus's mouth from his leather flask. The harness they were in was too snug to allow much movement, so he had to blindly feel for Corus's mouth from underneath him. The Champion was wrapped in Sorge's cloak, kept alive by a combination of Sorge's body heat and prayer. It was awkward. It was painful. Sorge breathed with difficulty in the cool, thin air. His gaze was fixed straight up toward the metal sky. Yet his was the easy part. The Highlanders were surely near to exhaustion. Gu'mo, especially, struggled to keep up. He was getting weaker.

Compared to the first flight, the temperature at least *was* warmer. They got another break—no more snow. The heaviness of winter was still some weeks off, and they were no longer high in the mountains. Sorge felt the steady, shallow movements of Corus's chest. He was still alive. They were all barely alive.

They chose a route balanced between survival, secrecy, and speed, sweeping south along the foothills of the Frostmarch, stopping only late at night for a few short hours of rest, a bite of food, more water if they could find it, snow if they couldn't. The villages of Vandöl and Faeborg passed in the distant depths far below, small, but bright with inviting fires. It was difficult not to give up. They only landed if they could find high enough, safe enough ground from which to launch again, and then huddled together for warmth through the cold nights. Sorge would warm the stone, as before. Every little bit helped. They refused to build a fire, fearing smoke signals to roaming Watchers. Sorge lost track of time. Day and night lost meaning. There was light and darkness, cool and cold, nothing more. He had no idea how the Bird Men kept going. Especially Gu'mo. Flight took so much strength. But they did.

On the sixth day of flight, he heard one of them cry out.

"Below!"

It was Va'nya. Sorge tried his best to crane his neck. What he saw chilled his blood even more than the wind in his face. A strange looking army was marching in loose formation ahead and below, trudging across the barren plains on the same course the Bird Men flew. Toward Röckval.

"Lower!" Sorge croaked.

It was a risk. They slowed, gliding lower. Sorge saw giant beasts with skin like rock and exposed ribs. They had no face, only a mouth. They had no armor. Metal spikes protruded from their clubbed hands. Sorge estimated their number.

Two thousand. Three? Aion have mercy.

"Enough!" he cried, as the wind began to falter. He gripped Corus tighter. His old friend groaned with the strain.

They caught a gust of air, which lifted them. The army faded swiftly into the distance. They flew hard, found a high promontory, a shelf of stone suitable for landing and taking off again. They slept another night, flew another day. By afternoon, as he fitfully dozed in his cradle, Sorge was awakened by Va'nya's cry.

"Röckval!" the Bird Man announced hopefully through cracked lips smeared with blood. His normal, brown-toned skin was chill and pale. "I see the city."

Röckval was a city in two parts: a fortress built into the yawning crags of the lower Frostmarch overshadowing a compact cluster of shops and dwellings on the plain below. Low Röckval was butted up against the sheer wall of the fortress like a chick nestling under its mother's wing. High Röckval was dark stone, almost black, formed of the mountain itself, with silver banners rippling in the breeze atop her turrets. There, like a wooden crown set amidst the black stone, rose the thick timbered warrior's hall with its great beams and soaring thatched roof.

A wide, winding path called the Hoofer's Road connected Low and High for the sake of commerce, legal disputes, and little else. Yet even with that division, all the citizens understood Röckval was one.

One people, one blood.

Röckval was home of Lady Odessa, ruler of the three kithlands of Bitterland, also called Vanír. Hers was a lineage of warriors, much like the fortress of her fathers, home to the red-haired, the bear-skinned, the axe-wielder, the round-shield. Bittermen viks were revered as warriors, along with their swift, carefully crossbred gorse. They protected the people, raised, trained, and sold the gorse, tended the Witemeld, crafted metal. The Witemeld was the fortress's water supply, a thing of legend in all the Five Dominions. Never in history had the Witemeld failed to flow. It was a great spring fed by high mountain streams, channeled clear and cold through the heart of the fortress before finally plunging as a thin, unceasing plume of water to a central reservoir used by the villagers below. The fortress had never been taken by siege or thirst. Once—once!—in the age of Hhyss One-Eye, the city had nearly fallen to hunger. It had been a desperate time, a story of shame told to scold young boys if ever they failed a test of courage. Thus and ever since, it had been required that vast stores of grain, dried beans, and salted meats be kept in huge caverns above, preserved by the cold and guarded unto the day of calamity.

Below, the townspeople lived very differently than their vik brothers above. They were short-season farmers, merchants, miners, trappers. The villagers lived a quieter life with a different purpose, to make sure their protectors were well stocked.

But it had not always been so.

In olden days, *all* men were expected to be viks. All men would train for battle on the high promontory of their mountain fortress, in gorse runs on Grym Field, then rotate with others from Low Röckval. Two years as a vik, two years in a common trade, as metal smith, baker, or gorseman. Then repeat, over and over. In this way, all the townsfolk knew how to fight. They kept their blades sharp. It was a matter of survival and pride. Viks were the first to come to the call of the king and the first to die in battle. But bloodshed had not been needed in a long time, at least not for any great cause. The realm had been quiet for generations now. The two-year rotations had been abandoned. Training had grown lax. Divisions of labor were more permanent. Battles, if there were any, consisted of feudal infighting and petty tribal conflicts, mere skirmishes. Nothing noble. Nothing glorious. Nothing deadly and dreadful enough to stir a Bitterman's blood.

And so, like their mountain fortress home, their warrior blood had slowly grown cold. For generations, the clang of steel had gradually been replaced by belching and bickering and drunken feasting so subtly, yet so completely, that the Bittermen legacy had largely become a laughingstock among the Five Dominions, rivaling even the Highlanders as objects of scorn.

It wasn't true of them all, of course. Those faithful to the lady kept their weapons sharp, their bodies trained. And Odessa, by all accounts, was steadily laboring to reawaken her people. She was cunning. Wise to the times, it was said. When she came to power as Vanír, she had gathered warriors of the old vik tradition to her council table. But the majority did not readily accept the rule of a woman, whatever title she claimed. Though they had loved her husband, when he was killed in an accident, it seemed the last of their fighting spirit had faded.

Odessa was under constant pressure. Down the coast as far as Stratamore, men whispered that she should give in to her station as a widow and marry the good Duke Pol Shyne of Greenland, himself a wifeless man. Their alliance would afford her the duke's greater military strength, and thus her land could be strong again, should rumblings from the Hödurspikes prove full of doom. But good rumors and two shil would still not buy any decent ale at the pub. Certainly nothing formal had been announced.

But tensions remained high, and Bittermen were hardly patient. For now they waited to see what their lady would do.

They would not wait forever.

The army of Goths on foot had a scout in the air. It flew far in advance to keep an eye on the city. Too late, the Bird Men saw, heard it. Va'nya was too focused on Röckval to notice. Over the roar of the wind, an unmistakable shriek rang out, high and loud—like a wild boar squealing after it is run through by a spear, or a hawk, screaming for prey. Sorge's heart sank. He knew that sound.

"Darkwing ahead!"

"How far to the city?" Sorge cried.

No answer. He strained, twisting. They were still miles away. Moving much slower than the vulturous creature behind them.

The city was visible over the blur of wet, spongy flatlands, but not close. The Watcher tore through the air toward them.

"Steady!" Va'nya commanded. "Stay the course! Veer right at the last—"

They never got the chance. The Watcher was simply too fast. It screeched past, raking its talons along Gu'mo's exposed backside. Sorge heard the sound of tearing flesh and cracking bone. Sensing the most vulnerable among them, the Watcher had gone for the easy kill. Gu'mo made no sound of pain. Sorge saw a fountain of red spray the air. Trapped in their wings, none of the Bird Men could defend themselves. They began to plummet.

"Hold! Hold! Even out!" Va'nya demanded. "Fight, Gu'mo!"

Gu'mo had nothing left to give. The other three Bird Men pulled on their wings with all their might, trying to catch enough air to slow their descent. Sorge knew he would take the hardest hit. He would try to soften the crash for Corus.

Their descent became erratic. He looked up. Gu'mo, pale and bloody and gasping for air, was writhing free of his wings. Sorge tried to warn him, but Va'nya watched coolly as Gu'mo unlashed himself from the bindings. The force of the wind against his wings caused vibrations that rattled all of them, pulling them leftward. Finally, as he slipped loose, Gu'mo tumbled head over heels in a slow, almost graceful descent, falling through the air like a stone dropping through water. There was a sudden lightening of the load. Sorge craned his neck, saw Gu'mo's body hit the ground hard, forming a small crater in the cold, water-soaked mud. The flatlands of Bitterland were vast, marshy fields of bog and peat this time of year, but the cushion wouldn't be enough if they couldn't slow their descent.

Circling round in the air ahead of them, the Watcher squawked with triumph. It dove.

"*Oka'ingapi!*" Va'nya cried at the last possible moment. All three remaining Bird Men heaved, arching their backs against the force of the wind created by their fall. They stretched their arms and cupped their fists, bowing the thin leather, hoping to expand the surface of resistance. The hard shift in angle popped their wings like sails catching a heavy gust. The change of speed was violent. One of the Bird Men cried out as his back snapped under the strain.

They slowed. The Watcher overshot, coming in fast and low. As it thrust at Corus, its claws became tangled in the mess of woven straps. Thrashing ensnared it even more. As the ground came rushing up to meet them, Sorge braced for impact, taking hold of its scaly ankle like a sapling in his hands. With one hand he cradled Corus, with the other, he tried to keep the Watcher from slicing Corus in half.

They struck at an angle. Sorge whiplashed, plowing into a patch of bog, with the body of the Watcher burrowing into the ground underneath him. The force of impact punched the wind out of his lungs, nearly knocking him unconscious. The world became a whirling tangle of bodies, mud, grass, sky, foul feathers. He felt a bone in his wrist snap, felt his ribs compress in grinding pain as they mashed together in a heap. The stench of the Watcher was terrible, but the impact had left it dazed and stuck in the mud.

Sorge tried to fill his lungs, couldn't. He would not release Corus. Never again.

The Champion was so silent that Sorge feared his friend's long torment might finally be over. He tasted blood in his own mouth, felt himself swooning. Dimly, he saw Va'nya's battered form rise on shaky legs, saw him as a blur, becoming a shadow among shadows. Saw him stumble forward, silently bury his jirq in the Watcher's skull.

A last scream. Then calm. Only the sound of wind, the smell of wet earth.

Röckval was ahead, an army of lumbering brutes behind. And Corus? Sorge struggled to stay alert. Shadows crept across his vision. He had no idea if the Champion was alive or not. He had no idea if *he* was alive. Maybe this is what it felt like to die.

Now came the darkness. He had done what he could. He could do no more.

CHAPTER 41

Röckval

Eight days later, the Gray elder awoke in a room of ash gray stone. The room was spare, with a bed, a small table, a bowl of water, and a hearth fire burning cedar, filling the room with the fragrance of resin, cinnamon, clove. Pure, honey-colored light dripped from a high, wide window over his head.

His *head*!

As soon as he opened his eyes, a splitting arc of pain moved from one temple to the other, up and over his brows. Groaning, he tried to perch on his elbows, but a wave of nausea pushed him back down. A thin layer of sweat dampened his skin.

"Hello?" he said weakly, his voice breaking. He reached up, touching the back of his head, felt a bandage wrapped around and over the crown of his bald pate. An old woman hobbled in

355

with wrinkled eyes and a fretting smile, dressed in a frumpy, long-sleeved frock.

"Ah, so you've finally rejoined the living, have you?" she said, mixing relief with surprise. Her voice was as wrinkled as her skin. "How goes your road now, young one? Better? You've been in the water for many days."

In the water. The journey to Isgurd—unconscious or nearly dead.

"Where am I?" Sorge mumbled. He hadn't been called young in a long time.

"High Röckval. Banged and bruised. Lucky your skull's not crushed, from what I can tell. A gorse herder found one of your Bird Men limping toward the city. My lady sent men back to retrieve you. All four of you are pretty bad off, but you were nearly the worst. Thought you might not make it, I did. But I've had help. Got a mirling with us a few weeks now, praying for all of you, helping me tend to your wounds. She's been particularly mindful of you. They call me Morny, just so you know."

Sorge lay still, breathing deeply, feeling a dull ache in his chest, side, and legs. His wrist throbbed, but no longer felt broken. He tried to grasp at memory. Bits of thought, like drops of oil, clung together, then slipped away. Within seconds, he was asleep again.

When he awoke later that evening, the light had turned from gold to dusky vermillion, and the fire had burned low. The same old woman was there by his bed, waiting.

"Good. Now stay awake this time. I'll fetch some soup."

She left in haste, returning with a bowl of warm broth mixed thinly with small chunks of chicken and brown rice. She dipped a wooden spoon and held it to his mouth.

"Here, eat. You need your strength. But small bites, and chew slow."

Sorge took a bite, swallowed. The soup was delicious. He was famished.

"By the Witemeld, you should be dead, you know. You should *all* be dead I reckon, all four of you. But Aion has smiled. Now . . . the lady will wish to speak with you when—"

"Four?" Sorge blurted out. "Only four returned?"

Morny bowed her gray head. "One of the Bird Men. He didn't make it. Broke his neck in the fall. I'm sorry."

"Wait, Gu'mo fell and died. Are you saying there was another?"

She seemed embarrassed, fussing over him like a mother hen. "I don't know names, Elder. They tell me your name is Sorge, and that's about all I know for sure. I've seen Bird Men before, but I don't speak their names too good. Strange looking aren't they, don't you think? And quiet." She checked his bandage, peeled it away, gently rubbed his head with something oily. "One of them lost two toes already, and a whole hand. Might lose an arm. Looks like you will keep all your parts, though I don't know how. The whole lot of you are a mess. The Bird Man leader's still fighting a terrible fever. He wants to see you soon as you're able. After he's stronger, I told him. And after the lady."

Sorge took two more bites. The warmth down his throat, in his belly, felt like life was returning.

"Get the lady," he said. "Please."

"Time enough for that after soup."

"No, now." With his good hand, he pushed the spoon away. As his fingers touched the wood, more memory came rushing in. First of an old man with his face pressed into Sorge's, lingering for an uncomfortably long period. He recalled the smell, the crooked teeth, the wild eyes. He remembered Barsonici's voice in Hel, strangely calm, guiding him to . . . Corus.

He sat up, made a noise without words, of yearning and fear. *Corus. The army! Coming.*

"Easy now," Morny said, placing a gentle, firm hand on his chest, pushing down. "Just lay back or you'll wear yourself out all over again. I'm not leaving till you eat your soup. Lady's orders."

"What news of Corus?" Sorge demanded, pushing the spoon away again, spilling broth on the bed. "The beaten man with the long beard? Tell me."

"Oh, now, that's not polite," Morny murmured disapprovingly, dabbing at the wet spot with a cloth. "He lives, thanks to you they tell me. But barely. Still in the water, if you know what I mean. It's a miracle he's breathing at all from the look of him, but I don't know if he'll ever awaken. It's a thin thread holding him, and Aion's got the other end." She grew quiet, feigning a smile. "Eat and gain your strength. You're no good to anyone as you are."

Sorge took a long, slow breath. He could hardly believe Corus survived the fall. How could a man endure so much? How had any of them survived the cold? He could still feel the cutting wind, still remember the numbness in his toes. His nurse threw another log on the fire, then came back to his bedside to unroll a cloth. Inside was an ornately carved dagger. The metal reflected the firelight even more than her eyes. Her voice was soft.

"I remember the Champion, from many years ago. The last great one. He looks so different now. Aion have mercy, is it really him?"

Sorge stared beyond Morny to the wall behind her.

She said, "He held this tight to his bosom, you know. Had to pry his fingers loose from it, even as he slept."

Sorge looked at the knife. Corus must have kept it in a pocket in his ratty robe. The blade was short and wide, with a gilded haft made of many open, overlapping circles. It looked ceremonial or decorative, perhaps an artisan's piece for display or a gift exchanged between kings. It was brilliantly wrought, with a clean, sharp edge.

Morny handed him the spoon. "You should finish your soup, Elder. Keep praying. Who knows? Maybe Corus will live to eat another day, though bones to stones, I don't know what it will take to save him now. Such terrible scars! So thin. I can hardly bear to look at him. So much sadness in those eyes. No fire. To tell you the truth, he looks more dead than alive." She gave a wan smile, then smoothed his blanket. "Now finish up. I'll fetch my lady."

The Lady Odessa was radiant—oddly out of place in a cold mountain fortress. Her deep flame of hair framed delicate features and pale, soft skin. She was thin, striking, in a black, high-collared dress that melted on the flagstone behind her. She wore no color but the shade of grief, save for the countless bracelets between her wrist and elbow—copper, silver, iron, wood. Bitterland's rulers wore the mark of their leadership on their arms, not their head.

"Elder Sorge," she said warmly. Morny had gone. The two were alone. Low embers on the hearth occasionally erupted in a fount of sparks.

Sorge sat up slowly, with pain, gritting his teeth. "Lady Odessa, forgive me, I have no time for pleasantries. If you do not already know it, you have in your care the Champion, Corus. He must not be allowed to die. Give him every aid, I beg you. More pressing, a war band is marching toward the city from Agasag—strange creatures I have never seen before. You must prepare for battle. Low Röckval is in danger."

Odessa's blue eyes glimmered. She lifted her chin. Sorge saw no evidence of surprise. "The Highlander named Va'nya informed us. I have sent my son Brodan with fifty warriors—"

"Fifty will be slaughtered!"

"—to *scout* their plans. They are a day's ride from the city. I will know more tomorrow morning."

Sorge shook his head. "Listen to me, I have seen their entire force. You must not wait for Brodan. Prepare now! They are not human. If Brodan has any sense, he will say the same."

Odessa took a half step forward, clasping her hands. The warmth began to leach out of her voice. "It is one thing to bring trouble to my house, Elder. No need to bring rudeness, also."

"The trouble is not mine. But I will be rude if needed to convince you to prepare. Because trouble *is* coming."

Odessa took a deep breath, slowly pouring herself a cup of wine from the flagon on the table. Her tone became hushed. "What are they, then? These creatures?"

"It will press your faith, I fear. Creatures of Helheim. Haurgne, the Stag Lord of old, has returned. These are his servants, a new sorcery at work. Hel was full of foul beasts." Almost to himself, he added, "S'Qoth slaves, too." That thought troubled Sorge as much as anything. Quil was a mighty nation. And utterly pagan.

In spite of her composure, Lady Odessa's fair complexion paled even further. "We have felt the mountains tremble. The trappers have told tales. I sent Thorlson, but Archibald will not listen to our pleas."

Sorge nodded grimly. "None of the dominions are prepared."

Almost hopefully, Odessa said, "Are you certain, Elder? The Stag Lord? Could it be some other?"

"The Fey would have no reason to lie on this point—none that I can discern. The queen said the Horned Lord took Corus from her. I fought S'Qoth and monsters of Hel to free Corus. Now, this army. The next wave of evil is loosed, my lady. Of that I am sure."

The Vanír's face hardened, her eyes grew distant. "Upon Röckval." Something wordless and silent, like regret, rose from the stone to fill the space between them. Odessa straightened her back, her voice quivered. "I did not realize . . ."

Her words trailed away. More silence.

"Fortify the walls," Sorge urged. "Cut new beams for the gates and pikes for the outer walls. Begin moving the people up the mountain. We can hold them out on the battlefield for a while at least, to see what spirit—"

"We?" Odessa scoffed. Something hardened in her winter blue eyes. "Do you think I cannot muster the people to this challenge, monk?" She took a sip of wine, gazing at Sorge over the rim of her cup with narrow eyes, put the cup down. "We do not need battle plans from a holy man."

Sorge clenched his jaw. "I am now a monk, not always. You know this."

"Now is all we have!"

She did not shout, but Sorge felt a wave vibrate up his spine into his head just the same. Though brief, their conversation had left him exhausted. He had no strength to argue.

Odessa grit her teeth. "My husband, Ragnar, was the child of warriors, but I no less. I will send Brodan to scout once more at dawn, and I will hear his tale. Then we shall fight as we must, as we always have. The viks shall drive these beasts back to Hel where they belong if needed. But who knows, monk? Maybe it is not needed. Perhaps they journey to the sea, or to the south? Perhaps they have another purpose altogether?"

"You cannot afford to entertain such thoughts, my lady. *Expect* battle."

Odessa smiled, but there was no warmth left. "You have done a great service to all the land, Elder, bringing Corus back from the grave. You have always been welcome in my hall, and you are welcome still. But here, you are a Gray. You carry no steel, which is the voice of war. In a time of peace, you have my ear. But this is not a time of peace."

She turned. "Rest until you are well. Röckval is a strong city. There is nothing to fear."

CHAPTER 42

The Last Calm

But there was.

Brodan returned to his mother with dire news. He was tall and muscular, but dark-haired, an unusual trait for a Bitterman. He was nineteen, skilled on a gorse. Like most young men, having seen too little for his liking, he was eager for battle. Thorlson Hammerföe was with him, pale as frost. Both were grimy from sweat and hard riding. Both snapped fist to chest in salute. They were in the feasting hall.

Thorlson spoke first, flatly. "My lady, this is a foe unlike any other. If we had ten thousand men of fighting spirit, we could not defeat them."

Odessa slowly swirled her finger in her goblet of wine, contemplating.

"What is so great about them?"

"They do not bleed," Brodan said, amazed. He was still breathing hard from the ride

"They are daemons of earth." Thorlson shrugged. "Ogres, with no eyes, no soul. They are the nightmares of old. Creatures of the One-Eye."

"Hhyss?" Odessa said, rising. "Goths?"

Thorlson did not answer. It was considered a bad omen to confirm evil aloud. Brodan unsheathed the sword at his waist and laid it on one of the many scarred wooden tables in the hall. "I took five men with me. We flanked them, snuck close enough to strike with bows. We shot *twenty* arrows at one creature. Half the arrows broke on its skin. The other half pierced but did nothing. The Goth—whatever it is—did not slow, nor cry out. Though we were easily within striking distance, it did nothing to retaliate. As if it didn't care."

"They are focused on Röckval, my lady. It is dreadful to behold. The earth shakes beneath them."

Odessa stood, robed in black. She wore a cloak of dark green, with a brooch of silver at her slender neck. "So said the monk." Her faraway eyes focused on Brodan. "How long?"

"They are slow, mother."

He hesitated to say more. Thorlson was more direct. "They do not rest nor veer in their path. Two more days—three if Aion smiles."

Odessa strolled to a window, gazing out at the morning light, across the gulf to the thick outer walls of the town below, beyond to the bogs of Grym Fields. "A poor time to have traded a thousand of our best gorse to Vineland."

"Poor indeed," Thorlson said. "The Outlander's warning was true."

"Does my war chief scold me?"

"Not at all, my lady. The deal was done. But it should spur you on. We must sharpen our swords and rally the viks. The other war chiefs will not be easily swayed. Helmor, Björn, will be with us. Maybe Magnus. The rest will resist. They will say you fabricate a crisis to gain sympathy. They see you as vulnerable; they will make up excuses to weaken you further."

"They play the dagger of politics in a time of war?" Odessa whispered.

"If needed, yes. They must have cause to fight."

"If Goths come to our gates, they will have their cause."

"No, the cause must be *now*. Later is too late."

"Then I will rally them," Odessa said. Her red hair flicked like a viper's tongue in the air.

"I will tell them Haurgne has returned and is sowing lies to weaken the blood of all Bittermen, to sow discord among us. The great deceiver of old would try to deceive us again."

"My lady, 'tis true, but it is not enough. You know their loyalty is not complete."

"Tell me something I do not know!" Odessa cried in frustration, spilling wine. Thorlson did not flinch. Brodan, too, stood his ground.

"Mother, we are with you. None more than Thorlson and I. But of the sixteen war chiefs, we have only three."

Odessa turned, angrily striking a bell on the wall. A young boy appeared at the door.

"Fetch me parchment," she commanded, "ink and wax."

The page dashed away, returning moments later with a sheaf of paper and a quill pen. Odessa scrawled a quick note, signed with a flourish, melted wax on the edge and pressed her ring into the soft puddle.

"Brodan, get your brother. You and Celdor ride hard, now. Fetch me Helmor and Björn. Forget Magnus; he will come begging soon enough, when his scouts tell him other chiefs are gaining glory in war, but we must let him think it is his idea. But Lothar owes me, get him. And Jomik—his wife is not pleased with him, and she adores me. Tell him a favor to me could restore him to her good graces. That's five, all close enough to matter. Bring them at once."

"What of Dâg, Thelgin, Godefroy? Perhaps they could be persuaded?"

"Too far. A week's ride. If it is truly Goths we fight, the outer wall may not hold that long."

She handed the scroll to Thorlson.

"Send your fastest rider to Yrgavien. If Brodan can gather my war chiefs, we may be able to hold the Goths off long enough for reinforcements to arrive. Tell them their brothers in the hills are preparing for a siege. Tell them the cold blood of the viks must rouse to war."

A cool, damp cloth touched Sorge's forehead, his cheek. He opened his eyes, expecting to see Morny again. Instead, he saw a young woman with dark hair, full lips like his own. She was draped in purple.

Asandra.

There was a rare tenderness in his daughter's eyes. She held up her fingers, blessing him with the shape of a circle. "You have walked a dark road since we last spoke, Elder."

Sorge sat up, unsure whether he was awake or dreaming.

"It's you," he murmured. "You're the one helping Morny."

"I managed to meld your wrist." She touched his face. Her fingers lingered on his skin. "I was scared. You were . . . not well."

Sorge felt an urge to embrace her, but awkwardness restrained him. Father and daughter, hardly friends. A strange contradiction; like so many other things, his fault. He tentatively reached out, then froze, his fingers suspended midair, unsure what to do next.

He cleared his throat. "It is good to see you, Mirling Asandra . . . daughter. Was your journey to Seabraith profitable? There and back, I guess?"

Asandra brushed a strand of hair from her eyes. "I arrived at Röckval only a few days before you, en route back to the abbey. I was set to depart the day you arrived, a half step from death."

Sorge's brow wrinkled. "Tell me of the mismyri."

A cloud passed over Asandra's face. "It is dreadful out there. After my business in Seabraith, Pol sent two men to accompany me, but of course I can see what they can't. I know the feel of them, even when they are in hiding. But they are hiding less. Each one that gains flesh makes room for more spirits to sway the people. More than one sacred grove has been built, and the darkness is thick around them. Poor folk are drawn to the power, hoping for rain, better crops, fish. Gates are opening every day. I fear the people will soon have released many more Watchers than Nemesia's thousand."

She fell silent. Sorge reached out, touched her hand. To his quiet surprise, she did not pull away. They looked into each other's faces, groping for the soul of a friend in the eyes of a stranger. Asandra was first to change the topic.

"Is it really Corus in the other room?"

Sorge nodded. For whatever reason—time, healing, his daughter's nearness—he felt better. For the first time since regaining consciousness, there was no dizziness, no fever. His head did not hurt. Not much, anyway.

The mirling's eyes dropped to the knife on the table by his bed, half wrapped in a small, white cloth. Sorge followed her gaze. He unwrapped the silver blade for her to study. The handle was a whorl of never-ending circles. A clear sign of Olfadr.

"Corus carried it out of Hel," he explained. "He would not let it go."

He noticed Asandra holding her breath, wide-eyed.

Sorge touched the haft more carefully. "I thought it might be a holy blade. What's wrong, is it cursed? Have you seen it before?"

"Only in dreams and old books. The seers have drawn pictures. Many years, many bishops. We *all* know this knife from the stories they tell. For nearly three hundred years, it has been lost."

Sorge's eyes darted left, right. He examined the knife again. "The Severing Blade?"

Asandra exhaled slowly. "We have been without it for so long."

Sorge lifted the blade with a new and delicate reverence. He spoke with hushed awe. "Tyr Taine. Gwyl, Ayl. The great festivals of cleansing have been—"

"Silent, because we did not have the Severing Blade."

Sorge found himself thinking a single thought, of Corus, his friend. Corus had held onto the knife, had kept it safe.

Even so weak, he thought. *Still a Champion.*

He had to speak with him. Soon. Emboldened, he told his daughter, "You must send word to Cassock. The Vanír will have a pigeon. Let it fly. Tell the bishop we have recovered the blade. Tell him plans must be made to immediately revive the Taines. Then you must depart before the battle begins."

"Battle?"

"No time to explain. Hel has unleashed a small army toward Röckval. Send the message and flee, or you will be trapped here with the rest of us. Go!"

Slowly, he pushed himself upright, swung his legs off the bed. Aching, he came to his feet. His head felt light. Asandra put her hands under his elbow. The monk groaned.

"Please," he said, sweating. "I do not want you to be here when they arrive. You have no time to waste. They are coming from the north where you must ride. Stay close to the foothills."

"If battle is coming, I will stay."

"No, I cannot bear it."

Asandra stubbornly crossed her arms. "The pigeon will fly faster than I, and the message it carries is what matters, not me. I want to be here."

Sorge's face grew taut as he fought to steady himself. As he prepared to speak more sternly, Asandra took his hand in her own, cutting him short. The gesture was as awkward as his own had been, but he was caught off guard by her gentleness.

"I have had months trapped in my own head," she said. "Time to think, to feel, to hate. Time to forgive." She met his eyes. "I want to be with *you*."

The tender moment passed. She squeezed his hand, rough and stubborn.

"And that's final."

Though Sorge could not see it, by the end of the next day, down the steep path carved into the mountain's side, where mules pulled lumbering, two-wheeled carts laden with goods and road-weary traders marched down the trail for the millionth time, a rider came at last to the city, dashing through the gates of Low Röckval. He rode a gray mare, and his cloak flapped wildly in the sharp wind. He dashed past the guarded entry, through the ten-foot-thick walls—made of huge blocks of mountain stone—just as the night watchmen were about to close the heavy iron-banded wooden gates.

His name was Win Shyne.

He came with a message. He would take it to the lady first. She would be grateful. Win Shyne was a curious man, a proxy plenipotentiary. A goodwill ambassador to four of the five dominions, he was habitually unrecognized by only one, his own. He was one of those men that found news, and news found him. In turn, he shared, giving and receiving dispatches and intelligence on semi-official terms, though never with formal recognition. Any more would be too risky. Might upset Pol Shyne. But Win had a way about him. Before he had even completed his mission to the Vanír, he caught the local swirl amongst chamberlains and stable boys— five different flavors of the same gossip. News of a daring raid, a grand theft. The Black Gates had been breached. Corus lived. Sorge and the Bird Men had done the impossible, the unthinkable.

And they were there, now, at Röckval.

Of course, the news would spur him to find Sorge. The two knew each other well from Sorge's days as a warrior. Win, like Cruedwyn, traveled the whole of Karac Tor. He made it his business to know people, the right people. The Gray elder had always been trustworthy and wise. Even more important, he had once been a friend to Corus—student to master. Win knew of the fallout, the bad blood. But now Sorge had rescued him. How? Corus was dead, wasn't he? How could this be? But maybe things were different.

Maybe miracles still happened. Regardless, Sorge would need to know. Corus needed to know. Win had news for them, too.

Artorius. The Sleeping King.

Had awakened.

CHAPTER 43

The Return of the King

I n the vaulted cedar halls of Brimshane, ringed with round shields, jackal heads, and banners of emerald green bearing a single silver tree in the middle of a golden circle, Har hosted a strange conglomerate of souls. For once, he was quiet about it. What could he do?

A pepper-haired man stood like an ox in his strength above the kneeling form of Cruedwyn Creed. Creed and Har knew many people, so it was no accident they knew each other. Hadyn watched as a quiet dread hammered in his chest. He barely remembered to keep his mouth closed.

Arthur, crownless now, was about to reclaim his sword.

Utilizing the mental link the twins had established—still very weird—he and Ewan had agreed to meet in Brimshane, as near to halfway as they could imagine. Both boys agreed: They trusted Har more than any of the land barons they had yet met. Recent events seemed too strange to trust Alethes's rather limited judgment. So over the course of the next week, Ewan, Gabe, and Arthur had journeyed north. On day two they had found Peg grazing in the fields east of the foothills in the shadow of Mount Bourne, still carrying their saddlebags. At the sight of them, she neighed pleasantly and came galloping up to Ewan. That night they devoured two days' worth of food from the packs she carried. Conversation with Arthur was halting at first. He was a stern, commanding presence. But he had a bit of wit about him, thank goodness, and told story after story that left both their jaws hanging. Even Gabe was starstruck.

Meanwhile, Hadyn, Garret, and Cruedwyn bid adieu to Win, who was determined that the wisest course of action would be to carry news to the Lady Odessa of all that was transpiring. He said her land would be the first to feel the brunt of any attack, if Hel had truly wakened. And there was more, great looming questions: If a king of legend from another world now strode the land, what would Archibald say to that? Would Arthur be viewed as an ally or a threat? How would the land barons react, especially his own father?

"He will take the news of Arthur better from Har, anyway," Win said. And he rode away.

Hadyn had tried to argue with him. The logic didn't make sense. But Win would have none of it, and Creed seemed content.

"That's just his way," the bard said as Win pounded away on his horse. "You'll not change his mind, so don't even bother."

They had continued on to the fishing village of Montmarling, caught a ferry across Avl-Argosee to Dungal on the other side, through the Shimlings by Dun Pass, then to Brimshane by foot, all without further event. The reunion between the four brothers was a grand, happy affair. Gabe cried. Ewan laughed. Even Hadyn was choked with emotion. And Garret, well, he just beamed and beamed, asking over and over, "When do we go home now?"

When no one seemed to be listening or answering, he changed tactics. "Dad will be worried, guys," he spoke louder. "We should head on back."

Eventually he gave up and joined in the fun. The boys talked nonstop, drowning out one another with louder and louder voices, exaggerating every story as needed to outdo the last. Weeks and months were compressed into exhausted minutes. Hadyn and Ewan paired up, the twins paired up, then all four again. When Ewan reached the point of describing how he lost his song, he struggled, and for a moment grew quiet, fumbling with the quartz key in his pocket. He hated the cursed relic but could not let it go. It was all he had to prove his loss. Yet as fantastic as all the stories were, Garret's seemed to take the high prize. He showed his brothers the necklace. Arthur peered close, recognizing the shape of it.

"It was you," he murmured, staring hard at Garret. From him to Gabe and back again. "I remember now. At Camlann. It does not seem so long ago. But I see. You look alike, but not entirely."

"We're twins," Gabe said, as if there was any doubt.

"So," Arthur mused aloud. He was beginning to grasp his own importance. The strange quilt of recent events was starting to make sense. "I am known . . . in the future of our world? And somehow here, beyond the shores of Breton?"

"Oh, definitely." Hadyn grinned. Of all the Barlow boys, he knew most to be impressed. "You're a legend. We come from fifteen hundred years after your time, so long that most people don't even believe you ever lived. Just a made-up story, like Santa Claus or something—" He cut himself short, wondering if Arthur even knew who Santa Claus was, or if the comparison would be insulting. "That's not really what I meant. I mean, you're still a legend in a good way, but it's been so long that no one knows for sure." He gave up. "Dad could explain it better."

Arthur did not comment on the story, sensing Hadyn's stress. He lifted Hadyn's chin, waiting for the oldest Barlow to meet his gaze. "We are all a long way from home. Be strong, eldest. This is a strange land, yet—*ab imo pectore*—from the depths of my chest, I feel . . ."

Har, who had watched in silence as this carnival of brothers and legends invaded his mead hall, grumbled, "Feel what?"

What else could he do or say? Har was generous and suspicious in equal measure. A man had come into his hall wearing a crown, claiming to be king of another land—to Brimshane, the Midlands capital, when there had been no royal blood on a throne in Karac Tor for a very long time. It was a dangerous thing. He kept his eyes fixed on Arthur.

Arthur finished his thought, regarding Har with respect, man to man. "*Absit invidia*. I feel in my bones that this world is not so different than our own."

Har rolled his eyes. "Does anyone know what he's talking about?"

The king's fingers continued to twitch at the place where his sword should hang. Until now, the bard had intentionally avoided nearly all interaction, seeming content to let the boys gab away. Hadyn had wondered at his unusual heaviness. Now he knew why.

As Creudwyn stepped forward into Arthur's line of sight, waiting awkwardly, looking guilty, a lump formed in Hadyn's throat.

Eventually, Arthur's steady gaze came to rest upon the bard. Almost instantly, his eyes spied the weapon at Cruedwyn's side. Amber drops on the haft gleamed in the waning light of Brimshane's hall. Hunger, dark as crow's wings, crept into the Sleeping King's troubled face. He shifted on his feet. He could not hide it. The sword drew him.

"I do not know you, sir," he said in a raspy voice, across the hall. "But I know that blade."

A hush fell upon the room.

Cruedwyn closed his eyes, took a deep breath. "I was afraid you might say so." He laughed, a fake, nervous sound. "I didn't know the truth of it until this very moment. Never heard the name ca'Libre until Quillian tried to kill me for it. Never except in legend and old Fey tales. And then one revealed herself to me and gave me the sword. And now, here we are." He laughed again, sadly. "I'm sorry this day has come."

Arthur's gaze narrowed, as if he were appraising the worth of the man before him.

"Why do you think she gave it to you?" he queried. "Morgiona."

Cruedwyn swallowed. The sword was quiet. "I have no idea, really. Perhaps the League had learned of your location . . . of the cave under the water, as Ewan described? On the one hand, I don't know how that could be. But then, maybe someone in the League had begun to feel them, like Har feels them." He wiped his brow. "I suppose it's possible that they gave the sword to me to protect you. But if you are asking why *me*, I have no idea. I was just in the right place at the right time."

"Let me see your hands, friend," Arthur demanded.

Cruedwyn hesitated, looking to Hadyn for support. He removed his gloves, holding up his open palms. Everyone in the hall gasped. The bard's skin was blistered and calloused.

"Seems I can't quite keep my mouth shut," he said sheepishly.

"A swordsman with a burning sword?" Arthur mused. "Word would get around quickly, would it not? A most effective diversion. My hands were blistered for five years after I gained that cursed sword." He smiled ruefully. More gently, he said, "On my world, every great swordsman names his blade."

It wasn't a statement but an invitation. Something passed between the two men. Cruedwyn cast off his brief humility. "What did I name it?" he grinned, more like his old self. "Oh, my lord . . . most names I can't repeat in front of the boys. *Mother-in-law* would be the kindest of them. She bites, you know?" He patted the sword. "*Stinger* was another. Sometimes, *Justice*. It just depended on my mood. On the sword's mood."

Arthur's lips pursed in quiet amusement. He shook his head and spoke softly, "Yes."

He filled his chest with a deep draft of air, letting his eyes roam around the room to each person. His voice was raw, strangely subdued. "You say I am legend. I am not. I am the son of a Roman officer and a Welsh maid. My father's Latin name was Artorius, and so it is mine. By the grace of God, when I became king and gathered my knights for the first time, I made a vow. My soul would be the Lord's, *a cruce salus*. But my name would be in the tongue of my mother. Arthur. When I was a boy, a strange, marvelous man named Taliesin came to me. He showed me that very sword, let me hold it, let it burn me, too." Arthur's gaze grew distant at the memory. "Then he drove it into a large, flat rock, placing magic on the rock so that only I could draw it forth. He called it stonemolding.

It was a dangerous time in my world. Everyone was looking to lead, but no one was willing to serve. I pulled the sword from the stone, and the people hailed me as king. I did not want to be king. I was a boy, not much older than you." He eyed Hadyn. "Nevertheless, I was willing to fight, and sometimes that is all it takes." He sighed. "I learned wisdom from that sword. It made me great. I dare not trust myself without it."

Driven by instinct, Cruedwyn stepped forward. Hadyn had to close his eyes as Cruedwyn withdrew ca'Libre and held it aloft, trembling. Giving a blade, especially to a king, was a holy thing indeed. A hush filled Har's hall.

"You are a fine swordsman," Arthur said, observing Cruedwyn's grip on the haft. "I can tell you have the love of metal in your hands." He stared into the distance, seeming lost and alone. An uncomfortably long period of time passed in silence. Only the sound of Ewan, cracking his knuckles. Finally, as if telling a secret, Arthur looked to Creed, to Har. He whispered, "Once, I had a brother. A comrade for my soul. The finest swordsman, and greatest warrior in my realm . . ."

He hesitated, as if he wanted to say more, but couldn't find the words. The entire room held it's breath, as if that might make space for his confession. Suddenly, Garret's high, thin voice rang out, breaking the reverie, "Oh my gosh, Tal! I almost forgot, the curse! Lancelot!"

It was a jarring moment.

"Swords and blood!" Har cried. "What's he talking about now?"

Garret rushed forward, eyes wide. "Tal told me to tell Arthur about Lahns of Lotsley, but I forgot in all the noise." He turned to Arthur. "Sorry."

Cruedwyn, at the peak of sacrifice, lowered his sword uncertainly.

Garret continued, "He explained stuff to me and I was supposed to remember to pass it along. See, the knight Lancelot was really from Karac Tor, not Breton. He told you, didn't he?"

"He said he was from another country," Arthur remembered. "I thought by his accent, Gaul."

Garret shook his head excitedly. "Tal said Lahns was there for a time during his youth, after sneaking into our world through one of Tal's portals. He came to love you and serve you. But his name was Lahns, from the city of Lotsley. *Here.* This world."

Ewan caught the train of thought. Quicker than the rest, he put the pieces together.

"Lord King," he coughed. All this royal talk. It was weird. "Arthur, sir. The city Garret's talking about is nothing but ruins now. For many generations, the second sons of this lineage have been driven to find someone called the Sleeping King. You see, a blood oath was laid upon them by their father, Lahns—Lancelot, I guess. After returning to this world in his old age, he had sons. The last of his line was the last great Champion of this realm, another second son. His name is Corus. Everyone thought he was dead. But my friend, Sorge, a monk, went to rescue him from Hel. He believed he might be ali—"

"What!" Har bellowed angrily. "By the hard, sharp sun . . . to Helheim?"

Hadyn began clenching and unclenching his fists at his side. It was all coming so fast. The room grew quiet as red-faced Har stared holes into Ewan.

"Hadn't quite had chance to get to that part," Ewan said weakly. The tension slowly eased. Everyone took a deep breath.

Har continued muttering. "Gray fool."

Arthur stroked his beard thoughtfully, almost didn't see Cruedwyn, still kneeling before him, holding forth the sword once more by the blade, with the haft extended toward the king. "My lord, take it." His voice wavered. His eyes glimmered. "But you will know I speak the truth, for the sword will bear witness. I would carry this sword to my death if I could."

Arthur gingerly placed his hands on the haft.

Garret asked, "So what does ca'Libre mean?"

Arthur rumbled. "It sounds like a perversion of its true name, *ex calor libera*. From burning, freedom."

The two men held each other's eyes—a moment only they could share. Each knew the pain and price of that freedom. One had been shaped over a lifetime. One had barely begun. Cruedwyn held on a moment longer, as if he could not manage the final release. Arthur waited patiently. Cruedwyn rose, shrugging with nonchalance.

"Good to be rid of it, really. Nothing but trouble, that sword."

The blade whined softly. Creed turned his face away quickly so that no one could see. Arthur did not mock. He knew.

"*Ad astra per aspera,*" the king whispered, sheathing the blade. "To the stars with difficulty, my friend. Morgiona chose you well."

Har called to one of his servants, ordered meat and mead and alm tea, apples, cheese, and wine. They had been so busy talking that none of them had eaten. It was getting late. Garret went over to Arthur and tugged on his shirt of mail.

"Mr. King, I need to give you something," he said. "In private."

As the others began to dine and converse, the two withdrew, man and boy, to a corner of the hall near a smoking torch and a window laced with the clean, cool smell of autumn pine. The leaves in the forest behind the city had begun to turn russet, gold, and crimson, rimmed with the light of the setting sun.

Garret fumbled over his words. "Like I said, I traveled a lot with Tal Yssen. We were at Ynys-Witrin together, after you had gone away with the ladies. I saw you, dying, by the river. And then we went back to the portal on the hill. A woman was there. I can't pronounce her name. Gwyn-something. Your wife. She was very sad. She gave Tal these to give to you. He gave them to me."

Garret held out his hand. He had carried these things as burdens for many weeks. *It's important*, Tal had told him over and over. *More than you know.* He offered Arthur a crumpled scrap of thick paper and a ring of two entwined serpents facing one another. Red rubies crusted the eyes.

As soon as he beheld them, all of Arthur's strength withered on his frame, drained into the floor. He took the items with trembling fingers.

His lips moved. No sound came out. *Gwenhwyfar.*

The king's chest swelled. Tears came to his eyes. He stared in pale silence, opened the note, read it. Read it again, moaning deep in his chest. He closed his fingers over the ring. Then sank to the floor. He pulled Garret down with him, held him tightly in his arms.

And wept.

CHAPTER 44

The First Battle

Ten men with curved gorse horns stood atop Signal
Rock, high on the cliff near the flood point where the
Witemeld plunged over and below. They filled their
lungs, held a moment, then pierced the air with five short blasts.
The sound of their horns echoed in the village below. Everyone
heard.

Odessa had given the order. The fortification of Low Röckval
had begun.

Within minutes, the entire town was scrambling. Signal horns
had not blown in many decades. Wherever people stood, whatever
they were engaged in, they stopped and tilted their heads toward
the ridge. Some snickered, thinking it a poor joke, or a mistake.
But then wives and mothers began to fret, gathering food, pulling
children to their skirts. Traders groused about losing money that

383

day. Old men looked to the sky, wondering what raider was strong enough to mount an assault. Many whispered, and not too quietly, that the lady had panicked, showing her womanly weakness.

But a call was a call. Five blasts on the gorse horn. They may scoff, but no one was foolish enough to ignore.

Röckval had a system. It wasn't well-rehearsed, which meant hours were lost in mobilization. But they had a system. Soon teams were venturing into the woods skirting the mountains, laying axe to wood, felling, stripping, dragging the poles by chain and gorse back to the city. Bitterman soldiers began trimming the ends to points, then burying the pikes outside the curtain wall, especially around the gate. The spikes intersected and overlapped, designed to slow the Goth assault and attempt to fracture their ranks. Heavier beams of maple and red oak were cut to length and squared, used to double the thickness of the gates, with more to reinforce as needed. Thicker, heavier hinges were forged.

Low Röckval's wall was not as tall or thick as some cities'. Twenty feet tall, ten feet thick. But that ten feet was solid stone, not cut-and-mortared. There was nothing harder than solid Frostmarch black granite. The wall curved around the front of the city, mountain to mountain, with the town nestling in the middle on a plateau of rock in the foothills. It was a natural defensive position. Even if Low Röckval should fall, there was always retreat to the fortress on the cliff above.

No one believed it would be needed. Young men looked eagerly down the tumbling land to the plains below, hoping to be the first to sight whatever threat approached. Most had no idea what to look for.

They labored all day. Young children cried because everyone seemed to be scurrying and nervous. Older children got caught up in the excitement, as if it were all a big game. They knew better when the weapons came. Swords were drawn out of the armory. Blacksmith fires burned all over the city. Monks in two shades of blue—acolytes and seers of the Black Abbey—milled about, offering words of encouragement, lending a hand, standing on street corners, murmuring prayers.

No one really knew how seriously to take this.

But they worked. Brodan and Celdor returned with old Helmor, limping Björn, red-bearded Jomik, who helped to oversee the work. All took positions along the wall, barking orders. They had the respect of the people—enough, it seemed, to make a difference. Ponytailed Mac'Kalok was there, too, with a strip of cloth bound around his head to cover his blind eyes. Once, he had been a fierce Champion, a vik who took a Highland wife and a Highland name. When his wife died and the League took his eyes, he returned to his homeland, a Champion no more. But he knew how to give orders; he did not need to see for that.

They worked until a band of twenty men on gorse came thundering down the mountain, past the women and children toward the gates. They came grim-faced, wearing armor and swords. Thorlson led them, like a white flame. Brodan rode hard beside him.

They passed through the gate, racing down the stony trail that led to the plains below.

A child held his mother's hand. "Where are they going, momma?"

The mother didn't answer.

The eastern sky heaped up like coals piled under a spit, ready to burst into flame. It had been a long night. At last dawn came, coloring the sky like harvest wheat. A few men wearing thick woolen breeches and fur-lined vests were already working, hammering stakes into the ground, gathering wood for the day's fires, placing a few more sharpened pikes along the outer walls. The town had gone to bed late and risen early.

"Open!" a voice cried outside the wall.

Mac'Kalok heard. He perked his ears. "Thorlson."

Mac'Kalok had sat through the bitter night by a roaring fire, smelling the burning of the wood, the snow gathering high on the mountain. His hand was on his sword. He would fight if needed.

"Open for the lady's war chief!" he demanded, rising, throwing his gray ponytail over his shoulder.

The heavy, iron-banded gates creaked open. Men who gathered around to welcome them fell silent, counting. Seventeen gorse plodded through the entry, but only sixteen men. About half were slumped forward on the necks of their steeds, utterly exhausted. All had fresh blood on their faces, their arms, blood matted in their beards. Their mail was torn. They wore dazed expressions of shock and disbelief. Brodan and Thorlson rode the lead, whispering to one another, heedless of the townspeople looking on. Both the albino warrior and the lady's dark-haired son bore shattered shields and helmets split in two.

Men and boys parted fearfully as the weary gorse passed by. A mixed breed of mountain goat and wild mustang, gorse were shaggy-haired, agile, strong—prized for their stamina and ability to adapt to numerous terrains. They were not as large as horses, but nearly so. Not quite as fast, but more nimble of foot, with a stubborn spirit. They looked frightened and exhausted.

"Tell me," Mac'Kalok demanded, tapping his stick on the ground as he picked his way to the front where Thorlson rode past. "Speak!"

The pale-skinned war chief did not shift his eyes nor slow his pace. He offered nothing but the numbness of his own words. "Evacuate the city. All able-bodied men to the wall. They will be here by nightfall."

True to his word, as the sun set, the Goths came.

They were enormous creatures. Eight, maybe nine feet tall, eyeless and earless with skin the muted tones of stone. Open, exposed bellies revealed bleached bones twisted into something resembling rib cages and bent spines. Their frames had been collected from countless graveyards, the corpses of bears, wolves, murdered slaves, kidnapped Nameless—whatever could be scavenged away to the Black Gates. Two sounds preceded them: the heaviness of their feet striking the earth and waves of high, lonely sighs. It was the sound a man might make who has just lost everything—a desperate, disbelieving strain of air.

The sight of them was dreadful, panic-inducing: three thousand strong making the slow, silent climb from the plains up the rocky ridges and foothills toward the plateau of Low Röckval. They did not march in formation. There was no general or lieutenant, no war drums, no battle cry. They were a horde of monsters, shaking the earth under their relentless advance.

Thorlson and Brodan had given Odessa a dire report. One Goth might slay a hundred men before they brought it down—*if* they could bring it down. His men had been utterly unable to halt the advance of the line or discover any weakness. The creatures felt no pain, shed no blood. They never stopped marching. And there were so many. By contrast, only a thousand vik warriors were garrisoned in the fortress at any one time; Helmor and Jomik had brought five hundred more; perhaps another thousand able-bodied men had been gathered from the town, but they weren't vik mettle. Even if Yrgavien sent aid, it would take days for the March Lords to arrive.

Still the Goths came.

Viks lined the walls, swords and axes ready. Thorlson had called down the archers, given them swords. No need to waste arrows. They would attempt to hold the wall. It was all they could do. He had checked the caves where the old catapults were stored, found them rotting and unkempt, the oil vats dry.

"A windy day is not the time to fix your thatch," he had told Lady Odessa before riding down once more to join his brothers at the wall. "But even if we had two months, it would not matter. The gates *will* fail."

Thus, the horn blasts. Thus, the exodus. Thus, the cold, lonely walk. Hoofer's Road was jammed. Mothers wept. Low Röckval was simply abandoned. And now, the battle was joined. The viks had to buy the townsfolk time.

The wooden spikes delayed their advance by a few hours, maybe two or three. But the Goths eventually chewed through, shattering the pikes with many blows, tromping over. Anything to reach the wall. As the first Goth arrived at the gates, it lifted its bald, featureless face to the sky, toward the place where the Wite-meld flowed down from the cliff. A dry wind came from its throat. It began to gnash the nails lining its gums. As if pained, it raised two beefy arms above its head, two fists of balled, fingerless rock, then brought them down upon the gates. The force of the impact rattled the new hinges, sending vibrations through the stone to the men standing on the ramparts above. Other Goths soon joined around it, clustered at the gate, spreading along the length of the wall. They needed no signal; none was given. They began to pound with the flat of their fists, or shred and gouge with their iron spikes. The wall shuddered with the force of their blows. Looking down upon them, the viks trembled.

"Hold steady!" Thorlson roared from his command position near the gates. "A high, windy gibbet for the first coward I see! Lean on the beams, men. Build another barricade."

Men lifted more beams, laid them against the door, then crossed more beams between the postern walls and pressure wedged them in, then laid their own bodies upon all the beams for weight. Blows rained down upon the door, bouncing the men. More men piled on. Up and down the wall, it sounded like thunder. Two massive square-cut beams were slid into the iron framework of the gate, locking into slots in the stone on either side. The bars groaned under the pressure, beginning to bow in the middle.

"Hold!" Thorlson cried. "You're viks! Born for battle!"

More men piled around the gate, straining their muscles. The veins on their necks bulged.

"It's holding!" a Bitterman shouted hopefully from the rampart.

Men cheered. The stone was solid. Thorlson had expected as much. But the gates were old timber. Too late he realized they should have rebuilt, not merely braced.

It didn't matter. The outcome would be the same.

Whether by blows, or by gashing and shredding until the gates were mashed into wooden pulp, the Goths would not stop. Thorlson knew this. He had watched them enough to know. But even he did not understand the depths of obsession woven into their making. He did not know that they carried dirt from High Röckval in their mix of bones, clay, metal, and rock. Stolen away, brought to life in the cauldron of Angwyn by the will of the Horned Lord, they would stop at nothing, destroy everything in their path, to reach the soil of their birth in the upper fortress. The swath of destruction would be wide.

Goths had no soul, one purpose: return.

Thorlson had one purpose too. There would be no fight here, no real battle. It would only lead to slaughter. All they could do was hold the gate and buy enough time for the people to find refuge in the fortress above the cliff where the Witemeld flowed. Then retreat. Defend the road up the mountain. Lay up for a siege. Wait.

And pray to Aion for reinforcements.

CHAPTER 45

Repentance

High on the cliff, away from the noise at the gate, Sorge the Gray sat near the bed of his former master. Corus was awake, eating food, looking placeless and uncomfortable. His gaze was fixed somewhere beyond, refusing to acknowledge the monk's presence. An awkward silence stretched out for several minutes. The Champion's body was still bruised, but Asandra's and Morny's ministry had brought color to his skin, had healed the freshest whippings. He even looked as if he might have put a little flesh on his thin ribs.

"I have no words," Sorge said finally, his voice catching.

"Then don't waste them on me. Leave. It's what you do."

Sorge shook his head. "Never again."

Corus shifted his weight, returning to a hard, sullen visage, as mournful winds whistling through the cracks in the rock of the

391

fortress stole away both their voices. Candles flickered, shadows danced. The room faced north, toward the standoff at the gates below. From Sorge's vantage point, he could only see a steady line of torches drifting up the mountain. The last of the townsfolk was nearing the top. Soon, the viks would be forced to abandon their post. The next few days, weeks—possibly months, if they could hold off the Goths so long—would not be easy.

Asandra had stayed, displeasing Sorge, but tenderly touching his heart.

"I do not deserve your mercy," he said softly, when he could bear the silence no longer. "Yet, Aion help me, I must ask: My brother, will you . . . forgive me?" His mouth felt dry and tasteless. "I know I can never make up for your pai—"

Corus, sneering, waved away his apology. "I would kill you if I had the strength. But there is no use pretending, Sorge. You knew the truth then; you know it now. My sins dragged me into Hel."

"No, you've paid your sins," Sorge whispered, closing his eyes, wishing Corus would let him take the blame onto himself. Nothing warranted the torment he had endured. Sorge sighed. "I was rash, stupid, and jealous. We could have talked. I might have seen it differently."

"Or it might have been the same. I was a traitor. About to be. You stayed true."

"True?" Sorge cried in anguish, rising. "A true friend would have found another way! A true friend would have supplanted judgment with loyalty and love. My feelings for Nemesia blinded me. Made me a fool! I wear your mark on my arm, just as you wear mine. We were brothers! That should have come first."

Corus did not answer, nor did he bother to glance at the tattoo on his upper arm, identical to Sorge's. But Sorge saw the heavily scarred skin around the tattoo, as if Corus had repeatedly scraped the mark with his own nails, or the edge of a rock. His eyes were dull and cold as the fortress stone, cold as the night.

"He whipped me and whipped me, but would not let me die," he said, to no one, "and I knew it was the judgment of Aion against me."

Sorge hung his head and began to weep. He slumped beside the bed onto his knees, taking Corus's unresponsive hand in his own. "I never wished this. Lost among the Fey, I thought, never this. Can you ever—" he choked on the words, kissed Corus's hand. "My vow as a Gray is a poor penance. I must have peace with you."

Corus looked more dead than alive. "I would have given it to her," he said. "The map. You know I would."

"Corus, the map was false!" Sorge wailed. "I only recently discovered it. Neither of us knew. All I did was betray you for a lie."

It was a slap in the face. Eyes met, beggar and broken man. "The Pillar Map was—?"

"A decoy planted in Lotsley by Soriah. Why, I don't know. To hide the truth, I guess. What you took to Nemesia was a harmless relic."

Corus blinked, exhaled. "It doesn't matter. She was turning to evil. You tried to warn me her voice could not be trusted. I wouldn't listen. I was a fool."

"You were my master, my friend. The greater wrong is mine."

"There is no greater wrong than trading your honor. She seduced me . . . for a map."

The room fell silent except for the snapping of the fire, the whistling wind. In the distance, there was another blast of horns. The polished stone floor became a mirror in which Sorge glimpsed his own face, like looking into the past. A memory teased the deep places of his mind. Of kneeling in a grassy circle of trees where a raven-haired woman struggled for life. He had once loved this woman—they had a daughter—but she came to love another. Dangling over a crater in the earth, she had given him a message. Her eyes had pled with his.

Tell Corus . . . Nemesia remains true. Tell Corus.

"It wasn't only for the map," Sorge said in a dry voice. "She loved you, I think."

Too many words. None seemed adequate to bridge the chasm between the two men, and more would only be futile. The ache, the pang of loss, gathered like a knot in Sorge's belly. He looked upon the shell of his friend's body, racked with years of suffering. And for what? Because Sorge had chosen the path of revenge. Nemesia's heart had turned to Corus, away from him. Jealous and blind, proud and rejected, he had given Corus to the Fey Queen. To protect the map from a Champion on the verge of defection—or so he had told himself twenty years ago. He had tried to persuade his friend that Nemesia was turning to the dark arts.

"Her heart is not true," he had told Corus, facing one another on a starry night.

By then it was too late. There was too much mistrust, too much bad blood. Since he could not best Corus in battle, he struck a deal with the Fey, and for twenty years, had assuaged his guilt by publicly maintaining the illusion of Corus's honor. Mourn the last great Champion! No one had to know what had really happened.

But now? Corus was rescued to a city under siege. It all seemed so pointless.

"Beasts from Hel have come to the city," he told him, not knowing what else to do.

Corus took a sip of water from a wooden cup near his bed. He rang a bell. A few minutes later, Morny came bustling in with a bowl of soup. She looked nervous, scattered. Corus took only two small sips before setting the bowl down.

"They are Goths," he said without emotion. "I have seen them. The Horned Lord will make thousands and tens of thousands, until there are no more bones in the earth. The pits of Angwyn will never sleep."

Sorge waited until Morny had departed again. "The viks do not know what to do. I spoke with Odessa today, with her war chief. I can see the fear. All the people are frightened."

"They should be. Soon they will die."

Sorge paced a slow circle around the room once, twice, feeling sick to his stomach. There was another matter. He didn't want to speak it, but Corus needed to know about the Sleeping King. It seemed cruel. The monk tried to think of another way, a better time.

"Artorius has been found," he said at last. "The Sleeping King. I received word from the Duke of Greenland's son earlier today. They call him Arthur. He is with Har Hallas as we speak."

He didn't dare face Corus, couldn't. To hear those words, he knew the color and energy of the room had drained away. But the Champion woodenly adjusted himself on the bed.

Just one more pain.

Sorge opened the door, dangling a soft-spoken challenge in the air.

"In case you need a reason to live."

Just one more pain.

Corus flung his bowl of soup across the room. It shattered on the wall, splattering broth and bits of chicken. "Do you think," he shouted, "by telling me of the Sleeping King I shall rise and draw my sword and fight evil again? Swine! Son of a rabid hog! Do not ever call me master or friend again! Would that you could rot in Hel as I have! Then speak to me of the price of living!" He reached for his cup of water and flung it also. The strain of the motion sent pain like a spasm across his face. He collapsed back onto the bed, panting. "Never enter this room again, Sorge," he said bitterly. "Let the world forget me. My battles are done. I will not forgive you for sentencing me to Hel, nor for rescuing me from it. You should not have done either."

Sorge closed the door behind him, stood in the hall for a long time. How does a man survive the collapse of his entire life? How does he recover? From inside the walls, behind the door, Sorge listened for sound. But there was no weeping. No rage. Only the silence of stone.

Sorge limped away.

CHAPTER 46

Things That Change

The silvery creature floating in the air resembled a flame flickering in the wind. Elysabel's wings flitted and sparkled like a bumblebee, catching gossamer arrows of light shooting through the foliage overhead. At any other time, she would have been beautiful to look upon. But now her hair was sickly yellow. Her eyes were downcast. She trembled. Thousands of hard, angry faces surrounded her, their hair all dark—dark purple, brown, black.

Before her, the queen rose to her full height with judgment etched on her elfin face. Deep, booming drums filled Fey Haven with a cadence of doom. All voices were silent.

Marielle drew near to Elysabel. Her ethereal beauty was winter cold and haughty.

"One of our own!" she cried aloud, turning a slow circle to encompass the outer ring of Fey with her angry gaze. "One of our own is a traitor!"

The crowd gasped. Their hair moved in the air as in water.

"The pixie Elysabel stands accused of fraternizing with humans to the harm of the haven. She led the boy who can see to the secret place of my mother's dwelling, where the Sleeping King has been kept for hundreds of years. She betrayed our secrets. She gave faerie dust to a mortal. She has done forbidden things. Do you deny any of this, Elysabel?"

Elysabel kept her eyes lowered to the ground.

"No."

Another gasp. The assembly erupted in rage. Marielle calmed them with an imperious wave of her hand. "Do you have any excuse? Any justification? Any reason by which I should offer you mercy or understanding?"

The only noise was the beating of Elysabel's shimmering wings. She thought a moment, raised her head, straightened her back. For a brief moment, her hair turned from sickly yellow to brilliant gold.

"You took his music. You took his soul. It was music more beautiful than even Fey could create. He did nothing to deserve it. You stole from him, so I stole from you. It is only fair."

Marielle grew dark with power. Her voice dropped to a smooth, deadly whisper.

"Be still," she commanded.

Elysabel grew still. Something unseen pulled her to the ground. The queen stretched out her hands, taking hold of the base of

Elysabel's wings where they joined at the scapula. Her eyes were a pale fire.

"You are Shorn," she hissed, then thrust her arms brutally downward, tearing with all her might. The ring of faces winced. Elysabel cried out as her wings broke from her body. Silver blood ran down her back, dripped from the wings. Marielle tossed them to the ground, pointing to the distance with a slender finger.

"Away," she said. "Forever."

"What do we do next?" Gabe asked.

It was morning in Brimshane, and the wind blowing from the north was cold. Arthur had been given a high honor—lodging in Har's own bedroom. The legendary king had retired to a long, lonely night clutching the letter and ring, the last tokens of love from a life that seemed at once so vivid in his mind and so lost in his dreams. He had not yet shown his face to the new day. Suddenly, the legend seemed more like a frail, old man.

"First thing, we need to find Sorge," Ewan insisted, chewing on a mouthful of scrambled eggs. They sat at a long table in the earl's expansive kitchen, a warm fire and a breakfast of eggs, cold beans, and thick slabs of salty bacon laid out before them. "We don't know if he's made it . . . if he found Corus or if Corus was alive. But I guarantee you, he was bound and determined. Next thing is we find Flogg. And then get Arthur and Corus together. Get Archibald to let Arthur take his place and finally get something done around here. Rally the people, build an army. Save the planet. It's that easy."

He grinned. The eggs tasted so good.

Hadyn rolled his eyes. He had a better idea. "Maybe we could use Gabe's power?"

"The mighty L'ka?" Ewan teased. "What do they call you again?"

"Wingtalker." Gabe grinned. "Hey, we need to find out about Va'nya, too, you know."

As one they realized how much there was to do, how large the task. They had each become attached—in one way or another—to someone or something in this strange new world.

"I'm thinking the birds could speed up the process," Hadyn explained.

"Okay, I'll bite," Ewan said. "How?"

"We could eat them," Cruedwyn suggested playfully. "It would sure make hunting easier if *they* came to us."

He was in surprisingly good spirits after giving his sword to Arthur. Maybe it was relief. Maybe it was all an act. Either way, Gabe looked horrified at his suggestion.

"Gotcha!" Creed smiled. "No worries, friend."

Hadyn groped for words. "I don't have it all figured out yet, just an idea. You see—wait, what are we going to call that thing you do, Gabe? The talk-to-birds-stuff? I need a name."

Hadyn, naming. It couldn't be helped.

"Birdspeech?" Gabe proposed.

"Good, let's call it Birdspeech. That'll be easier."

Garret had been sitting quietly, picking at his food. Cruedwyn leaned over.

"You okay, little friend?" he said softly.

"When can we go home?" Garret didn't look up from his plate, but tears welled in his eyes. Wind power was cool and all, but couldn't take the place of Dad. Of all the boys, Garret had formed his bonds with Karac Tor mainly through Tal . . . on *Earth*.

Creed laid a comforting hand on his shoulder.

"Listen to me," he answered. "We have not forgotten. The friends you have made—Sorge, Har, me—we will find a way. I promise."

The other boys continued to talk. Har eventually joined them, stomping into the room like a grizzly roused from hibernation, growling about another band of Fey roaming his borders, turning a village's milk green. Arthur was left to sort out his private pain. No one troubled him, mainly because no one knew quite what to do with him. The legends spoke of a sleeping king, but what then? What was he here for? The fact that Morgiona had referred to him as the Future King didn't help make things any clearer.

Hadyn put his arm around Garret. "I know it feels scary. But we're together. Remember that."

They did. They all remembered. It had been a strange journey. Four Calls, four brothers. In a wave of fresh emotion, the reality of this strange new life settled upon them all with a sudden chill, and no one wanted to talk anymore.

"I have a weird feeling, a bad feeling," Gabe said. "Like it's about to get worse."

Invisible to their eyes, but almost due north of Brimshane at that very moment, a messenger pigeon lofted in the cold mountain winds, flapping hard toward the reclusive Black Abbey. White as the snow beneath her, she carried a note of thin, brittle rice paper carefully rolled and stuffed into a tiny tin tube tied to her leg. A message from Asandra the mirling, composed at her father's side as Goths pressed against Low Röckval:

> *Corus rescued alive. Sleeping King awakened.*
> *Consult Ravna—'Blade Which Breaks'—we have.*
> *Taines must be renewed. Anoint, attack.*
> *Röckval under siege.*

Against a flurry of wind and snow, the bird winged her way east. Cassock, Bishop of the Black Abbey, would understand the import of the words all too well.

Groaning loudly from a long night of brutal pounding, the interior bars of the gate suddenly cracked. The thick, wooden planks splintered.

It was dawn.

The men of Röckval had toiled all night, taking shifts at the gate, dropping heavy stones from the ramparts. A few Goths were laid upon the ground from having their heads bashed in. Then, late in the night, Brodan had commanded that all extra beams be dropped over the wall in front of the gate to try to clog the path, to make the Goths' footing uncertain. If they could not stop them, perhaps they could slow them. And so they did. It had been another long night.

Come dawn, the Goths came crashing through anyway. Men cried out, slashing with their swords. Thorlson blew his horn to sound the retreat up the mountain, not before five men were felled by the deadly first wave entering the city. The rest escaped easily enough. Goths were slow, and the gate allowed only four abreast. Now the viks would have to hold Hoofer's Road.

Fortunately, holding the road was the basis of High Röckval's defense. They had many tactics. Above all, they had Kveld's Fence.

Thorlson looked at his men. They were weary, and there would be little rest for them anytime soon. He could see their fear. They had the look of men expecting to die soon.

In Corus's room high above, Morny described the scene to the Champion as she gazed down toward the gate, fretfully pulling on a handkerchief. She saw the gates yield, saw the Goths enter, the men flee. From here, they looked so small.

"Like wild rabbits," she muttered nervously. "But the pass is steep. It'll keep them. It'll have to."

She spread his tray of toast, butter, more soup. Thicker soup this time. Meatier. Then bustled off, using busyness as a distraction, leaving Corus to the silence of his room. In the far distance, he heard the muffled voices of the men below.

It was a strange thing to be alive. No more whipping post. No more cage surrounded by growling beasts in the blindness of Hel. No more taunting. No more frozen nights on the cliff.

No more Kr'Nunos. And somewhere . . . Arthur. Awakened.

Corus shook his head. He was alive. Against all odds, he was alive. For what?

If you need a reason to live, maybe that is it.

He had scoffed at escape. Thought it impossible to sprout wings, fly away. Then wings came for him, and he flew. How could it be so easy? But that was too easy. He had endured too much. Nothing could ever be that easy again. Living was a curse, freedom a punishment; different than the curse of whips and chains, but equal. And there, pressed right up against that realization, came the echo of another voice, vile and bitter, tempting him with words as sweet as honey.

Find the king. Destroy him. No one would ever have to know.

Corus wanted peace, wanted to simply forget everything. He had lain in bed for many days now, gaining a little bit of strength, fighting nightmares. Wishing he were dead. His soul was a tangle of thorns.

Sorge!

The shame of his past came rushing at him like a flood breaking a levee. The secret he could not tell, that had cost him twenty years of his life—that once he nearly yielded the honor of his name for the love of a witch—had been safe in the prison of Hel. As much as he hated Sorge, as much as he nursed the desire to kill him and finally take his revenge, he also could not shake a simple fact: he *deserved* Kr'Nunos's lash. Every cruel day and every long night, he deserved.

No, he was no Champion. Not anymore, maybe not ever.

But he was still a second son of Lotsley, and while reputations changed, curses did not.

The juxtaposition of his fate seemed irreconcilable. How dare Sorge taunt him with redemption! What did he want? What did *anyone* want from him? Had he not paid the price of his folly, in blood no less? Was he not older, scarred, made frail with suffering?

And yet, how can a man escape his destiny?

There upon his bed, his own words rose from the shadows of Hel to trouble him. He felt again the clarity in his own mind. One brief moment, weeks ago, when his strength had risen to challenge the Horned Lord. A moment without despair or shame. A moment of knowing.

One day I shall stand beside a king, he had said, bleeding. *The land will unite, and you will fall.* A voice. From a cave of torment. His own. In that moment, he had thought, *If I must suffer, then so be it.*

And he had suffered. He clenched his fist over and over, feeling rage, fear. He felt trapped in his room, as the walls closed in upon him. All he wanted to do was die. But something in his blood refused to yield.

"Morny!" he shouted. "Morny!"

Eventually, the old woman came.

"Get Thorlson. Get Odessa," he growled. He sat up slowly, put his feet on the floor. He was weak, thin, pale, unshaven. He winced at the effort of movement. His entire body ached.

"Find a boy, too. Tell him to run to the armory and bring me a sword. A good sword."

The Champion shifted his weight, rose to his feet. There was nothing to do but to do it. Do something. War was all he knew. With that thought, he reached for the bowl of soup, tilted his head, and drank it all in one swallow.

"More," he said. Morny hurried off.

CHAPTER 47

The Lodestone

For the twentieth time, Reggie Barlow made his way through the woods, across the fields to the briar patch. He wore a heavy coat, gloves, a scarf, and his breath made a cloud in the air under his runny nose. It was four days until Thanksgiving. He was still battling some sinus thing, hadn't slept in two days. The weekend had come and gone. Hadyn, Ewan— now Garret and Gabe—gone.

He was going crazy.

A dozen times, he had picked up the phone to call the police. Had pressed nine, then one . . . then paused, fingers quivering over the dial pad. He never added the last one. What would he tell the police, anyway? There was no kidnapping. He knew that. The boys had been asleep in his house. No break-in. No mess in their rooms. Over and over, a single thought played itself out in his mind.

Not my boys, not my boys.

Already, Anna had been taken from him, to a land he could not visit. Now this. Why had he been so stubborn? He had *insisted* they come to this place, buy this land, even when he knew the boys didn't want to move away from their friends. Hadyn had found the runestone, just as the old Viking map had indicated. But what was it? What did the runes mean? What had happened to his sons?

Calm, breathe. Stay calm.

Not a chance. All over again, Reggie began to choke on his own fear.

He sped up his pace, found the briar patch, the tunnels. He fought back a wave of nausea in his stomach, a film of tears in his eyes. He had not seen his boys for two days now. The house was a grave of silence. What in the world had he caused?

The tunnel mocked him. He bent low, crawled to the back. His flashlight illuminated the arch, the strange runes.

"What have you done with my boys?!" he shouted at the rock, striking the surface with the flat of his palm. He bent over double, pounded the earth. His body began to convulse with tears.

Anna, I'm sorry!

He could not live alone. Anger rose inside, demanding release. He began to claw at the ground, grasping handfuls of dead, moldy leaves. He could *not* live alone! A fury rose inside, a desperation. The last time he had felt such intense emotion was the night Anna breathed her last. It was the last time he had felt anything, really. That night he had discovered a vast canyon of darkness inside, a bottomless pit. Now, before the runestone, he felt himself falling into it again.

It was not good for man to live alone. After Anna died, at least he had his sons. He was so proud of his boys. *No!*

He clawed and scratched and tore at the cold, damp soil beneath the arch, like a wild man, possessed. Like a dog, growling at the earth. He used the handle of his flashlight as a shovel. He tore at branches, clawed the stone. Dug deeper. All random—no point, no meaning.

Thunk.

A sound. What sound? Something in the earth. Reggie paused, wiped his tears with a dirty hand, streaking his face with mud. Something metal, no . . . ceramic? He traced the edges with his finger, scraped away the dirt, lifting a small, fired-clay vase out of the earth. It was whole, and the top was plugged with something thick and waxy. It was very old, not cracked. Waterproof from the wax. Not Indian, but European. He recognized the design. Scandinavian, perhaps? He didn't care. He struck it against the arch of the runestone. The vase shattered, and he heard two things hit the earth. He shined his light. Felt his heart stop.

Impossible.

It had been a Christmas gift, last year. *Last year.* To Garret, who loved the Chiefs. They all loved the Chiefs. A way of remembering Anna, mom's favorite team. He stared at the same watch. The face was cracked. The leather band was crumbly and dry.

Reggie had to remind himself to put air into his lungs, then push it out.

It was Garret's watch. Buried for hundreds of years.

He stared in disbelief. Picked up the watch. The leather dissolved. His fingers trembled. Nothing made sense. He didn't understand, didn't know that a man named Taliesin on his world had placed into the hands of a Viking named Rögnvaldr a map to the new world, and a watch from the future. Taliesin had sent him on his way, with his men, as penance for their ancestor's sins.

At great cost, the men had found their way to Vineland, across long, angry waters. Then down what would come to be known as Hudson Bay, along several narrowing waterways, across land, until they came to the headwaters of another great river. And then, on the banks of that river, many, many miles inland from the sea, they had built a stone arch, crafted it with runes, marking the place to claim it as their own. Tal had told them.

It was a message. Over his racing pulse, Reggie felt a surge of hope.

There was something else, tinkling with light beside the watch. A little pebble of rock or tile, differently colored than the clay. It had a strange mark on it, like one of the runes on the arch. Reggie reached down, pinched the stone in his fingers. It was shaped like a hexagon, an obviously intentional design. As he held it in his palm, a soft light filled the tunnel. The light was a brighter, different color than his flashlight.

The runes on the arch began faintly to glow.

The empty space under the arch became fluid to look at. Reggie didn't hesitate. This was part of the mystery. He wasn't going to miss his moment. His boys were somewhere. Out there. He crawled through. A sickening sensation of motion and space. Colors and blackness. Then light. His eyes adjusted.

He was on the tiled floor of a room, still on all fours in the crawling position. The blurry form of a grizzled man took shape in front of him. The man was lifting a weapon. A sword. Focus came slowly. Reggie staggered to his feet. The man looked haggard and worn, like a prisoner of war, with ragged, hollow eyes. He was dreadful and terrible, full of determination and fury. Lifting the sword in his hands, he studied its lines, felt it for balance.

"Who are you?" Reggie croaked. He had never been here before. Had no idea what was happening. The man turned. The voice that answered him was rough as sandpaper.

"I am Corus. The Champion."

TO BE CONTINUED
in Book 3
The Song of Unmaking

VIEW A PORTION OF CHAPTER 1 OF
The Song of Unmaking ON PAGE 415 OF THIS BOOK

About the Author

Dean Barkley Briggs has worked in radio, marketing, and new product development. He also pastored for eleven years. After losing his beautiful wife at an early age, Briggs decided an epic fantasy might help his four boys live courageously through their loss. *Corus the Champion* is the second in a series of adventures set in the Hidden Lands of Karac Tor. Briggs has since remarried a beautiful widow named Jeanie, and now has eight amazing kids. Enter Karac Tor at www.hiddenlands. net.

THE SONG OF UNMAKING

A NOVEL

D. BARKLEY BRIGGS

LEGENDS OF KARAC TOR

CHAPTER 1

Beginnings

The machine was a series of huge, curving tubes. Circles. Not the holy circles branded onto the foreheads of Gray monks in homage to Aion, but alloyed cylinders of strange design.

"Put...tension on it!" Gorker of the Huldáfolk shouted angrily, cog to a troop of twelve burly gnomes. In the high, thin air, his voice whipped away from his throat, dying in the blustery snow. He yelled again. "Not all at once! I'll turn into the Stag Lord himself, buncha' nimwits! Take the slack out first!"

Coils of fist-thick hemp were everywhere. At Gorker's command, the mountain-bred gnomes heaved upon the rope until it vibrated like a taut lute string. One end was lashed to a long tube of metal. The other ran through a system of pulleys bolted here and there to the stone. This was to be the first real test of their assembly process: to dominate the wind without taming it. Raging gales were part of Vishgar; it was why the gnomes had come.

Far below their vantage, dead trees bulged from the shoulders of the mountains like hackles on a dog, while snow lay clean and bright on every angled surface. As the gnomes heaved the fifty foot long metal tube into the air, they strained to keep slack out of the line. It was gigantic, swelling from ten feet in diameter on the southern end to nearly twenty five feet at the north, where the mouth suddenly flared wide. Of three main cylinders, this was the first to be raised, and smallest. For weeks they had toiled on a platform to anchor the machine. Before that, long months had passed in careful preparation: clearing, chipping, leveling, properly orienting the base for maximum effect, gathering wood, raw ore and other resources. Gnomes were renowned builders, meticulous in their engineering. But it was slow, dangerous work. Most of the crafting was done inside the mountain, whether harvesting coal for the smelter or casting the metal, or forging nails and bolts. All according to the plan. They had been threatened and beaten: Measure, measure, measure again! *Exactitude!* Obey!

"Watch it now— lift!" shouted Gorker. He was an older gnome, with gray hair shooting from underneath his cap as if an explosion had been set off on top his head. His beard, like all gnomes, was thick and tough as iron, and he had old skin like leather. His native tongue was as bleak and brutal as the landscape about them.

"Hold steady, grunts! Damage the flare and I'll serve yer heads on a platter."

Huddled into their furs and fitted skullcaps, the gnomes carefully manuevered the metal toward the best angle for the mouth to drink the wind.

"Steady, steady! Ya got rocks for brains, Thum? Easy over there!"

A blast of swirling eddies threatened to fling the pipe over the jagged cliff edge. Again Gorker boomed. Gnomes on the windlass doubled their grip, grumbling and cursing. Fortunately, the broad, flat ledge allowed for plenty of bracing. Everything was put to use, a small derrick and several winches. When at last the pipe finally settled against the vertical uprights, three gnomes scurried up the scaffolding to quickly fasten the welded brackets to the uprights. At the cog's command, the others released their grip, watching nervously. But the pipe held firm. Immediately, a low rumble of noise added a deep base tone to the high soprano winds as gusts of air filled the tube.

Gorker began sorting through several flapping pages and scrolls tucked messily under his arm until he located the one he needed. Holding it tight against the wind, he studied the position of the surrounding peaks, the angle of the tube. He shuffled forward, sweeping snow with his foot. It had taken a long time digging through the ice to find the old stamping rods of Hhyss One-Eye. Using that as a guide, he checked his compass, made a note; looked through two other instruments mounted on poles. One had a lens that looked like a telescope, the other dials and sliders like a transit. He pressed his eye to the lens.

"We done checked a hundred times, Gorker!" one of the workers shouted impatiently into the wind, still bearing weight on the rope just to be sure.

"I'll be checkin' a hundred more!" Gorker snapped. "So shut your face, unless you want yer beard shaved to line my gloves."

The complaints faded to mumbles. Gorker began rummaging through a pile of brass fittings scattered in the snow, searching for the next transition piece. Most of the parts scheduled for assembly were heaped together in the large cavern abutting the ledge: various levers, valves, hydraulic cylinders, leather bladders and baffles. His troop had lived, worked and slept in that cave for months. Now the parts were ready, matching Gorker's drawing, revealing a complex, enormous machine the size of a small, two-story château. The main feature was three long pipes.

Windcatchers, Gorker called them.

They were like giant coiled snakes, ending in a progression of three massive horns, each larger than the next. Nine total, pointed south toward Karac Tor. Greedy windcatchers. That was the plan.

At long last, the first one was laid to bed, set in place.

It was more than a machine. It was a great instrument of noise and terror. Gorker checked his notes again, seeming satisfied. He could not afford mistakes.

"Alright, grunts!" he belched. "She'll be on us 'fore ya know it, and we're behind. Get on. Circles, fetch the first circle!"